"LEAVE ME ALONE, TREVOR. I DO NOT WANT YOU."

His breathing came in short, ragged pulls. "You want me as much as I want you, Celine."

"Do you think every woman wants you? Well, I don't."

A muscle in his jaw twitched. "Yes, you do. Why don't you admit it? Life's too short to play little virginal games, and that's something you and I both know you are not."

Raw emotion shot through her, sharpening her tongue to a knife's edge. "If it is illicit pleasure you seek, you've had the perfect partner on your arm all evening. Go to her for your dirty little games."

He pivoted on his heel and left her, but after a few steps, he paused. "You little fool. I spent the entire evening keeping jealous Giselle Beaudrée from sinking her vicious claws into you."

Celine

Kathleen Bittner Roth

ZEBRA BOOKS
KENSINGTON PUBLISHING CORP.
http://www.kensingtonbooks.com

ZEBRA BOOKS are published by

Kensington Publishing Corp.
119 West 40th Street
New York, NY 10018

First Printing: October 2014
ISBN-13: 978-1-4201-3528-2
ISBN-10: 1-4201-3528-7

First Electronic Edition: October 2014
eISBN-13: 978-1-4201-3529-9
eISBN-10: 1-4201-3529-5

10 9 8 7 6 5 4 3 2 1

Printed in the United States of America

To my wonderful niece Connie.
If not for you and your one a.m. phone call,
the pages of this story would have stoked
the flames in my fireplace.
Thanks for getting the time zones mixed up.

Chapter One

April 1853, St. James Parish, Louisiana

Celine Kirkland stared down at the simple wooden casket. Rain drummed against the lid, turning the open grave into a muddy pit. The pungent smell of wet earth and the film of grit in her mouth nauseated her. The wind kicked up. Icy rain swirled around her and stung her cheeks. She shivered and pulled her full-length, hooded cape tight against her body. It seemed as if nature was bidding her mother-in-law a raucous farewell.

Stephen touched her arm. "The weather is worsening. We need to make our way home."

Numb from grief and cold, she climbed into the wagon with her husband and father-in-law. Lightning fractured the sky, and ear-splitting thunder shook the ground. She clutched her swollen belly as if to soothe the babe kicking inside.

The rain turned into a deluge.

"God, this is foul weather," Stephen groaned as he snapped the whip in the air and urged the two draft horses into a trot.

Celine shifted about in her seat. How could he possibly

see beyond the horses? "Shouldn't we be coming upon the bridge soon?"

The horses jerked and danced to the left, wild-eyed and whinnying.

"Whoa!" Stephen yelled through a roar of thunder.

The wagon tipped sideways. Celine gasped and gripped the edge of the rough sideboard, her blood running as cold as the pelting rain.

The beasts pawed the ground. One of them whinnied again, nostrils flaring, and braced itself against forward motion. The other twisted hard against the reins, trying to turn back. Stephen lashed out with the whip just as a flash of lightning lit the path in front of them.

Too late, Celine spied the gaping hole where the bridge had been. She screamed.

The horses and wagon jackknifed against each other. The wild shriek of animals and metal grinding against wood vibrated through the air as the wagon careened toward the river.

"Miss Celine!"

Celine jerked awake, and caught herself before tumbling out of the window seat. Rubbing her eyes against the light streaming through the window, she glanced at Marie. Her maid stood near the bed, folding clothes and appraising Celine with a worried frown.

"Sorry, did I moan?" She rubbed her stiff neck.

"Did you have another one of those bad dreams—in broad daylight?"

Celine nodded.

"And sittin' up, no less. Begging your pardon, mam'selle, but if you kept to your bed nights, you might work into a habit of sleepin' during proper hours instead of catnapping in the window seat."

"You know what keeps me awake." Celine slid off the blue velvet cushions and made her way to the dressing table.

"Only been a year since Mister Andrews found you trapped under that broken-up wagon." Marie's voice softened. "That ain't so long for a bad memory to haunt a person. Especially considering your terrible loss and all."

Young Lindsey Andrews poked his head through the doorway to Celine's bedroom, his face aglow. "Trevor's coming home, Trevor's coming home!"

His loud voice jarred her senses, and she winced. He paused, the grin on his freckled face even wider. "Hello, Miss Celine. My brother's coming home."

With a nod, she managed a meager smile. "I'm well aware of the fact, Lindsey."

He disappeared, laughter trailing behind him.

She went back to tossing her toilette articles in one basket, ribbons, combs, and brushes in another, and wondered at her glum mood.

The maid gathered a stack of Celine's unmentionables and laid them in the basket she'd set on the bed. "That scoundrel Mischie Trevor. Did you know he's been in New Orleans a week now and didn't even bother letting his father know he's coming until last night? Tch, tch, tch."

"How would I know that?" Celine caught Marie's reference to Justin Andrews's eldest son as *mischie*, a localized version of *monsieur* reserved for someone favored. Marie's mahogany skin glowed from the effort of transporting Celine's things next door. "Do you need to rest a bit, Marie?"

"I'm fine, mam'selle." She grinned, and stuck with her subject. "Like as not, Mischie Trevor's been busy waking up N'awlins. I'll bet most of England sleeps like a babe since he done left. Likewise, papas in these parts won't be getting much sleep now."

Celine threw a brush in the basket and missed. It landed

on the floor with a clatter. She swept it up, tossed it back in, and went to sorting ribbons.

Marie lightened her tone. *"Pardonnez-moi. Ne vous en faites pas."*

Celine stared at the colorful ribbons tangled in her hand and then tossed them in the basket with a sigh. "Yes, I may as well leave everything to you since I'm only making a mess."

Marie used the lilting dialect straight out of the French Quarter whenever she attempted to soothe Celine. The maid was a mimic. She could imitate any accent after hearing a few words. Celine couldn't decide if the crisp French inflections Marie called her own might not be contrived as well. A day in Marie's company seemed more like a day among a small crowd.

The maid frowned. "You feeling all right?"

"I'm fine," Celine lied. She traipsed to the window seat along the outer wall and sank into it. With another sigh, she set her elbows to the ledge, propped her chin in her hands, and stared at a circle of children playing below, offspring of the field workers and household staff. They danced to the snappy rhythm of an older boy's clicking tongue and the tap of his foot. Their clever song spun a tale about Trevor that Celine couldn't quite decipher. Everyone seemed caught up in the enthusiasm of his return—everyone, that was, except her.

Zola stepped outside the cookhouse and wiped her wide forehead with the corner of her apron. Most likely working herself to a frazzle on account of Trevor's arrival. There would be pots hanging over the fire in that kitchen, rumbling and sputtering, as if they, too, shared in the excitement. Even from where Celine sat, the rich aroma of roux, filé, and the holy trinity of Louisiana cooking—celery, bell pepper, and onion—tantalized her senses. Her stomach rumbled.

"Do I smell gumbo?"

"And jambalaya," Marie added. "Mischie Trevor's favorites."

Celine shot her a scowl.

Marie raised a brow in return. "You know how Zola always fixes someone their special dishes when they comes to call."

Come to call? Trevor wasn't a visitor, for heaven's sake. He'd merely been gone two years. When she'd visited the kitchens, she'd noticed the cook referred to him as *mischie,* as well. Why did everyone speak of him with such favor? From what she'd heard, he was quite the rakehell.

Well, what did she know? Marie and the cook had been around all of Trevor's life while she had never met him. After all, if anyone was a guest here, it was she. She'd only met Justin last year, the day of her mother-in-law's funeral. Since Celine had no living relatives to go to, and she'd been too injured to return to an empty house, Justin had taken her in.

Melancholy tugged at her heart. What the devil was wrong with her of late? She rubbed at her arm. A thin red scar ran from shoulder to wrist, a grim reminder of the accident that had left her widowed and childless.

Marie moved to stand beside Celine. "Mam'selle, you haven't said a word about the beautiful clothes Mister Andrews had sent upriver for you. Don't you care for them?"

"Of course, I do."

"Then, what be the matter?"

She shrugged. How could she tell Marie what was amiss when Celine didn't know herself?

"Mischie Trevor used to sit in that window seat after his mother died, his chin propped in his hands and staring out at nothing, just like you be doing, Miss Celine."

Celine's elbows came off the windowsill like a finger off a hot stove.

Marie frowned. "Seems to me the new wardrobe might not be what's bothering you. The letter from Mischie Trevor came on the same boat as what brought your clothes." Her features softened. She reached out and fussed with a tendril on the nape of Celine's neck. "You be worried about Mischie Trevor and his wicked ways you been hearing of?"

Heat pricked Celine's cheeks. With a shrug of her shoulder, she cast the maid's fingers off her hair. "Don't be a dolt."

Marie dropped her hand and stepped back. She slipped into Louisiana Creole, a whimsical dialect that never failed to lighten Celine's spirits. "Doan you be worrying 'bout Mischie Trevor. He won't be botherin' wif you none. Maybe he be a scoundrel, and mayhap he a fool at times, but I ain't never heard of him botherin' no female what doan want no botherin' wif."

Celine laughed. "I hadn't given any thought to your Mischie Trevor *bothering me.*" She caught sight of Marie's toothy grin before she turned to the window again. "For heaven's sake, I didn't just crawl out from under some rock." Maybe Marie's teasing had lightened her mood, or perhaps her bright smile brought a ray of sunshine, Celine didn't know, but her disposition shifted.

"Would you care for a hot bath, Miss Celine?"

"I'd prefer you continue to remove my things from Trevor's room and put them in the guest room before he arrives."

Marie flashed a wide grin. "Oh, he ain't due till near sunset, and we've yet to see high noon." With a small grunt, she lifted the largest basket and headed out the door.

Justin's bellow echoed through the hallway, startling Celine. "What in the name of Glory are you up to, Marie?"

"I'm removing mam'selle's things from Trevor's room and transferring them to the guest room, sir," Marie said matter-of-factly.

"Put them back directly."

Celine shot off the window seat and flew to the doorway, her gaze fixed on Justin while she spoke. “Marie, do as I say.”

Justin’s set jaw gave a silent command.

Marie nodded at Justin and trudged past Celine and back into the room.

He raked his fingers through his thick silver hair and pinched the bridge of his large nose. “May I ask why you are going to all the trouble of having your things transferred to the guest room?”

Celine crossed her arms and tapped her foot. “Haven’t you heard? Your son is returning.”

Justin’s bushy brows knitted together in a hooded frown. “He’ll only be here a few days.”

Confusion scattered Celine’s thoughts. “Oh?”

He cocked his head. “Did you actually think my thirty-year-old son would be moving back in with his father? He’s come from London on business—in New Orleans, not here.”

An odd sense of isolation gripped her. How had she missed all of this? Even the servants must know Trevor would remain for only a few days, but she hadn’t a clue. She was out of the circle—a gloomy reminder that she didn’t really belong here. Not permanently, anyway.

She squared her shoulders. “I prefer the guest room anyway. This one is too masculine for my taste.”

Justin stepped closer, using his great height to tower over her. “You don’t fool me.”

His dominant gesture, usually reserved for his unruly children, startled Celine. “Don’t think to bully me.”

He stood there for a moment and then chuckled, backed up a step, and gave her a fatherly pat on the shoulder. “Beg pardon, Celine. Perhaps I didn’t make clear the situation.”

He headed for the stairwell, talking all the while. “Since Trevor’s dealings will take place at our offices in New Orleans, he’ll reside in our townhouse there. As will his cousin and uncle, also due to arrive this week from England.

Our shipping company is expecting a new clipper to be delivered soon, so we're all chomping at the bit."

Celine called out after him. "Situating your son in the guest quarters still doesn't seem quite right."

He paused a few steps down, his hand on the cherrywood rail, and glanced up. "Hush. Trevor's a grown man. In spite of what you've doubtless heard, he was raised with decent manners."

He continued at a fast clip along the stairs, his voice growing louder as he descended. "Try to tolerate an old man's wishes, Celine. I purposely placed you in his old room because you needed the privacy during your recuperation. Admit it, you have the best views of the back gardens—not to mention the gallery at this end is virtually yours alone."

Even though he couldn't see her, she bit her bottom lip and nodded. "All right then." She turned and stood in the doorway, surveying the room that had been hers these past twelve months.

Trevor was obviously partial to blue. Except for the burgundy in the Persian carpet, the deep cobalt color dominated. Even the ceramic pitcher and basin on the marble-topped commode were of the same rich hue. She adored the dark, carved cherrywood of the sumptuous four-poster bed and side tables. And the wingback chair—cobalt blue velvet—angled next to the fireplace. She'd spent many a night curled up there with a book.

Too masculine for her tastes? Not really. She loved everything about her quarters.

She suddenly wished Marie wasn't still around. For some odd reason, she was absurdly close to tears.

Steam swirled around Celine, the tension in her muscles slipping away while Marie scrubbed her skin until it glistened. Sometimes being pampered felt simply grand.

"What a beautiful day, Marie. Open the doors to the gallery so we can get more of the scent of roses from the garden instead of Zola's cooking, will you please?"

Marie flung the French doors wide. A balmy breeze floated in, rustling the lace curtains hanging at the doors' sides until they floated like the lacy wings of a butterfly. The heady fragrance of roses wafted in and mixed with the mélange of robust smells drifting in from the cookhouse.

"I love this time of year, don't you? The spring flowers are in bloom. Everything looks so clean and fresh, and with nights still cool enough to curl up in front of a cozy fire. I'm so glad to be alive. How different things are from a year ago." Celine hummed to herself.

Marie pulled a chair behind the tub and brushed Celine's thick tresses. "Your hair looked half-dead those first few months with us. Like a string mop dipped in mud."

"That's because I *was* half-dead."

"Now the color reminds me of rich coffee. And so shiny. Like it's been shot through with gold. Lovely to look at. Same as you, mam'selle." Marie ceased her chatter and continued to brush in slow, even strokes.

Celine slipped deeper into the tub and closed her eyes, immersed in the busy sounds and smells of plantation life. A sharp clang of three bells jolted her out of her reverie. They sounded again, a signal that the captain of a sternwheeler had stopped to unload passengers.

Marie jumped. "Lordy, three bells, not two—passengers, not goods. Don't tell me Mischie Trevor got here so soon?"

The steady pounding of feet down the hallway caught both women's attention. "Trevor's home!" Lindsey shouted with a quick rap on the door. The sound of his footsteps disappeared down the stairs along with his whoops and hollers.

Celine sat up, her heart pounding. "I thought you said he wasn't due until the last steamboat?"

Marie leapt to her feet and waved the brush about as she

paced. "Oh, Miss Celine, how can I ever manage to get you dressed and your hair done up before he gets to the house?"

"For heaven's sake, such a state you're working yourself into. Settle down and hand me a towel." Celine stood amidst a cascade of water, wrapped the towel around herself, and stepped from the tub. "I have no intention of greeting your *Mischie Trevor* with the others. Introductions can be made over . . ." She gave a flip of her hand. "Over his favorite gumbo and jambalaya."

She dried herself, and then held her new lavender-sprigged muslin dress to her body. Relieved wasn't an adequate word to describe what it felt like to shed the oppressive black she'd worn for the past year. "What do you think?"

Marie stood at one corner of the bed, fidgeting and watching Celine twirl naked around the room.

She ignored the maid and picked up a purple sash and matching kid slippers. "Perfect. Help me into everything, and you can be off. No need to bother with my hair until evening."

Chemise and corset in hand, Marie frowned. "You'd best not be running around here nekkid and with the balcony doors open now that Mischie Trevor's arrived."

"This corner of the house is private," Celine said while Marie helped her into her clothing. "He'd have no need to wander around the gallery outside my door, would he? Besides, as you said, *he doan bother no woman what doan want no botherin' wif.*"

Marie laughed at Celine's exaggerated impression of her and slipped into Louisiana Cajun. "Yessah, but Mischie Trevor? Well, he's got him a way what makes the ladies *want* to be bothered wif, beggin' your pardon." She gave a small curtsy, giggled, and hurried off.

Celine made her way over to the cheval mirror and scrutinized her appearance. Satisfied, she patted a light fragrance of lily of the valley behind her ears and at the hollow of her neck. Then she slipped onto the gallery and headed toward the front of the mansion in hopes of surreptitiously observing Trevor's arrival.

She made her way to the front of the gallery and stood, hidden behind one of the ponderous Doric columns surrounding the two-story mansion. The open carriage ready to transport Trevor stood some two hundred yards away in front of *La Belle Créole*, the queen of the Mississippi.

The sight of the regal two-deck paddleboat gliding past Carlton Oaks during its regular runs between New Orleans and Baton Rouge never failed to stir Celine. What wasn't decorated with ornate iron scrollwork gleamed with fresh white paint. Her elegant twin stacks rose high in the air, billowing thick, white steam into the afternoon sky, her paddles at the stern churning the dark waters around her into white froth. Fashionably turned out passengers lined the upper deck, hoping to catch sight of the parade of ostentatious plantations up and down the river.

A man Celine assumed to be Trevor strolled down the gangplank and climbed into the carriage. She couldn't quite tell from this distance, but he appeared tall, like his father and brothers, but with dark hair like his sister, whose excited chatter from below gained cadence.

The gangplank behind him disappeared into the boat. A tender closed the gate and with three clangs of the bell, the paddles reversed, waters churned, and the sternwheeler floated gracefully upriver.

The carriage slowly approached, looming larger as the driver made his way along the shaded drive. Majestic oaks lined both sides of the narrow road, their boughs forming a vaulted corridor leading to the mansion. Celine backed away from the rail, hoping the colorful Brasilia vines clinging to the railing and column she stood behind hid the lavender of her wide skirt. Blasted hoops.

Lindsey scrambled down a tree, and ran and skipped

behind the carriage, calling excited greetings. Trevor turned, situating himself with his back to the house and toward his brother. Lindsey picked up his pace.

The carriage drew closer, and Trevor turned back to the small crowd of family and servants gathered in front of the grand plantation house. Celine caught a faltering breath. Good Lord! If that wasn't the most attractive man she had ever seen.

The driver pulled to a stop in front of the gathering. Trevor swung one long, muscular leg down from the carriage and twisted to reach for his valise. The muscles in his wide shoulders rippled beneath his dark blue broadcloth jacket. In one swift motion, he lifted the bag, sprang from the carriage, and set the baggage to the ground. He ran his hand down one thigh, smoothing his tight fawn-colored breeches tucked into shiny black boots that rose to his knees.

Celine's gaze roved the length of his body in hypnotized fascination. She stepped closer to the edge of the balcony for a better view of this enigma, who now leaned casually against the carriage as if he'd leisurely strolled in. His eyes crinkled at the corners when he smiled, and his full mouth displayed a set of even white teeth against golden skin. Dark eyes flashed merriment.

Lindsey reached his brother first. Trevor swung him easily in the air. He set the boy down and tousled his hair. Michel, the second oldest son, and Justin, gathered around Trevor. Finally Felicité, his sister, waiting on the sidelines, could stand still no longer. She pushed through the men and threw her arms around her brother.

"*Je t'aime, je t'aime,*" she cried, smothering her brother with affectionate kisses. Her dark curls bounced gaily about a petite and lovely face. "I missed you so much, *mon frère.*"

An easy grin settled about Trevor's startlingly handsome face as he held court with the family. He and Felicité shared similar features, both of them bearing a striking resemblance to the painting of their beautiful French mother hanging in the parlor.

Suddenly confused, Celine leaned into the pillar and pressed her hot cheek against the cool column. He wasn't anything like she had imagined. He was tall and wide in the shoulders like Justin, but any resemblance ended there. He had neither the Andrews hawk nose of his father and brothers, nor the hard edge about him she had anticipated. Oh, she'd expected him to be handsome enough—the men in the family were—but she'd thought he would mirror those wealthy dandies she used to sidestep at the parties she'd attended before her marriage. No matter how suave they appeared, something usually lurked beneath their façades that repelled her. She'd been curious as to why the other young ladies failed to notice, until she figured out why—they didn't want to, not where wealth was concerned. Trevor's demeanor held not a speck of the deceitful dandy.

Felicité stood on tiptoe, one arm hooked in Trevor's, and whispered something in his ear. He chuckled deeply, lifted her at the waist, and twirled her around in circles. Her dress danced about her ankles, the hems of her petticoats fluttering.

"Put me down!" Felicité squealed merrily, not meaning a word. Trevor laughed and tossed his head back. His gaze caught Celine's. He ceased swinging his sister in midair and set her down gently, never once taking his eyes off Celine. His lips parted and he stood as if transfixed.

Her breath caught in her throat. A vague fire smoldered in her belly. What a sensual man. He carried an aura of personal magnetism so powerful, a sensation close to fright swept through her. She stood still and aloof, masking her emotions. His intense gaze seemed almost a physical touch. She held her head at a proud, haughty angle, not flinching from his bold scrutiny.

In seconds, Trevor regained his cool, casual air. A lusty grin caught at the corners of his mouth, and fire danced in his eyes as he bent ever so slightly at the waist, tipped an imaginary hat, and strode casually into the house.

Damnation! Celine hurried along the gallery back to her room.

Slamming the French doors behind her, she kicked off her slippers in a fury, sending one crashing against the door across the room, the other falling squarely in the fireplace. She sat on the cushions in the window seat, still in a frazzle over being caught spying. Her face heated at the embarrassing thought. She wrapped her arms around her legs, set her chin to knees, and stared blankly out the window, her emotions in a whirl.

Being caught lurking on the gallery wasn't all that bothered her.

Puzzlement washed through her. Why be so upset because a man returned home? An aqueous haze clouded her vision. She swiped at one corner of her eye. How in heaven's name could there be any tears left? Hadn't she cried them all out two weeks ago over Stephen's grave? Here she thought she'd healed in mind and body, but she'd only managed to fool herself into thinking so.

It suddenly dawned on her that in the year she'd lived with the Andrews family, she'd never stepped off the land but to visit the cemetery. Life at bucolic Carlton Oaks was busy, but predictable as the setting sun. And safe. Had this predictability given her a false sense of how to face the world again once she ventured beyond the plantation's borders? So, she wasn't angry at Trevor's return after all. She was frightened of venturing forward in life; that's what all the unwanted emotion was about.

Trevor's returning to Carlton Oaks had upset the plantation's daily routine—including hers. Worse though was what the mere sight of him did to her insides. Good Lord, from where had those volcanic feelings erupted? Such unrealistic yearnings had been buried so deep before her marriage, she had all but forgotten them.

There had been a time when she and her best friend, Dianah Morgan, had sat under a tree reading erotic books they'd clandestinely transported in their closed parasols. She'd often awaken at night covered in a sheen of perspiration after one of her sensuous dreams. But when she married, she sadly decided the authors had played a cruel trick on her. Reality proved to be little more than a few minutes of fumbling around in the dark under bunched up nightclothes.

Mere fantasy—that's what Trevor Andrews represented. Any debonair man stepping off a jewel of a sternwheeler, and making his way along a lovely tree-shrouded path to one of the most beautiful plantations in all of Louisiana, was bound to stir romantic notions. Especially in a woman spying on him who'd spent her idle hours as a youth tasting forbidden fruit in the form of unmentionable books.

She reached into a pocket hidden in the seam of her dress and pulled out a letter from Dianah, one she'd carried around far too long. The Morgan family, having recently relocated to San Francisco, had invited Celine to live with them in their new luxury hotel.

A shaft of pain shot through her heart at the idea of leaving a place—and people—she had grown to love. But there was no family left, nothing to tie her to Louisiana any longer. Tonight she would cease her procrastinations and accept Dianah's invitation.

Celine sat in the window seat for nearly an hour, sorting through her thoughts and fitting all the past year's events into a jigsaw puzzle in her mind, Trevor's coming home being the final piece. She convinced herself that with all the confidence she had gained over this past year she could handle him in proper perspective, not like some schoolgirl sitting under a tree reading romantic fantasies—she was a grown woman, nearly twenty-one.

And a widow, for heaven's sake.

She smiled to herself, still staring intently out the window at nothing in particular when something startled her attention back to the moment. She turned and looked straight up into the beguiling face of Trevor Brandon Andrews.

The man stood before her, his booted feet planted slightly apart, fists on hips. "Lost in thought?"

Celine's mouth turned to cotton. She swallowed hard. Whether she was widowed or not, how dare he enter her quarters without permission? She stood and faced him, aloof and unswayed. Oh, God, they stood so close. He smelled of sandalwood and musk. And . . . and of a delicious body heat that nearly dizzied her. She gazed into midnight eyes framed with thick black lashes.

Something flickered in them, some knowing or realization that set her heart reeling. She tore her gaze from his only to survey his full, lush mouth. The strange smoldering that had nearly burst into flames on the balcony swept through her once again. Surreptitiously, she clasped her hands in front of her to prevent their trembling and diverted her prurient thoughts.

When she forced herself to look back into his eyes, she wasn't quite sure what she saw, but there was a curious edge to them now. And mischief?

"I thought I had better see for myself this fair maid I've been hearing about. Seems you've charmed my family so entirely, I've been ordered to keep my distance." One corner of his mouth lifted. "Mustn't sully your propriety with my presence, you know."

Oh, Lord. His voice, rich and husky, vibrated right through her. She prayed her vocal cords worked. "I do not know what you mean, sir." Glancing over Trevor's shoulder, she spied Marie standing in the doorway, arms crossed and a scowl on her face.

Trevor followed her gaze. "Nothing to fear, Marie, she's safe."

The maid tapped her foot. "I came to see if you be needin' help with your things in the *other* room, Mister Andrews."

Trevor's brows furrowed. "Oh, so now I am *mister* instead of *mischie?*"

He returned his attention to Celine. "Seems you have enough pull around here to get whatever you want, including my quarters, whilst I'm hustled off to the guest room by a sullen maid with whom I have quickly lost favor."

His mouth eased into a slow, seductive grin. Celine's heart pounded out a nervous tattoo in her throat. His gaze settled on the small vee in her neck where her blood pulsated. *He sees.* Fainting dead away would work. She'd be out of her misery, at least.

He tilted his head. "On second thought, right next door in the guest room may not be so bad, after all. If you need anything . . ." He issued a throaty laugh, raising one eyebrow slightly as he reached for her hair. Long, tapered fingers gently flicked a thick curl resting on Celine's shoulder. His fringed lashes lowered, veiling his dark eyes.

She stood stoically before him, fascinated with what mischief he might be up to. Especially with Marie standing right there. *What a bold one he is*. No wonder the women were quite taken with him.

Trevor cocked his head slightly to one side, as if he heard her thoughts. He hooked one thumb in the top of his trousers and raised his chin a notch until he regarded her through half-closed lids. The corner of his mouth curled into a sardonic grin. "What's the matter? Don't you like what you see close up as well as when you were sneaking around on the gallery?"

She hadn't expected that. A bucket of cold river water tossed in her face couldn't have shocked her more. Well, she wasn't letting him get to her.

He regarded her from head to toe, mischief skirting his features. “Madam, if you were any more controlled, you’d become a statue.”

She stood still and reserved for a second longer, then turned abruptly and went to where one of her shoes lay. She slipped it on and then searched the room.

Trevor chuckled, walked over to the fireplace, and retrieved the other. He blew the ashes off and handed it to her. “My visit might prove to be rather interesting after all, Mrs. Kirkland.” He sauntered past Marie without a backward glance.

Marie stepped into the room. “Told you he could be a rascal.”

With a huff, Celine stuffed her foot into the shoe Trevor had handed her, turned on her heel, and without a word, exited the French doors and flew down the back stairs.

Chapter Two

Trevor sat in one of the two oversize brown leather wingback chairs in front of his father's desk, his back to the door. He'd spread himself casually over the chair while they reviewed shipping manifests.

He tapped a riding crop lightly against a booted leg crossed over his knee. "The wealthy Malones out of Boston signed a new contract while we were there. They've increased business with us twofold. And they aren't the only ones. I'm telling you, the mounting tension between the states isn't the only reason to move our New Orleans office to San Francisco. China trade is growing faster than we can have ships delivered."

His father drummed his fingers on the top of his burl wood desk. "Simon won't leave New Orleans. Who will run our affairs way out there?"

"Cameron."

His father's jaw dropped. "You mean to say your cousin, of all people, agreed to leave sophisticated England for a rugged town still in its infancy?"

"We drew straws."

"Drew straws?"

"Yes, Father. Two pieces of hay from the stable."

"Good God. For a vital business venture?"

"It was either that or draw swords."

"Christ Almighty. What if you had lost? Cameron is capable, mind you, but he isn't seasoned like you, hasn't had time to acquire the business acumen you possess to run the entire company."

Trevor grinned. "I cheated."

"You did *what?*"

Trevor continued to idly tap the riding crop against his boot. "You'd have done the same had you been in my place."

His father chuckled. "Most likely. You'll remain in England?"

"Not permanently. Uncle Miles will manage both the Liverpool and London offices. I'll travel every year between England and San Francisco to oversee everything. However, when our new clippers are delivered, I intend to be aboard when the first one makes her maiden voyage to China."

He brushed a hand over his knee, smoothing the fabric of his suede riding breeches as an indecipherable niggling shot through him again. "I've grown somewhat restless of late."

His father leaned back in his chair and heaved a deep sigh. "I can't fault your judgment thus far. Not with the way you've increased business fourfold since taking the reins." A wistfulness gathered about his countenance. He turned his head and stared out the window. "I know I'm retired, Trevor, but giving up our office in town does yank at the old heartstrings. More business and good will went through there in my time than I can likely recall."

"I think you should consider selling the plantation."

His father's head snapped back toward Trevor. "Get rid of Carlton Oaks? Never!"

A familiar irritation raced through Trevor's blood. He took in a slow breath to settle himself. "From what I heard in the coffeehouses in Boston, there's bound to come a time when all hell breaks loose between the states. When that happens, you could wake up one morning and find every abolitionist from here to Canada swarming through the South and torching everything he can get his hands on."

His father's mouth settled into a grim slit. "I'm no blasted slave owner. You know full well how vigorously I oppose the filthy practice. My employees are free and I give them—"

"The abolitionists won't know that, which is exactly my point." Trevor stretched his legs out in front of him and settled lower in the chair. "They'll not stop to question you. I know you enjoy life here, but you really should consider selling and moving on or you may not get a dollar for the whole of the place in a few years."

"Where the devil would I go?"

Trevor shrugged. "I don't know. Out West, since you're not inclined to return to your roots in England. All I know is I'm concerned about my family. I hope you aren't going to trust my instincts only when it pleases you."

His father shot him a piercing glance before he went back to staring out the window. "I don't give a damn about political rumor in some Northern coffeehouse. Felicité and Lindsey shall remain in America. I will see to raising them on Carlton Oaks land, and that is final."

Trevor despised bringing up such a dour subject, especially after arriving only a few hours earlier, but the opportunity might not present itself again. Besides, this would give his father time to ponder.

"Would you look at your sister," his father murmured. "Isn't she the image of your mother?"

Trevor spied Felicité through the window as she strolled past on the gallery outside. She stopped short, waved to someone, and then stood still, as if waiting for their approach. Ebullience shone from her profiled face.

Mrs. Kirkland moved into view, the window framing her like a portrait. His full attention shifted to the two women. He watched, fascinated, as Felicité chattered soundlessly.

The woman gazed intently into his sister's face, smiling warmly.

A pulse in Trevor's groin quickened. He couldn't take his eyes off her. What a strange charisma he found in her. The aloof haughtiness he'd encountered earlier had evaporated. Was her coldness intended for him alone? For all men? Or maybe for anyone she did not like, for the affection she showered on his sister appeared sincere enough. A muscle in his cheek hardened.

"There's Celine Kirkland," his father said. "She's the young widow I told you about. Looks as though she's headed inside. I'll call her in so you can meet her."

As if on cue, she floated in. "Oh, Justin, I've just been with Felicité. She is so excited about the ball we've been invited to, and . . ."

Her voice trailed off as Trevor casually rose from the high-back chair and turned to face her. For a moment, it looked as though she'd seen a ghost. But her recovery was so swift, his father most likely hadn't noticed.

Trevor ran one hand down his thigh, smoothing a crease in his tight breeches. To his surprise, her gaze followed his movement and then landed squarely at his crotch. For the scant seconds that she stared, her cheeks flushed.

She regained her composure, but not before the tip of her tongue traced over her lips. He'd bet her mouth had gone dry at being caught staring. Wouldn't he like to be the one to wet those lovely lips, though?

With a flick of her head, she all but dismissed him and approached his father's desk.

"Celine, I'd like you to meet my eldest son. Trevor, this is our Mrs. Kirkland."

Our Mrs. Kirkland?

She extended a hand to shake his, but Trevor turned it over and pressed his lips lightly against her flesh.

She snatched her hand away and refused to look at him.

"I've heard so much about you, Mrs. Kirkland. You seem to have enchanted my family."

Her eyes lit with fire—like the sun ricocheting off green bottle-glass. Was she one of those whose eyes tended to change color along with her moods or with whatever she wore? He stared back, sending a silent message—yes, he also intended to ignore his rude entry into her room earlier.

Belligerence flickered across her face as if to say two could play the same game. She smiled warmly.

Her magical eyes seemed to shift color again, returning to a green flecked with gold. They weren't quite hazel, those eyes, but they sure spoke a language of their own.

"Please sit, Celine," his father urged.

"I mustn't. I've been at the river, and I need to change before dinner." She sat, however.

Trevor glanced at her slippers peeking from beneath the hem of her skirts. The one he'd rescued from the fireplace still showed signs of soot while both were wet around the edges. As was the hem of her dress. He chuckled lightly. Celine drew her feet under her chair.

He swore the color of her eyes shifted once again. He moved to behind his father's desk, picked a book from the shelf, and turned back to face Celine, positioning himself slightly behind and to the left of his father. Nonchalantly, he sifted through the pages, not reading a word.

Celine turned her full attention on Justin. Trevor knew she meant to obliterate him from her peripheral vision, but he'd seen to it that would not happen. Not from where he stood. *Foolish woman, you are up against the master of game playing.*

His father leaned forward, clasping his hands on the desk. "I have more exciting news, Celine. My brother, Miles, and his son, Cameron, are here, as well. I thought they'd lag a week behind on their journey from England, but they arrived in New Orleans aboard the same clipper as Trevor. They had business to attend to in the city before they caught the next steamboat, which is due shortly. We have cause for celebration this evening. Miles, a widower for ten years, has taken a new wife."

"How exciting." Celine's eyes sparkled, and she looked into Trevor's father's face with the same unaffected quality Trevor had observed when she spoke with Felicité. His jaw twitched.

"My entire family will be here for your birthday next month, Celine." Justin glanced back at Trevor. "I've arranged a formal ball on behalf of Mrs. Kirkland. It's time to ease her back into society now that her mourning period is over. I'll be expecting you to travel back up from New Orleans, of course. In the meantime, there is a soirée a couple evenings from now at the Verrette plantation."

Trevor said nothing, only watched Celine's fascinating eyes.

She leaned forward. "Does Cameron have a wife I might meet, as well?"

"Not as yet," Trevor's father responded, glancing Trevor's way again with a grin. "Apparently, the two cousins haven't been so inclined."

Trevor shrugged one shoulder. Hell, had he known of Celine's existence, he would have made sure Cameron remained in New Orleans. The rutting stag had a penchant for young widows.

Not that Trevor's tastes ran much different.

His father turned back to Celine. "I shall arrange for Cameron to be your escort at these functions."

Cameron? Why the hell Cameron? Something odd pinched deep in Trevor's chest.

"Oh, please, there's no need. I am already spoken for," Celine said.

Both men's heads shot up at her remark. Trevor quickly hooded his eyes and went back to pretending to read the book in his hand. Casually, he flipped the pages.

"Lindsey is to squire me about," Celine laughed. "He's quite excited. Thinks he's a grown-up gentleman, he does." Her skin glowed and her eyes danced.

Trevor shoved the book back on the shelf, no longer feigning interest. He leaned back, one shoulder against the bookcase, his arms crossed over his chest. A small, disturbing knot tightened in his stomach as he observed the warm, intimate scene before him.

Celine stood and made her excuses to leave. "Oh, and thank you for the perfume, Justin. I couldn't have chosen a more perfect scent. You do know me well, don't you?"

You know me well? He gives her perfume? A chill ran through Trevor. What the hell was going on between these two?

Good God, was he reading things right? He'd never remotely considered the idea that his father might remarry, especially to someone so young. But Uncle Miles had—not to one as young as this, but certainly much younger than his first wife. No wonder Celine fussed over Lindsey and Felicité. *Mon Dieu,* if she hadn't wormed her way into their good graces. And here he'd entertained thoughts of . . . oh, hell.

"I'm going to dismiss myself, too," he said. "Allow me to see you to your room, Mrs. Kirkland." He walked past his father and lightly touched Celine's elbow, guiding her gently from the room and up the stairs in silence.

"Cozy little scene you were playing back there with my father," he growled as they approached her bedchamber.

Celine whirled around, her back against the door. "What do you mean by that remark?"

"Perhaps I should be asking you that question. Just what do you have in mind, working your way into my family the way you have? Lindsey this, Felicité that, and, oh, Justin," Trevor mocked her. "Are you in the market to become the next Mrs. Justin Andrews?"

She raised her hand to strike him. He caught her wrist.

Emerald eyes blazed dangerously through narrow slits. "Why, you—"

"Bastard?" Trevor lifted an eyebrow. "Why don't you say it? Everyone else does." His grip tightened on her thin wrist. Her rapid pulse coursed through him. Despite his anger, he couldn't seem to release her.

"Let me go," she demanded in a wintry voice.

Trevor's grip tightened in response. He stared down at her, saying nothing and fighting a terrible urge to kiss her. What the hell was wrong with him? His gut churned at the idea of desiring someone his father was interested in.

"Apparently you do not know your father very well," she retorted. "You have no idea what he has done for me. He has been gracious enough to allow me to live here during my mourning period, which is now over. He has arranged for several social functions this month, which will allow me to feel comfortable in society again. Also, he has arranged for the sale of my property, which will be final in one month and which will provide me the funds to live out my days in peace. Alone."

Christ, he had things all wrong. He opened his mouth to apologize, but she cut him off.

"Your father knew my husband's parents before they were deceased. He took me in, a near stranger, because I had no one to turn to after I was widowed and in no position to run a small plantation alone. I will soon leave here, as has been my plan all along. Most likely I will never see your father again. He and I share a friendship that will last forever in our hearts, no matter how many miles separate us. But I doubt you would understand a simple camaraderie between two people of opposite genders. From what I hear, and have observed, all you are able to perceive in a woman is a night's shallow pleasure. I should feel sorry for you, but instead I find you despicable."

Despite her cutting words, relief flooded his chest, followed by a spike of guilt. "I beg your pardon, I misunderstood." His grip on Celine relaxed, and he slowly let her arm down, never shifting his gaze from her cold green eyes, void of the golden flecks he'd seen before.

She turned and rushed into her room, slamming the door behind her.

A slow grin settled about his mouth. He'd deduced one emotion that made the color of her eyes shift about like a kaleidoscope. Now to figure out a few more. He whistled lightly as he strolled to his bedchamber.

Chapter Three

Celine paused at the bottom of the grand staircase and peered across the hall into the dining room. Her grip tightened on Lindsey's arm when she saw the family gathered in a small circle. Michel, on break from Jefferson University and full of the political bent of youth, held court. Trevor and his cousin stood with their backs to the entry. Thank God, no one noticed her. She wasn't up to being caught spying again.

She counted six people. Where the devil was Justin?

He emerged from the library. "Ah, Celine, there you are. And aren't you a sight to behold?"

"Thank you." She relaxed now that he was at her side.

He moved in front of her, blocking her view of the others, regarding her with a gentle smile. "Your gown is beautiful. As are you, of course."

She brushed a hand over the rows of delicate Belgian lace cascading from her waist to her toes. "I would have preferred something less dramatic, but Marie insisted. You know how she can be sometimes. At least the beige is a subdued color."

She touched the narrow row of lace gathered around the top of the dress that left her shoulders bare and the top of her breasts exposed. There wasn't an inch to spare for slippage.

The chocolate-colored silk sash tied around her corseted waist matched her doeskin slippers. She wiggled her toes just to feel the comfort.

Justin gave her hand a squeeze. "Relax. This is an informal family gathering."

Lindsey fidgeted. "May I go to the others, Father?"

"As you wish."

He bolted across the hallway like a horse let out of a paddock.

"That's what boys do at thirteen." Justin chuckled and presented his arm. "Shall we join them?"

Celine slipped her hand in the crook of his elbow and steadied herself. "Of course."

The massive room never failed to impress her. Glittering candlelight danced off the prisms of the twin chandeliers overhead. Tall candelabras graced the table, high enough to allow the diners an unobstructed view. Roses, the color of a pink morning sunrise, floated in a shallow bowl in the center.

The others were assembled near the French doors and sipped either mint juleps or sangria. They turned in unison at her approach.

Her stomach gave an isolated lurch, and then quieted. Michel moved quickly to her side and blew a kiss across her cheek. "Aren't you a wondrous sight." Removing her arm from his father's, he took it and whispered wickedly in her ear. "Come, allow me to introduce you to my cousin and his parents. You are going to drive Cameron absolutely wild."

Celine's cheeks prickled with heat when she found herself standing beside a man who was unnervingly handsome. What appeared to be surprise flickered over Cameron's countenance before a cool, almost arrogant demeanor settled around him.

Trevor stood just behind and to the left of him. She ignored Trevor and focused her attention on Cameron. Sweet heavens. Except for the hazel eyes fringed with the same sooty lashes as Trevor's and the neatly manicured moustache, the two could be brothers. Cameron's height was nearly the same as his cousin's, his hair the same mass of thick black waves. His large frame showed to advantage in finely tailored clothing as well.

She shot a quick glance at Trevor. He gave her a small nod. Were they both haughty men? She went back to acknowledging Trevor's cousin while Michel made the introductions.

Cameron was all charm. No, arrogance was not what the two men displayed—this was power. And mischief. And confidence. Along with dazzling charisma. Lord, the two of them together must be a formidable force in business matters. And when they stepped out together in the evening, surely they melted hearts along the way. They wore their power like their clothing—impeccably.

She struggled to inhale. Drat the tight lacing on her corset. She extended her hand in greeting. Oh, wouldn't her daring friend, Dianah, have appreciated these two? And wouldn't Celine feel so much more comfortable with Dianah demanding all the attention.

Cameron took her hand and brushed the back of her knuckles lightly with his lips, his manner faultless. What a relief—his touch didn't burn her skin as Trevor's had. And his nearness didn't weaken her knees. She smiled at him. "I am pleased to meet you."

"I'll bet you are," Trevor said, studying her with those damnable heavy-lidded eyes.

She was forced to acknowledge him. "Good evening."

Instead of taking her hand as Cameron had, Trevor clasped his behind his back and slowly regarded every inch of her. "Indeed, it is."

His neatly combed hair appeared as black as his velvet jacket. His charcoal trousers were molded to his narrow hips and long legs. This Trevor was even more handsome and magnetic than the man who had left her so confused a few hours earlier. She had to force herself to breathe. What was the matter with her? For pity's sake, she wasn't a schoolgirl.

Something wavered in his countenance. "Excuse me." He turned on his heel, and stepped out to the terrace.

What in the world had just happened to make him walk away so abruptly? Squaring her shoulders, she smiled and turned back to Cameron.

He slid his hand gracefully into hers, and guided her to his parents. "I'd like you to meet my father and his new wife."

Celine exhaled softly, thankful Cameron was friendly—and that he didn't have the same effect on her as Trevor.

Cameron's father, Miles, was a younger version of Justin, the gray only beginning to appear at his temples. A short, squat woman stood next to him. Elizabeth Andrews bent her head to Celine when they were introduced, but said nothing. Her cheeks turned crimson, and she cast her gaze to the floor.

Why, she's painfully shy.

Cameron still held Celine's hand when Trevor returned a few moments later. An odd smile turned up the corners of his mouth. "Nice to see you two have become fast friends."

"Shall we be seated?" Justin broke in, ending Trevor's game.

Dear Lord, give me strength. Celine slowly let out her breath and moved to the table. She stood behind the chair in front of a place card bearing her name.

"Ah, delightful." Cameron pulled her chair out along with the one to her right.

"I believe that's where Michel is to sit," Celine said, indicating the place setting next to hers. "Yours is to the right of his."

Cameron nonchalantly switched place cards. "So it was."

Lindsey scurried into his seat to her left as if he feared someone might snatch his place card away too.

Trevor sat down opposite her. Her fingers gripped the

sides of her chair. She'd sneaked in earlier in the day and made certain he was seated as far from her as possible. How did the scoundrel come to sit directly across from her? It chafed her temper to know he would be in her direct line of vision the entire evening and there was little she could do about it.

Miles and Justin sat at opposite ends of the table, Elizabeth next to Miles. The chair to Justin's right stood empty. Justin glowered at Trevor. "Who changed the seating arrangement around?"

A corner of Trevor's mouth twitched. He raised the glass of sangria to his lips. It did little good—his eyes laughed at her over the rim.

Justin's demeanor shifted, as if he had second thoughts, and he mumbled, "Won't this be an evening worth watching."

Felicité made her grand entrance dressed in a silvery blue silk gown trimmed in white lace, a string of perfectly matched pearls at her throat. She sat in the vacant seat next to her father and began to chatter in French.

"*Mon Dieu,*" her father muttered. Then his face brightened. "Elizabeth only speaks English. To speak in any other language would be tantamount to whispering behind her back. Would everyone agree?"

"That should hold the little one's tongue a while," Trevor said dryly. Felicité's command of English was not yet strong. He was back to studying Celine as he spoke to his sister. "And stop pouting. It ruins your ensemble."

Celine couldn't help herself. She laughed. The scamp.

A deep red wine replaced the sangria and mint juleps. Platters of crusty French bread appeared along with steaming tureens of jambalaya, shrimp gumbo, and crawfish étoufée. The air was redolent with the savory smells Celine had grown up with. The room took on a cozy air as everyone around her broke into noisy, relaxed conversation.

Cameron waved a servant off and filled Celine's plate. He

tore a thick chunk of bread from a loaf still hot from the oven and made a soft, appreciative noise at the back of his throat. "There's nothing like good Creole cooking to bring back family memories."

The chatter around the table and the clink of utensils against china faded into a backdrop for Celine's internal world. How alike he and Trevor were, but how differently each affected her. She wondered if they kissed alike.

Oh, Lord, where had such a wicked thought come from? She took up her wineglass, hoping to dismiss the bloom that must have appeared in her cheeks.

Cameron tore off another piece of bread and set the piece on her plate, openly studying her.

"Do you intend to feed her as well?" Trevor said dryly.

Something wild and playfully arousing swept through Celine. Fixing her eyes on Trevor, she picked up her spoon, dipped it into the savory jambalaya, and slowly, ever so slowly, brought the spoonful to her lips.

He stilled. Despite the bold game she played, she nearly swooned at the burst of robust flavors. He wasn't the only one who favored the brown jambalaya over red. It was thick with chicken, andouille sausage, and tasso—the spicy, smoky Cajun pork that gave this dish its rich color. The full-bodied taste penetrated her senses in layers. Memories of life in the French Quarter cleaved a path through her mind and tugged at her heart. She couldn't help herself; she closed her eyes in pleasure.

Trevor chuckled at her reaction.

She opened her eyes.

He pulled off a chunk of bread, dunked it into the thick broth, then dipped his head just enough to pop the laden piece into his mouth without spilling a drop. "Mmm. *Voilà comment savourer un plat digne des dieux.*" The only way to eat food from the gods.

How many times had she heard that phrase along with the

first bite of anything Creole or Cajun in the French Quarter? But never had anyone performing that little ritual caused a wave of raw, pagan pleasure to grip her.

Perhaps those erotic books she and Dianah had read beneath her parents' oak tree held a mustard seed of truth after all. Odd, but tension that had held her back rigid drained from her, and she found herself suddenly enjoying the evening. "How is it your speech carries a hint of our Colonial French while Cameron has a decidedly English bent to his? I notice the two of you exchange colloquialisms from both England and the Quarter with ease."

Cameron jumped in. "We spent our youth between the plantation and the French Quarter before I went off to school in England."

"He had to go," Trevor responded.

"They separated us," Cameron put in. "God only knows what would have happened had we—"

"So, Mrs. Kirkland," Miles interrupted. "I understand you are giving consideration to relocating to San Francisco."

Trevor and Cameron shot speaking glances at one another and stopped eating. Trevor still held a piece of bread over his plate.

Cameron draped one arm over the back of Celine's chair and with an ever-broadening grin said, "Fancy that, so am I."

Trevor brought his wineglass to his smirking lips. "On second thought . . ."

Cameron lifted his in toast to Trevor. "That's what you get for cheating when drawing straws, dear cousin." He turned to Celine. "But why the move? Are you not content here?"

Justin took over the conversation. "Eustace Morgan built a luxury hotel in San Francisco, and relocated his family there." He paused. "Surely, Trevor, *both* you and Cameron remember *Judge* Morgan?"

Trevor and Cameron exchanged knowing glances before Justin continued.

"Celine is close friends with his daughter and has been invited to live with them since she has no family left in these parts." He paused and turned to Celine, his voice deepening. "However, since she has a home at Carlton Oaks for as long as she pleases, I do hope she decides to decline their offer."

Cameron sat a little straighter at Justin's aggressive delivery, as though he'd just been given the cut direct, and signaled for more wine. "Do tell. Far be it for me to question life's little twists and turns." He leaned toward Celine, his moustache tickling her ear. "However, I do hope you'll choose to become an intrepid traveler and move West. In the meantime, would you care to join me in a ride about the plantation tomorrow? It's been quite some time since I've seen the old place."

His cheek was so close, she caught the scent of clean citrus laced with musk. His nearness did nothing to stir her senses. The man sitting directly across from her might as well have been the one whose cheek had just touched hers, for she could feel his heat, could recall his scent from where she sat.

"How did you come to know the Morgan family?" Trevor asked before she had a chance to respond to Cameron's invitation. "They lived in the French Quarter."

"As did I," she responded.

"Really? You're not French."

A jolt ran through her; defiance followed. Oh, hell's bells, what did she care what he assumed of her meager upbringing? "Neither is Dianah. While she was born into wealth, I was raised in the Quarter by my grandmother. She was a dressmaker for the upper echelons of society, which could well have included your mother, Mr. Andrews. We lived behind her tiny shop."

"Ah," Miles put in. "Don't tell me you speak of Mrs. Rogers?"

Celine's heart lurched at the mere mention of her grandmother's name. "I do, Mr. Andrews."

"Then you're the little Rogers girl." His words were more a statement than a question. "I remember you." His smile could not have been warmer. "And since there are six male members of the Andrews family in attendance, you may call me Miles."

"You may call me Celine then."

"Does that include all of us?" Cameron asked with a sultry grin.

Trevor leaned toward his father, changing the subject. "Do you know why Judge Morgan sold out and left the South?"

Celine stopped listening when the subject turned to the strained political climate. She observed Elizabeth, a painfully shy and decidedly plain woman. What did Miles see in her? Her mousy brown hair strained to break out of the tight little bun sitting at the nape of her neck. Her fingers shook slightly as they rested uncomfortably around the bowl of her wineglass. Her downcast eyes avoided everyone, and her cheeks bloomed whenever any attention was cast her way.

The poor dear was totally out of her element. Celine's chest tightened at Elizabeth's discomfiture. A sudden dawning struck. Why, Celine was likely not much different from Elizabeth. Probably they came from similarly modest circumstances. If it hadn't been for Celine's grandmother, so intent on sacrificing everything to train Celine in the manner of gentility, she could just as easily be sitting here as uncomfortable and awkward as Elizabeth.

A shudder ran down Celine's spine as the full realization of the unselfish gift her grandmother had bestowed upon her settled in. Her grandmother had studied the manners of the elite of New Orleans and brought them home to Celine, fashioned her clothing after theirs, even managed to save some of the finest leftover materials to sneak home. When the time came for Celine to step into society, the deed was accomplished with little effort—thanks to her grandmother—and Dianah Morgan's insistence that they become friends. Celine's heart squeezed with compassion for Elizabeth.

Out of the corner of her eye, Celine became painfully aware that Trevor studied her intently while he chatted with the others. Her heart lost its rhythm. If ever there was a dangerous man, here sat one. She'd be leaving soon. All the sooner if it wasn't for that blasted ball Justin had already planned. But Trevor would only remain here for a few days. Surely she could allow him to be her friend for Justin's sake. Couldn't she? Her breath caught at the intensity in Trevor's gaze before she forced a smile, willing herself to forget her wildly thumping heart.

He smiled back in the same easy fashion Celine had seen the first time she laid eyes on him. He raised his wineglass slightly in a toast to her and murmured, "That's two times your eyes have shifted color."

"I beg your pardon, what did you say?"

Trevor leaned forward and responded in a hushed voice, his gaze never leaving hers. "I said touché."

Puzzled, she turned away from him, suddenly uncomfortable. She signaled for another glass of wine. She held the glass to her lips and drank half its contents, nervously aware that Trevor's attention was still fixed on her, the din of conversation around her a dull roar. She stared into the glass as if she held a crystal ball.

Dear Lord, what an intense response he stirred deep in her belly. For a brief moment, she let herself wonder what it would be like to lie in his arms, to feel his naked body next to hers, to kiss those soft-looking lips. She was sure, somehow, that he slept naked and that his lovemaking would be gentle, his kisses sweet. Her cheeks flamed.

What foolishness. How could she know such intimate

things? She had never lain naked next to a man. Throughout her marriage she and Stephen had worn nightclothes, each dressing in private. Married a full year, and she had never seen a man unclothed. For heaven's sake. Why, no man had ever seen her naked, either, and here she was, a widow. She giggled at the absurdity of it all.

The others turned to her. "Oh, my, I may have had a little too much to drink on an empty stomach." Damnation, her nose was probably red, too. She touched the tip, only to find it numb. Cameron reached over and gave her hand a gentle, knowing squeeze.

Trevor leaned back in his chair, his visage unreadable.

Miles brought the conversation to a halt when he tapped his glass with a spoon. He announced to all that he had turned the leadership of the shipping business over to Trevor. "I am by no means too smug to admit when someone else is more adept than am I."

"Well said," Trevor announced with mock arrogance.

Miles raised his wineglass. "Trevor is the one who has been responsible for the great financial gains we have experienced these past two years. And I, quite frankly, admit to a strong desire to spend more time in England with Elizabeth."

"Here, here," Justin put in. All glasses were raised.

Miles patted Elizabeth's hand affectionately. She smiled sweetly at him.

There were more toasts, and Celine drank more wine. She hadn't been this relaxed since . . . well . . . never.

The men began swapping sea stories, each trying to top the other. Cameron's arm still rested lightly on the back of Celine's chair.

"Do you suppose there are actually such things as mermaids?" Celine asked.

"Indeed," Trevor responded with Cameron and Miles heartily agreeing.

"Where might one find them?" she queried.

"Oh, you don't find them. They find you," Cameron said, joining in the teasing. "And you don't usually sight them until you are well away from shore."

"Aye, about a month out to sea, that is," someone added.

Celine turned to Elizabeth, who mouthed the words *sea cow*. At first, Celine didn't understand, thinking Elizabeth had said *seek how*.

"Oh, sea cow," Celine laughed, picturing lovesick sailors lined up at the ship's rails staring lovingly at some blubbery old mammal, all the while imagining it to be a graceful mermaid beckoning to them. She had definitely drunk too much wine.

Felicité stared at her plate and pouted, not understanding much of what was going on.

Celine started to explain the story to Felicité in French, but Trevor chided her.

"Now, Trevor," she scolded lightly, the wine allowing her to drop her guard a bit. "Don't be so hard on your sister."

He leaned back in his chair, raising its front legs. He hooked his thumbs in the top of his trousers, his fringed lashes failing to screen the intimacy of his gaze. His eyes crinkled at the corners. In the space between them, a current was building.

Like a fly in a spider's web, she was captured by strange sensations—the giddiness of the wine, Trevor's commanding presence—so caught up that an ache, deep in the soft, secret recesses of her being, throbbed. Using every ounce of willpower she could muster, she tore her gaze from his and peered into the safety of her wineglass. Again, she wondered what it would be like to lie with him. If only she had no pride, if only she didn't care that she would end up like his other lovers.

If only.

* * *

A storm gathered force deep within Trevor as he watched Celine's pulse beat lightly in the soft hollow of her throat. Her breasts rose and fell with every shallow, quick breath she took. Her lashes swept nearly closed as she smiled into her wineglass. Somewhere in that smile was the knowledge that he wanted her. And when he had her—and he would—it would be what she wanted, as well.

Christ, she did something to him. It was more than her beauty. He'd known plenty of beautiful women. Yet every one of them who'd ever succumbed to him paled in comparison. Even the way her body moved when she'd first walked into the room this evening had stirred his blood. Unable to control the embarrassing tug to his groin, he'd walked away. And remained on the terrace until he was composed enough to rejoin the group.

"What about Etienne Beaudrée, Father?" At the mention of his neighbor's name, Trevor's attention focused on the conversation at hand.

"I said, he passed on nearly six months ago. Heart failure, they say. He left his widow to run things on her own."

"Widow? I wasn't aware he'd married."

"He was only wed a little over two months. You wouldn't have had any reason to know. He married Giselle Beauvalet."

Cameron whistled through his teeth. "I think we can guess what killed the old boy."

Trevor chuckled. "So, it's the Widow Beaudrée now, is it? Here she is mourning away at the plantation right next door, and I haven't even had the courtesy to pay my respects. Perhaps I should do so on behalf of the family. Would tomorrow be too soon, Cousin?"

He watched for Celine's reaction out of the corner of his eye. Now why the hell had he gone and said that? What was he, an overzealous schoolboy? *Mon Dieu.*

Cameron laughed derisively. "Not at all, Cousin, not at

all." He raised his glass in a toast to Trevor, wicked signals passing between them.

Celine visibly stiffened and turned to Cameron. "Do you recall your earlier offer to take me riding in the morning?"

"Why, yes, dear heart."

Had Cameron just slurred his words? At any rate, he'd had more wine than was good for him. And was Trevor's cousin having trouble focusing on Celine, as well? He appeared as though he was about to plant a kiss on her mouth right then and there, but he pulled back as if checking the impulse.

Some dark emotion Trevor couldn't identify swept through him.

"How could I remember? I mean, not remember?" Cameron had composed himself and was smiling at her.

Celine laughed lightly.

Trevor could stand it no longer. He stood and pushed his chair back. "If you'll excuse me, I'm off for some fresh air before I retire. It's nearly midnight, and I've had a long day."

Chapter Four

Celine fidgeted in the firelight while Marie undressed her and slipped a thin night rail over her head. The fabric brushed lightly against her breasts. A shaft of lightning skittered through her body. Her nipples hardened. She turned her back on the keen-eyed maid.

"Throw my things on the window seat until morning and take yourself to bed, it's late."

"And wrinkle this pretty little thing?" Marie headed for the wardrobe with the gown in her hand. "I'll only be a minute, and then I'll see to your coiffure."

Celine huffed, sat down at the dressing table, and pulled pins from her hair. "I can manage on my own tonight." Oh, how she'd love to broach the subject of the Widow Beaudrée with Marie, who seemed to know everything that went on up and down the river. But not now, not after barely leaving the dinner table. Celine would bide her time until just the right moment.

"Things not go well at dinner, mam'selle?" Marie called out from the closet.

Blast it all, did nothing get past her? "Everything went well enough, thank you. Better than I expected, actually. I merely drank too much wine and ate little."

"Now *that* I can fix for you. I'll see to—"

"No, please." Celine stood. "I really want my bed. By morning I'll be fine."

"You're sure?" Marie stepped from the wardrobe with a peach-colored peignoir in her hand and stepped over to the dressing table. She draped the satin dressing gown over Celine's shoulders.

"I am going to bed directly, so I hardly need a robe." Celine pulled the brush through her hair.

"It'll keep you from taking any loose hair to bed." Marie set the back of her hand to Celine's forehead.

She rolled her eyes. "Don't treat me as if I were a child."

Marie smiled. "Even though you're acting like one? The wine will help you sleep. Good night then, mam'selle." She closed the door gently behind her.

Celine laid the dressing gown across the foot of her bed and crawled in. She curled onto her side and watched the orange and yellow flames dance in the fireplace. Soon, it would be too warm for a fire, and then she would be forced to fall asleep in the dark—something she wasn't comfortable doing, not since the accident anyway. Not since she'd been trapped beneath the splintered wagon alongside her dead husband. Not since she'd spent the entire night chilled to the bone, her legs dangling in a swollen river thick with debris and water moccasins.

Her body gave an involuntary shudder. Well, she'd be gone to San Francisco before the muggy heat of summer settled in. According to the Morgans, the weather there was cool year-round.

Trevor invaded her thoughts. She grew restless. Damnation, but the man had a way about him.

She tossed and turned until the covers lay in a tangle. With a frustrated kick, she cast them aside, and rose. As she paced, a dull throbbing struck her temples. She flopped onto the bed for a while, then stood and paced again.

An aching, unfulfilled hollowness burned deep within. Hungry—she felt hungry. Digging the robe from the twisted pile of covers, she put it on, and slipped down the stairs and out the back door.

The house was as dark as the night, but as always, the cookhouse was lit. She worked her way along the stone path bathed in moonlight, stubbed her toe, and cursed softly.

Zola was sure to have a conniption about Celine's running around barefoot. But the cook wouldn't be a bit surprised to see Celine, who had spent many long, sleepless nights in front of one of the twin fireplaces that stood at each end of the room. Zola would bake and listen while Celine poured her heart out. Gradually, her nightmares lessened, and she was able to sleep some, however badly. While she'd learned to cope with the nightmares somewhat, she hadn't gotten used to thunderstorms. They still terrified her.

In the beginning, Marie used to curl up in a chair beside Celine's bed whenever lightning and thunder crashed. Lately, though, Celine had taken to riding out the storms in front of one of the fireplaces while Zola worked.

"Zola?" Celine called out softly. She stepped over the threshold. The warm, yeasty smell of baking bread filled the air. Fires blazed in both fireplaces. An empty chair sat in front of one of them. Zola couldn't have gone far.

Celine wandered to a table filled with fresh loaves of bread. She touched a top. That's what she wanted, hot bread slathered with butter and jam. One loaf stood on the table, an end missing, a knife lying beside it. A butter dish and jam pot stood next to the cutlery. She helped herself to a thick slice, spread the soft butter on top, and after the yellow blob melted into the bread, she lifted the jam jar's lid. Empty.

Blast it all.

"Zola, where are you?" Remembering the preserves were kept on the top shelf of the pantry, she went in search.

Stretching on tiptoe, Celine felt around with both hands for a jar. A soft rustle told her someone else was in the room. Instinctively, she knew who it was.

Thought scattered.

God give me strength.

She heard the whisper of clothing against skin, felt body heat engulf her, caught his scent. Strong, firm hands reached over her head and nudged a jar forward.

"This what you're looking for?" His words, barely above a husky whisper, wafted hot across her cheek.

She struggled for an answer, her arms still outstretched.

He picked up the jar, moved it one shelf lower, and then closed his hands around her wrists. *God, the wildfire heat of his touch—it coursed right through her.*

Her breath hitched.

Still holding her by her wrists, he slowly turned her around to face him.

She tried to step back, but had no place to go and found the pantry shelves digging into her back. He was so close his entire body nearly touched the length of hers.

He still wore dark trousers, but no jacket. His shirt was open at the collar, his sleeves rolled up, exposing his forearms. She caught a glimpse of his broad chest and a patch of dark curls. A wave of unexpected want swept through her. She stared into his shadowed face, so close she could feel his breath on her cheek, could smell his clothes and skin.

"Leave me alone, Trevor."

His eyes glittered like diamonds on black velvet. "Do you really want me to leave you alone, Celine? Or do you want me as I want you?" His gaze shifted to her mouth.

Slowly, he leaned forward, his thick lashes veiling his eyes, his intentions obvious when his lips parted.

Dear God!

She bit down on her lip so that all he encountered was a

straight, tight, uninviting slit. Nonetheless, when his lips touched her skin and his breath mingled with hers, her mind altered.

His mouth grazed her cheek, traced a seductive path along her jaw—soft, warm, and tender.

"So that's the way it's going to be," he whispered.

His teeth tugged at the lobe of her ear—gently, ever so gently, but the reaction he provoked was anything but gentle—his touch seared her like a branding iron.

Wild, primitive urges she didn't know she possessed pounded in her veins. Her body stiffened, then shook slightly.

A quiet force emanated from him, a power unlike anything she'd ever experienced as he held her. She knew it was useless to struggle. He could easily overwhelm her.

She closed her eyes to him.

To think.

But she couldn't seem to pull her thoughts together. Oh, she was definitely over her head here. This kind of seduction was clearly Trevor's territory. She must have been insane to think she could handle him.

Panic licked at her heels.

His lips caressed the curve of her shoulder, and then came to rest at the hollow of her neck. She needed to stop him, but she couldn't seem to move. Did she dare to embrace a bit of the rapture her erotic books had touched upon?

They stood together quietly, not moving. But his lips remained, soft and sweet on her neck, his breath a hot rush across her flesh. The air around her turned thick with passion, and her knees turned to liquid.

The battle was lost to her.

Trevor's mouth moved slowly along her neck, leaving a hot trail as he went. "You smell so good, so tempting." He kissed her ear, and then moved up to press gentle kisses against her eyelids.

He clasped her wrists closer together, holding them easily over her head with one hand, leaving his other free to stroke her hair. He ran his thumb gently along her ear, then along her jaw, before sliding his fingers behind her neck.

She held still, trying one last time to find the strength to reject him. But her insides burned, and all she knew was that her desire for him was deepening.

Gently, he pushed her chin up with his thumb, tilted her face to his. His lips came down on hers, this time meeting no resistance. His mouth, warm against hers, engulfed her. For a moment all that existed was his supple lips on hers as he softly murmured her name.

His hand left her neck and moved down the front of her, loosening the sash of her robe. The top of his hand brushed against her ribcage—and God, she wanted more of his touch.

The tips of her breasts stiffened and tugged at her womb as though they were connected by a thin thread. Aching with desire, she fought a moan.

Her robe fell open.

The flat of his hand settled on the curve of her waist, his fingers splaying to her navel.

Hot—so hot it was as if the thin fabric of her night rail had all but disintegrated. She leaned her head back against the vertical panel holding the shelves, unaware she had exposed the column of her neck until his mouth grazed her skin.

His eyes were downcast as he regarded her. "You are so beautiful, Celine," he whispered, as he drew her arms around his neck. He slid his hand under her robe to the small of her back, tilting her pelvis toward him. Slowly, deliberately, he leaned into her body, pressing his male hardness gently against her.

Celine gasped as his mouth came down on hers once again, his heated tongue exploring its depths.

She kissed him back, her arms wrapped tight around his

neck, her fingers curling into his hair. Liquid fire pumped wildly through her veins. She was in danger of losing herself to him, yet she was experiencing the sweetest, most loving moment she had ever known.

He lifted his mouth from hers.

And then he smiled.

Shocked disbelief ran through her like ice water. That was triumph she saw. Oh God, no. Why, this was nothing to him but idle sport. He was indeed a bastard.

She leaned forward as if to kiss him again, but when his mouth touched hers, she bit down, hard and quick.

He jumped back, grabbing his lip. The passion in his countenance faded to puzzlement. "What the hell was that about?"

"If you ever try to touch me again, I swear, I'll castrate you." Celine wrapped her robe around herself and tied the ribbons together. "Get away from me."

"What be all dis ruckus?" Zola stalked through the kitchen and set her fists on her wide hips, a deep scowl on her broad face. "And excuse me while I tend to my jam pot," she said. Reaching around them, Zola grabbed the jar of preserves off the shelf with a grunt and stomped off.

"Here, now, both you sit down." She dragged another chair to the fireplace. "If you two intend to be living in the same house, then you better be a gettin' along, you hear?"

She frowned at Trevor's rapidly swelling lip. Tossing a couple of plates on the table with a clatter, she sawed on the loaf of bread. "Only be one footstool here, so you best share it like the gentleman you are."

She tossed the bread on the plates and grunted as she gave the lid on the jam jar a hard twist. "Lordy, but you two can't be living here fighting and scratching. Here, have some a dis bread I baked up." She spread the hot bread liberally with butter and jam and plopped a plate onto each of their laps. Then she bent over and picked up their feet, plunking both pairs on the same footstool. "Tch, tch, tch. Don't you ever wear shoes, girl? You're gonna get bit by a big old cottonmouth one of these days."

"I've already been bit," Celine muttered.

Trevor gingerly touched his lip. "As have I."

Zola leaned over and examined his lip with a scowl still painted on her face. "Likely serves you right. Humph."

When the cook moved back to the table, Trevor eased back into his casual manner. "I know full well what you're up to, Zola. I got caught, and you're about to make me pay the piper." He rested his head against the back of the chair.

Celine sat staring at the fire in stony silence, aware Trevor watched her. She turned to him, shot him the biggest frown she could muster, and then resumed her cool indifference.

Trevor laughed that same easy laughter she'd heard when she saw him twirl Felicité through the air.

"You have spunk, Celine, I'll hand you that." He boldly studied her before his expression changed subtly. He turned his attention to the fire.

Celine went back to staring at the dancing flames as well, but she couldn't seem to get her mind off his powerful presence. Or what had just transpired. The flames blurred as her peripheral vision took over. His countenance drew her like a magnet. She fought an inner battle to keep from looking his way.

She lost.

Barely turning her head, she attempted to focus on the footstool they shared. But slowly, her gaze inched up his crossed ankles, then moved to his iron-hard thighs, and came to rest on the mound of maleness that just moments before had been hard and pressed against her stomach, turning her into a helpless wanton. Lord, she should find such a sight indecent, but her blood stirred and a ridiculous urge ran through her—what would it be like to lay her hand over the seductive mass? His body was a work of art.

"Does the lady care for anything else this evening?" Trevor offered softly. "Dessert perhaps?"

Celine's cheeks burned with the shame of being caught staring.

That was the last straw.

She jumped up, regained her composure, and shot Trevor one final glare of disgust before striding from the room. "I'm out for a walk before I go to my room, Zola," she said, and stepped over the threshold. "It's stifling in here."

"What do you mean, *your* room?" Trevor called out.

Celine was barely out the door when Zola lit into him. "Best you don't go gettin' no ideas about dat girl."

Didn't she realize Celine could hear her? *For God's sake.* Nonetheless, Celine paused in the darkness.

"She ain't like those good-for-nuthin' womens you be takin' up with," Zola said. "Your papa gonna skin you alive if'n you touch her."

Trevor's soft laughter trailed behind Celine as she disappeared around the corner of the house and found the garden. She wandered along the floral-scented paths, confused, and still trembling.

What was happening? Everything about Carlton Oaks had been so quiet, so peaceful—until that scoundrel showed up. Finding a bench, she sat. For how long, she didn't have a clue, but when the horizon over the trees took on a shifting light, she slipped back into her room. A fire burned low in the fireplace. She had hoped she wouldn't rouse Marie—again. But the maid had instincts whenever Celine wandered about at odd hours. She would be sure to thank her maid for lighting the fire when Marie delivered breakfast.

Celine removed her robe, threw it on the floor beside the bed, and separated the mosquito netting. A rose and note lay on her pillow. She opened the note.

"Dormez bien, mon amour." Sleep well, my love.

Trevor's bold signature trailed beneath the words.

She regarded the blazing fire, the neatly made bed, one

corner of the covers pulled back to receive her. So this was all *his* doing, not Marie's. Heaving a great, tired sigh, she walked over to the door and locked it before making her way to the wingback chair angled before the fire. She curled up with the note in her lap and stared into the flames.

She'd wanted to surrender to Trevor tonight, plain and simple. Could mere desire actually be so stunning as to completely tangle the mind? Could temptation be so powerful as to make a person want to sink to the floor with someone they'd barely met and give in to wantonness for the sheer pleasure of touching and being touched?

Here she'd thought she'd experienced true desire reading those erotic books, but now she knew what she'd experienced had been without substance. She finally knew what fantasy was—it was the idea that she could be in control with a man like Trevor.

What an unexpected twist to her life.

If she'd been overwhelmed when she'd caught sight of him climbing out of the carriage, this was devastation. In the instant he touched her, reality left her and pieces of her scattered like leaves in the wind. What would have happened if she hadn't come to her senses? Mercy, but the two of them lived in such different worlds—and he was only passing through hers. What would she have sacrificed had she succumbed? No need to try and ponder—some things were better left alone.

But what about tomorrow? How would she react if he approached her again? She knew full well what could happen. He was temptation, that's what he was.

And sweet deceit.

Well, whatever measures she had to take, there would be no repeating tonight. If only she could somehow disappear into the ethers, magically transport herself to the next waiting ship bound for San Francisco. Well, she couldn't do that, could she? But what she could do was show him she took no interest in him. Not a speck. She would seek Cameron out in the morning, take him up on his offer to spend the day riding.

She wrapped her arms around her waist and surveyed the room. Trevor's power was everywhere—in the note, in the bedding he'd straightened for her, in the flames dancing in the fire he'd lit. He'd done it all for her.

Tears welled.

The last thing she needed was a glimpse of tenderness in a man who was most likely the most dangerous person she had ever met.

Chapter Five

Celine slid off her horse and into Cameron's outstretched arms. He set her gently to the ground, waited for her to straighten her skirts, and then offered his arm. She was glad she'd approached him at breakfast before Trevor arrived. In the far reaches of the plantation, away from the beehive of activity at the house, she could think clearly again. And here, surrounded by oak trees and silence, Trevor did not exist.

"Come," Cameron said. "There's a marvelous tree over here I'd like to show you. It was my favorite as a child."

She placed her hand about his elbow and allowed him to escort her off the path. "How in the world did you find this place? You seem to know every inch of Carlton Oaks. Did you visit often?"

His mouth hitched into a grin. "Indeed. We were a close family. My mother and Trevor's mother were sisters as well as our fathers being brothers."

"No wonder your resemblance to one another is so remarkable. Trevor is your senior by how many years?"

"Two. He and I were inseparable most of our lives. Ah, here we are, what do you think?"

A majestic old oak rose high into the sky, gnarled and weathered with age, its massive branches an umbrella. Hazy shafts of sunlight filtered through the velvet green leaves. Moss, like the gray beards of old wise men, hung heavy from the branches.

"Oh, my. I doubt I've ever seen anything quite so grand. And to think you grew up with it." Her lips formed a smile. No doubt Trevor had played here as well.

One massive branch curved so low to the ground, a part of it provided a wide bench before curving upward again. "We used to sit here oftentimes to regroup, and to eat whatever we managed to snatch from the cookhouse. Have a seat."

Celine shifted about on the limb until she found a comfortable position leaning against the upswing of the tree's grand bough. Cameron rested a bent leg across the branch and his arm across his knee.

"Comfortable?"

"Quite." She relaxed her head against the bark. Cameron was so easy to be around—and certainly kind to one's eyes. The same fondness she treasured for Justin crept into her heart.

"I'm curious, Cameron. If you and Trevor were so close, how is it you went off to school in England?"

"Our fathers separated us."

"Oh yes, that was mentioned over dinner." She dared not ask why, but hoped he'd say.

He touched his thumb and forefinger to the middle of his upper lip, smoothing his moustache to the corners.

"We both lost our mothers two years apart, nearly to the month. We were each aged fifteen when it happened. Trevor had already become a handful by the time my mother died, and it didn't take long for me to catch up. We joined forces in raising holy you-know-what in New Orleans."

"I'm sorry, I shouldn't have asked—"

He raised a hand to stop her words. "Actually, we had quite a jolly time of it until things got out of hand."

"Meaning you were rascals?"

He shrugged. “We got into some rather nasty altercations.” He grinned. “Among other things.”

“Other things?”

He laughed. “Suffice it to say, we . . . ah . . . celebrated the gods of wine and ecstasy to our fullest potential. Things escalated until one night our overindulgence resulted in Madame Olympée’s establishment requiring a rather extensive overhaul.”

Celine’s hands shot to her mouth. Everyone knew what went on at *that* particular gentlemen’s club. “Oh, dear. The Madame allowed young boys inside?”

He looked at her as if she’d lost her mind. “The night of which I speak was my seventeenth birthday. I’ll have you know, I was very much a man—at least in my own eyes. However, before I knew what had happened, I was on the next Andrews Company ship bound for England.”

“And you didn’t set eyes on Trevor again until two years ago? But you were so close.”

He shrugged, picked up a fallen leaf, and then tossed it aside.

“Tell me,” she said.

He studied her for a moment. “I was only in school a couple of months when I became sick as a dog. The doctors surmised that losing a mother and being sent away from the rest of my family was too much for me. So, my father, who was born and raised in England, returned. He brought Trevor along.”

He chuckled again. “But Trevor’s stay barely lasted a few weeks before my father shipped him back to New Orleans.”

“Oh, dear. You must have done quite a bit of making up for lost time once Trevor returned to England permanently.”

Cameron curled his fingers and studied them in mock boredom. “The Parisians revoked our keys to the city that first month. And the whole of Italy won’t have a thing to do with us.” He shrugged. “I suppose if it weren’t for the wealth we provided to some well-placed Asians, a few ports in the Orient wouldn't have us either."

"Oh, and aren't you full of yourself though."

He grew quiet, merriment lingering in his eyes.

She settled a smile on him. "You're a good man, sir. A lady would be fortunate to have you, should you ever decide to settle down."

Cameron leaned forward over his knee and took her hand in his. "Then marry me, Celine. We'll sail the world over. My wealth shall be yours, my wishes your command."

He flipped his hand in the air. "Or is it your wish would be my command? Oh, some such drivel."

Celine laughed softly. "Why, Cameron, you've only recently met me."

"Who cares?" He winked playfully. "Think of the interesting time we'd have getting to know one another." He leaned over and planted a gentleman's kiss on her forehead.

"Sweet. Real sweet, Cousin," Trevor said dryly.

Celine jumped and twisted around to catch Trevor's indolent gaze. "How in the world did you find us clear out here?" Her heart skipped beats at the sight of him sitting casually on that magnificent horse she'd spied earlier in the barn. It was a European Friesian, the stable master had said, and its name was Panther. What a stunning creature with its black coat shimmering in the sun, and a thick curling mane that fell nearly to its knees. Leave it to Trevor to own a horse so striking it turned heads. He sat with one leg hitched over the front of the saddle. He appeared bored, but his dark eyes held fire.

Cameron simply tilted his head backward, peering at his cousin. "Greetings, Trev, old boy. Didn't hear you approach, I was so busy. On your way home from the Widow Beaudrée's?"

Trevor snorted as he swung down from the huge black beast he rode with the same ease and grace as when he'd climbed out of the carriage the day before. He removed his coat and tossed it over the saddle. He was left wearing a white lawn shirt open at the neck and tan buckskin breeches tucked into his boots. A quick glance at his jacket and Celine caught sight of a white stock tie peeking out of the pocket.

Dear Lord, no waistcoat? He didn't even have the decency to finish dressing.

She was appalled at her body's crude response to the thick muscles rippling beneath his thin cambric shirt. She willed herself not to glance at his tight breeches, her stomach knotting. The roar of blood in her ears sounded more like a howling wind. She didn't know if what was happening to her was from the sight of him, and the ever-present sensuousness that clung to him like a musky fog, or if it was because of where she was sure he'd just been. She tried not to think of him and Mrs. Beaudrée wrapped in each other's arms.

Indecent!

Cameron lifted his legs over the branch and switched positions so he faced Trevor. Celine walked around rather than climb over. She moved closer to Cameron, which did little to ease her discomfort. Drat.

Trevor picked up a blade of grass and slipped it between those lush lips of his before he sat down in front of them. He rested an arm on one cocked knee.

Cameron broke into a thick British accent. "I do say, Celine, I think the old boy is about to rudely impose upon us."

"Just keeping an eye on you, Cam." Trevor cocked his head toward Celine. "Has no one told you he has a terrible reputation with regard to young women? One takes quite the risk being alone with him."

Celine set her jaw. As if Trevor were a winged angel. Cornering a lady in the dead of night was more the devil's work. His gaze ran the length of her. Blast it all, a fishing line cast her way could not have hooked her any better than his sultry regard.

Something new and forbidden stirred in her. Damn her unruly emotions.

She blinked, and swore she heard a soft chuckle. Lord, she only hoped she appeared a little more composed than she felt.

A silly schoolgirl, that's what she was. No, schoolgirls didn't get their senses roused at the mere sight of a man. Damnation, he'd just been with another woman. If she were any closer, she could probably smell the other woman's perfume. His musk. Her mouth went dry and an odd misery settled in the pit of her stomach.

Trevor shifted his attention from Celine back to Cameron. "By the way, don't you have anything better to do, Cousin, than sit around in a tree?"

"Such as?"

"Such as perform a bit of work?"

"Egads. You know what they say, Trev, the meek shall inherit the work."

They both laughed easily.

Celine sat quiet and aloof, feeling left out of the camaraderie the cousins shared as they playfully bantered back and forth. Still, she wasn't able to shake the image of what Trevor had so recently been doing with Mrs. Beaudrée, her imagination lowering her previous fine spirits.

"You weren't at the Beaudrées' very long, Trev. What's the matter, somebody beat you there?" Cameron taunted.

"Her barrister came to call. Guess I'll pay my . . . ah . . . respects later."

Celine's heart gave a leap. She heard a rustle in the bushes to her left. "Shh. A rabbit." The animal was gone as fast as she had seen it. She glanced toward the men to see if they, too, had caught a glimpse, but Trevor's cheek rested on his knee and his head was bent in her direction. He studied her as if he held secret thoughts. A corner of his mouth curled upward.

He was thinking of last night, she just knew he was.

Well, she would ignore him and his silent messages. After spending most of the night in contemplation, she had decided not to acknowledge what had occurred. She was determined to keep some measure of control. Nonetheless, a light-headedness crept in as she regarded those dark, almost midnight-black eyes.

Trevor leaned back. Arms crossed behind his head as a pillow, he stretched his long sinewy legs out in front of him, and crossed them at the ankles. His magnificent body lay before her like a banquet. He certainly was well made. Longing, dark as sin, threatened to break through her years of repressed emotions.

He smiled—a knowing smile.

Enough of being toyed with! Lord, but she wanted to bolt. Climb on her horse and ride away from both of them. No, from *him.* She rose and brushed at her skirts. "I need to be on my way, Cameron. I am to meet with Justin to finalize my trip to San Francisco," she lied.

True, she intended to meet with him regarding her plans to leave Carlton Oaks, but it would be his first knowledge that her plans were imminent.

Cameron stood, but Trevor was already on his feet and beside her horse. "I'll help you mount."

There was little she could do to refuse without being rude, but when she placed her booted foot in his cupped hands and touched his shoulder, her pulse tripped.

She nearly laughed out loud when she spied Cameron on his horse and ready to ride. Once beside her gelding, Cameron nudged Trevor out of the way. "Sorry, old chap," he jested.

Trevor only grunted and made for his own horse. The three of them headed back down the narrow ribbon of road to the plantation house, with Trevor forced to ride slightly behind Celine and Cameron.

* * *

Justin handed a pink camellia to Celine and continued to stroll silently along the garden walkway, a slight twitch in his jaw the only indication of his distress.

She wished he would say something—anything.

The silence wore on her. The cloying scent of the flowers grew heavier by the moment until she wondered if she could manage another breath. "Justin, please—"

A deep frown hooded his brow. "Why now, Celine? I hoped you might wait a year, if you went at all. Now I realize when the discussion came up over dinner that you meant sooner. Does Trevor have anything to do with your sudden decision?"

"Yes, and no." Celine decided to be as honest with Justin as she could. He deserved that much. "Elizabeth, Miles, Cameron, Trevor—what does it matter who is involved in my decision? The point is, I've lived quietly, mending slowly. I'll be forever grateful to you for giving me the time to do so in such peaceful surroundings. But I cannot carry on this way. Perhaps your family's arrival hastened my awakening, I don't know, but we both knew from the outset I would leave."

She placed her hand on his arm. "I must find my place in the world, Justin. Staying here would merely continue my . . . my hibernation. I'd be hiding. Stagnating. Something deep within tells me the time to leave here has come."

She squeezed his arm. "Please try to understand. Don't make things harder for me."

He tucked his hand under her chin and raised her face to his. "I do understand, my dear. More than you probably realize. It's just that . . . this selfish old man doesn't want to lose you. I have come to think of you as family. You've filled the gaping hole in my life that opened when I lost my eldest daughter to influenza."

"I must leave."

"I know."

Tears glistened in both their eyes as, arm in arm, they made their way back through the garden.

Suddenly, her senses alerted her that someone watched them. She glanced up to the second-floor gallery. Trevor stood in the afternoon shadows, leaning against the wall in silent observation.

A chill ran through her. “Do you mind if we go inside?”

Justin gave her arm a pat. “Not at all. In fact, come to my office. There’s something I’d like to discuss with you.”

They exchanged small talk as they made their way to his office. He retrieved a thick journal from the bookcase behind him and nodded to the leather chair in front of the desk. “Please, sit.”

The clock on a shelf ticked the silent moments by as Justin thumbed through the book. “Our company has a ship sailing for San Francisco from New Orleans in six weeks. Do an old man one last favor and take passage on it?” He smiled tenderly. “I’ll see you to town myself when the time comes.”

Dear Lord, six long weeks? “Of course,” Celine responded, wondering how in the world she would be able to put up with Trevor’s advances. How the devil long were those two cousins planning to extend their stay at Carlton Oaks? She dared not ask. Not at the moment, anyway.

She thought of suggesting they leave for New Orleans at once, telling Justin she would like to spend a bit of time in the city where she’d grown up before leaving forever. But then, Trevor and Cameron would soon return there on business, and wouldn’t they reside in the family townhouse? Which was where Justin would expect her to stay. Oh, dear, what a predicament.

Chapter Six

Despite the formidable gray skies that moved in before sunset, spirits ran high, for the family would soon travel upriver to attend the soirée at the Verrette plantation. Celine couldn't remember when she'd tasted such delicious excitement.

She sat at the dressing table fidgeting while Marie put the finishing touches on her hair. She tried for as much nonchalance as she could muster. "Tell me about the Widow Beaudrée."

Marie grunted and spoke through the pins in her mouth. "Oh, that woman is something, I'll tell you." Her gaze connected with Celine's through the mirror. Her pursed lips contained a sly smile. "That woman wasn't even half Mister Beaudrée's age."

She wound the last section of hair, pinned the curl in place, and removing the pins from her mouth, patted the sides of Celine's head. "There now, let's see to your gown."

Celine stepped over to the full-length cheval mirror and removed her robe.

"If you ask me," Marie continued while she dressed Celine, "she was only after his money, because she doesn't seem too put out now there's no man around. No ma'am.

Soon's poor Mister Beaudrée was in the ground, she started spendin' his money like the world wouldn't see another Sunday."

"Is she attractive?"

"Well—" She drew out the word, savoring it like sweet chocolate on her tongue. "I suppose she's pretty enough. But she knows it, and that kills any hope the woman has of impressin' most people. Doesn't dress much like a widow, neither. Even the frock she wore to Mr. Beaudrée's funeral was cut so low you could spy her toes when she bent over. And believe me, she managed a lot of bendin' that day."

Marie grinned wide through the mirror at Celine. And then she giggled.

Oh, dear. Celine wouldn't dare laugh along with Marie.

She simply couldn't.

She did.

"You were there?"

Marie was all teeth and sparkling eyes as she nodded. "Hold still, mam'selle. With all your fidgeting, I've had to do these corset laces three times. I know the truth of which I speak, because there was a crowd here followin' the funeral. Zola was fit to be tied having to prepare anything on behalf of that woman. Mrs. Beaudrée spent her entire stay crying in her hanky, with the men putting their arms around her and saying, 'There, there. Don't be weepin' so.' And all the while they was gawkin' right down the front of her." She winked. "Right to her toes."

Celine laughed harder. "So, she's pretty enough, then."

Marie carried Celine's gown over to her. "Oh, she's pretty, all right. Well shaped in the body, too. But she goes and ruins it by that look she always has about her."

"What look?"

"Like she's just waitin' for someone to be givin' her a poke right 'tween her legs."

Celine's jaw dropped. "Marie!" And then she guffawed at the maid's frankness.

"She is nowhere near as lovely as you, though, mam'selle." Marie patted a bow on the gown's puffed sleeve, a gesture indicating the toilette was complete.

"There you go. *Ravissante.*"

"Thank you for the kind compliment, Marie, but I hardly think I am ravishing."

"*Mais oui.* Look in the mirror."

Celine made a pirouette in front of the looking glass. She stepped closer and paused to study the deep turquoise moiré silk gown with a bateau neckline cut so low she wondered if *she* dared bend over lest someone see *her* toes. The bodice fit tightly down to her hips, accenting every curve before billowing out to the floor. A string of pearls snaked through the shining curls piled atop her head. "Oh, the gown is beautiful, isn't it?"

Lindsey's knock sounded at the door. He flushed when the door opened and he spied Celine. "You are . . . well, you are breathtaking."

She slipped her hand over his elbow and bid Marie a good evening.

Cameron called out from below when the two descended the stairs. "And I am supposed to escort my cousin while little Lindsey gets you? Unfair, I say."

She met him at the bottom and held her gloved hand to him for his perfunctory kiss.

"At least may I have the honor of riding in the same carriage, madame?"

"Of course," Celine laughed softly. "Whatever did I do for entertainment before I met you?"

Trevor's gaze burned into her as he joined them. "You're lovely, Celine. Your dress matches your eyes."

Cameron shot a curious glance at Celine's turquoise gown

and then to her eyes. He raised an inquisitive brow at Trevor, but made no comment.

Two covered carriages stood at the ready in front of the manse. Justin assisted Felicité and Celine into the first carriage and then went about seeing to the other.

Felicité began to chatter. Celine leaned over and whispered, “Remember, well-bred ladies do not talk over much.” Justin often referred to his daughter as sixteen, going on twelve, and Celine worried he might be right at times.

Trevor slid gracefully into the seat next to Celine, his movements as sleek as a cat’s.

She grew instantly light-headed. “Isn’t Lindsey supposed to ride in this carriage?”

Trevor shifted to the corner in order to fit his wide expanse of shoulder next to Celine. “Lindsey wanted his papa.” He slid his arm along the back of the seat behind her, his fingers brushing her bare flesh ever so slightly as he took in every detail of her.

Despite the heat of his body, shivers ran down her arm.

Cameron vaulted into the carriage next to Felicité and regarded Trevor. “*Mon Dieu,* how much did you have to pay your little brother, old boy?”

Celine sensed a sting to Cameron’s taunting words. He smiled, but his eyes were cold.

The ominous sky caused Celine to shudder. She pulled her cape around her.

Felicité leaned over and touched Celine’s knee, her brows knit together.

Celine shook her head to the girl.

“Chilled?” Trevor asked.

“I’m fine, thank you.” She prayed they would arrive soon. The air felt heavy inside the carriage, and she thought she heard a rumble of thunder.

They rode the distance in silence. Every jostle of the carriage pressed Trevor’s hard, sinewy thigh to hers, burning through the layers of clothing. Her cheeks prickled with heat. He could be Satan himself tonight. He was dressed entirely in black, except for his white shirt and white silk stock. His raven hair and midnight eyes made him appear almost sinister, albeit exceedingly handsome. And there seemed to be an even greater intensity about him this evening than usual.

She thought of his sensuous mouth.

Her loins quickened.

Once again, chaos reigned in her mind.

At last they arrived, and soon, Celine found herself standing inside the entrance between Cameron and Trevor. The others stood behind them, waiting to be announced.

All attention in the room was riveted on Celine as Trevor removed her cape and handed it to a footman. The buzz of conversation increased. She stood, regal and proud, while she was announced—as her grandmother had taught her. Hopefully, no one would guess how violently her insides churned.

"Hold on, Celine," Cameron said through a clenched jaw. "Here comes the Widow Beaudrée with her claws out, and she's headed straight for you."

Giselle Beaudrée smiled through even, white teeth. "Cameron, Trevor, how nice to see you. And you must be Mrs. Kirkland. I've heard so much about you. We really must take tea, my dear. We widows have to stick together, you know."

Giselle's condescending manner did little to hide her obvious jealousy. Her cold blue eyes boldly pierced Celine like two ice picks.

The woman was more beautiful than Celine had anticipated with her ivory skin and pale yellow hair. She was dressed in a low-cut black gown that revealed every line and curve of her body. Her ample breasts lay practically bare.

Celine's breath suddenly felt shorter when she saw

Trevor's quick appraisal of Giselle. Oooh, that damnable lazy smile of his. She willed herself to remain calm, aloof, while a subtle grin settled around her mouth. Marie was right. The widow did look as though she was just *waitin' to get poked.*

Uncertainty seemed to wash over Giselle Beaudrée at Celine's regard of her. Her brows drew together slightly, and she backed away a step. Suddenly, she faced Celine again with fury in her eyes and a red blotch on each cheek.

Trevor left Celine's side and stepped between the two women. Giselle slid her arm through the crook of Trevor's elbow and raised her nose in the air. "See me to the refreshment table, will you, dear?"

The woman brazenly hung on Trevor's arm the entire evening while a long line of potential *beaux* and curious married gentlemen kept Celine occupied on the dance floor. Cameron and Lindsey simply got back in line after each turn and jockeyed for their fair share of her attention.

Michel and Felicité were lost in their own fantasies and spared little time for their family. Celine would have enjoyed herself immensely but for her constant vexation whenever Trevor and Giselle danced by. He seemed oblivious to Celine's very presence.

Why should she care? Those two deserved one another. A rutting bull and a cow in heat. Nonetheless, as the night wore on, Celine felt drained.

Justin, who kept constant vigil over her, must have sensed her fatigue, for he finally cut in on one of her smitten partners. He escorted her to the terrace for a breath of fresh air.

"Thank heavens for my knight in shining armor." She grimaced when she noticed black clouds hanging low and threatening in the sky.

Justin made note as well. "Stay here while I round up

the others. It's nearing midnight anyway, and I've no desire to get caught in a cloudburst."

He knew she still had a great fear of storms, and although she did not want to be responsible for their early departure, relief flooded her. She looked for the moon, and, not finding it, wrapped her arms about herself, feeling very alone.

A hand slid gently around her waist. She shivered. Trevor's hot breath fell against her ear. This time she grew angry. How dare he try his seductions after spending the entire evening with that . . . that bovine? She steeled herself against any reaction. "Don't touch me."

"You don't really mean that, do you, Celine?"

"Indeed, I do." She brushed his hand off her.

"You speak as though your tongue dripped ice water." He grasped her shoulders and forced her to face him. "Look at me, *ma petite.*"

"I do believe you've had too much to drink." She attempted to push him away, but he may as well have been a wall. "And you do not have permission to refer to me so intimately."

His mouth crushed down on hers. The heady scent of brandy filled her nostrils. She gave a strangled cry and struggled for release. But the more she writhed, the tighter he held her, until she was sure he would rob the very breath from her lungs.

She ceased fighting him.

His tongue deftly parted her lips and probed the soft recesses of her trembling mouth. Each hot thrust felt as though he were deep inside her, touching from within. Primal desire shot through her, jagged and hot.

God, what was he doing to her? How could she be reacting this way? His hand slipped down to the small of her back, and tilted her pelvis forward. She gasped as he leaned his hard shaft against her in the same manner as he'd done in the cookhouse. He pulled his mouth from hers and looked through the shadows, searching her face.

"Leave me alone, Trevor. I do not want you."

His breathing came in short, ragged pulls. "You want me as much as I want you, Celine."

"Do you think every woman wants you? Well, I don't."

A muscle in his jaw twitched. "Yes, you do. Why don't you admit it? Life's too short to play little virginal games, and that's something you and I both know you are not."

Raw emotion shot through her, sharpening her tongue to a knife's edge. "If it is illicit pleasure you seek, you've had the perfect partner on your arm all evening. Go to her for your dirty little games."

He pivoted on his heel and left her, but after a few steps, he paused. "You little fool. I spent the entire evening keeping jealous Giselle Beaudrée from sinking her vicious claws into you." He disappeared.

Justin found Celine again and moments later the Andrews family departed under the blanket of an impending storm. She tried to jockey the seating around to make sure she rode next to Lindsey, but this time Justin intervened.

He scowled at the sky. "Celine, I want you in the carriage next to me. Trevor, you and Felicité ride with us. The rest of you take the other carriage."

Trevor frowned at the concerned mantle his father wore as the carriages rolled into the night.

A rumble in the distance brought huge drops of rain down on the coach. The wind kicked up and howled like a great wolf.

Celine stiffened.

Justin slipped his arm around her. "Everything's under control."

What the devil?

A bolt of lightning lit the sky followed by an ear-splitting crack of thunder.

Celine whimpered.

Justin pulled her closer.

Lightning lit the night again and the horses whinnied and shied. The carriage swayed sideways. Celine's horrifying shriek reverberated through the night.

Trevor leaned forward, puzzled, but his father didn't see him, so intent was he on trying to calm a cowering Celine.

"It's all right," Justin soothed. "You're fine, Celine." He kept talking to her, rocking her in his arms as the storm hit with a fury. Her cries melted into pitiful low moans.

The tempest howled, growing fiercer with the journey. With each fire bolt that illuminated the blackness, Celine disintegrated a little further. The band around Trevor's chest cinched tighter at every roar of thunder.

As soon as they reached the manor, he intercepted his father, swooping Celine up in his arms and dashing for the door Marie held open.

"I've been waiting for her. Quick, get her to her quarters."

Trevor rushed a whimpering Celine up the stairs, taking them two at a time. As he laid her gently on the bed, he wrenched the wet cape from her shoulders.

Marie rudely cast Trevor aside. "Now git!" she ordered, before slamming the door in his face.

"What the hell was that about?" Trevor demanded as his father mounted the stairs.

Justin dismissed the others to their rooms before addressing Trevor. Sparing no detail, he told his son how a stable hand had found Celine in the storm, how if it weren't for Old Jim, she would not be alive. "All of Celine's blood relatives had been deceased for some time, and after that terrible day, she was left with no one, so I took her in."

Speechless, a shudder ran through Trevor.

"We never did find her father-in-law, but Old Jim dug

him a grave next to Celine's husband anyway. He mounded the earth back on top of the empty pit, so she would think he was in there."

Justin caught his breath, and then continued. "He buried the infant, as well."

A jolt spiked through Trevor. "Infant?"

Justin nodded. "I think that was the hardest part. Her child wasn't due for another three months, but she gave birth to the babe while she lay trapped under the wagon. Old Jim lifted that child from Celine's bloody body, wrapped it in a blanket, and buried it alongside its father. The physician told us she would never bear another child, her injuries were so severe."

Nausea bit at Trevor's gut. He ran a trembling hand through his wet hair, shoving the curls away from his damp forehead. "Good God, I had no idea. You told me she was a widow. I . . . I simply assumed—"

"Assumed what, Trevor? That she was like your Mrs. Beaudrée, or any of the other questionable women you frequent? Marrying some old man for his money and helping him to a premature grave so she can romp with the likes of you? Is that what you thought? Celine isn't made of such thin fabric. And don't you for one second assume otherwise."

His father stood taller, drew in an audible breath, and shot Trevor a scowl that could have frozen the Mississippi. Christ. Trevor bit back a sharp retort. Not since his mother's death, when he'd blamed his father for not calling in a physician soon enough, had he been the recipient of such animosity. Blast it all, he'd only been fifteen at the time. When would the past stop haunting them? He stood for a long moment, not knowing what to do with the raw emotion fogging his brain. All he knew was he wanted to go to Celine.

Marie opened the door and Trevor stalked in, his father right behind. A fist hit Trevor's gut at the sight of Celine.

She lay silent and limp beneath the covers, as pale as the nightgown she wore. Her eyes were closed in apparent slumber.

"I got a good dose of laudanum in her, but looks like this storm has a mind to carry on all night by the sound of it. She'll be needin' someone, so I'd best spend the night with her. No tellin' when that stuff wears off a person when they're so upset."

She regarded the sleeping figure. "Tch, tch. Poor thing. What she's been through."

Trevor couldn't bear the thought of leaving her. "You go along, Marie. I'll watch over her."

Marie's jaw dropped. Wide-eyed, she looked at Trevor and then at Justin. She scowled and opened her mouth to speak.

Trevor raised a hand to stop her before she got the words out. "*Mon Dieu,* woman. What do you take me for?"

His foul temper caused even Marie to back away.

"Trevor's right," Justin broke in, heaving a tired sigh. "Actually, with his size and strength, he's probably the best one to handle her if she becomes hysterical. Remember how it took both of us at one time? Should that happen, you'd only have to call him in anyway, since his bedchamber is closest. Besides, we have a house full of guests you'll need to be tending to come morning and Trevor can sleep the day away."

Marie shook her head in disapproval, but went around pulling the drapes and securing doors. "It'd be best to keep the lightnin' out as much as you can. And lock the doors so they don't rattle and shake. That gives her such a fright." She nodded to the chair by the fireplace. "I usually pull that chair right up beside the bed, pat her hand when needed."

She surveyed the men, giving in to them. "Lordy, but you two had better get out of those wet clothes before you catch your deaths. I'll bring your robe, Mischie Trevor." She walked off, shaking her head and muttering.

"Sure talks a lot when she's nervous, doesn't she, Father?"

Justin smiled tiredly at Trevor's attempt to bridge the gap between them. He studied Trevor thoughtfully before bidding him good night.

Perhaps, Trevor thought, the hollow relationship they'd had since his mother's death was about to change.

By the time Marie returned, carrying a thick towel and robe, Trevor had a fire blazing. He was stripped to his trousers, his hands held over the flames when she walked in. She threw the robe and towels onto the chair and hurried to Celine's side, as if to shield her from the sight of him.

"Don't worry, she's asleep." Trevor spoke in a hushed, annoyed voice as he grabbed the towel and dried his hair and arms. "Now turn around while I disrobe, or get out."

Marie put her back to him. "I near raised you, Trevor. It ain't like I never seen you nekkid."

A small smile passed over his lips. He stepped out of his sodden trousers and reached for his robe. "I never thanked you for all those nights you waited up for me and made excuses regarding my whereabouts."

When she didn't deign to reply, he said, "You can leave and take this wet heap with you."

She walked over to the clothing on the floor, wrapped everything in the towel, and started for the door.

"Why did you?"

She stopped and turned to face him. "Why did I what?"

"What made you risk standing by me back then? I think I was quite mad, you know—the effects of an angry young man filled with liquor."

The scowl left her face and her words softened. "That and the mating call."

"I never thanked you for saving my skin on several occasions."

"Savin' your skin while I risked my own hide? I'll have you know my covering for you wasn't because of all the liquor you were pickling your liver with, or the loose women you were seducing like a damned jack rabbit." She stepped closer. "So don't go thanking me, 'cause I didn't do nuthin' for you. Whatever I did was for your father's sake."

"Father?"

"Don't you remember the night Thérèse Dubois's husband lit up the front yard with his torch lookin' for you? I always feared after that night that a time would come when your papa would wake up to a passel of torches, and it would be more than a bush being put to flame. That's why I fibbed the skin right off my teeth every time the sheriff showed up."

She glanced over Trevor's shoulder at Celine and then back to him. "Things are mighty peaceful around here. Maybe you'd best get back to your business in N'awlins. I don't see nuthin' but trouble for Miss Celine if'n you stay here."

"Maybe I've changed," he said.

"And maybe you haven't."

Trevor glanced to where Celine lay. A desire to protect her crept through his bones. But this wasn't just about protecting her. He was growing damn tired of carousing. "What if I change whatever needs changing?"

Marie paused, holding the door's handle. "What if you can't?"

When the door closed, Trevor lifted the chair over to the side of the bed and settled in. He studied Celine while she slept. He wondered what it was about her that made him want her so much. Desire flooded through him at the very thought. He picked up her limp hand and pressed a kiss on the back. He caught the scent of her skin before tucking the covers around her.

He leaned back in the chair. His desire for her went beyond the physical. How had she gotten under his skin so quickly? What was it about her that made him hunger so, that filled him with an aching need that wouldn't dissipate? Maybe it was nothing more than his growing restlessness of late. Hell, he didn't know.

A shutter banged in the wind and Celine moaned.

"Everything's all right," he murmured. "I'm here." He hoped the damn storm was almost over, and they weren't merely in the eye of a hurricane running up from New Orleans.

He recalled the time he'd broken his leg as a child. He'd been given laudanum to help him through the worst of it. Frightened and disoriented, he'd wanted someone to hold him, to comfort him in his pain and fear. But even though his fogged brain could think, and his eyes could see, his thick tongue refused to move in his mouth, so he lay there, staring up at his mother, suffering in mute terror. He wondered if Celine wasn't experiencing the same thing.

He slipped his hand under the covers and, finding hers again, gave it a small squeeze. The weak pressure he felt in return gave him the answer. His heart pumped hard as concern grew into quiet alarm. Moving atop the covers next to her, he stroked her hair, combed through the mass with his fingers, all the while whispering soft, gentle words of comfort.

The edges of the shutters lit up, followed by a crack of thunder that shook the rafters. Christ, they'd been in a lull after all. The worst of the storm was most likely moving overhead.

A shutter tore loose and hammered against the house. A thunderbolt split the air again. Celine's eyes flew wide in terror, focusing on nothing.

"There, there, Celine. It's all right." Trevor leaned over her, squeezed her hand in his.

She shivered and her teeth chattered.

"Hush." He tucked the covers up under her chin and ran his hand across her forehead in soothing strokes.

A low moan escaped her lips.

"Celine, listen to me. You're all right. Everything's fine now. You're safe."

Panic bit at his gut. *Mon Dieu.* Maybe she would have

been better off with Marie. At least the maid would know what the hell to do now.

Celine's body curled up like a child's, and she began to moan and thrash about. He didn't know what else to do, so he crawled under the covers, shushing and nurturing as he went.

Slowly, gently, he straightened her quivering body, rolled her onto her side, and nestled her against him. He buried her head in his chest and rocked her.

She shook and trembled. Her teeth chattered, but her skin was almost hot to the touch. Trevor knew from experience she was gripped by a fear beyond rational thought.

"It's all right, *ma petite*. I'm taking care of you." He stroked her hair and placed soft, tender kisses on her eyelids. "*Mon amour, mon amour,* you are safe."

She managed enough movement to slip her arms under his, wrapped them tightly around his back as though she couldn't get close enough, nearly bringing him atop her. He lay firm but gently against her, the quaking in her body lessening by the sheer force of him.

Trevor? Was that Trevor? No, it must be a hazy dream. Yet, a sense of great comfort settled over her. The wind whispered her name as it blew across her eyelids.

"*Mon amour, mon amour,* you are safe with me."

In her foggy haze, clouds gathered together, descended upon her, body and soul. Warm, safe, cotton clouds. Gently, they pressed her down, a warm blanket of protection. She dreamed the storm was Trevor enfolding her, protecting her, loving her. And she ceased to be frightened, for now it was a gentle storm, a loving storm, a nurturing storm.

The storm gentled further and pressed closer. She relaxed against it, let the warmth envelop her, let the tenderness sweep her into its depths until she was completely surrounded, possessed entirely.

In the far reaches of her mind, she heard herself moan as

she tried to receive more of the storm's warmth, wanting it to enter her, to become a part of her.

The wind continued to whisper her name, and slowly, she pulled her head back, searching.

Lightning struck her mouth. Soft and cool and sweet, it pulsated through her, filled her with a velvet glow. She felt supremely safe, warm and loved.

Thunder roared through the night like a wild bear. And the wind—like a hungry wolf—howled and beat its claws against the shutters.

She whimpered and he held her closer.

Was she dreaming?

Had she heard Trevor murmur to her? Was he actually holding her tightly to him—so safe?

The wind howled louder and beat against the walls.

His whispers soothed, his arms held.

This could only be a dream. But let the reverie continue, for she felt so safe and warm.

And in her dream she was snuggled against Trevor. Her quaking body ceased its tremors. She pulled him closer, sought his comfort.

Did he just say he ached for her? That he ached to taste her sweetness, but not now, not tonight?

Somewhere in the recesses of her fogged brain, she again questioned if she was only dreaming.

She didn't care.

His male hardness pressed against her. Her legs parted beneath her gown as she urged him to enter her.

"No, Celine. No."

Was that the wind?

It could not be, for Trevor gasped her name again and again until his mouth found hers. He kissed her cheeks, her forehead, tenderly, lovingly. And then he cradled her against him and gently rocked her. While she was wrapped in the warmth of his arms, her fears dissipated and the world faded into nothingness.

Chapter Seven

"Open the door, Miss Celine!"

Celine shot straight up in bed, peering through the darkened room. Numb from sleep, she dragged herself to the door and unlocked it. Hazy memories trickled to the periphery of her mind.

"Tch, tch, tch." Marie shook her head as she set the tray of coffee and toast down and flung the draperies aside, letting in a bright swath of golden sunlight.

"I'll take breakfast on the gallery." Celine fumbled for a robe, then changed her mind and let Marie help her into a simple green cotton dress. "Leave my hair."

She walked over to the basin, splashed cold water on her face, and then picked up a brush to unsnarl the tangled mass about her shoulders. "On second thought, can you brush the snarls out?"

"Marie?" She was surprised to find herself alone. "Marie, where in the world did you run off to?" Oh well, she'd rather be by herself anyway. Scrutinizing herself in the mirror, she recalled her vivid, physically stimulating dreams from the night before.

They'd seemed so real.

Could Trevor have possibly been with her in the flesh?

Of course not.

The aroma of strong, black Creole coffee tickled her senses. A cup of the *petit noir* would clear her head. As she walked toward the French doors leading to the gallery, she spied a brown bottle of laudanum on the table next to the bed. And then the blue satin sheets with indentations where two bodies had lain.

A rush of emotion swept through her like a hot wind.

She swept her trembling hands over her breasts, and then slowly trailed them down her body, her mind clearing. Memories flooded in—of his warm body next to hers, of gentle words whispered in her ear, of strong arms enfolding her, and soothing kisses. God, they were sweet, and wonderful. But nothing had happened beyond that. Relief calmed her fluttering heart. She breathed an audible sigh.

Her stomach grumbled. She moved toward the gallery, but then hesitated and turned to stare at the bedroom door, its key still hanging in the lock. She looked to the French doors, and raised an eyebrow in question.

Had she not unlocked the bedroom door to admit Marie? And had she not observed the maid unlocking the French doors in order to take the breakfast tray outside? If so, how then had Trevor exited? Did he have an extra set of keys? With a shrug, she decided that was likely the answer since the room had originally been his. She stepped onto the gallery.

Trevor sat at the table, casually sipping a cup of coffee, his broad shoulders sheathed in a pale yellow lawn shirt and tan jacket, his long legs in suede breeches and boots.

"Good morning," she said, as nonchalantly as she could manage, and seated herself across from him.

He smiled easily, but Celine sensed a seriousness in him she hadn't felt before. Perhaps if she pretended not to recall anything from the night before . . . After all, there was the laudanum. "Marie tells me you remained the night to watch over me," she fibbed. "That was very kind." Lord, her heart thumped so.

Trevor's eyes narrowed. And then he looked to his coffee. "Ah, I see. I suppose things are better left that way."

A heated flush crawled up her neck. He knew she'd lied. She fidgeted with the napkin that lay next to her plate, and then slipped the square of cotton onto her lap. "I . . . ah . . . had dreams that you comforted me in the night, Trevor. I—" Her words caught in her throat.

He covered her hand with his—warm and strong. And familiar.

He brushed his thumb slowly back and forth across her sensitive skin—a loving, comforting gesture that sent bursts of pleasure up her arm.

Then she remembered. Everything. How well she'd fit into the wondrous circle of his protection, how her hand had slid between the folds of his robe to tangle with curls on his chest before she drifted away to the sound of his soothing murmurs.

Oh, how she would love to be able to relax, allow the sheer joy of being touched by him to take them where it would. Instead, she turned away, barely aware of the sun-kissed day, cognizant only of his exquisite touch blurring her thoughts.

"Look at me," he commanded softly.

She was afraid to do so. Would he see raw desire in her eyes? The confusing longing that went beyond anything she had the ability to cope with? And what if he did? She couldn't avoid his scrutiny forever. Not until she removed herself from Carlton Oaks, at least.

Her bottom lip quivered when she took in a breath. Surely he noticed. She wrapped her pride cape-like around her, so intimidated was she by the feelings this man evoked in her.

His thumb ceased stroking her; his cupped hand applied a gentle pressure. "Now, Celine."

She returned her gaze to his, the tension so great that she closed her lids and swallowed hard.

The pressure on her hand increased.

He would be relentless.

She opened her eyes.

Her lips went dry. She wet them with her tongue. He watched her every movement, like a cat stalking a mouse.

A fickle wave of desire swept through her.

If he carried her to a bed this very instant, she doubted she could refuse him. And then she would be sorry later. So very sorry when he'd had his taste of her and moved on.

"We're not finished, you and I," he murmured huskily. "It's time we admitted our mutual attraction, *ma petite.*"

She didn't feel very brave right now, not with her womb like tinder about to ignite.

Something more than desire emanated from the depths of him. A force she couldn't quite translate into thought. Could it be the same kind of compelling energy gathering in her?

He leaned forward and pressed his cheek to hers. "*Mon amour.* I want you as you want me."

Yes, she wanted him. A part of her wished he would take her up in his arms and end all her frustration—carry her back to the blue satin sheets. Yet, another part of her wanted to run, to protect herself from what she could not have. Had any other human felt so vulnerable?

Good God, he was a rakehell, a man merely passing through her life. Which meant only one thing—a tryst. "I . . . I cannot, Trevor." Hot pain clogged her heart. "I'm not made of the same fabric as you. I cannot lie casually with a man and then carry on as if nothing happened. It's not in me."

He eased back, a vague shadow crossing over his features. "We are more alike than you realize, Celine."

For a split second, she saw him in all his desperate loneliness, a solitary figure of a man whose passions ran as deep as his pride.

He was hugely successful by every social standard—an instinctive genius with business, a fine figure of a man whom many admired, despite his questionable behavior. But from what Celine had gathered at last night's event, even his improper deportment garnered secret admiration—from men who silently wished they had the courage to commit half of what they heard gossiped about him, and from women who secretly wished to share his scandalous conduct.

Yet did he still struggle with life? Was he trying to find meaning and purpose—like her? If that was what he meant by his remark, then perhaps they were alike. She dared not ask—she feared his answer.

"What do you want from me that most other women wouldn't freely give you?" She withdrew her hand from his and placed it in her lap, well away from his reach. "Because I sense your desires are more complicated than simply bedding an available female."

She sat back, found the strength to butter a piece of toast, and waited.

He did not deign to answer. He himself did not know what it was he truly wanted from her, what compelled him to seek her out, to taunt her.

His desire to make love to her was undeniable. But even that seemed strangely secondary since last night.

Frustration curdled his gut. He had always enjoyed the company of women, had taken their pleasure on his terms, amused himself with their passions at will. Yet, he pursued this woman as though he were a smitten schoolboy. Was he merely trying to capture the bird that insisted on remaining just out of reach? Or was there more—much more?

He physically turned away from her question, toward the view of the gardens. A vague anger he didn't understand rose in him like thin smoke from a chimney. He wanted to strike back at her blatant rejection of him, and at her maddeningly superior calm.

"You'll never have me on your terms, Trevor," she said softly.

Primal emotion ran through him at her last remark, turning his blood cold. He regretted his whim to take breakfast on the balcony with her. What the hell was wrong with him anyway?

"And just what are your terms, Mrs. Kirkland? Marriage?"

His words stung; he knew it by the shock sweeping over her face. He was instantly sorry. But it was too late to retract them—a crisp click of heels sounded along the gallery, coming from the front of the house.

Cameron rounded the corner and bore down on the two of them.

"Ah, there you are, old boy. You have a guest eagerly awaiting your appearance in your father's office. A certain Mrs. Beaudrée."

Cameron focused on Celine, smiling. "Care to go for a ride, my dear?"

"Perhaps you and your guest would like to join us?" Celine offered Trevor, her words dripping with sarcasm.

Trevor barked a cynical laugh. He rose, pushed the wrinkles of his brown suede breeches down his leg, and ran the other hand carelessly through his hair. He stretched, catlike, and covered a yawn, feeling perversely mischievous. "No, thank you. Mrs. Beaudrée and I have . . . ah . . . other plans."

Celine's cheeks flushed and her mouth opened to speak, but then she hesitated. "A pity."

She turned to Cameron. "Meet me at the stables in an hour's time. You showed me the marvelous oak; now I have a special place I would like to take you."

Trevor could have spit. He feigned lack of interest instead.

"At your service, *ma chérie.*" Cameron bent and kissed

the back of Celine's hand, then whispered something in her ear, which Trevor couldn't quite catch. She laughed softly and stood.

Well, he'd be damned if he was going to play this game. Where the hell could she be taking Cameron? He turned to leave before the muscle twitching at his set jaw gave him away.

"Wait, Trev, old boy. I'll walk with you." Cameron slapped him on the back.

"Keep your hands to yourself," Trevor muttered, suddenly wanting to knock the smirk off his cousin's face.

"Oh, and see if you can round up a bottle of champagne, will you?" Celine called after Cameron.

Both men turned at her words.

"We can cool it in the stream." Straight-backed and with an elevated chin, she disappeared into her quarters.

Once inside, she disintegrated and flung herself onto the bed in tears. She was so sick of playing games, of being on edge all the time, pretending one emotion while feeling another, looking for Trevor in every shadow.

She wanted to run as far away as she could.

San Francisco. She couldn't get there fast enough. Had she not lingered over Dianah's invitation, she would already be there. But it wouldn't do to try and book passage quicker—to do so would break Justin's heart. Her emotions were in shreds, all because of some rutting bull of a man wishing to bed her.

And why had she agreed to go riding with Cameron? The *garçonnière* was her little secret, her private world, and now she was taking him there? The last thing she felt like doing was carrying out the little farce she'd created with him. Enjoying his friendship was one thing. Using him to taunt another man was beneath her. The headache she'd barely gotten rid of returned with a vengeance. A good reason to beg off.

Bring champagne, Cameron, she mocked herself. God, she wished she'd never been rescued from under the wheels of that wagon. She was a widow, but worse, she'd been left barren by the accident. She could never consider life with a man wanting a family. Loving, or being loved by such a man, was out of the question.

Trevor sat in his father's office pretending to listen to Giselle and her ramblings while he racked his brain for answers. Where the hell was Celine taking Cameron that she could cool a bottle of champagne in a stream?

He was well aware that the meeting Giselle Beaudrée had requested was pretense. She had claimed she wanted to go over their agreement to ship furniture from Europe on the Andrews Company shipping line. Everything was already in order. He knew it. She knew it.

He wished he'd taken Celine up on her offer to join them on their ride instead of implying that there was something going on between him and Giselle.

Frustrated, he shifted in his seat and flung a leg over the arm of his chair, causing Giselle to look up from the records she and Justin were poring over.

She threw Trevor a bold glance aimed at his crotch, and then worked her gaze slowly up to his eyes. A knowing smile played upon her mouth.

They'd been insatiable together at one time. His mind flickered back two years earlier—to the last time he'd been with her. Both had drunk far too much champagne, and he'd taken her on the bare floor in a wild frenzy. She raked his back with her fingernails and announced she was pleased he would sail off to England bearing the distinct markings of their mutual passion.

She'd been an addiction then. The more he got, the more he wanted. Revulsion stirred in his gut at the memory of his past behavior. Her low-cut widow's weeds, heavy perfume, and come hither look disgusted him. He fought the urge to walk out, knowing full well what she was up to, bending over the bills of lading in such a wanton manner.

Suddenly, something caught in his mind. The old *garçonnière* in the woods. Of course, that's where Celine and Cameron were, damn it! The stream there was man-made, designed so a fresh, cool backflow from the Mississippi provided water for the old bachelor's quarters. And after last night's heavy rains, it would indeed be swollen and cold.

He stood, and rudely dismissed himself. His father, accustomed to Trevor's showing less than punctilious French Creole manners, scowled at Trevor's actions. Giselle wrapped up the paperwork, eager to join him.

"I'll see you out," he said, ignoring the displeasure washing over her face. "I have some business I must attend to."

He walked her to the carriage and then turned on his heel and headed for the stable. He intended to ride as far in the opposite direction from the *garçonnière* as he could manage in a day. To hell with both of them.

Trevor carried his foul mood to the dinner table, dampening everyone's spirits. He didn't bother to acknowledge Cameron's efforts to tease him into a more jocular mood. The only one he bothered to regard was Celine, and he did that with a coldness that even to him felt menacing.

She fidgeted openly and ignored him. There were shadows under her eyes.

"Tired, Celine?" he asked directly.

When she turned her gaze on him, it was without passion. "I find the evening to be strangely cool. Truth be told, I have a keen desire to curl up by a fire in my room and pull an interesting book from the shelf."

Why, to get away from him?

She looked away.

Cameron asked Trevor a question. He didn't bother to respond.

"Well, Trev," Cameron finally put in after another try at bringing him into the conversation, "the nice thing about apathy is you don't have to exert yourself to show you're sincere."

Trevor twisted one corner of his mouth up and snorted lightly.

Cameron was delighted. "Well, then, it only took all evening, but I finally elicited a response from the grouch."

Justin was unusually quiet, but he missed nothing. He rarely did. Irritation soured Trevor's stomach. His father was like a guard dog sleeping with one eye open.

"Well, now, how was, ah, Mrs. Beaudrée?" Cameron continued. "Does she have anything to do with your black mood?"

A flush crawled up Celine's neck.

"Don't ask," Trevor snapped, and then a sardonic reply left his tongue. "Or I might tell you. And we wouldn't want to embarrass the ladies, now would we, Cam?"

"Oh, do tell." Cameron leaned forward to refill his wineglass. "You know the old saying—if you can't say anything nice about someone, then you're probably delightful company."

Felicité tittered. Cameron's perverse humor even elicited a small smile from Celine. She stood, though. "With that, I beg to be excused," she announced. "I'm fatigued and would dearly love to retire."

The men rose as she departed. Cameron turned to her. "I do hope you're feeling chipper by morning so we can take the ride we missed out on today."

Odd, but when he heard the news that she was turning in,

Trevor's mood lightened even more than when he'd learned she hadn't gone riding with Cameron after all. He took himself off to bed.

He tossed fitfully for what seemed hours before he finally slept. In his dreams a vision of Celine swam before him in a watercolor fantasy.

Her arms opened to accept him, her turquoise eyes huge pools of love and passion from which he drank thirstily. She floated forward and embraced him, pressing her lips softly against his. She spoke loving words he could not understand. She kissed him again, and then her mouth moved from his and traveled languidly down his body, coming to rest on his manhood. He hardened as her lips parted to accept him.

He awoke with a start, perspiring profusely, his body aching for release. Why hadn't he taken Giselle up on her offer to meet him in the stable? A few minutes in the hay with her would at least have taken away some of the pressure about to explode inside him. But that idea excited him about as much as a cold bath. What the hell had gone wrong with him since meeting Celine?

Agitated, he flung back the covers and removed himself from the bed. He prowled around his room like a caged lion. It was the third straight night he'd been awakened by the same dream. Try as he might, he couldn't get Celine out of his system. Even in sleep she haunted him.

He donned his robe and poured a brandy, eyeing the closet door as he paced back and forth, until, finally, he moved toward it, his body overtaking his mind. He opened the door, pressed lightly on one of the carved dados on the fireplace, and watched as a hidden panel in the wall separating the two closets slid silently open. He slipped through into Celine's room.

He sat in the wingback chair before the fire, watching her slumber. She had fallen asleep atop the covers, wearing only a filmy wrap. The night had grown cooler, and he could tell by the way she tried to tuck her feet beneath her and cradle her arms under her that she would soon stir.

Celine came awake slowly, her feet like blocks of ice. Her brain focused on the crackling of the fire, and she wondered how long she'd been asleep; she was surprised that the wood was still burning so brightly. She removed herself from the bed and padded sleepily to the fire, rubbing her eyes. Trevor sat calmly in the chair, sipping on a glass of brandy. She nearly tripped when she caught sight of him.

"Good Lord, it's the devil himself!"

She rushed first to the bedroom door, where the key was still in the lock, and then to the French doors, where the latch was secure. Returning to the chair, she planted herself directly in front of Trevor and narrowed her eyes.

"How did you manage to get in here?"

He leaned his head back against the chair, regarding her with heavy-lidded eyes, a lusty grin on his mouth. "My dear, with your hands on your hips and your hair hanging about your shoulders, you remind me of those wild Cajun women."

Despite herself, a smile almost passed over her lips. Lord, but he had a way. She reminded herself of her anger. "And how would you know about wild Cajun women?" Her face heated. "Oh, never mind."

"When you stand in front of the fire like that, one can see right through that flimsy material you're wearing."

She looked down, could see her own parted legs silhouetted through the fabric as though she wore nothing. She flushed and moved aside quickly.

He lifted his glass in toast.

"What the devil do you want?" Instantly, she was sorry she'd asked.

"You." His eyes crinkled merrily at the corners.

Not liking him was difficult when he was in such a playful mood. Celine responded with a smile in spite of herself. "You never give up, do you?"

"Come sit with me, *ma petite,* and I'll share my brandy with you." He patted his knee.

Warm memories of him holding her through the night tugged at her core. How she would love to sit close, to feel his heat surround her. Desire washed through her.

"Don't be silly, I couldn't possibly fit next to you on that chair." She suddenly wished there were room, for she delighted in his mood. He was certainly a dangerous man for her to be alone with, but she enjoyed his presence so terribly much.

Trevor caught her off guard, reaching over and grasping her wrist to pull her down onto his lap. "I didn't say next to me, *ma petite.*" He placed his brandy glass on the table, and then wrapped his arms around her, pulling her tighter to him.

God, he felt good. That heated scent, his actual warmth. His arms. Her body filled so quickly and fiercely with desire, her thoughts scattered. Dangerous. This was very dangerous. She struggled to remove herself from his lap, but his arms only tightened around her.

"You had better let me go, or I'll call for Marie."

He chuckled and nibbled at her ear, sending a delicious shock through her. "You do, and she's going to wonder how I got in here." His eyes sparkled with merriment. "She'll assume you let me in, and then, not liking what you had gotten yourself into, called for help."

Trevor's skewed reasoning made her laugh. "I've an idea Marie would think otherwise."

He shrugged. He continually scanned every inch of her face, sending her senses reeling. She could barely manage words. "Aren't you the one full of mischief?"

"I try to be." He ran a finger along her jawline. The tender act sent a quiver through her bones.

"I suggest you cease wriggling around on my lap, Celine. It's guaranteed to make trouble for both of us."

She settled down abruptly and looked into his beguiling face. "How *did* you get in here?"

He blatantly ignored her question. "Just this once, Celine, relax. Remember our walk in the garden the other night, when I promised not to touch you?"

She nodded her head warily.

"Did I touch you?"

She shook her head.

"Well, *mon amour,* I extend a promise to you now that I will not make love to you."

There was truth in his words. The clean scent of his clothes and skin sent her heart drumming. She yearned to snuggle against his neck and chest, to feel the same comfort he had given her the night before.

"Promise?"

"I think you instinctively know I am a man of my word." He toyed with her hair.

She shouldn't, she really shouldn't. But, oh, it felt so wonderful to relax against his warmth. Being held was something she dearly missed—had missed for most of her life.

Cupping her chin, he lifted her face to his. His breath fell softly on her mouth, mingling with hers. "I won't make love to you. I want you too badly to have you any other way than wanting me without question."

He raised a brow. "And when you surrender to your desires, which I truly hope you will, the sweet agony I have suffered will have been well worth the wait." His voice rasped and his nostrils flared. "I know your lovemaking will be as sweet as I have imagined."

Something hard pressed against her bottom, sending a delicious quiver through her. She should remove herself from his lap, she really should, but she dismissed the idea, so badly did she wish to remain. "You shouldn't speak of such things." Her body gave a tiny, involuntary shudder as desire wended through her like slow-moving lava.

"Don't fight me, Celine. Enjoy the moment."

They grew silent. She stared into the dancing flames. Again, she wondered what it would be like to lie with him. If only there was no pride in her, if only she didn't care that she would end up like the others. If only.

A thought of Dianah Morgan flashed through Celine's mind. She remembered what Dianah had done her last night in New Orleans. The young officer had been as much a womanizer as Trevor. Dianah, who knew how to have her way, bided her time, enjoyed the flirtations, teased the officer over dinners, danced too close to him at parties, but never quite stepped beyond the boundaries. Then, on the night before her departure for San Francisco, she sent for him, and they spent the night together. Celine had accompanied Dianah and her parents to the wharf the next morning. Dianah rode in the carriage, her head held high, with an air of mystery and serenity cloaking her.

She sailed off that morning, but not before she pressed the nosegay she carried into Celine's hand with a wicked little wink.

Of course, here was Celine's solution. There would be a last night before Trevor and she went off in different directions. She could savor the anticipation as Dianah had. And waiting until the last night would spare her from having to face him the next day.

She could do this.

She could bide her time just as Dianah had. And Celine's moments with Trevor would be far more satisfying than any novel. She would be left with irrevocable memories to carry her far into her winter years.

Trevor touched his fingers to the pulse beating at the soft

hollow of her throat. Then he took her chin between his thumb and curled fingers and gently turned her face to his. "Something changed in you just now. What is it?"

Here she was, sitting on the lap of the most handsome, most devastatingly exciting man she had ever encountered, and she had decided to allow him to seduce her—in her own way. There wasn't a chance in Hades she was about to share such a revelation with him.

"I like your promise," was all she said.

"Are you aware your eyes appear to change color according to what you wear, or your moods?" His voice was husky and low in his throat.

She nodded. "My grandmother always said that."

His breath left him in a small laugh. "I doubt your grandmother could possibly have been aware that your eyes take on a certain dark turquoise coloring when you are filled with passion."

Her fingers shot to her lips. "Oh, dear!" And then she reminded herself what she was about. A new resolve gripped her. Like Dianah, she would have what she wanted.

For the first time, she regarded Trevor openly, without guile. Their faces were so close, their breaths mingled. She did what she'd wanted to do since the first day she'd laid eyes on him—she touched her fingertips lightly to his bottom lip.

Trevor went back to playing with the tendrils of her hair, tickling her neck and ear with the ends, sending delicious shivers down her body. Her nipples stood rigid under her wrap. His lashes veiled his eyes as his gaze settled on her breasts.

His breath hitched.

Firelight danced on his skin, and she marveled at his male beauty.

Releasing her hair from his grasp, he lightly traced small circles at the base of her throat with one finger. At the sharp intake of her breath, he slowly widened the circles, trailing downward as he went until his finger rested between her breasts, where the fabric of her robe came together.

Her body throbbed and floated, yielding to him.

Slowly, he pulled her wrap open, exposing her breasts beneath her thin night rail to his experienced, sensuous fingers. He moved his hand to cup one breast, sending a thousand exploding sparks throughout her body. He bent his head to her chest, his breath coasting across her skin. Touching her breast lightly with his mouth, he teased her with languorous kisses.

And then he sucked.

"Unfair," she gasped as hot pleasure ran from her breast to her inner thighs and to the place she had been keeping secret from him.

He drew more circles around her breast with his tongue. The velvety softness of his mouth closed over the tip of the mound.

"You said—"

He sucked again.

She hissed. He was about to overwhelm her.

His mouth left her breast and trailed slowly up her neck, and closed down on hers. She supped on his sweet heat. Then she pulled away, panting. "You promised."

Gently, he raked his fingers through her hair, tucked a lock behind her ear. "And I am keeping that promise, Celine, for I will not enter you until you ask me."

He smiled down at her, gathered her to his chest, and closed her wrap back over her breasts.

"Are you trying to get me to beg for your favors?"

He stilled for a moment, then buried his hand in her hair and gently eased her cheek to his chest. "Supplication is the last thing I want from you, *ma petite.*" Time was suspended as he held her, combing his fingers through her hair, staring silently into the flames until they were mere embers.

She couldn't move—didn't want to. How very different this night had turned out to be from the morning.

"To bed," he whispered in her ear. "Alone, unfortunately."

He carried her to the four-poster and gently tucked her under the covers.

She felt like a babe.

He lifted a single rose from the vase by the bed and placed it beside her pillow. *"Dormez bien, mon coeur."*

Chapter Eight

Trevor exited the house alongside Cameron and stepped silently into the cool morning mist. Jewel-like droplets of water beaded across the toes of their smartly polished boots as they made their way through the dew-kissed grass to the carriage that would transport them to the waiting ship.

Like a giant firefly dancing in the air, a lamp waved slowly back and forth from shore, signaling to the riverboat captain that there were passengers waiting to board. The ship's tender hastened the familiar clang of three bells to indicate a light had been seen and that the prospective passengers should make their way from the plantation house to the shore. The huge sternwheeler loomed from the center of the Mississippi—an enchanted castle, the river's turgid waters her protective moat.

A mystical haze clung to the ship's sides and hovered, cloudlike, over the dark waters as a pale dawn overtook the night. Moss-laden cypress trees crooked along the riverbanks at odd, ghostly angles.

While Cameron eagerly disappeared into his cabin, Trevor boarded with hesitation, shrouded in a peculiar kind of melancholy. Three weeks in New Orleans seemed a long while.

He leaned against the ship's railing with his forearms resting on the rich oak trim, and peered through the vaulted corridor of oaks to his childhood home, as if he could see beyond the façade, straight through to the far corner room where Celine lay sleeping. A deep, dull ache tugged at him.

Two stout seamen hauled in the cumbersome gangplank. The gate closed behind them with a solid clang. The safety bar dropped in place, and they disappeared into the bowels of the sternwheeler, leaving Trevor alone on deck. The mighty steam engines belched thick, white clouds into the air, and the huge paddles hitched, readying themselves for the journey.

He stared into the water's depths, only to see Celine's image floating on the surface, smiling sweetly at him with beckoning, turquoise eyes.

What the devil *was* it about her? When he'd returned to Carlton Oaks, he hadn't expected to find a mysterious beauty standing on the balcony, peering down at him from behind a fat Doric column. Even then, he could tell she had spirit. She'd fascinated him enough to draw him into the house and right up the stairs after her. And when he got to her, those captivating, kaleidoscopic eyes that seemed to change color along with her moods kept him finding one reason after another to be in her company.

His groin tightened at the memory of her in his lap last night. A twinge of guilt coursed through him. He should have told her that he'd be gone in the morning.

A light in the manor house was but a mere speck now as the sternwheeler slipped through the water. He stared at the twinkling dot. Cobwebbed memories of his mother and father strolling along the river's edge hand in hand crept into Trevor's contemplations. Where had *that* come from, and what the devil did it have to do with Celine?

He pushed away from the banister and sought his stateroom. He would see to putting his things in order and then meet up with Cam. Business matters were sure to distract him from haunting thoughts of *her.*

"Ah, there you are." Cameron leaned against the door to the stateroom next to Trevor's. "I was beginning to think you fell overboard. I'm famished. What about you?"

"Indeed." What the hell, putting everything in order could wait. They headed to the opulent dining room at the ship's stern.

Breakfast with Cameron began pleasantly enough. A hunger, more ravenous than usual, consumed Trevor. He blamed it on the fresh air and the fabulous French chef on board.

Cameron lifted a brow. "I say, old boy, I can't recall ever seeing you so preoccupied with food. You seem to be quite lost in thought, as well. Is it the excellent fare, or have you other reasons for such heartiness this morning?"

"Hmm?" Trevor took another mouthful of eggs. "Can't imagine what's got into me. Guess I've a lot on my mind."

Cameron lifted his cup of *petit noir* and sipped. "Like what? Or, should I say, like whom?"

His quip was light, but his eyes were intense, as though he was trying to discern what Trevor was thinking without disturbing the mantle of privacy he'd purposely erected these past few days.

Trevor adjusted his weight in his chair, and with the shift in posture came a change in demeanor that he hoped signaled Cameron to back off. Pulling an agenda from his waistcoat, Trevor brought business to the forefront. "Regarding the founding of the Bank of New Orleans—Father was adamant that both our signatures appear on the original mandate rather than his or your father's. Any objections?"

Cameron shook his head. "That ought to be our first item of business to dispense with."

Trevor nodded, but there was something unsettling in Cameron's demeanor. "What's on your mind?"

Cameron took a sip of coffee and shifted in his seat. "Actually, it's the new clipper ships due in that have me chomping at the bit."

Until then, Trevor had only been tending to the conversation with half a mind. "My sentiments exactly."

He had commissioned Donald McKay out of Boston to design and construct the fastest merchant sailing ships ever built. McKay had a reputation for building clippers that were achieving unheard of runs of more than three hundred fifty miles a day. Trevor had told him to build theirs to run four hundred.

"Hell, Cameron, Captain Waterman skippered the *Sea Witch* from New York to San Francisco in ninety-seven days. He now commands four times more money than anyone else sailing the China seas. If we can cut the time from New Orleans to San Francisco down to thirty-seven days, we'll lock in the China trade. With all three ships due within the month, our slower ships can then be used to ship sugar to Australia and bring that country's wool back to the port of New Orleans. A couple of months out, and we'll have secured worldwide trade."

Cameron only nodded.

"How does it feel, Cam? A shipping empire unmatched in England or America, and neither of us beyond thirty." Trevor leaned forward, a sense of victory already pounding in his veins.

"I am in total agreement." Cameron spoke with a quiet authority while unconsciously running a fingertip over the rim of his cup, which meant he had his own agenda, which would somehow run contrary to Trevor's. "However, I do want to make one thing clear."

Trevor's gut tightened. He had an ugly feeling about what was to come.

Cameron smoothed his mustache with the tips of his thumb and index finger. "I feel I am the best man to captain the lead ship on its maiden voyage to San Francisco. Especially since I have agreed to relocate there."

Just as Trevor figured. A peculiar anger percolated in him. "Do I have to remind you that we are *both* required to inspect all three ships upon their arrival?"

When Cameron set his jaw and failed to respond, the air grew so thick with tension, the passengers dining immediately adjacent shifted about in their chairs and either grew silent themselves, or lowered the volume of their conversations.

Trevor stirred his already stirred coffee and dropped his spoon onto the porcelain plate with a clatter. "And do I have to remind you that when we head for San Francisco, you and I need to be on the last clipper out in case something goes wrong with those leading the pack? And since our first ship out is the one needing to break all records, we cannot afford to sail for sport. I had someone else in mind. You know Captain Thompson is the best man. . . ."

Cameron's face blanched. He leaned forward and listed cogent reasons for his captaining the first ship out of New Orleans. The cadence of his speech was deliberately paced, the tone low, but aggressive. He had the unruly habit of openly rebelling whenever someone tried to direct him.

Trevor leaned back in his chair, locked eyes with Cameron, and spoke quietly. "Celine is to be on that first ship." He paused for a beat. "But then, you knew that."

The two men glared at each other in deadly silence.

And then Cameron leaned back in his chair as well. "You, Cousin, can be such an insufferable bastard."

Like tinder set alight, Trevor's anger flamed. "Oh, goddamn it, get off your high horse. We have records to break. I can't have a captain of one of our ships running after a woman's petticoats when I need his full attention. Jesus, man, we stand to lose millions if we aren't on top of that maiden voyage every minute of the day."

"Why don't you mind your own business, Trev, *old chap?* After all, your business is supposed to be running the entire shipping company, not taking a magnifying glass to my actions."

"I am minding my own business!" Trevor slammed a fist on the table. Coffee cups rattled in their saucers, and pieces of silverware jangled nervously against one another.

Passengers hushed. Trevor shifted in his chair. The idea of his cousin and Celine sharing anything close to what Trevor had shared with her last night—and over a period of weeks—was intolerable.

He leaned over the table and spoke in a hoarse whisper. "I know you are one hell of a sailor. But I also see that you are overly preoccupied with Mrs. Kirkland. I'll say this one more time—none of us can afford to have you divide your time between a woman and the ship. Likely as not, you'd end up losing both at sea. Be reasonable, man."

By now the dining room was nearly empty, save for a few stragglers hanging about to eavesdrop on the heated argument.

Red blotches marked Cameron's cheeks. "You fool. Perhaps it is *you* who wants to captain the ship because Celine will be aboard, and this talk of hiring on another captain is a ruse."

He cocked an eyebrow at Trevor. "It's been you with that randy air about you, not me. You have that demeanor of . . . how did I hear Celine put it the other night . . . of a bull looking for a cow in heat?"

In order to keep from reaching across the table and pummeling Cameron, Trevor pulled himself to his full height and stalked off, knocking his chair over as he went. He growled at the nosy passenger sitting nearest. The rotund man skittered from the dining room through the opposite door.

Retreating to his quarters, Trevor yanked his jacket off, threw it in a heap on a chair, and flopped on the bed, suddenly weary. Pillowing his hands behind his neck, he stared at the ceiling.

What the hell had just happened? Aside from the ordinary scuffles of childhood, he and Cameron shared a comfortable relationship filled with high regard for one another. Lately, however, they seemed to be at one another's throats.

Of late? Only since green-eyed trouble arrived.

He knew full well Cameron could captain the lead clipper as well as Thompson, and see to it records were broken during that first sail. Hell, the ship hadn't even reached port yet and Celine—no, Mrs. Kirkland's presence—was already wreaking havoc. Why the devil had his father insisted she be on the lead ship?

Somehow, referring to Celine as Mrs. Kirkland set her apart from him, left him cold, unfeeling—gave her less dimension.

Cameron and he had shared many things in life, but never women. And damn it, Cameron and Celine were both heading for a life in San Francisco while he was going where? To China, and then back to England. What made him think he had shared anything with Celine? Or ever would? Or wanted to?

He lay there for a long while, thinking. He'd never seen his cousin so taken with anyone. And she certainly displayed what appeared to be genuine affection toward Cameron, while he wanted . . . what *did* he ultimately want other than to bed a woman who sent a few extra sparks through him? She was merely a temptation that laid bare his weakness for a beautiful woman. And now she had become a hindrance.

To hell with it. He knew exactly how to solve the dilemma—he would not return to Carlton Oaks—not even for that blasted ball his father had planned for her. His decision left him strangely numb, but he'd be damned if he allowed anything or anyone to tear his family apart.

He rose from the bed and dashed off a note to Cameron, congratulating him on being captain of the lead clipper to San Francisco, while Trevor would have the privilege of being the first to sail her to China.

A clean-smelling, slightly humid breeze puffed marshmallow clouds across the sky as Trevor stepped onto the wooden banquette of Canal Street with Cameron by his side. They peered boldly into each passing carriage. Mysterious-looking ladies hid behind elaborately carved and painted oriental fans—the very same fans their shipping company would import by the tens of thousands from Whampoa and Hong Kong, along with fresh teas, fireworks, and furniture.

Their banking business completed, and their meetings regarding the clipper ships delayed until the morrow, the two stood together improvising plans.

Cameron crossed his arms and rocked back on his heels. "It's been a long while since we enjoyed New Orleans together. Which would you prefer tonight, the quadroon ball or Madame Olympée's?"

Trevor snorted. "Do you think Madame will remember us and call out her burly guards?"

"I doubt it since neither one of us was yet twenty when we nearly destroyed the place." Cameron gave a nod toward Royal Street. "Walk with me to the jewelry store. There's something I need to purchase. So what's it to be, the ball or the brothel?"

Trevor shrugged. "Dinner at Antoine's, followed by a night at Madame Olympée's suits me." He could damn well use a bloody outlet.

Cameron grinned and slapped Trevor on the back, resting

his hand there to guide him into *Maison d'Orléans,* the finest jewelry store in the city.

"What are we doing here?" Trevor asked. "Madame Olympée demands cold, hard coin."

Cameron chuckled. "Your father had a necklace made for Celine for her birthday next week, and asked me to retrieve it for him. Thought I might find a pair of earrings to match."

Trevor stood quietly against the jamb of the door with his arms crossed casually over his broad chest while Cameron spoke to the jeweler.

"One moment, monsieur." The shop owner disappeared into the back of the establishment, and then quickly reappeared, carrying a small black velvet box. He set it on the counter before Cameron and opened the lid. "A perfect complement to the exquisite diamond-and-pearl necklace commissioned by your uncle." The Frenchman rubbed his slender, well-manicured fingers together, anticipating Cameron's reaction.

Cameron lifted the earrings from the case and held them in the air against imaginary ears. At the sight of the pearl-drop earrings ablaze with diamonds, Trevor's jaw clenched. A strange, sardonic mood fell over him. He focused his attention on the shopgirl who'd been eyeing him covertly. She dropped her head and busied herself with a piece of jewelry. Her cheeks flushed when Trevor moved toward her end of the display case. Subtly, he flirted with her as he passed the time inspecting rare pieces of jewelry imported from exotic ports around the world.

One piece caught his eye. He removed the thin gold bracelet from the girl's outstretched hand. Turning it this way and that, he examined the unusual piece while the girl gave him an explanation of its mysterious origins. He stood in silence for a moment while a strange sense of satisfaction settled in. He purchased the item and placed the thin velvet box in his breast pocket.

He and Cameron left the premises and headed west from

Royal, to the dressmaker where they were to check on an order of ball gowns that was to be shipped back to Carlton Oaks.

Madame Charmontès had been a friend of the family for decades. Many considered her to be the finest modiste in America. According to the petite Frenchwoman, she was actually the finest dressmaker in the entire world.

She claimed to be able to touch a piece of fabric with her eyes closed, and the vision of what it should become, and the kind of woman who should wear it, appeared in her mind's eye. Every item that left her shop, she considered a work of art. Trevor couldn't help wondering what she would come up with for Çeline's ball gown.

Oh, what the hell did he care? He wouldn't be there.

He and Cameron sauntered into the shop, the little bell over the door announcing their arrival. Madame stepped from the back room. Her mouth opened and closed soundlessly.

Trevor chuckled.

"You are nearly a week early," she gasped.

At once she came alive, scurrying about and wildly waving her arms around. "*Mais, non, mais non,* you naughty boys. You are not to be here for six more days. Go! Scat! Do not reappear until you are meant to." She tried to scoot them out the door like puppies at the end of a broom. "Do you not hear me? Be gone!"

Trevor and Cameron laughed and sidestepped her flailing hands.

Heads poked every which way from behind the curtains leading to the back room. Those who recognized the two cousins pulled the others back to their work, and a buzz of gossip ensued. The idle chatter came to an abrupt halt when the two men ushered themselves through the curtained doorway.

"Get on with your work, ladies. We were simply making

sure Madame Charmontès will complete her assignment on time." Trevor winked at the reigning queen of couture.

She smiled back, somewhat reassured by his manner. She wiggled a finger at them. "At least you aren't expecting to carry anything away. Every aspect of the family's order must be perfect before so much as a stitch goes out the door."

Trevor touched her shoulders and blew a kiss on each cheek. "We came to pay our respects and to let you know we've arrived."

"Such a flirt you are, *chéri*." She stretched up on her toes and pinched Trevor's cheek in return. "I will only allow you to carry my creations away hidden in boxes. Do I need to remind you that every item I create must be properly draped on its female wearer before a gentleman sets his eyes on it? Only then can you receive the full benefit of its loveliness."

"Be damned, woman. One of the ladies is my sister."

"And one is my stepmother," Cameron added.

The seamstresses tittered and giggled, thoroughly enjoying the two cousins and their friendly diversion.

Madame chatted with them about her upcoming trip to France, and of the new clipper ships due to arrive that had everyone in New Orleans gossiping. Trevor offhandedly watched the seamstresses, and every now and then casually reached out to touch the fineness of a particular fabric. The sensation of the different textures between his fingertips did subtle things to his insides that he rather liked.

He caught sight of a filmy turquoise-colored garment already completed and folded in its box, the lid beside it. His senses sharpened. He reached over and touched the sheer fabric. Blood drained from his head and went straight to his groin. Slowly, he pulled the long, filmy nightgown from the container. As he held the translucent chiffon in his hands, something akin to pain and desire settled in his chest. Celine's eyes were this color when she was filled with passion. He'd seen as much just last night when he'd toyed with those firm breasts of hers.

Madame stepped forward, watching him, her spine rigid. He didn't care. She requested Cameron's assistance with a bookkeeping matter, and escorted him to the front of the shop. Just as Trevor returned the nightgown to the box and was fitting the lid on it, she reappeared.

She placed her hand over his. *"Non."*

"You can make another, madame." Trevor's voice was low and measured. Something untamed and dangerous stirred within him.

"I do not duplicate."

The drumming in his pulse quickened. "You will now."

The two studied one another in a room that had grown silent as a cave, her hand still resting atop his.

"You have six days," he murmured.

She lifted her chin. "The fabric for that particular gown has been in my possession for some time." Her words sounded stilted, but were filled with an underlying heat. "I laid it aside, patiently waiting for the perfect woman whose depth of soul and passion matched its turquoise color. I finally found her."

A fist in his gut clawed and twisted.

Her eyes narrowed and she studied him for a long moment. "There is only one way you could possibly know to whom this special garment belongs."

"I beg you to make another, madame." He nearly choked on his words.

By removing her hand from his, she gave him silent permission to take what he somehow desperately needed. He left quietly with the box under his arm.

Trevor never should have switched from drinking Sazeracs, with their less potent mixture of cognac and absinthe, to straight absinthe. *La fée verte*—the green fairy—they called it. But whatever the name, the mind-altering properties that caused the walls to shift and faces to blur did nothing to make him believe that the woman he had pinned to the wall was anything other than what she was—a skilled professional.

The finest brothel in the city employed beautiful women who knew more tricks and offered more favors than any man could dream up. None of it did any good. Not the absinthe. Not Madame Olympée's elaborate establishment. Not this woman.

Her hair was nearly the same color, and her eyes were a similar hazel-green, but they didn't change color when she smiled, or when she pretended arousal. He drew a breath through his nose to quell his disgust. Even her scent was wrong. What the hell did he want? What was he doing?

He dropped the hands that caged her in and stepped back. "You're free to go."

"Monsieur?"

He managed to shove his arms into the sleeves of his jacket. "I'll see that you receive extra compensation."

She frowned and her dark eyebrows seemed to snake across her forehead. "But we have done nothing, monsieur. I must earn my wage or Madame—"

"We're finished here. At least I am." The walls moved about, and the turquoise nightgown lying across the end of the bed undulated. He swiped his hand over his eyes and reached for the box he'd brought from Madame Charmontès's.

Her chin jutted out, and it did an odd, pointy little twist. "I keep whatever clothing men bring to me." Was it the absinthe, or had her voice just gone from sweet to hard enough to crack glass? "That exquisite peignoir is mine, and I intend to lure many lovers with it."

He wasn't about to leave something behind that was meant for Celine. But he couldn't return it when he'd told Madame Charmontès to duplicate it. What the devil had he been thinking?

"Give me the gown, monsieur."

"No," he said quietly. "I've doubled your money for nothing more than a few minutes' conversation. That's enough."

She ran to the bedside commode, picked up a vase full of flowers, and held it in the air. "Give it to me or I shall scream and throw this and then scream again. I shall accuse you of horrid acts, and in the end, you will be carried off, and I will be left with this gown."

"Like hell." He tore the flimsy fabric in two.

"Bastard." She flung the vase. It landed at his feet with a resounding crash, the water soaking his pant legs. Coldly, deliberately, she opened her mouth and screamed.

Christ! In seconds, two burly guards burst through the door. Trevor raised the flat of his hand to them. "No need, gentlemen. I was just leaving." He leaned over and picked up the gown, nearly stumbling over himself. He shredded what was left of it and stuffed it into the box. He'd be damned if she'd use it for so much as a dusting rag.

He shoved the box under his arm, and using the soft glow in the corridor as his target, he headed for the exit.

Madame Olympée stood in the corridor across from the open door. She took a slow, long drag on the cigarillo she held between her fingers. "Mr. Andrews."

"Madame."

She plucked bits of tobacco from the end of her tongue with her scarlet nails. "A pity. It was a lovely work of art."

He repositioned the box under his arm. "I'll see to it your employee is further compensated. Although I don't know why. She turned into quite a witch."

Madame Olympée took another drag on her cigarillo. "Your cousin is waiting for you in the parlor."

He nodded.

"Should you think to return, you will not be welcome."

"I shan't be back, madame. You can count on it." Only one woman would give him what he needed, and he wasn't about to find her here.

Chapter Nine

Celine crossed the small footbridge over the stream in front of the *garçonnière,* and headed down the crooked, nearly overgrown path through the woods toward the main house. She'd spent the better part of three days there in contemplation. Lord, but she missed Trevor. Actually, she missed both him *and* Cameron. There had definitely been a void in her life when she'd awoken to find them gone. But it was Trevor who caused her to toss and turn at night. She was convinced that he'd fully intended to leave her with a lusty memory of that last night together. And he'd done a crack job of it.

Something shifted inside her after that. She was a widow. Widows had more freedom than unmarried women. When she departed here, she would damn well have her own memories to take with her. And if he made no further overtures, well, *she* would seduce *him.* Her decision coursed through her like a slow, sweet poison, dissolving her fear and turning her longing into a hot, formless hunger.

She'd sent a letter off to Dianah, letting her know Celine would soon set sail for San Francisco. Would Dianah catch on when she read that Celine intended the same kind of departure Dianah had?

She smiled to herself. Yes, she was going to do it. She was going to give in to Trevor. She was not about to spend her winter years regretting that she had not known the pleasure of lying with him.

Zola stepped from the cookhouse and called out to Celine as she passed. "Got your favorite hot biscuits and honey inside."

"Mmm. In a bit. I need to speak with Justin first."

Not finding him in his office, Celine took a book from the shelf and headed for the window seat to wait for his return. She enjoyed their afternoon visits, especially his more frequent conversations regarding Trevor. And now, after she had decided to have an affair with Trevor, she was even more eager to hear Justin's tales.

Celine fairly jumped onto the window seat. She missed and crashed to the floor on her backside, the book and cushion landing on top of her. Despite the pain, she had to giggle. She stood, gathered the book, and went to replace the cushion.

She frowned at the hinged top to the window seat, which had been hidden by the velvet cushion. She lifted the lid and peered inside. With the top of the seat up against the window, the shadow it cast obscured her vision, so she reached in and fumbled around. Her hand came to rest on a large rolled scroll of paper.

Extracting it from the cubbyhole, she untied the ribbon and unrolled the large parchment only to find several detailed architectural renderings. The original plans to Carlton Oaks?

She pored over them, sheet by sheet, noting nothing out of the ordinary. When she came to the sheet marked *Second Level*, she discovered that none of the current occupants were in any of the rooms originally assigned to them. What was once the nursery, Felicité now claimed as hers. Justin's current room was marked *Additional Sleeping Quarters*.

Had he rearranged things after his wife died? Feeling like a snoop, she started to roll the sheets back up but stopped with a gasp. The room she resided in was marked *Mr. Andrews' Quarters*, while the room Trevor occupied was marked *Mrs. Andrews' Quarters*.

The rooms were mirror images of each other—and connecting them was a secret passage through the closets, operable by twisting a certain carved dado on the fireplace. So, that was how Trevor had been coming and going. Why, that sneaking—

Quickly, she rolled the parchment, returned it to its hiding place, settled the cushion back where it belonged, and raced up the stairs to her room, passing Justin halfway up. "Afternoon, Justin."

He turned to her as she flew past like a whirlwind. "And a good afternoon to you, too, young lady."

She locked the door to her room, made certain the key cover was over the lock, and then ran to the French doors and locked them as well. She drew the drapes with such haste she nearly yanked them from their moorings. Next, she rushed to the fireplace and twisted at one carving, then another, and another, until one gave way. Heart pounding, she sucked in her breath and stood silent for a moment before hurrying into the closet. Pushing past her clothes, she slipped through an open panel, and worked her way through a closet that mirrored hers.

Rich, masculine aromas of leather and suede, mixed with the faint scent of Trevor, left Celine light-headed. His shirts of silk, lawn, and chambray brushed her cheek as she moved forward. She pushed aside a woven jacket and touching the sleeve, recalled how it had felt on Trevor's arm the evening he walked with her in the garden. Taking in a deep breath for courage, she stepped into the silence of his room.

Blood thundered in her ears, and her arms and legs tingled with a mixture of trepidation and excitement. If she thought peeking at the drawings of the plantation house was snooping, this was positively wicked. She perched on the edge of the huge accoutrement bed—a near likeness to the one she slept in. She lay down for a moment, trying to imagine what had passed through Trevor's mind before he went to the fireplace and turned the dado to gain entrance to her room.

Mischief coursed through her veins. Her mind was already scheming of ways to repay him when she heard Marie's loud knocking and shrill voice echo through the closet. Quickly, she straightened the covers, ran back through the closet, and twisted the dado on the fireplace.

"Oh, for heaven's sake, hush your carrying on so, Marie. Whatever is the matter out there?" Celine pulled the drapes back and opened the French doors.

"What do you mean *out here,* mam'selle? What's the matter in here is what I be askin'. I knock on your locked door and when I don't get no response, I come all the way around and find the drapes pulled tight. Back again to your door and you still don't answer. I wondered if something terrible went wrong in here."

She glanced sideways at Celine with a great exaggerated huff, one that would have created guilt in even the innocent, and Celine by no means felt guiltless. Marie held her expression for effect, and then surveyed the room as she entered. "You haven't been yourself lately, Miss Celine. Is anything wrong?"

"Please try to remember you are supposed to be here to help me, not to spy on me."

"Aren't you in a mood?" Marie mumbled as she placed Celine's laundered linens in the wardrobe. "Zola says she'll be glad when the boys get back to make you normal again."

"What?"

"Nothing, Miss Celine. I'm only doing my share of grumbling. I figure everybody is grumbling, so I might as well join in."

Marie heaved a sigh and continued sorting the clean clothing. "I'm fatigued from trying to get everything fixed up for the ball and haven't been myself, neither. I'm terrible sorry, Miss Celine. I was looking for you because you never showed up for Zola's hot biscuits and honey, so we both figured somethin' was wrong."

She picked up the bottle of laudanum still sitting on Celine's dressing table and opened her pocket to deposit it inside.

"Wait, Marie, give me that." Celine snatched the opiate from Marie's hand and studied it, as a wicked thought settled in. She grinned and shoved it into her pocket.

Marie squared her shoulders. "I don't have anything to say about anything that ain't none of my business, Miss Celine, but I can surely think all I want."

Throaty laughter escaped Celine's lips.

Marie stared at her as though she'd seen the devil.

"Oh, stop that, Marie. You look as though something dreadful is about to happen. It's not, I promise. There's just some . . . squaring of accounts that needs doing. Nothing harmful, so put your eyes back in your head and come along. It's time for those biscuits and honey."

Trevor stood on the bank of the levee, waiting for his cousin to disembark. He peered through the vaulted corridor of oaks to the columned mansion ahead.

Damn it, why had he returned? Telling himself he owed it to his father to see Celine's birthday ball through was a bloody thin excuse. Well, he'd sure as hell return to New Orleans as soon as it was over.

There appeared to be no one in sight. Perhaps it was nothing more than their late arrival on the last boat of the day, but the same vague gloom that had haunted him his entire time in New Orleans tugged at him again.

"Where the hell are you, Cameron?"

"Right here." Cameron trotted down the gangplank and stepped into the carriage. "Ah, ever the lighthearted one, hey, Cousin?" Cameron chuckled as Trevor shot him an icy scowl.

As the carriage pulled up to the steps, the front doors of the plantation house swung open and Lindsey and Felicité jostled one another in their haste to reach the men. Trevor's mood rose and he chuckled at Felicité's theatrics when she lost out. The servants, faces brightened as much by the break in their routines as the return of the cousins, gathered to greet the men and unload the many boxes that had arrived with them.

There wasn't the excitement of his previous arrival, but Trevor nonetheless lifted Felicité up in the air and twirled her around. He stole a glance toward the upper gallery. Empty. His chest tightened. He put on an easy smile and headed for the front door.

He begged fatigue and ordered a bath. While he waited, he sat in his father's office, discussing business with him, Cameron, and Miles. He guessed Celine must be upstairs with his sister and Elizabeth, going through the boxes from Madame Charmontès.

When a servant notified him that his bath was ready, Trevor left the office and climbed the stairs. Glancing only momentarily at the closed door next to his, he strode purposefully toward his own room. The upper floor felt strangely hollow. He'd be damned if he'd inquire about her.

He disrobed and started for the bath, then stopped, and paced the room naked, eyeing the carved dado on the fireplace with a roiling in his gut. Frustrated, he raked his fingers through his hair. What the hell was the matter with him? He slammed his fist against the wall next to the fireplace, and fought the terrible urge to reach out and twist the carving.

He climbed into the tub and lay back with his eyes closed, his thoughts on the night at Madame Olympée's. He'd been extremely intoxicated. In fact, there were pieces of that awful night still missing. Damn the absinthe. But he did recall describing to Madame Olympée the kind of woman he wanted. She'd produced three of her finest, all with the same color hair and skin. As soon as he was alone with the one he'd chosen, he produced the nightgown and asked her to put it on. He couldn't bring himself to touch her, and what he'd done next still disgusted him.

His bath completed, he dressed and headed for the stables. A good ride around the plantation always worked to settle his mind.

Dinner went no better than had the afternoon, for Celine was nowhere in sight. He fought the urge to discover her whereabouts. He figured Cameron had, for he never mentioned her either. Damn it. Trevor grew even surlier as the evening wore on. Finally, he excused himself early, blaming his dark mood on the long days in New Orleans.

He retreated to his room, where he removed his jacket and stock tie, and unbuttoned the front of his pleated silk shirt before taking his usual glass of sherry at his bedside. He downed the amber liquid in a single gulp. Still fully clothed, he lay on the bed, crossed his arms behind his neck, and flung one leg carelessly across the bed. He eyed the dado on the fireplace. Damn it, he was here to attend the ball and fulfill a duty to his father, and then he would be gone. That was all, damn it.

He grew suddenly weary.

In minutes, any attempt to lift his head became such an effort that he didn't bother. A sense of detachment came over him. Soon, he didn't seem to know, or care, if he was awake or asleep.

His head fell limply to one side, directing his half-closed

eyes toward the closet. It stood open. He hadn't opened it. Had he? Oh, well, nothing seemed to matter, nor make sense. The opening changed size, loomed large and distorted, then contracted and began to move about the wall, reminding him of the damnable absinthe he'd ingested while in New Orleans. He tried to still the movement by focusing intently on the door, but he could not make it stand still.

He tried to move and couldn't do that either.

A vision of Celine, beautiful and ethereal, appeared to float through the wall and move toward the bed.

She was dressed in the sheer turquoise nightgown he'd torn to shreds. Or had Madame Charmontès reconstructed it as he'd ordered her to? Celine's hair hung in soft, radiant curls about her shoulders. She smiled sweetly down at him, leaned over, and kissed him softly on the mouth.

Oh, Celine, how beautiful you are. He thought the words, but try as he might, he could not vocalize them. What the devil was wrong with him?

The faint scent that was hers alone drifted over him, and his heart nearly burst. He must be dreaming. His thoughts swirled randomly, disjointed. He was helpless before this vision.

Gently, she stroked his brow, then ran a hand ever so lightly past his cheek and down his chest, tracing circles around his nipples with a fingertip. And then she parted his shirt and splayed her warm hand across his stomach.

His loins were on fire, and still he could not move. She lifted his hand to her shoulder, guided his fingers slowly, gently down the front of her gossamer gown. Her turquoise gaze never left his as the delicate fabric melded with silken skin and passed beneath his fingertips, filling every crevice of his being like water through smooth pebbles.

Her soft, gentle mouth, so cool and sweet, pressed down on his again, and he heard himself moan. Never had he wanted a woman so much. But why could he not move if he was awake? And if he was indeed asleep, why could he not awaken?

Somewhere deep in the night, Trevor came awake. His head felt like it was filled with cotton. He ran his hand down his front. He was still fully clothed. The candle had burned to nothing, so by touch he retrieved another from the bedside drawer and replaced it. He lit it and inspected the closet door. Closed tight.

What the hell kind of dream was that?

He was thirsty beyond belief and reached for the water pitcher. His movements were leaden, awkward. There was something awfully familiar about this feeling, but he couldn't quite name it. He picked up the empty sherry glass, ran a finger across the bottom of the bowl, and licked the tip.

Laudanum!

No wonder. He fell back on the bed. His hand landed on . . . what? Hoisting himself up on his elbows, he picked up a single red rose and a note with one word written on it—*touché*.

"Damn it!" He grabbed the crystal glass and hurled it at the carved dado. It hit its mark and disintegrated into a thousand shards.

Blinking hard, he attempted to focus on the dado that would allow him entrance to Celine's quarters. He shouldn't.

He should just let it all go.

But he could not. He stood, moved woodenly to the fireplace, and reached out to caress the rich, dark wood of the dado. He gave it a twist, and then slipped silently through the closet and into the next room.

He moved, still somewhat clumsily, until he stood by the edge of the four-poster bed. Blood pounded in his ears as he carefully parted the mosquito netting.

Felicité!

He snatched his hand away from the netting as though it were made of nettles. What the hell was his sister doing in Celine's bed? He glanced at the window seat, half-expecting to see Celine curled up there, smugly mocking him. She was nowhere in sight.

He made a hasty retreat.

Once back through the closet, he closed the door, twisted the dado back in place, and strode to his bed, shaking the cobwebs from his head. He stood for a moment, staring at the closet door.

And then he laughed.

Chapter Ten

Tonight was the formal ball, but today held just as much excitement. A bit nervous for more reasons then she dared to confess, Celine paused at the open front doors of the plantation house, smoothed the skirts of her green day dress, and stepped out to greet Justin. She didn't expect to see Trevor, not before breakfast, anyway. Just the thought of what she'd done last night made her heart jump to her throat.

Justin rose from where he was seated and made a sweeping gesture at the elegantly decorated veranda and grounds. "What do you think?"

The shaded lawn was graced with small groupings of wrought iron furniture. The veranda contained more of the same, all painted pristine white. Even the red Chinese lanterns strung overhead managed to appear regal with all their gold braid and tassels. "You've thought of everything."

"No, I merely told the experts to create something fetching."

"Hardly fetching." She laughed. "This is exquisite. What more could I ask for?"

Justin smiled and withdrew a narrow black velvet box from his jacket and opened it. "You didn't ask, but I have a little something for you."

Celine caught her breath, speechless at the sight of the glittering diamond-and-pearl necklace resting on black velvet. "Oh, my, I couldn't possibly—"

"Hush, Celine. Don't steal my pleasure by refusing." He laid the diamond-and-pearl necklace against her throat and fastened the clasp.

Running her fingers over the jewels, she swallowed tears. "How can I ever thank you for everything?"

A small smile graced his mouth. "Well, now that you mention it." He paused, took in a deep breath, and exhaled slowly. "The quality of your friendship makes you very special, my dear." His carefully chosen words puzzled Celine.

"You honor everyone without prejudice," he continued. "Everyone, that is, except Trevor."

Startled, Celine's breath caught in her throat. "I . . . I don't know what you mean. I—" Guilt flooded in. Lord, had Justin found out what she'd done to his son last night?

"Please, Celine." Justin's words grew even more measured. "I am not a naive man. I know there is conflict between the two of you. I don't understand what it could be since you said he has never made advances toward you, but could you do your best to treat him as you would treat anyone else today? That's all the thanks I ask for."

Her voice barely made it above a whisper as she acknowledged him. "Of course." If he only knew she planned to seduce Trevor—and soon, he wouldn't think so highly of her.

She swallowed hard and slipped her arm through his. With a toss of her head, she changed the subject. "Isn't this necklace a bit ostentatious to be wearing to breakfast?"

"Decidedly so."

"I thought so."

"Shall we?"

"Yes, let's."

Together, they strolled into the dining room. She was startled to see how many people had already gathered at the long table. They'd begun arriving from New Orleans and upriver since the past evening, but she hadn't realized until they collected together that at least ten couples and two bachelors were already in attendance. Two of the three larger *garçonnières* on the plantation were filled, and the family was doubling up in bedrooms, Felicité sharing with her.

Justin made a round of introductions. Celine knew few in attendance—except, of course, the Widow Beaudrée, who appeared none too pleased to be seated between two older men.

Celine gritted her teeth at the sight of Giselle. How could she expect the woman to be excluded? After all, she was a neighbor who had opened her home to the overflow of guests. And would likely seduce the male half of them before the festivities came to a close.

Justin's chair was at the head of the table. He seated Celine to his right and excused himself to chat with guests up and down the table. Trevor was already seated directly opposite her. There was amusement in his eyes. "Sleep well, Celine?"

She couldn't help but laugh. "Indeed I did. What of you? Did you sleep well despite your . . . ah . . . lengthy trip upriver and what must have been tedious business in New Orleans?"

He brought his glass to his lips, but not before a lazy smile touched them. Amusement flickered through his eyes. "You're quite the scamp. Do you enjoy playing dangerous games?"

"Dangerous?" This was it, this was the beginning of the seduction, and she was going to savor every moment of it. She had to part her lips to breathe properly.

He lifted a brow.

"You were missed," she said, offering him a smile.

"By you?"

"Oh, I was flattened by grief."

His husky chuckle rolled through her, touching every

nerve in her body. "I was flattened as well recently, but not by grief, it would seem."

Oh, this was delicious. "You don't say."

Justin returned to his seat, the color in his cheeks high. "Ah, I see you two are getting on. Splendid."

From the ballroom came the faint but clear strains of a violin as platters of cornbread smothered in honey, eggs in every fashion, biscuits covered in sausage gravy, chops of smoked pork, and fresh-caught catfish appeared on the plates and filled satisfied stomachs. Conversation flowed effortlessly—and noisily.

The clinking of empty cups being nestled onto their plates indicated breakfast was complete. Justin stood, thanked his guests, dipped his head to Celine, and departed the dining room. Dresses rustled as chairs were slid back and everyone except Celine, Trevor, and Cameron departed.

Cameron helped himself to a vacated chair next to Celine. He touched the necklace, his sigh exaggerated. "Exquisite, but sadly, you lack earrings to match."

"I hardly—" Celine's stomach lurched. She stood. "Oh no, Cameron, you cannot mean to—"

"Indeed, I can." He stood as well, and after smoothing his moustache, as was his habit, lifted a black velvet box from an inside jacket pocket. "And I did."

Trevor excused himself, but not entirely. He moved to the carved fireplace at the far end of the room, leaned against its Italian marble frame, draped an arm on the mantel, and much to Celine's discomfort, waited.

Cameron opened the box, revealing the dazzling set of earrings.

Her hand went to her heart. Was that uncertainty she saw in Cameron? How could she possibly reject his gift when she hadn't rejected his uncle's? And Lord, but was Trevor standing in line with one as well?

Oh, dear.

Cameron took his time fastening the diamond-and-pearl earrings to each of Celine's earlobes. The sheer size of him was nearly overwhelming this close, but knowing Trevor stood behind her, watching everything, was more disconcerting than Cameron's heated nearness.

"I am simply at a loss for words, Cameron."

"Then allow me to prompt you." His lips curved into a jaunty smile; his eyes danced. "Thank you, Cameron. I will be certain to wear them in your presence in San Francisco."

Before she could respond, Trevor's life force swept around her like a cloak, nearly shrouding Cameron's presence.

The light in Cameron's eyes dimmed. He glanced over his shoulder at his cousin, then back to Celine. A different kind of light flickered, one laced with what—anger?

Could it be he had intentions? She closed her eyes for a brief moment, as if the act would erase the implications that had struck her.

His words were terse when he spoke. "It seems there might be others in line." With only a nod, he left the room, leaving her and Trevor alone.

"Cameron," she called out, but he was gone. A cold arrow of pain shot through her heart at his hasty retreat. She must seek him out, set him straight—but after she met with Trevor.

She stood with her back to him in order to collect herself. When the beat of her heart returned to something that resembled normal, she moved to where he stood.

He gave her a half-smile.

There was something definitely different about him since he'd returned, but try as she might, she couldn't put her finger on the change. But then, she had changed as well, hadn't she? Her decision had been made and she would not back down.

Gently, he flicked an earring with his finger, then reached for the other, but not without caressing the underside of her chin along the way. Was he more serious now? Or was it only the moment? "There's no way out with him, but to face the truth. Whatever the truth may be."

What did he mean by that? She nodded and swallowed hard. "I am . . . I have . . . I see things plainly now. Cameron is a dear, dear man, but he will never be anything other than a friend. Here, or in San Francisco."

Something indefinable flickered through his eyes. "Your heart would know."

"I'll have a word with him." A desire to lean into Trevor, to ask him to wrap his arms around her and pull her close, threatened to overwhelm her. She ached to bury her head in the warmth of his chest, if for no other reason than for comfort after what had just transpired. Oh, how she had missed him. And oh, she was determined to take this slow. Very slow.

He tucked his curled fingers under her chin, and tilted her compliant head back. The very air around them shifted, his action dispelling the heaviness of the last few moments.

"As I said earlier, you were a little scamp last night, but oh, so sweet this morning." His voice rasped husky and low in his throat. "Thus, I have no alternative but to forgive you. However, forgiveness does carry a price."

"Last night? Forgiveness?" Celine's heart lightened. "And what might that be, Mr. Andrews?" Had he gone to her room, only to find Felicité in Celine's bed?

Dark lashes swept lazily over smoldering eyes. "I should extract a kiss from you as your penance. But then, since it's your birthday, perhaps you should be on the receiving end." He bent his head. "Either way, I win."

She didn't protest as his lips pressed ever so gently against hers—only the barest of touches—but as sweet and tender a gesture as she'd ever known. After all, there was no one around to see them, so why not taste him once again? If only for the briefest of moments.

He lifted his mouth from hers, studied her.

She couldn't help but wonder what he was thinking. "I'll

consider your kiss one of the nicest birthday presents, sir." Her lips tingled, and she came away a bit light-headed.

"Was that better than last night, *ma petite?*" Trevor's voice grew even huskier.

She bit down on her lower lip to keep from laughing. "What are you talking about?"

"You would certainly remember far better than I what went on since I was the victim of a wicked dose of laudanum. And a lovely turquoise nightgown that matched the depths of your eyes. Will you wear it for me again when I am more in control of my senses? Tonight, perhaps?"

"You must be mad. I wasn't even on the premises last night. I gave up my room to . . . to accommodate other guests." She wasn't about to tell him she'd slept in her cabin.

He tilted his head, amused. "Other guests? Come now."

Again, she bit down on her bottom lip.

Trevor's fingers slipped into her mass of unbound hair. He twisted a lock, brought the tip under his nose. His nostrils flared. "Why didn't you stay, *ma petite?*" he murmured. "Why did you leave me?"

Celine drew the curl back. "Probably for the same reason you never remained when you made your midnight calls through your little passageway."

He toyed with the curl. "So, sweet Celine, what shall it be, truce or stalemate?"

"Hmmm." She drew out the moment, tilting her head this way and that. "How about checkmate?"

He laughed. "I'm afraid we're both far too strong-willed to ever acquiesce to a checkmate."

They stood for a moment, contemplating one another amid a charged atmosphere. If he could read her thoughts, would he be surprised at their wickedness?

Something shifted in him. He slipped his hand into his waistcoat, and brought out a small, thin box in the same black velvet as those Justin and Cameron had presented. He opened it.

Inside, Celine found a simple gold bracelet resting on black velvet. When she lifted it from the box, she noticed a clasp unlike any she'd ever seen.

"Thank you. This is certainly unusual."

Trevor took the bangle and slid it onto her wrist, sending little shivers up her arm at the touch of his fingers on her bare skin. He held the bracelet open. "The clasp is unique. See the little pin on this side?"

She nodded. Breathing was difficult with his nearness. She wished she could lean into his warmth and set her mouth to his neck.

"When it's inserted into the other side, the bracelet is permanently sealed onto the wrist."

A jolt ran through her.

She regarded the circle of gold glinting at her wrist, then gazed back up at Trevor, searching for an answer to the intangible something that had shifted in him a moment ago. She tensed, the air she breathed mingling with his. The heat from his body increased, as if it were charged with a new kind of energy.

She did not move away.

She did not say no.

The click at her wrist sealed the bracelet on her arm.

Her heart quivered.

She leaned her flushed cheek against his chest for support. His arms encircled her, and he enveloped her in his heat, in his scent. If only she could stay like this forever.

Time stood still for a moment before his words floated across the top of her head. "Could this have been what my father meant when he asked us to respect one another today?"

She lifted her head in surprise, but he only smiled and eased her cheek back to his chest. "My father can be infuriating with his controlling ways, but he can also be very wise.

This is a special day for you, Celine. Let's neither one of us be so foolish as to muck it up."

He gave her a quick hug and then stepped back. "What are your immediate plans?"

"None, at present. I am supposed to take a long nap this afternoon so I'll be presentable, or so Madame Charmontès says. If you think your father is controlling, humph. One would think this was Madame's ball the way she pays attention to every detail. She even insists on dressing me personally. Marie says it's because the woman has been a friend of the family for over twenty years and used to dress your mother. I very much wanted to take in everything today, but she says it's rude to follow the workers around as they make ready."

"I know a private place where you can rest and still observe the goings-on."

Celine pulled away from him, her interest piqued. "And just what other *secret* little places besides my closet do you know?"

"Up in the loft, over the stable. The hay is soft, and the loft door swings open toward the house. It's a vantage point unsurpassed."

"Oh, and I suppose you would have to escort me to this observatory to make certain I get there safely?"

"But of course."

"That's indecent."

"Only in your mind. I have no ulterior motives other than to share the day with you."

Celine gaped at him. "Only in *my* mind? And only in the minds of everyone else, should we be discovered. My word, a day in the hayloft with you would be most inappropriate." Not to mention dangerous. She didn't want today to be the day she gave herself to him. Her heart fluttered in her chest.

Trevor grew suddenly serious. "Have you never done

something simply because you wanted to, and the rules of society be damned?"

Celine thought of Dianah and the books they'd hidden in her parasol. She laughed and stuck her chin out in defiance. "As a matter of fact, I have."

"Ah, a little mystery? You'll be perfectly safe with me today."

He was sincere, she could sense it, yet she searched his face for signs of betrayal. His breath fell rhythmically onto her lips as he patiently allowed her to study him.

"Yes, I believe I am safe—for today. But you are not."

Trevor smiled that devilish, easy smile. "Go. Remove those earrings and necklace. They're rather inappropriate for hay lounging. In about a half-hour's time, wander through the garden, and then make your way to the stables."

He gave her a chuck under the chin, and then strode off.

Was she daft to be doing this? Celine pushed open the door to the stable. Inside, she paused while her eyes adjusted to the dim light. Hazy shafts of sunlight filtered through the loft from above. Peaceful silence hushed her uncertain heart.

Along the way to the loft's ladder, she stopped at the stall holding Trevor's horse, Panther, and ran a hand over his velvet nose. He nickered softly. What awesome power. Even Trevor's horse held a dignity above the rest of the beasts in the stable.

She climbed the ladder, lifting her skirts as she went, glad she'd left behind her hoops and half her petticoats—another defiant act.

Where in heaven was he?

She knew he was up there, could sense him. And yet, there was only silence. Biting her lip, she continued on, refusing to allow doubt to creep in.

Apprehension vanished as she stepped on the final rung

of the ladder. There he was, lifting her up with surprising ease. In one swift motion, he helped her off the ladder and onto a quilt spread flat upon the hay.

He looked even more at ease than back in the dining room. He wore a blue chambray shirt and tan pants. At the edge of the quilt rested a basket of food and a bottle of wine. Off to the side stood his boots.

He'd fashioned a bed of sorts.

Trepidation set in. Was she ready for this?

"Stop looking like a bird about to become a cat's trophy. I thought the hay would be too harsh for your skin. If I had it in mind to bed you, I'd have found a more private place."

She paused, and then she laughed at the absurdity of her apprehension. If he only knew. Stretching out on the quilt, she rested her chin on folded arms, peered out the portal, and mimicked Cameron. "You're quite right, Trev, old boy, this is quite a magnificent view.

"And you certainly thought of everything." She nodded to the basket. "I ate practically nothing at breakfast."

"I noticed."

She went back to scanning the scenery, trying to ignore his clean scent. "Who do you suppose that is arriving by carriage?"

Trevor stretched out on his side next to her, and propped himself on an elbow. He slipped a piece of straw between his teeth and twirled it nonchalantly with his fingertips.

"The Verrettes. They're from upriver, remember? You were at their home for the soirée."

"Of course."

A desire to be physically closer to him swept over her with such a powerful force, it was as if a part of her detached from her body and moved into oneness with him. A churning in the center of her chest discomfited her.

Turning her cheek onto her arm, she studied him. His bold gaze caught her off guard. But this time, she put up no barriers.

He removed the piece of straw from between his lips and used it to tease a wisp of hair from her cheek. "Tell me what you intend to do with yourself once you reach San Francisco? What's out there that's not here, if you've no ties to either place? You aren't exactly a poor man's catch, you know. You could do just as well for yourself in New Orleans."

Frustration swept through her veins at his remark.

Trevor ducked as she threw a handful of hay at him. "What did I just say that made you do that?"

She studied him for a moment. "I suppose I'm somewhat touchy about being termed someone's *catch.* The idea rankles me. I think that's the part I resent about being a woman."

"What part?"

"The part about having to have a man in my life to be content. Can I not be happy left to my own devices?"

He shrugged. "Can you?"

"Tell me this, Trevor—if a man is unmarried, he is called a bachelor, and no one questions his state of well-being. But if a woman is not wed, she is referred to as a miserable old maid."

"It doesn't sound like you have it in mind to marry again."

"I don't."

He frowned. "Was your marriage that bad?"

She tried to turn her head, but he would not let her. "Did your husband mistreat you?"

"Heavens, no. He was perfectly kind to me. It's just that . . ." She shrugged.

He squeezed her arm when her words trailed off. "Go on."

"The accident not only took my husband and unborn child from me, it took the lives of any future children as well."

"You're certain?"

She nodded. "The physician said the fever that followed took care of that."

Trevor gave her hand a squeeze. "I am sorry."

"Don't be. I don't wallow in self-pity. I prefer the reality that there are few men who would care to marry a barren woman—unless he has one foot in the grave." She smiled. "And perhaps even then."

"That wasn't funny, Celine. I think there must be numerous men who would welcome all your attention, and wouldn't miss having children. And what about a widower who already has his own family? Besides, I'm not so sure it's always in a child's best interest if both parents are so caught up in one another, the children are excluded. Perhaps it's only possible to have one or the other, but never both." It was about time to bring this part of the discussion to a close—he was beginning to feel uncomfortable.

Celine reached out and touched his arm. "Your thinking is skewed because of your own childhood."

Now he was *really* uncomfortable. "What the hell do you mean by that?"

"Your father and I had many conversations while I was grieving, Trevor. I am quite aware of what went on in your family. Your father has much regretted his exclusion of you when he was so deeply in love with your mother. He knows you cherished your mother's time when you had it, and that you had no one after she died. At the time, your father couldn't comprehend that the love of a son is different from the love of a husband."

"Are you insinuating that my father was jealous of a mother's love for her son?"

"It wouldn't be the first time such jealousy occurred. Perhaps it is more common than we realize. He certainly is deeply sorry, and has many regrets."

"I never knew."

"And that would be because you two never spoke of the past, which is typical of men."

"Humph."

For some strange reason, he needed her right then. He

moved his body closer to hers, but was quickly aroused by nothing more than the simple curve of her back, and the smooth touch of her skin. He shifted to his stomach to conceal his growing ardor, and in doing so, his body touched the length of hers.

It set him on fire—the last thing he wanted to occur today. He fully intended to fulfill his father's request to treat Celine with dignity. Bedding her in the hayloft was not part of his plans. No, that he would do later.

Oh, hell. His body had a mind of its own. He got up and fumbled around in the wicker basket. He retrieved the bottle of wine and two glasses and settled back next to her.

She smiled.

For the first time, he noticed that her smile started out at the right corner of her mouth, the left corner lagging behind, giving it an ever-so-slightly crooked appearance before it appeared fully. The wonderful little flaw only accentuated her beauty. Without thinking, he leaned over and touched the crooked corner of her mouth with his lips.

She stiffened.

He pulled back. "Pardon."

With only a slight nod, she set about watching the workers place the finishing touches on the outdoor decorations, seemingly unfazed by his action.

Trevor regarded her profile. "You're very pretty." Christ, such trite words for the mighty feelings in his heart.

Her cheeks flushed. "Thank you."

He poured a little more wine in her glass. The ruby liquid spilled down the edge. With the tip of her tongue, she caught the overflow.

"Ah." She smiled, and then held the glass to her lips.

He wanted to drink from the side she'd just caressed with her tongue.

She intrigued him, captivated him with her mind as well as with her sheer physical presence. His hand enclosed hers.

He held it to his constricted chest and let his heart beat into her hand. How the hell was he going to let her sail off with Cameron?

His gaze swept over her length, touched skirts draped over shapely legs, up over a flat stomach and round breasts that moved subtly with her gentle breaths. Then his gaze came to rest upon her face again. He became brutally aware of the quickened tempo of her breathing.

The electricity in the air surged as though a storm had gathered. He regarded her for a long while, watching for some slight gesture or movement. Her pulse throbbed at the base of her throat, and he knew that one day very soon, they would have to have one another.

But not now, not in the purity of this moment.

A sudden ache in the hollow of his heart compelled him to reach for her. His voice was uneven as he spoke. "Have you ever wanted to be held, Celine? Simply held in a man's arms, and nothing more?"

Her lips parted and she took in an audible breath. "And have you ever wanted to hold someone, Trevor? Simply hold them, and nothing more?"

He embraced her—as if the embrace would discharge an entire lifetime of inconsolable hunger and emptiness.

She buried her head in his chest, relaxed into him as though her bones had dissolved. Then she pulled her head back, studied him for a moment. "What happened to you in New Orleans? You are . . . different."

"Shh. I missed you."

In one languid movement, his mouth came down on hers, feather light, and then deepened into a passionate, complete kiss. It was warm and wonderful, drinking her in. Deeper and deeper into her essence he dove until he felt as though the ground gave way beneath them.

On the brink of losing control, he broke the kiss. "Time

for the nap Madame Charmontès ordered, *ma petite*." He held her, just held her until she drifted off to sleep.

Celine awoke with muffled sounds drifting up from below. Confused, she sat up, then realized where she was. Alone in the loft, she crawled over to the ledge and peered down.

Trevor was tending to Panther. She watched for a moment, beguiled by his gentle manner with the horse.

He glanced upward and grinned. "Sleepyhead."

Her heart bloomed. How could he have grown more handsome in such a short time? She returned his smile, and then started down the ladder.

Trevor turned his back to her and continued brushing the horse. "You should probably help yourself down. You may save yourself some embarrassment that way."

His honey-soft laughter rushed into her heart. His teasing was as intimate as a kiss.

She stood beside him, quietly observed as he swept a wide brush across the horse's shiny black coat. Soon, Panther became a mere backdrop to the sleek man at work. She checked an urge to reach out and sweep away the ebony locks tumbling over his forehead.

The air stirred with his movements, filled the space around her with the unmistakable, heady scent that was part of his allure. It was a timeless, intimate painting. She hung suspended in the magical moment.

"Would you care for an afternoon ride?" he asked.

Celine started. "Afternoon? Oh, wonderful, just wonderful. What time is it?"

"Around two o'clock, I would suppose."

"Oh, Lord. Madame Charmontès is absolutely going to kill me." She raised her skirts to run.

He grabbed her arm. "Whoa. The little woman has you on a leash. What time were you supposed to meet with her?"

"Half past two."

He brushed her forehead with his lips and smiled. "Get on with you, then, but relax, it's not the end of the world."

"Thank you." She was off and running, her skirts swirling the dust as she exited the stables.

As soon as she was inside the house and halfway up the stairs, she could hear wailing. "Good heavens, what in the world is the matter?"

There stood Felicité in the upstairs hall, sobbing loudly while Cameron attempted to calm her. Madame Charmontès stepped from Celine's room, clucking her tongue.

"I lost my earrings," Felicité sniffled. "The . . . the earrings I was supposed to wear tonight."

Celine put an arm around the sobbing girl. "Do you have any idea where you might have lost them?"

"Now, then," Cameron interjected. "If she knew where she lost them, then they wouldn't be lost, would they?"

Felicité stomped her foot. "This is no time for your tomfoolery, Cameron."

"And this is no time for a temper tantrum, Felicité," Celine broke in. "Where were you when you last recall wearing them?"

"Aha!" Cameron punctuated the air with his finger. "That's what's so upsetting to the little dear. She was wearing her mother's expensive earrings, which, I might add, her father does not know she'd gotten her little fingers on, and then she was off wearing them someplace she shouldn't have been. And now the little goat doesn't want to tell you where that someplace is."

"Where were you, Felicité?" Celine demanded.

Felicité howled louder.

Madame Charmontès glowered at the threesome. "I cannot tend to you when you are in such a state, little one. Go. Off with you. Find the earrings while I work on Celine."

"Enough!" Celine startled everyone into silence with her sharp cry.

"Where were you, Felicité? Oh, I think I understand. Somewhere you are not supposed to be, *oui?* You couldn't possibly have taken the key to my cabin from my room?"

Felicité twisted one toe into the floor.

Celine took a deep breath and turned to Madame Charmontès. "You work on Felicité while I go in search of the earrings. I'll only worry if she goes alone."

"Cameron may go with her," Madame Charmontès responded sharply. "I must work on you."

Celine rolled her eyes. "Marvelous, a goat and a ninny looking for a needle in a haystack."

Cameron shot Celine a hard glance. "How about you and I see if we can find them?"

"Good idea. I have a private matter I wish to speak with you about anyway."

Felicité stopped sniffling, her wide gaze flickering from Celine to Cameron and back again.

"Oh?" Cameron smoothed his mustache. "Now why is it I find your tone a little worrisome?"

"Hush." Celine hugged Felicité. "Wash the tears off your face, and go about your business. Nothing is going to spoil our day."

"I'll get the horses," Cameron said, heading for the stairs. "Meet me at the back entrance."

Trevor glanced up from Panther when Cameron roared into the stable.

"Going someplace?"

Cameron threw a blanket and saddle on the gray. "What are you doing in here, Trev? Widow Beaudrée hidden somewhere under the hay, or are you actually tending to your horse?"

"You can't think of anything saltier than that? You're slipping."

"How about kiss my sweet *derrière.*" Cameron grinned and lifted another saddle onto a roan. When he finished, he led the two horses toward the stable doors.

Trevor felt relaxed, affable. "You're in a hurry."

As Cameron exited the stable, he called over his shoulder. "Why should I remain here with the likes of you when I've got something sweet and beautiful waiting for me?"

Curious, Trevor followed Cameron from the stable and watched him ride to the rear of the house, dismount, and help Celine onto the other horse. Hastily, he remounted and the two rode off in the direction of the woods.

Trevor stood still, his ears ringing, his blood running cold. He pulled a watch from his left pocket and checked the time.

"Well, I'll be damned, you lying little fool."

Chapter Eleven

Celine was still in the tub when Marie returned to the room.

"You're not out of there yet? Lordy, but I don't know how you dare dawdle with that crazy Madame Charmontès takin' charge like she's a general and we're her troops. You know she'll have a conniption if'n I don't have you any further along than this."

Marie held up a towel, and Celine stepped from the tub.

As if on cue, Madame Charmontès burst into the room, clucking and badgering poor Marie for running late, and pushing her hands in the air in front of her. "Quickly, please, quickly."

Celine laughed at the absurd expressions on both their faces. "You two. I would hope to have a little peace after all the chaos over Felicité's antics this afternoon. I was exhausted by the time I found those earrings."

Madame Charmontès wrung her hands and pursed her lips as she paced and watched Marie complete her toweling of Celine. Together, the petite tornado and Marie fussed over Celine.

Oil and vinegar, those two.

They stepped on one another's toes, each blaming the other, until Celine was forced to intervene. She assured

Madame Charmontès that Marie could prepare Celine. And since Madame Charmontès was the very finest of all dressmakers in the world, she need not be present for the simple administering of the toilette. She would, however, be much needed for the final inspection. Placated, Madame Charmontès retreated.

As the door closed behind Madame, Marie wheezed a great sigh of relief. "Lordy, but there must have been a black moon risin' the night that woman was born. I'll bet she came out screechin' and been at it ever since."

In her serenity, Celine's mind wandered little from the events in the hayloft. She barely heard her maid's grumblings.

Trevor.

The memory of his essence swept through her, quickening the beating of her heart. The remainder of the afternoon without him had inched by. A desire to be near him once again welled inside her with such force, she thought she might burst.

The strain of violins wafted through the upper hallways, blending with the sounds of the guests wandering through the house. When had that all started? How long had she been off in her own world? "Are you nearly finished, Marie?"

"One more little pin in your hair and there you be." Marie stepped back and walked a circle around Celine. "Oh, my. I don't think I've ever seen anything so beautiful as you. Have a look-see."

Celine moved to the mirror, and gasped. The flesh-colored silk of her ballgown played host to thousands of tiny crystal beads strung together in one-inch strands. The entire gown was covered with them, from the low-cut bodice that shimmered with the rise and fall of every breath, to the soft folds of the full skirt. She turned a slow pirouette and the beads danced like fireflies. She raised an arm and the fitted sleeves winked at her. So much glitter, yet the gown seemed to weigh nothing. "Say what you will, but Madame Charmontès is a veritable genius."

The same beads, strung on combs, were tucked into the soft curls just behind her ears, creating a halo effect.

Marie touched Celine on the elbow. "I'll fetch Mr. Andrews to see you downstairs." She opened the door and nearly fell over Madame Charmontès.

The couturiere sucked in her breath at the sight of Celine. Her eyes glistened as she rushed into the room. She clasped her hands in front of her, prayerlike, and pressed them to her lips. Lines, carved and tunneled over the years, slipped away from the dressmaker's face, while her chin quivered, then jutted upward in exultation. "The result is far more exquisite than I had envisioned. I have created my masterpiece—a *Michel-Ange de couture.*"

Marie scowled at her.

Justin stepped into the room. His jaw slackened. "I am beyond words."

The strains of a Viennese waltz sounded from below. He bowed. "It would be my pleasure to escort you to your ball, Celine. I pray I have done you justice."

Celine's heart could have burst just then. She twirled once for him and then slipped her arm into his and together they descended the stairs.

He paused with Celine at the entrance to the crowded ballroom and waited for her to be announced. The music seemed to grow louder, but then she realized it had actually ceased, and the crowd hushed. The roaring in her ears was what she heard.

Trevor mingled with the crowd in front. He didn't smile and a muscle twitched alongside his jaw. Was he angry about something? He turned away. Celine corrected her expression before shock had time to register on her face.

On cue, the orchestra resumed. Celine stepped into the ballroom, instantly surrounded by eager well-wishers. Cameron begged for the first dance. When they danced past Trevor, he ignored them.

Why? Because she danced with Cameron? Because she hadn't had a chance to inform Trevor she'd spoken to Cameron about her feelings toward him? She would tell Trevor straight away that Cameron claimed to have no designs on her. Nonetheless, her spirits flagged.

The widow Beaudrée sidled up to Trevor. He smiled down at her. Her arm slipped through his.

That dreadful woman.

Could she possibly be the reason he was acting so strangely? Was he actually with her? Perhaps to protect Celine, like at the last fete? But that couldn't be—they'd had a discussion and he knew she needed no protection from another woman.

Nothing made sense.

The widow leaned toward Trevor's ear, brushing her mouth against his cheek while she spoke. Whatever she said, he laughed. He was so mercurial, so shallow after this afternoon, so blatant in ignoring her presence. And tonight of all nights.

A sullen sense of betrayal crept in. Sorely disappointed, she couldn't take another step on the dance floor without speaking her mind to him directly.

"Cameron, please, I could use a little refreshment and a bit of a rest."

"I thought you'd never ask, my dear. Ah, there's Trevor and our, ahem, good neighbor." Cameron coughed into his fist, and then guided Celine toward the other couple while whispering wickedly through his teeth. "Wonder what he sees in her? Everyone knows she's so fickle even her towels are monogrammed *hers* and *next.*"

Celine laughed and gave Cameron's arm a squeeze. "You are positively wicked."

Menacing eyes, as black as sin, raked over them as they

approached. Nonetheless, Celine managed to hold her composure, even though her smile felt wooden.

What the devil was wrong with him? It couldn't all be because he assumed she hadn't yet spoken with Cameron.

Cameron bent at the waist and pecked the back of the widow's hand. "Madame Beaudrée, aren't you the stunning one this evening?" He turned to Trevor and cocked a brow at his dark mood. "Be a good chap, *s'il vous plait,* and take care of Celine while I see to quenching her thirst."

The widow Beaudrée responded in Trevor's stead, her honeyed voice tinged with a kind of sarcasm only another woman would detect. "Certainly, Cameron. We'll see she's kept safe and waiting for you, won't we, Trevor, dear?"

She clasped her hand over the one she had twined about Trevor's curved elbow and leaned closer to him.

Celine bristled. A sense of being an uninvited third party turned her mouth to cotton. She glanced to the floor lest Trevor guess her mood from her eyes. Forcing a relaxed demeanor, she raised her head.

"Thank you, Madame Beaudrée. Whatever would I do without your generous concern? And I am ever so grateful you are here this evening. Trevor would have been quite bored had you declined the invitation."

She looked around the room, then back to Giselle. "I dare say there isn't anyone here who comes close to your social station." She fought the smirk trying to curl the corners of her mouth.

The widow shifted her stance. Her eyes narrowed and her hold on Trevor's arm tightened.

Trevor had genuinely anticipated Celine's arrival this evening, despite her damnable afternoon ride with Cameron. Their morning together had struck a chord deep in his heart.

No matter how hard he tried, he could not get her out of his thoughts. The feelings she'd stirred in him when she finally made her grand entrance were nearly more than he could handle. He had not yet asked her to dance, so unsure was he of what actions he might take. He was still furious with her. He didn't take much to liars.

In the meantime, Giselle, like a sequined tick, laid claim to him, and caused his mood to turn even more disagreeable.

And then he caught sight of Celine flirting and dancing with Cameron. For an instant, his own vulnerability had crushed him. He hadn't trusted himself enough to talk to her after that, for fear he would demand an explanation as to why she had gone off with his cousin after their glorious morning together. And most importantly, it was painfully obvious from Cameron's attitude that she'd failed to settle anything with him. On the contrary, damn it.

Trevor's mood dipped lower. God, she had the capacity to knock him totally off balance.

His mind wrestled with the morning's events. He'd left her napping in the loft and tended to Panther in order to restrain himself. She'd rested so easily in his arms, all soft and woman-scented. He'd lain there as long as was possible, holding her, secretly capturing her every feature, every sweet breath she took, burning her essence into his memory. Until, in her slumbering innocence, she slipped an arm around his neck and edged closer to him, nuzzled him until the heat of her womanly body entranced him.

Everything had felt so comfortable, as though they'd lain in each other's arms a thousand times. A deep desire for something intangible worked its mysterious pull on him—something that seducing her right then would have surely destroyed. Fire had mixed with the blood in his veins until he could no longer contain or trust himself. It had taken all his strength to retreat.

But now he'd be damned if he would let her get away with marching right up to him on Cameron's arm with such cold indifference. Especially after she'd toyed with his emotions all morning while knowing full well she would meet with Cameron. Why did she have to lie? Once trust was gone . . .

He started to speak, but his father appeared from nowhere.

"Madame Beaudrée." Justin held his arm out and smiled. "Would you kindly grace this old man's arm for a twirl around the dance floor?"

There was not a thing she could do but accept, which left Celine and Trevor to themselves.

He looked to Celine for a scant second, then raised his glass to his mouth and perused the room over its rim. He took small sips of the amber contents, and ignored her.

Celine's cheeks flushed. She was angry. Good. Let her suffer a little. What did he care?

Damn it, he did care, that was the worst of it.

"Just because you have a beautiful woman on your arm, Trevor, that is no excuse for your rudeness toward me. Perhaps you owe me an apology."

He lowered his glass and surveyed the room one more time before he regarded her. "Madame, if memory serves me, I do believe it was you who approached the two of us in a less than courteous manner. Correct me if I am wrong, but I do not recall speaking to you."

He did not know what to do with his anger. "As for apologies, Mrs. Kirkland, perhaps an apology would be more appropriate coming from you."

He set his glass to his mouth once again, disarmed at how quickly she could fracture his composure. How easily she destroyed his steely intention of ignoring her by simply standing in front of him, staring with those damnable eyes of hers. He forced himself to look away, knowing he was now fighting the urge to ask her why the hell she'd lied to him, knowing he was combating the even more powerful desire to hold her once again, despite his anger with her.

Mentally, he compared the other women in the room to Celine, tried to determine what it was about her that had him so captivated. There were others in attendance that, by anyone's standards, could be considered more beautiful than Celine. Besides, he usually preferred taller, longer-legged women. Didn't he? He couldn't seem to recall.

His father and Giselle glided around the dance floor. Trevor noted her chiseled beauty. Her white-blond hair, curled and laden with jewels. Her flawless body, barely disguised beneath the gown she wore. Giselle noticed his gaze and with a seductive smile, raised long, tapered fingers from his father's shoulder in discreet response. He tipped his glass to her and returned the smile, yet she stirred not a modicum of emotion in him.

He returned his attention to Celine. Slowly, from her toes upward, he boldly drank her in. The intoxicating results pounded through his veins. Now, this one moved him—only she—and hadn't he known it all along? Fire and ice, that's what she was.

Pressure tightened his chest, heat coursed through his groin. *Damn it!* He nearly groaned aloud in his fight not to reach for her. He had to do something to right the situation.

"Before we continue this tedious demand for apologies, Celine, or before your temper gets the best of you, I would like to tell you, by the way, that Madame Charmontès has outdone herself with the gown you wear."

Oh, hell, that didn't sound right, either. And she was still angry.

* * *

Celine squeezed her eyes shut for a second, then opened them, hoping she was casting emerald green shards into every pore of Trevor's body.

Her hands had begun to tremble when he'd had the audacity to blatantly eye the other females in attendance right in front of her. But when he'd brazenly turned his scrutiny toward her, as if he were deciding to take his pick, she could not control their shaking. She hid her hands behind her back. "That's all you have to say to me, that Madame Charmontès has created a beautiful gown?"

He stared over the heads of the crowd. A muscle twitched in his jaw.

"Trevor, I do not understand. We had such a beautiful morning and afternoon together, and now you act like this."

"Like what?"

"Like an arrogant, presumptuous cad. What happened? I think you owe me an explanation."

"First I owe you an apology. Now I owe you an explanation? Reality can be such a terrible thing, my naive little bird. We suspended it for a bit today, but it seems to have descended upon us once again. And with a vengeance."

If she didn't walk away right this minute, she would weep. Or slap him. Without a word, she stalked off, elbowing her way through the crowd. Memories of their shared intimacy in the loft trailed through her consciousness. She couldn't get out of the room fast enough.

Her attempt to make an exit was intercepted by an aggressive beau-in-waiting, asking for a dance. Giving it a moment's thought, she decided Trevor would be the last person to tarnish her evening. She noted the tall blond man standing hesitantly in front of her. He was rather handsome.

"I would very much enjoy a dance with you, sir."

The stranger took her in his arms and swung her onto the dance floor.

* * *

Trevor felt as though he'd sliced himself to ribbons as well as her. She hadn't deserved his ugly diatribe, yet his wounded pride wouldn't allow him to back down. He had to do something to mend the situation—and fast.

But before he could make his way to Celine, Felicité cornered him, begging for a dance. Grudgingly, he led his verbose little sister to the dance floor.

"Oh, I am having such a wonderful time, Trevor. This is a fairy tale come true, in spite of the mess I made of things this afternoon. I thought I was in for it this time, but Cameron and Celine saved me. *Merde!*"

"Do not curse, *ma soeur.* It does not become you. And from what little mess did Cameron and Celine rescue you?"

He whirled her around the dance floor, his interest piqued. As they danced, he tried to catch a glimpse of Celine. He decided to apologize for his belligerent behavior as soon as he was through dancing with his sister.

"Please promise not to tell Papa?"

Impatiently, he nodded his head, still scanning the room for Celine. "Get on with it."

"I took *Maman's* garnet earrings. I didn't see any harm since they are meant to be mine one day. But I took them with me to Celine's cabin, which, by the way, she says I am not allowed to visit for some silly reason. Anyway, I don't know what happened, but I misplaced them . . . the earrings, that is. Then, Cameron told Celine what I did, and did she ever get furious. And then Madame Charmontès got mad at Celine because she took off with that ninny Cameron to find them. And I don't know what the private matter she had to talk to him about was, but she had her temper up and then—"

"Whoa, Felice, take a breath." Relief washed away his anger. He led his sister off the dance floor and over to where Cameron stood holding Celine's drink.

"What's this about having to find lost earrings today, Cam? Felicité's been trying to tell me, but I'm not quite following. Did you or did you not find my mother's earrings?"

Not that he gave a damn about the bloody earrings.

Felicité clapped her hands together. "Yes, yes, they did, Trevor. They found them, but hush, or Papa—"

Cameron looked down his nose at his young cousin. "Oh, *you* hush, little goat. There you go again with that nasty little habit of yours."

"What nasty habit?" She stuck out her bottom lip.

"Breathing." He sniffed and turned his nose up at her.

"You aren't one bit humorous. And guess what, Trevor? Celine got quite angry at him, called him a ninny for treating me the way he does. And then Madame Charmontès started ordering everyone around, including me, and Celine got mad at her, too, and started shouting at everybody, telling us we ruined her birthday, and then she threatened to stomp off to her room and not talk to anyone until we calmed down. I've never seen her in such a fit."

Felicité's eyes widened with her exaggerated performance until Trevor broke into hearty laughter.

Cameron snorted. "Speaks English rather well when she wants to, wouldn't you say?"

"Would you two excuse me. I have some unfinished business . . ." Trevor began a visual search of the room.

Cameron groaned. "Oh, please. Don't leave me here to child-sit, I beg of you."

"Ninny." Felicité turned and walked off.

"Why does that sister of yours have to follow me on my coattails day and night? She's like a sore toe in tight boots. And where the devil did Celine go? This punch is growing mold it's been in my hand so long."

"Don't have the slightest idea on either count. Wait here, Cameron. I'll find her for you." Trevor smirked at his cousin.

"Ninny, eh? Hmm. I have a feeling that moniker is going to stick for a while."

He patted Cameron on the shoulder and went looking for Celine—with no intention of finding her for his cousin. In fact, he was eager to apologize and then transport her somewhere secluded.

An urgency to get to her, to hold her, hit like a gale. He intended to have a full heart-to-heart talk with her. He believed what they'd shared in the loft had been genuine. He needed to know if it meant as much to her as it had to him.

But he never got that far. He spied her on one of the settees in the upper hall, sitting close—too close—to a blond man. She was gazing into his eyes the way she'd looked at Trevor up in the loft.

Celine was still blazing with anger when Trevor hiked up the stairs. Damn him! She planted a kiss on her surprised companion's cheek. He wasted no time returning the favor.

Trevor stopped in his tracks. His eyes, like black clouds cast over a moon, bored into her.

And then he retreated.

Celine made her way over to the railing to get a full view of him. The Widow Beaudrée stood at the bottom of the curved stairway, one hand resting on a seductively turned hip, the other holding a fresh drink.

Trevor paused midway down the stairs, one foot poised over the next step. He leaned against the railing and openly appraised the widow.

Celine's heart caught in her throat as Giselle raised her drink to Trevor in toast. A sultry grin curled the corner of his mouth, then spread over his dark visage before he swaggered down the stairs toward her and drank from the glass she held to his lips.

Madame Charmontès came out of nowhere and laid a hand on Celine's shoulder, startling her. "Come. You have a small tear in your gown." She turned to the man sitting next to Celine. "Please excuse us while I see to Mrs. Kirkland."

If Celine had wanted to refuse, she couldn't have. The grip Madame Charmontès had on her was like a vise.

Once inside the bedroom, Madame sat Celine gently down in the window seat. Too gently. Madame was not her high-strung, aggressive self. Not at all.

"What do you think you are doing, toying with that man's emotions in such a wicked way? It is not what will turn him into a suitor. *Non,* it will only drive him off so quickly you will not know where he has disappeared to. There is so very much you have yet to learn."

"That little kiss I gave that man meant nothing, and I couldn't care less about him as a suitor."

"*Non,* Madame Celine, I do not speak of the young man, Charles. I speak of your other suitor, the one you spurned with your false show of affection toward this one who means nothing to you."

Celine's spine stiffened. Nervous fingers stroked the jewels on her gown. "What do you mean?"

"I speak of Trevor, madame."

"He is hardly my suitor. Nor will he ever be, by . . . by mutual consent . . ." Her words trailed off in a small whisper.

The dressmaker reached out and covered Celine's hands with hers. Celine saw wisdom shining through pensive, wizened eyes.

"Ah, that is not the truth as I see it. Trust one who has the gift of vision, one who knows a well-finished garment long before the pattern has been cut. Believe me, little one, the pieces of the pattern here are just barely being fitted between the two of you. It will take time before they are in final form. Have patience."

Celine leaned forward and rested her head on Madame's shoulder, feeling suddenly weary. "This is all too much for me. I am nothing more than a plaything to him. He . . . he—"

"Frightens you?"

Celine stiffened. She started to protest, but instead, at Madame's resolute manner, she slumped. "I suppose you are right. I am completely incapable of conquering a man such as he. I am so inept at all of this."

"So inept that you give up before the first piece of the pattern is cut? Ah, did it ever come to mind that he is as much afraid of you as you are of him?"

"That's absurd. Why should Trevor Andrews, of all men, be afraid of me? He's been with women the world over. And then there is Madame Beaudrée—why, I can't even begin to compete with her."

"Hear my words, and hear them well, madame. You have no competition from her. Be as you are, and do not hold back in fear."

Madame tapped a bony finger emphatically on her own chest. "Trust what I tell you. The beast of fear is your only competition, and it is sad to see that the monster attacks both of you. You have great presence, Celine. And you have a certain . . . mystery about you. But when you are afraid? Ah, that is when the light in you wavers. And I tell you, this suitor of yours whom you deny, I have known him since his birth, and I will share a secret—Trevor is terrified of love. You must show him he has nothing to fear from you."

Madame stood and exited so quickly, Celine had no time to respond. She was left with a myriad of unanswered questions. Frustrated, she twisted the gold bracelet around her wrist and heaved a great sigh.

Fear? She thought about Madame's words and then about Trevor. Her memory was so sharp and clear, she could recall, in each of her senses, his very essence.

And then she knew. She cared for Trevor far more than she

wanted to admit. But she was barren and he was a restless man who sailed the seas. What could they possibly want with one another other than an affair? Her pulse speeded at the thought. Blast it all. Despite everything, she still wanted that one night with him.

Celine left her room, deciding to ask Trevor to dance so she could make amends. But he was nowhere in sight. Neither was Giselle Beaudrée.

"There you are," Justin said.

"I slipped away to my quarters for a moment's rest."

"Ah, and here I was looking for you so I could ask for a dance."

She forced a smile. "Please do."

After two full dances, neither Trevor nor *that woman* appeared to be anywhere in the ballroom. Celine's heart fell as she slipped quietly onto the veranda.

The night was clear, the air warm. Stars were scattered across the sky like diamonds on black velvet. With soft strains of the orchestra riding the night's still air, she meandered aimlessly about the garden, wishing she could go back in time, crawl into her grandmother's lap, and grow up differently. Perhaps then she wouldn't be so blasted sensitive.

Wandering to the edge of the garden, she caught sight of a golden shaft of light streaming from the stable. Either the stablemaster was waiting up to hand off carriages to departing guests, or he'd left a lantern lit. She went to investigate.

The huge door stood slightly ajar, allowing Celine to slip through. "Thomas?"

She saw them.

Giselle was stretched out languidly in the hay, her body still clothed, but half hidden under Trevor's. Her triumphant smile was directed at Celine.

"Won't you join us, darling?"

Stunned, Celine could not tear her eyes away from the scene before her. Trevor rolled onto his back, his face hidden in shadow.

With all the calm and control she could summon, Celine breathed deeply, then exhaled very slowly, remembering Madame Charmontès's instruction about fear. "Why, Trevor," she said, "I thought you only rode thoroughbreds."

Giselle's body pitched forward. "Why, you little—"

Trevor's low laughter interrupted Giselle's counterattack. "And what pedigree does your friend have, Celine?"

His words cut through her like a hot knife. Head held high, she walked out of the stable.

The night air was now a shock, as though cold water had been thrown in her face. She headed straight through the garden toward the rear of the house. Before she could reach the house, her knees buckled. She leaned against a mimosa tree for support. Sick to her stomach, she purged its contents. Tears spilled down her cheeks as she quietly and desperately sobbed.

Her arms stretched around the smooth trunk of the small tree, and she hugged it for solace. The cool bark against her cheek drank her tears. How utterly and completely alone she was. She couldn't begin to find the words to describe her pain.

Wiping her eyes, she retreated to the back stairs and to her room, each step heavier than the one before.

Chapter Twelve

Morning gave way to a somber gray sky and humidity that hung heavy in the air. Overnight guests streamed aboard the early riverboat, hoping to reach New Orleans before nightfall. Just as well. Celine was in no mood for stragglers.

She was curled up in a chair in the cookhouse, twisting a loose tendril through her fingers and chewing on her lower lip as she watched Zola cook.

"I hate days like this," Zola grumbled. "The air is so heavy even my bread dough refuses to rise proper." She cast a frown at Celine. "Miss Celine, don't you think you ought to take lunch with the family?"

"Huh? Oh, I . . . I don't feel like eating. Guess I had too much champagne."

"But you'll be missed."

"I won't be the only one to pass up food. You outdid yourself last night, Zola."

"You don't look so happy today. Did something go wrong last night?"

When Celine failed to answer, only curled up like a cat in the chair and went back to reading her book, Zola said nothing, but produced a quilt and tucked it around Celine. It wasn't the first time she'd spent the day in the cookhouse.

When Marie walked in, it was late afternoon. Zola's shushing woke Celine, but she kept her eyes closed and feigned sleep while Marie and Zola gossiped in hushed whispers.

"Best if'n I take Miss Celine's dinner on up to her room," Marie said. "By the way she was sittin' up there at the window starin' out at nuthin' this morning, she don't plan to see herself to the table."

"Too much champagne at the ball," Zola sing-songed.

Marie humphed. "If'n you ask me, there's somethin' besides too much champagne wrong with her. And it started last night. I know, 'cause she went to bed lookin' like someone done punched the life out of her. Of course, it couldn't possibly have anythin' to do with that *sweet li'l ol' punkin' head* you favor, now could it?"

"Hush. What goes on between those two ain't none of our business."

Celine stretched, yawned, and stood. Silence filled the room. "I'll be off to my chambers." She didn't care what they had to say. In fact, she didn't care about much of anything.

Near the dinner hour she wandered back into the cookhouse, again refusing to join the others. She curled up in the same chair she'd occupied earlier, and sat with her back to the door while Marie hovered about, cross as a cow that hadn't been milked in three days.

Zola's eyes widened.

At Zola's odd expression, Celine glanced over her shoulder. Trevor's broad shoulders shadowed the entry. He leaned against the door's frame and folded his arms over his chest. "Seems you have been entertaining a guest, Zola."

Marie, standing next to Celine, muttered. "Seems to me he doesn't look any too good, neither."

Trevor's brow furrowed, and his eyes lacked their normal fire. "Come, Celine. My father wants you to sit with the family at dinner."

She wished he would leave. "Tell your father I had more than enough food and drink at the ball, thank you very much. A day's fast is my usual panacea."

Trevor dropped his arms to his sides, one hand fisting and unfisting. "May I speak with you for a moment, Celine?"

"Why?"

"There's something I wish to discuss with you privately."

"There is nothing you could possibly have to say that would interest me in the least. Besides, I honestly find you despicable." Her voice sounded as flat as she felt.

He shifted his stance, stood straight. A muscle rippled along his jawline. "What a coincidence. I find you—"

Marie hissed and Zola chewed on her lip.

Celine stood and turned on Trevor. "I am soon gone from here, Mr. Andrews. In the meantime, you go straight to hell."

She made for the exit, but Trevor blocked it.

Zola chewed her lip again, likely to keep from blurting out something she had no right saying. But then she sucked in a deep breath and, on the exhale, spoke. "Best maybe you be joining the others like your papa requests, mischie. Food'll be on the table in an hour and we don't want him disappointed. I'll send Miss Celine along right soon."

Trevor turned on his heel and stalked off.

Zola clucked her tongue. She shot a scowl at Marie when the maid slammed a pot on the worktable. "Don't say nuthin'. I don't want to hear it."

Marie huffed.

Blast it all, the last thing she needed was to spend the night in her room with that secret closet door between her and Trevor . . . Well, she could do something about that little problem.

Zola shuffled over to where Celine sat and lifted the quilt. "You'd best git to the big house, Miss Celine."

Celine tossed the quilt aside and stood. "I was just leaving."

* * *

Trevor was acutely aware of the empty chair at the dinner table. He was also painfully aware his father eyed it with a grim countenance. His father had said nothing, other than to order him to collect Celine for dinner rather than have Marie perform the task—which told Trevor his father knew something had happened between them.

The silence throughout dinner was deafening. Trevor's gut was so tight he wasn't even aware of what he'd eaten. *Oh, hell.* He'd leave in the morning. He should have known returning to Carlton Oaks was a mistake.

Lightning split the air with a searing hiss, followed instantly by a boom of thunder, so close it shook the chandeliers.

Cameron dropped his silverware onto his plate. "Where's Celine?"

Marie's frantic voice and slapping feet echoed down the hallway. "Mister Andrews! Mister Andrews!"

Justin glared at Trevor. "Where the devil is Celine?"

Marie barreled into the dining room, wild-eyed, with Zola close behind.

Trevor stood, and nearly collided with Marie. She spoke to Justin but glared at Trevor. "Sir, the stable master done said Miss Celine left the barn an hour ago on that bay and headed for the woods—most likely to that *garçonnière* she calls her cabin."

Another round of lightning and thunder fractured the air.

Zola jumped. "Somebody better fetch her right fast. We can't let nuthin' happen to that girl."

Marie shook as she tried to control herself. "She's not in a good way." She glared harder at Trevor.

Zola swatted at Marie's arm. "Hush."

Cameron was out of his chair and halfway through the door when Trevor caught up with him and grabbed his arm. "I'll take care of this."

Cameron shrugged off Trevor's hold. "Keep your bloody hands off me. I'll see to her."

Justin slammed his fist on the table. The vein in his right temple pulsed thickly. "Be damned! I have held my temper in check these past few days, but I have had enough. Trevor, if you have anything to do with Celine's disappearance, you had better move fast."

Felicité whimpered. Elizabeth kept her head bowed. The others sat in stunned silence.

Damn it, Trevor knew exactly what was wrong with Celine, and he had to be the one to see to her.

Seeing the silent determination on his face, Cameron stepped back. "You had better make this right."

"I won't come back without her." Trevor bolted from the house and ran to the stables, taking no coat or wrap, not bothering with anything other than a bridle for Panther.

The winds nearly knocked him off his horse when he rode out. After the last storm he'd seen her through, and what it had done to her, his only concern was for Celine. He raced for the *garçonnière,* praying she'd made it there and wasn't lost in the blinding rain. Lightning and thunder shattered the night around him, the bolts crashing louder with each snap across the sky. Wind lashed and hurled the rain at him from every direction.

"I'm so sorry, so sorry. Please let me find you safe."

The rain pelted his face with such force, his eyes were mere slits. Bushes and branches blew across his path, the sky and ground trembled beneath the onslaught. He hoped to hell this wasn't a hurricane blowing across the gulf. Tree limbs tore at his clothing as he rode. Panther tried to pull back, whinnying and dancing about.

"Come on, boy. Come on," he urged. "You can make it, not much farther."

The horse bolted and pulled sideways as the riderless bay nearly knocked them over in a frantic search for shelter.

Nausea knotted Trevor's throat. He knew for certain now that Celine was in trouble. He dug his heels into Panther's flanks and called out her name. The horse pushed through the wind and lancing rain. What the bloody hell was she thinking, going off in a storm?

They crossed the swollen stream, and by memory, more than by sight, he pulled up in front of the *garçonnière.* Lightning struck nearby, splitting a tree. Thunder engulfed them. The earth beneath him trembled as the heavens let loose another angry deluge.

Trevor dismounted, and raced up the steps into the cabin, feeling for the front door in the darkness, hoping she was in there and hadn't fallen off the horse, lying injured somewhere.

"Celine! God, Celine, where are you?"

The storm howled and swirled around the small house with such ferocity, he could not have heard had she answered. He fumbled with the door's handle and stumbled inside. A blaze of lightning lit the room. There she was, curled up in a corner, arms hugging her knees against her chest.

He fastened the door, and in two long strides, knelt beside her. Lightning flickered around the banging shutters, and thunder boomed. Celine whimpered, grasping at him in stark terror. He swept her up in his arms and carried her to the chair by the fireplace.

"*Ma petite,* it's all right. It's all right, *mon amour.*" He sat with her in his lap, cradled her in his arms, rocking her back and forth.

"Celine, listen to me. I've got to get a fire going and get those wet clothes off you before you catch a chill, all right?" He attempted to pull away, but she clutched at him like a small waif and moaned.

"Everything's all right now, I'm here." He pushed her

hair from her face and tenderly wiped the dampness from her cheeks.

She clung to him, disoriented and shivering. At another blaze of lightning, her teeth chattered. She wrapped her arms around him and buried her face in the curve of his neck.

"Celine," he said, grasping her shoulder, "let me light the fire, sweetheart. I won't be but a couple of feet from you."

He pulled her hands away, kissed her cheek, and then brushed his lips back and forth over her damp skin. "There, there. It's all right, everything's all right now."

He sensed her trust in him and stood, placing her in the chair. Quickly, he lit the fire, relieved when the seasoned wood ignited without a problem. He crossed the room in long, quick strides and latched the shutters, then bolted the door lest the storm blow them open.

Gathering blankets and pillows from the bed, along with quilts stored in the cedar chest at its foot, he fashioned a pallet as close as possible to the crackling fire.

Already, the room was losing some of its dampness. He reached for Celine's wet clothing. "Let me help you."

She nodded.

He stripped off her clothing, and rubbed her dry with the cloth he'd wrenched from the table, not allowing his eyes to linger on her naked form. The light was poor, but still, he couldn't help but note the satin of her skin, the graceful swell of her hips, the perfect roundness of her breasts. A hunger passed through him. He shoved the emotion aside and tucked her into the pallet, bunching the covers around her shoulders until just her face, from the chin up, was visible.

Silently, she watched him. He smiled down at her, then reached out with the back of his hand and gently caressed her cheek.

He spoke, hoping to reassure her. "It sounds as though the lightning and thunder aren't going to give up. And the rain is coming down in torrents. I have a hunch we're here for the night."

His hand left her cheek, and he gently combed through her tangled, wet hair with his fingers.

"You're wet too," she whispered.

He cocked his head to one side and grinned, relieved to hear her quiet voice. "I know." He hesitated, unsure whether he should say what he had to say. *Oh hell.* "I can't tell you how relieved I am you are safe."

"I am safe, aren't I?"

He nodded.

"Tell me, Trevor, what did you want to speak to me about in the cookhouse?"

The last thing he wanted to discuss right now was the mess he'd made of things. He continued to run his fingers through her hair. "Later, *ma petite.*"

"Now."

He sighed and dropped his hand. "I wanted to tell you what happened last night—when you walked into the stables."

She stared blankly at him.

Uncomfortable at not being able to read her, he shifted his weight. "Nothing happened, Celine. Nor would it have, whether you'd walked in or not. I . . . I don't know what was wrong with me, why I did what I did. Lately, I can't figure out much of anything I do. I was angry over—" He let out an exasperated sigh. "Over something that never actually took place. I've never before been possessive of another. I . . ."

Struggling with his words, Trevor took in a heavy breath and shoved his hand through his wet hair. "I only know that after Giselle and I went to the stables, the whole idea of what we'd gone there to do—including the woman I was with—disgusted me. All I could think of was you and the time we'd spent together that morning. I'd had too much to drink, I was jealous, and I was angry, but I was calling it a night when you walked in.

"Don't you see? Nothing could have happened, because you were all I saw. Then you walked in. I knew how awful everything looked, and I felt guilty . . . angry. After you left, I told Mrs. Beaudrée that I never wanted to see her again. I saw to it that she was properly escorted home."

He hesitated, but still she said nothing, only stared at him with a turquoise gaze so deep his heart ached.

"I can't blame you at all, Celine. I . . . damn, I made a fine mess of the wonderful morning we shared, and I ruined the ball you so looked forward to all this time."

When she still said nothing, a haunting pain tore at his gut. "Celine, please understand. I am sorry, so damn sorry."

She brought her arm out from under the covers and slowly ran her hand through his hair, mirroring his previous movements. "It was nothing."

His heart slammed against his chest. He closed his eyes and heaved in a deep breath.

Even with his eyes closed, he saw nothing but the vision of her lying there by the fire. And then other visions beckoned. The magical moment he'd first laid eyes on her mingled with their erotic encounter in the kitchen pantry. Tinkling laughter echoed in his memory along with a vision of her floating upon the waters the day he'd left for New Orleans.

He raised his eyelids and drank in the beauty of her face in all its sweet surrender. He watched, hypnotized, as turquoise flames deepened until they became languid, beckoning pools he fought to resist.

Self-control won out over the desire that coursed through him. His breathing labored from the strain of forbidden hungers firing his blood. Gently, he removed her hand and tucked it back under the covers.

He smiled down at her and spoke softly. "I know I'm a bit wet, but I was waiting for you to go to sleep before I disrobed. Close your eyes and get some rest, if not for yourself, then I beg you, for my sorry sake."

* * *

Celine must have dozed. For how long she did not know, but she felt Trevor move silently away from her. Opening her eyes, she watched as he took great pains draping her clothing around the fireplace. He seemed so understanding, so caring, much as he'd been in the hayloft. Familiar, yet . . . different.

Then she remembered. Another stormy night, and equally attentive ministrations. When the façades were down, when there was a real need, he would be there—compassionate and tender.

Lightning and thunder shook the small house. But Trevor was here and she was safe.

Trevor, with his back to her, disrobed. She knew she should close her eyes, but she could not. He removed his drenched shirt and draped it on the fireplace, used the bootjack to rid himself of his boots. His soaked breeches and unmentionables came last before he dried himself with the tablecloth he'd used on her.

For the first time in her life, Celine was seeing a man naked. Firelight danced across broad, muscled shoulders and flickered along smooth, hard flanks. A heated wanting pricked at her womb. Her heart tightened in her chest. Her lungs no longer accommodated proper breathing.

If this was all she could have of him—one night—she didn't want any regrets. And she wanted her memories. They were hers to take now.

He must have sensed her because he turned from the waist. "Celine." Her name floated through the air in a bubble of troubled emotion.

She watched him, unblinking.

He turned back to the fire and groaned. "Don't look at me that way."

The crackling of the burning logs and the steady drum of rain were his only answers.

"God help me, I don't want to take advantage of you." His voice was filled with pained exasperation.

Still, she was silent.

He moved to the pallet. Her eyelids did not so much as flutter as she stared at him. He knelt by the makeshift bed and touched her cheek. Bending forward, he kissed her gently on the forehead, and reached to stroke her hair. He ran his fingers, ever so softly, from her ear down to her chin, over the curve of her lips, caressing them.

The way he touched her, as if he found her fragile, the way he gazed at her through heavy lids, the way his breath fell rhythmically on her bare skin, unleashed a spontaneous urge in Celine, and charged her with an electricity as powerful as the lightning outside. She slipped her arms around his neck and tried to pull him to her.

He stopped her, lifted her arms away. "Don't, Celine. I cannot help myself—"

"Trevor?"

He stroked her cheek with the back of his hand. "Yes, *ma petite?*"

"I want you to make love to me."

He sucked in his breath. Fierce eyes, filled with a blend of fiery intensity and painful questioning, studied her. "Do you know what you're saying?"

She touched a finger to his upper lip, traced the arc of his mouth, and nodded. "I've wanted you since the moment I saw you step from the carriage. But I haven't been true to my own feelings, not once since we've met. And tonight I desperately need you."

With a small groan, he stretched his naked body the length of her blanketed form and relaxed his weight onto her.

Boldly, she returned to the task of tracing his lips with her fingertips, pressing into them now and again to test their sensuous fullness. She remembered how skillfully he had used them in his first attempt to seduce her.

"You asked me if I know what I am saying, and the answer is yes. But if you were to ask me if I know what I am doing, in all honesty, I would have to answer no. I haven't the faintest idea what I am about to get myself into. But I am perplexed enough to quit fighting this . . . this feeling I have for you is very much like a sickness. I know of only one way to be healed."

A deep shudder rippled through him. His breath quickened against her skin. He drew very still for a long while, absorbed in studying her.

Whatever he was thinking created an energy that emanated from him in throbbing concentric waves. He grew incredibly hot against her skin.

Long, tapered fingers laced themselves through hers. Slowly, he withdrew her hand from his lips. His mouth, lush, warm, and soft, found hers.

A moan escaped his lips. Thick lashes closed over eyes shimmering dark with an incandescent flame. His riveting kiss plunged deep into her being. She inhaled his scent, the animal heat of him, and her heart nearly burst.

His hand left hers, came to rest along her cheek, teasing the corner of her mouth while his lips still covered hers.

Such a slight movement was this, but what incredible delight it brought.

He made to pull the blankets back. She clutched at the covers, surprised by his intentions, suddenly frightened at the enormity of what she was about to do. "I . . . Trevor—"

He frowned. "You weren't married long, were you?"

She shook her head.

"How many times did your husband make love to you?" His voice was tender, but throaty.

She cast her eyes downward.

Gently, he nudged her chin up with his fist, holding her

closer in a gesture of security. "I think you know, don't you?" He blew a soft kiss in her ear.

"Four times, I think. Perhaps five."

"And did he ever kiss you the way I do?" Slowly, he pressed his full, sensuous lips against her muffled answer.

"No."

She gasped when his hand slipped under the covers and he caressed her leg before moving to the soft inside of her thigh. His fingers traced along her sensitive flesh and cupped between her thighs.

"And did he ever touch you the way I have . . . the way I will?"

"No," she moaned and tried to pull his hand away, but he persisted until his fingers came to rest on her dampness.

He paused, not invading her, but gently moving his fingers in small, hot circles, capturing the velvet of her until her legs vibrated with exquisite currents of pleasure.

She bit her lower lip to keep from crying out, shut her eyes tightly against her crumbling emotions. She wanted to pull away, to move closer, to reject him, to never let him go.

A cry from deep within her private world let loose. She buried her fingers in his hair and called out his name. Her hips moved against his hand, her body quivered in his hold, longing for some unknown, singular release.

"You were both virgins?" His hand came back up and around her hip, squeezing and caressing her with a gentle rhythm that matched the pulsating currents galvanizing her being. His quickened breath fell hot upon her mouth.

"Yes," she whispered.

"He never even saw his bride naked, did he?"

"No . . . no." Her hips flexed involuntarily.

Sliding his teeth over her bottom lip, he sucked its fullness into his mouth and gently slid his tongue back and forth, teasing her. Delicious sensations ran through her in places she'd never known existed. Soon, he was sure to drive her mad.

"Ah, so much better this way. Don't you see, *ma petite?* No pain, only pleasure such as you have never known." He buried his head into her neck again and murmured and kissed her, trailing his tongue around in circles, blowing gently against her skin.

He let the blanket fall back on her chest and stretched out against the bundled length of her, then pulled her close. "Relax, *ma petite,* like in the loft." He swept his mouth over her forehead and wrapped his other arm around her, massaging the back of her neck until her tension slackened. "I want to touch every part of you. I want to taste you. I want to make you understand how utterly beautiful you are to me."

She nearly wept at his words and didn't resist when he gently loosened the covers from around her and slid in beside her, enfolding her against him. When his hot nakedness rocked against her, when his hard arousal pressed against her stomach, all thought dissipated.

Another wave of passion gripped her. His hand slid down the arc of her back and over the swell of her hip before his mouth came down upon hers once more, drugging her with his aching tenderness.

She tasted his honey sweetness as his tongue traced her parted lips, then plunged between them. He pulled her tighter against him, his hand rocking her hips gently into his. Her nails slid the length of his back, and up again to tangle in his hair. She heard her own sighs and moans mingle with his husky murmurings.

His mouth trailed down her neck, to her breast, as his hand slid along her skin, coming up under the swollen mound, cupping its roundness into his mouth. His lips closed around the tip. He sucked quick and hard.

"Oh!" she gasped, as mindless sensations screamed through her. She was now all but powerless against his skill.

He kissed the corner of her mouth, then opened his own slightly, as if to inhale her essence. He breathed deeply, erratically now.

Lifting his head, he gazed into her eyes, taking in the torrid emotions churning up from the depths of her soul. Soft laughter rumbled through his chest. "Didn't I tell you that just beneath your surface lies a passion you cannot control?"

He kissed the tip of her nose, then closed his teeth over her chin, nipping playfully, surprising her with the explosive arousal his act provoked.

"I know what you are feeling, Celine, because I am caught up as well. There is lust and fire and a gnawing hunger so bad inside you, it has to be fed, or you will be driven mad." His tender lips and hot breath swept over her face, barely grazing her skin as his throaty voice formed the potent words that left her senses both reeling and strangely flourishing.

She didn't answer him, but drew a hand up to feel the beat of his heart, burrowed her fingers through a cluster of dark curls, kneaded the muscles on his chest.

A deep desire to know what he felt when he touched her urged her onward, and the nails of her thumb and forefinger closed over his hardened nipple, duplicating what he'd done to her with his teeth. She let go and ran her hand down his back, pulled his hips to hers. A shudder flickered through his flanks and stomach, twitching at his male arousal. His quick, ragged intake of breath betrayed him.

A surge of erotic dominance and confidence tore through her veins. At once she understood why he smiled or laughed after performing such maneuvers on her, for those reactions were the heady result of controlling power.

Her own aroused half-murmur, half-chuckle escaped through mischievous lips. She knew he fought to control himself, barely hanging on to the brink of reason. His heavy-lidded eyes glowed with a primitive blaze, pulled her into their hypnotic depths.

Heightened senses magnified details, scents, in a peculiar way she had never before experienced, almost as though events were unfolding in dizzying slow motion, yet with crystalline clarity.

Boldly, she inched her hand downward, across the ripples of his stomach, until she paused under the tip of his hard manhood. With the back of her fingers, she barely brushed against his arousal, taunting him.

He moaned and she caught the feral shift of his energy.

Had she just forced him off the edge? Had she just cast them both into the depths of some erotic, carnal abyss?

Instinctively, she knew he would reclaim his dominance over her, would lead her on this journey that was beyond her understanding.

His strength expanded, intensified. Muscles in his arms quivered, and his iron-hard body began its conquest. One swift, aggressive movement of his leg, and he engulfed her, poised above her on his knees and hands. She stared into diamond-black eyes flashing with passion.

His nostrils flared, and his whisper was little more than a rasp in his throat. "You are a quick study, *mon amour.*"

Between murmurs that were both commanding yet mild, he smothered her face, her ears, her throat, with kisses that sent her into insatiable need.

"Let yourself go now, *ma petite.* And we shall go wherever your passion leads us. I'll be so careful with you, my sweet, ever so careful."

Tenderly, he brought his mouth to hers, tasting her with his tongue. Kitten-soft noises erupted from her throat. She wrapped her arms around his neck, tried to pull him down onto her, as she eagerly returned his kisses. The urgent, involuntary thrust of her hips searched for his. Her flesh connected with his, ignited every cell in her body, as if she were gunpowder set alight.

She had moved into that place where no such thing as logic existed—totally vulnerable and completely free to be guided by the natural forces that would direct whatever destiny had brought them together.

Trevor bent his head back and opened his throat for more air. Unbearable pleasure washed over him. His heart ached once again with that frightening, mysterious desire, a need that transcended mere lust, a craving that filled his every pore.

The last thread of logic slipped away. He was not himself. Had he slid into some vague dream state?

Sweet Jesus, what was happening to him?

He traced a finger along the pulse at her throat, trailed his languid caress around and between her breasts, then down, stroking the naked skin of her stomach. He went slowly, his fingers feeding the flames deep within him.

He moved his hand ever farther until it came to rest over the soft mound of curls cloaking a part of her that had caused him so many sleepless nights. He bent until his lips captured her breast, sweet and delicious, and sucked the tip into his mouth. He slipped his fingers inside her and caressed her with the same, erotic deliberateness as when he'd tugged at her nipple.

Slowly, he began to move his mouth downward. "You feel so good, so sweet." Releasing his hold, he cradled her hips in his hands. He closed his teeth over the flesh just below her waist, swirled his tongue as his mouth swept from hip to hip.

And lower.

Her breath exploded from her lungs. "No!"

"Let me, *mon amour,*" he murmured.

And she did.

When she surrendered, he clasped her wrists, held them captive as he placed a tender kiss on that throbbing, sensitive place that begged for release.

She cried out in pained ecstasy as he tasted her velvet softness, pressed his tongue rhythmically into her warm recesses, over and over again.

Then he released her and brought his full weight over her, pressing her into the pallet, overwhelming her with his body.

He wrapped himself close around her and brought his mouth to hers once again. He tasted of the earth and the sea and of their seductive concert. She found this strangely enticing, for it allowed her to once again know what he had experienced of her in their lovemaking. His lithe body molded itself to hers—fervent heat enveloped her, dizzied her senses.

His breath came intense and quick as he planted kisses all over her face, her mouth, her eyes, all the while uttering deep, unintelligible groans.

Celine's own will leapt up to meet his as Trevor shifted his body and drew her leg around his hip until her parted thighs cradled him intimately.

"Open your eyes, Celine." His insistent command, the timbre of his voice, sent a renewed fever through her veins, stealing her breath away. "I want you to look at me when I enter you."

The silver shimmer of desire, of senses in full bloom, lay in his luminous dark gaze, beckoning her into the depths of his very soul. The sheer strength and power he emanated was all around her, overwhelming her will as though it were a tangible coercion.

The earth beneath her disintegrated.

He tightened his hold on the swell of her hip and slowly eased himself into her. Her tight, hot flesh closed around him. Exquisite ardor rushed through her. Unmerciful ecstasy slammed the core of her being.

She cried out in rapture with his tender entry. She exploded with the unspent passion held in reserve all her years. Thrusting her hips up to meet his, she slid her hands down either side of him, feeling his body move in unison with hers.

"Keep looking at me, sweetheart." His demand for full possession released a deep hunger in her far beyond any surface yearnings. "And tell me what you feel while I make love to you. Tell me, Celine. I crave to hear it."

Slowly, rhythmically, he moved inside her, sending thousands upon thousands of tiny sparks exploding within her. And she responded as he demanded, telling him how wonderful he felt inside her, moving with him. He murmured of her sweetness, of how exciting she was to him, all the while the tender, unspoken core of her confused heart cried out from somewhere deep within—*I love you. Please love me back.*

He paused for a moment, pulled the pillow from beneath her head, and tucked it under her hips. He thrust down again, this time harder. And again. And again.

She gasped, as each new level of arousal deepened with every thrust of his hips.

Suddenly, a quickening radiated from the center of her. She whimpered, her breath coming in shallow pants as her body gave itself over in final submission to whatever he wanted, totally subservient to the passions that had engulfed her.

She was drowning, going down for the last time.

"Please, Trevor, please!" she begged, not knowing why or for what she was begging. The quickening increased until a tingling radiated from deep within. She could only whimper his name as millions of sparks ignited flames that swirled from her loins and exploded throughout her body.

Trevor buried his head in her shoulder, whispering to her in his ecstasy. "Come for me, *ma petite,* give all of yourself to me now."

The stars from the heavens rained down around them, the earth opened up, and the universe became theirs for the taking. Two souls, blended into one for but a timeless moment.

Her body arched up, she pulled his hips hard into hers and she cried out as her climactic response quivered uncontrollably through her.

He groaned, ground his hips into her and stilled as his own flashpoint washed over him. A shudder, and then he collapsed onto his side, rolling her with him, holding her tight against him. She reveled in knowing that he, too, had exploded into a thousand fragmented pieces.

Firelight danced around them as they lay, still entwined. Trevor marveled at Celine's strength. Her small body nestled against his, while one arm, wrapped around Trevor's back, held him in a tight grip.

He tried to gently withdraw from her.

"No," was all she said, and pulled his hips even closer to hers.

He understood. If she felt anywhere near to what he was experiencing, she could not bear to release herself from their physical union.

Relaxed, he reached to her wrist and touched the gold bracelet, turned it slightly to catch a glint of firelight. "Ah, *ma petite,* I'm afraid if you refuse to release me, you will experience a very long, very sleepless night."

He reveled in the smooth contours of her face. Already his lust was stirring again. He'd imagined that once he'd sated himself with her, there would be a complete release from such burning desire. Instead, his heart beat with her very life spirit. He lay with her, somewhere between fantasy and reality, yearning to safeguard and pleasure and worship her with even greater dedication.

He'd never felt such comfort lying next to a woman. He wished the night would never end, that he could hold her in his arms forever.

She rubbed her cheek against his naked chest. "Is it wicked to want you again?"

Chapter Thirteen

Celine slowly awoke. A lazy sense of contentment held her suspended somewhere between nocturnal shadows and drowsy consciousness. The rich aroma of freshly brewed coffee filled her senses. Pushing up on one arm, she swept a veil of tangled locks from her eyes and looked around. She was alone.

He made coffee and then left?

No, she heard him out front just then, speaking to . . . to whom? She laughed under her breath. He was talking to his horse. Panther had not spooked in the storm and turned back to the barn, after all. Lord, what a night! Her cheeks heated. She ran the tip of a finger over her bottom lip at the memory of his kisses. His hands, his body, they'd been all over her—in her. The aftermath of their night sent a delicious shiver through her. He knew every inch of her better than she knew herself. Her heart raced in her chest and she took in gulps of air. What could he be thinking this morning?

Trevor opened the door and leaned a shoulder against the jamb. He regarded her in that sensuous way that was his alone. "Celine."

Waves of desire washed through her. Oh dear, she could easily invite him to her bed again—right this minute.

Embarrassed, she gathered the blankets around her and lifted her gaze.

Trevor chuckled. "How quaint, Celine. After what we've been through together?"

She had to grin. "Ridiculous of me, I suppose."

"I suppose." His smile disarmed her as he crossed the room and poured a cup of coffee. "Get dressed and let's get out of here before I ravish you one last time." He raised an eyebrow to punctuate the order.

Her eyes widened. She caught a sharp breath and pulled the bedding to her chin.

Trevor chuckled and blew across the cup to cool its contents. "At least you saw fit to store some coffee in this place—pathetically old as it is."

When she didn't respond, his voice softened. "Lighten your mood a bit, *ma petite.*" The more quietly he spoke, the more commanding he seemed. "Let me know when you want me to help with your buttons, or whatever else needs doing, because those blankets up to your chin are ridiculous."

"Oh, ridiculous, am I?" Her heart danced.

"A bit."

"Do you intend to watch me dress?" Another shiver went through her at the idea. This one going straight to her womb.

"You do know that's a challenge to every ounce of discipline I possess?" His voice turned husky. "However, we'd never make it back to the house today, and since the storm has passed, someone's sure to come looking for us if we remain much longer."

She rose, and with Trevor's back to her, dressed as much as she was able. When it came time to ask for his help with the buttons on the back of her gown, he came to her with the cup of coffee in his hand.

He offered it to her. She sipped and made a face. "You're right, it is old."

He pressed his forehead to hers. "Shall we beg a fresh cup off Zola?"

She pulled back. He was so close she couldn't help it—she touched her lips to his. "I don't know that I want to appear in public just yet."

"Turn around and let me see to your buttons," he groaned. "Or you know what will happen." He took the cup from her hand, but before he turned her around, he pressed her hand to the front of his breeches.

She gave a soft moan as her hunger announced itself again. She squeezed.

His breath hitched, and he took her by the shoulders and turned her about. "Enough. We need to be getting these buttons done up."

They made their way back to the big house on Panther with her sitting in front of Trevor. Melancholy crept in at the idea of never seeing him again once she left for San Francisco. Had the mere dawning of a new day slanted her perspective?

Should she confess that she had never known two people could make love in such erotic splendor? How would he react if she were to confess how utterly magical their night was, and that she would never forget it or the love she felt for him? No, the beautiful memories she'd made last night were hers alone.

A man like Trevor was used to this kind of encounter. To him, their affair was most likely no different from any of his other numerous trysts—perhaps worse, thanks to her naiveté. He probably never gave his liaisons an ounce of attention once they were over.

Her stomach gave a sickening lurch at the idea that what she considered an intense union might have been mere sport to him.

No matter how she twisted and turned her thoughts to arrive at one conclusion or another, one realization crystallized from the gray mists of her consciousness—she was on the brink of falling in love with him.

Trevor controlled a strong impulse to slide his hands over her breasts, willed his flesh away from impending hardness. He enjoyed the comfortable manner in which she'd relaxed against him, welcomed the silence.

But what was he supposed to do now? He needed time to himself, time to think things through. He fought the urge to bury his face in the sweet-smelling softness of her hair.

The morning hadn't given him enough time to collect his thoughts—they kept getting scattered by raw emotion. Earlier, he'd experienced a moment of regret, for her sake, coupled with a vague misgiving that he didn't want to leave Carlton Oaks if it meant never seeing her again. He'd even entertained a maverick thought of taking her with him to China. After all, she'd told him she wanted to sail around the world.

What the devil was wrong with him? He would be sailing for months on end, and she was headed to a life in San Francisco. They'd go their separate ways and that would be that.

Wouldn't it?

Oh, devil take it. The last thing someone like Celine needed was him in her life.

The plantation house came into view, and Celine stiffened. "Why do I feel like a child getting caught with her hand in the cookie jar? We're both adults and I'm a widow, for heaven's sake."

He pulled her tighter against him. "Remember what I told you about handling Madame Charmontès. This situation isn't any different now than when you left the hayloft. If she is still on the premises, then walk in with dignity, and let me handle everything."

"Thank you." She slid her hand to her stomach, covered his splayed fingers and squeezed.

The stable master hurried to the rear of the house when they approached. Trevor handed the reins to the man, helped Celine off the horse, and carried her onto the veranda. Somehow during the storm, she'd lost her shoes.

The house seemed unusually quiet, bereft of its usual sounds. Only the loud ticking of the great clock in the front hall gave any indication there was life inside. Trevor guided Celine to her quarters and opened the door.

Marie stood just inside, balancing a stack of folded linens on her forearms. At the sight of Trevor and Celine, she quickly deposited the laundry on the window seat, and sped through the French doors.

Trevor placed a hand at the small of Celine's back and nudged her into the bedroom, closing the door behind them. "Marie, get back here."

Marie stopped in her tracks, but didn't turn around.

"If I have to come after you, there's going to be hell to pay."

Celine openly winced at his sharp tone.

Marie returned, her face filled with dread. "I don't want any trouble, Monsieur Trevor. I only wish to do my job."

He walked over to the wingback chair by the fireplace and leaned his forearms against the wings for support. "Close the door, Marie, and tell me what's going on around this morgue."

Marie eyed Celine's tattered dress and bare feet, and then cast Trevor a scathing look.

He deliberately ignored her rudeness. "Celine's all right, Marie. You don't have to protect her. Where is everyone, and what's going on?"

Marie's spine stiffened. "Everybody's gone, that's where they is." She pursed her lips and crossed her arms over her chest. "Gone by the first boat downriver this mornin'."

"Everyone?" He cocked a quizzical eyebrow. "Including my father?"

He'd get Marie to talk, but he would have to go slow. He knew her well, knew how to get whatever information he wanted from her, and how much patience it would take.

Marie leaned on one hip and tapped her foot on the floor in irritation. "No, not Mister Andrews."

Trevor figured she couldn't keep her silence much longer, so he waited.

She shifted her weight and huffed. "He's holed up in his office. The guests were gone before the storm hit, but your relatives left this morning, including that Madame Charmontès who likes to think she's family."

"Cameron and my siblings?"

Marie nodded her head. "Gone. Mister Andrews told your uncle to see the family to N'awlins, until things blow over. Besides, there is a family shipping business down there, which you are supposed to be running, in case you haven't heard."

"Marie!" Celine cried.

Trevor raised a hand, signaling her to silence. "I told you, Celine is fine."

"Oh, we all know Celine is *just fine.*" Marie huffed, and her eyes narrowed.

Good, Trevor thought, the floodgates are opening. "Why did my father send the entire family away?"

Marie went to tapping her foot again. "As you well know, that Madame Charmontès claims to have the sight. Seems she got a vision of just how *fine* you were takin' care of Miss Celine, if'n you git my meanin'." She changed her stance and planted one hand firmly on each hip.

Celine's cheeks flushed.

"Christ." Right or wrong, Madame would have given every detail she thought she perceived to anyone who would listen—ten times over.

"Well, Mister Andrews was so worried about Miss Celine, he let that mad woman tell him what she saw. They were locked in the study for the longest time, and then they got into a shouting match, which is when I ceased being privy to anythin' more."

"Why is that?"

Marie looked sheepish. "Madame Charmontès did her shouting with her hand on the door's handle, so the parlor maid had to jump away in case the door opened, that's why. I don't know what happened after the argument started. I only know she left madder than a bull what got no breedin' time."

Celine covered her mouth with both hands.

"I told Celine that woman was born under a black moon," Marie said. "Caused nuthin' but trouble, giving Mister Andrews outlandish information. Even told him a wild story about you taking something of Miss Celine's to a brothel."

Good God!

Celine tilted her head at Trevor quizzically.

Marie shifted her stance in defiance. "Even if it was all true, I can't—"

"It's not Madame Charmontès's fault." Trevor brought his hand to his heart. "All the fault lies here."

The maid stood there, her mouth agape.

"Thank you, Marie, you may go." He'd spoken to Marie, but his focus was on Celine. "You might want to bring something for Celine. She hasn't eaten in a while."

Marie looked from one to the other, and then back again before she made a hasty retreat out the French doors. "I'll see to it Miss Celine is fed."

Trevor moved from where he leaned against the back of the chair. He lifted Celine's chin with a curled finger and regarded her for a long while. Whatever transpired next, he had to protect her. "It would be best if you remained in your quarters while I take care of matters. I'll come to you this evening." He nodded toward the closet and its secret passage.

"I understand," she said. "At any rate, I wouldn't care to see a soul anyway."

He turned to take his leave, then hesitated and returned to stand before her once again. He touched her cheek, brushed his thumb across the skin beneath her earlobe. For a long moment he stood there, remembering what they had shared.

She stared at him in silent trust.

What incredible eyes. He'd never seen anything remotely like them. His throat tightened, suppressing what he had to say. He wanted to hold her, to cradle her and shut the world away. He fought to put his feelings into words. He had to speak. He had to tell her.

"For what it's worth, *ma petite,* I want you to know that whatever price I may be forced to pay for my indiscretion, it will never destroy the memory of what we shared last night. And if it is at all within my power, I shall see to it that your honor remains intact, that you do not suffer because of my uncontrolled desire for you."

He was gone before she could speak, but not before tears filled her eyes and splashed over her cheeks. She paced the floor for what seemed like hours. But the mantel clock showed only twenty minutes had passed. *I'll come to you this evening*. She heard his words in her mind over and over, savoring them, tasting their sweetness. Their union had meant something to him, after all.

She thought she heard muffled sounds and stopped to listen. She couldn't be certain. Unable to stand the tension any longer, she flung open the door, determined to face Justin. What was wrong with him? A widow wasn't expected to live by the same standards as a girl who'd never married. And why try to control her life, for heaven's sake?

When angry voices boomed from Justin's office, she paused midway down the stairs. Her heart leapt into her throat as she tiptoed down the stairs and over to the office door.

Trevor and Justin hurled savage words at each other. Justin tore viscerally at his son, and Trevor fought back. "You made a mockery of the word *family,* the way you kept your children from their own mother."

"She was my wife!" Justin shouted. "I worked hard at building this plantation and the shipping company. I had a right to want my privacy without gawking children interfering. You had her to yourself when I was gone from here. Wasn't that enough?"

"At least I wasn't so wrapped up in myself that I couldn't tell she was sick enough to call in a physician."

"Don't start with that again, Trevor. I won't hear it."

"You don't want to face the truth that she might have been saved if not for your arrogance?"

"That's a lie."

"You had me shoved so far aside, you couldn't begin to hear my pleas when I begged you to call for help."

"I did call in a physician."

"How pathetic you sound. By the time she lost consciousness it was too late, and you know it. I will *never* forgive you for her death."

"Not forgiving me is no excuse for what you've turned into. You not only humiliated me, you mortified everyone around you. What kind of behavior caused every husband with a young wife to lock their doors? Or try to burn our house down? Even bordellos shut you out, for God's sake. And now you turn your whoring ways on someone I took in when she was near death? I won't have it!"

Bile rose in Celine's throat and her heart pounded so hard it stole her breath. She couldn't take any more and made her way back up the stairs and to her bedchamber. Marie was waiting for her with a bath and a tray of sandwiches and milk. In silence, Marie removed Celine's tattered dress, and then helped her into the tub.

It wasn't until her bath was complete and she was dressed and perched in the window seat that the muffled noises from below ceased. Through the window, she spied Trevor. The heels of his boots bit into the earth as long, purposeful strides carried him quickly toward the stable. She had a feeling he would ride out and not come to her that evening as he'd said. She knew he could not go to anyone. Not yet, anyway.

Nonetheless, when night came, she lay awake, waiting, listening for his return, her eyes fastened to the closet door. She ached to go to him, but knew she must wait for him to come to her. However, she'd made a decision—no matter what went on between Trevor and his father, she would speak to Justin in the morning on her own behalf.

She'd only managed to doze when Marie brought her a breakfast tray. "Where's Justin this morning, Marie?"

Marie yanked undergarments from the armoire and slapped them on the bed, a frown wrinkling her forehead. "In his office. At least that's where he said to send his breakfast, so I suspect he's still there." She removed a yellow chemise from the cupboard, and with a few quick snaps of her wrists, shook out the folds, all the while muttering under her breath.

"Good heavens, what's wrong with you?"

The maid took a deep breath, pain etched on her face. "Oh, Miss Celine. I am so sorry. Mister Andrews banned Trevor from the plantation. He's gone."

Celine's heart tripped a beat and then it froze. "When?"

"Yesterday."

"Damnation!"

Celine's skirts swirled around her ankles as she flew down the stairs and into Justin's office, slamming the door behind her. "How dare you meddle in my life!"

Deep lines furrowed his brow and his skin had a pale cast to it. His eyes were flat. Dull.

"Dear God." She sank into the big leather chair in front of the desk he sat behind. A tear slid down her cheek. "What have you done, Justin?" She buried her face in her hands. "What have I done?"

He leaned his head against the back of his chair and stared out the window. "I've always been a man who thought long and hard about making decisions, and once made, I never looked back. But this time I'm not so sure."

He turned and faced her. Celine almost wished he had not, for the raw pain etched on his face was terrible to see. She opened her mouth to speak, but he shook his head, stopping her.

"I tried to play God. I purposely asked Trevor to come home because I wanted him to discover you. And he did. But I banished him because I thought he used you and intended to leave without looking back."

Celine tried to swallow the lump in her throat but failed. She brought her hand to her throat. "You wanted him with me?"

He nodded. "I thought you would suit one another. I saw qualities in you that I thought he would admire. And I had an idea you would take to him—differently than the other women he has a reputation for collecting."

He heaved a sigh. "In essence, I thought you two might find love together. But I fell apart at the thought of Trevor taking advantage of you. I suppose I am unlikely ever to see him again."

Hot tears scalded Celine's cheeks. She stood, moved behind Justin's chair, and slid her arms around his slumped shoulders. "What happened was not his fault. I am as guilty, if not more so, as your son for what transpired. He was an honorable man the night before last. I need you to know that. I was the one who—"

She clasped her hands over the center of his chest and squeezed tightly. She cried hard, no longer able to separate sobs from words. "It was . . . as though a force . . . pulled me to him. I . . . I could not stay away." She inhaled a ragged breath.

Tears dripped from her chin, staining his shirt, but he did not seem to notice. She rocked him gently back and forth, weeping without restraint. His age-spotted hand moved to cover hers locked over his heart.

"I did not say no to him because of my own selfish feelings, not his, Justin. Do you hear me? Because I wanted him. I was the one who took from him." She squeezed him hard.

He buried his head in his other hand and grew silent. They both stared silently out the window for a long while as if hoping some winged messenger might ride in on a golden shaft of sunlight and restore what had already been destroyed.

"Let's go after him, the two of us," Celine whispered into Justin's ear.

He remained silent.

"Think about it, Justin. Your son cannot possibly be anywhere else right now, but in New Orleans, waiting for the new ships to arrive. We can go after him. Both of us owe him an apology," she finished softly.

"He would never return to Carlton Oaks. He is too proud."

"Not now, perhaps." Celine waited for Justin's full attention. "I know he's proud, but you'll have time to make amends before the ships arrive. Then, while he's sailing the seas, he'll have plenty of time to mellow. By his next homecoming, he can easily return with his dignity intact. Justin, this is your eldest son, your flesh and blood. Please, let's do what we can, before it's too late."

Her voice softened with his continued silence. "I know

you have your pride too. And so do I. But I'll be leaving soon, and my pride doesn't matter nearly as much as thinking I left a broken family behind." Celine squeezed his shoulders again and waited.

Justin stood and walked to the window, peering out toward the levee. "If you care for Trevor as you claim, then how could you entertain thoughts of sending him off to sea while you disappear to the other side of the country? It would seem to me, if you truly care for him, your natural inclination would lean toward remaining here."

He turned then, an intense question burning in his eyes. "Wouldn't you think so?"

Celine paced as she sorted out the tangle of thoughts in her brain. "I . . . I . . . that is . . . you know it takes two caring people to make love last. Just because I care for Trevor does not mean he—"

"Enough." Justin fanned his hand through the air, as if swatting flies. "It's as if a powerful current connects the two of you whenever you are in the same room. And I'm not alone in noticing the fireworks."

Celine opened her mouth to speak, but was hushed again.

"No one wanted a union between the two of you more than I, because I love you both. But something has held each of you back, Celine. I could figure Trevor out, somewhat. But, for the life of me, I have not been able to decipher you." He paused. "I can be an old fool at times, but I cannot be fooled very often. Something doesn't ring quite true here."

She spoke barely above a whisper. "You know I am a barren woman because of the accident. I would never do as a wife for Trevor."

"Did Trevor tell you he wouldn't have you because of that?"

"We did not speak of such matters in depth."

"But he did not say no, did he?"

Celine raised her chin. "How could you possibly think our relationship had gotten to that stage?"

"Then perhaps it should have. Trevor is a sailor at heart. He doesn't require a family in the traditional sense, but rather he needs the singular love of a fine woman. He needs someone who is devoted and loyal to him, yet strong enough, independent enough not to be buried under his great strength."

The lines in Justin's face softened. "Trevor needs someone as adventuresome as he is. God knows, if you're willing enough to traipse off to San Francisco all alone, then you certainly have that spirit in you."

Justin's eyes took on a glint. "Besides, didn't you once say you wanted to sail the world?"

When she failed to respond, he said, "It seems I have been an old fool, Celine. I'm leaving on the morrow. It would behoove you to have Marie see to your packing if you've a mind to come along." Before she could reply, he exited the room, leaving his words lingering in the air.

Chapter Fourteen

Celine could barely sit still in the boudoir chair. Even her teeth hurt she was so agitated. She pressed tiny circles against the hinges of her jaw. Soon, Justin would arrive to escort her to the opera house where Lola Montez, the famous actress and "Spanish dancer," would perform. Tickets had been hard to come by. In the three weeks since Celine and Justin had arrived in New Orleans, every attempt on his part to confer with Trevor had been met with contempt. So when Trevor sent a note inquiring about an extra ticket for the opera, Justin invited him to join the family. At the same time, Justin requested a meeting. Waiting for the outcome was excruciating.

Marie set her hands on Celine's shoulders. "You keep wigglin' like that, Missy Celine, and I won't never get your hair done."

Celine stilled. "Sorry. Things haven't turned out as I had hoped. This meeting might be the only opportunity Justin will have to bring the family together before I depart New Orleans."

"Well, worrying ain't gonna do nuthin' but give you wrinkles. I'm near done, and then you can relax in here all by yourself, or you can sip a nice calmin' toddy in the parlor."

Celine offered Marie a faint smile through the mirror. "I'm afraid one of your toddies might do me in. Besides, I can hear the carriage from here."

Justin had insisted she become the sole resident of his townhouse until her departure for San Francisco. At first, she had been reluctant to accept, but Lindsey and Felicité loved the novelty of hotel life, and Celine sorely needed her privacy. At Celine's request, Marie was the only servant in residence.

The compact townhouse was nothing like the sprawling plantation. The smaller rooms with their rich, dark woods and heavy velvet drapes were more intimate. The ornate filigreed balconies, the modest courtyard filled with a sea of roses, the protective wrought iron gate at the porte cochere—all of it wrapped Celine in a warm cocoon. Here was a safe haven in which she could retreat during the day and face the onslaught of her turbulent emotions during her empty, fitful nights.

Even though she'd been sorely disillusioned, Celine had been determined to stick with Justin's plan. Trevor had taken up residence in the elegant St. Charles Hotel and proceeded to carouse with a different woman on his arm every evening. There were times Celine seethed with jealousy, while at other times she managed to maintain a cool, dignified demeanor. Still, her patience had worn thin and until tonight, hope had all but faded.

The bracelet locked on her wrist caught the firelight and winked at her. She twisted it about. Was the golden band a curse? She could have it cut off. But in her heart she knew she never would. The bracelet was a constant reminder that whatever the future might hold, she had shared an exquisite moment in time when she'd loved someone and he had loved her back.

Marie patted one of Celine's curls. "There now, all done. You gonna be the loveliest lady at the opera tonight."

"Thank you. You're free to go." Celine stood and smoothed the front of her turquoise gown, the one she'd worn to the

Verrette soirée. A hundred years could have passed since that night. How long ago it all seemed. She issued a soft sigh and adjusted one of the diamond-and-pearl earrings Cameron had given her. She glanced at the mantel clock. The hour was growing late, and still no sign of Justin.

Marie turned to leave, and then paused with her hand on the door handle. "I know things ain't been so good since you arrived, but I do believe Mischie Trevor will come around. There's still nearly a week left afore you leave us."

Celine nodded. Six days was not very much time. Not at all.

A click of the door and she was alone. A warm breeze wafting through the open French doors carried the sweet scent of roses from the courtyard below. The moon, full and white, shone as a misty haze through billowing sheer curtains. She stepped past the curtains and onto the balcony. Here was the same moon under which she and Trevor once walked peacefully in the garden, yet now he passed her by without speaking. Each time, another little piece of her heart broke off. She swallowed tears. It wouldn't do to weep with Justin arriving any moment.

How would tonight unfold? Society in New Orleans seemed to have a singular goal—to collect en masse at one function after another. Trevor and Celine often ended up at the same crowded function. Even though he kept his distance, she could feel his presence, as if he drew her to him with some profound, heady power. On occasion, she'd caught him staring at her from across a room. He never bothered turning away. Instead, his gaze intensified until it penetrated her with an energy all its own.

His actions were not to be confused as an invitation, however. The few times she tried to approach him, he left the premises. After that, whenever he spent his time observing her, she let him. In some queer way, it maintained an abstract bond.

Whenever she was with Justin, Trevor acted mannerly,

but kept his distance. When Cameron escorted her, however, Trevor displayed an acerbic, bitter edge. At times it was difficult to determine to whom he directed his sarcasm.

Soon, the cousins barely spoke to one another. Even though Cameron insisted there was something else going on between them, the continued deterioration in their once easy relationship left Celine mired in guilt.

And then there was the bothersome situation with Cameron. Even though he'd acquiesced to an amicable relationship, she suspected he cared for her more than he wanted to admit, which made her uncomfortable. Increasingly so. And he'd changed. No longer was he the humorous, fun-loving man she once knew; he'd become surly and overly protective.

The door to the porte cochere swung open with a creaking of heavy wood. A jangle of metal, an echo of hoofbeats, and the carriage rolled in. Celine hurried down to the parlor. Justin entered the room, and his relaxed smile sent Celine flying into his arms.

"Whoa! Don't knock me over, young lady." He gave her a squeeze, and then gently eased her away. He pulled a handkerchief from his waistcoat and handed it to her. "If those tears spill over, you'll have to wash your face, and we'll be late for the curtain's rising. We must hurry if we are to make it at all."

"Things went well?"

He helped her into the carriage and slid in beside her. "Quite well, as a matter of fact." The buggy pulled onto Royal Street and moved toward the opera house. Justin looked tired and his eyes were red-rimmed. "He'll be joining us."

A sharp current ran through Celine and gripped her rapidly beating heart. She sat back and exhaled with a whoosh. "Oh, thank the Lord."

"He'll come along with Cameron."

"Oh!" Celine exhaled again. "Things must have gone very well, indeed." Justin offered nothing further and Celine dared not ask. In reality, this was a family matter, not hers. All she wanted was to help heal the family so she could leave in peace. They rode the rest of the way in silence.

Celine's mood was light when they entered Justin's box seats. His younger children were already seated in the second row behind her, Miles and Elizabeth in the third. She and Justin occupied two of the four front row seats, leaving the two beside Celine empty. She hoped it would be Trevor who took the seat closest to her.

Justin excused himself to speak to Elizabeth and Miles. Michel and Lindsey turned to listen. Felicité, seated directly behind Celine, leaned over, and whispered in her ear. "Trevor's coming tonight."

Celine nodded, patted Felicité's hand in response, and then nudged it away, hoping to send Felicité back into her seat. She was grateful the conversation around her muffled the noisy girl.

Instead, Felicité only leaned closer. "Here's hoping you give Trevor another opportunity to repeat his offenses."

What? Celine turned around and whispered, "What in the world are you talking about?"

Felicité grinned broadly. "So he can make you a mother, and I won't lose you forever."

Celine gasped. "Hush with your scandalous nonsense. And do sit back in your seat."

Felicité did as she was told, but in seconds she leaned forward again. "I've been a good girl and said my prayers." She giggled.

Speechless, Celine turned to face the curtain.

Justin slipped into his seat beside her. "Enjoying yourself?"

If only he knew how her mind flew in a hundred directions and she could barely breathe for how wound up she was. "Immensely, but I must admit I'm a bit nervous."

"As am I," he responded.

Celine glanced at the two empty seats next to her and wondered what was keeping Trevor and Cameron. The curtain would rise at any moment.

Trevor slipped silently into the seat beside her with Cameron taking the end seat. Thought scattered like fall leaves in a brisk wind. Trevor offered her a tentative grin, the first docile smile she had seen from him since their night together. Her heart was about to jump right through her ribs. Nonetheless, she turned to study him. "How much more handsome you are when you smile like that."

Trevor visibly relaxed. He leaned one elbow on the arm of his chair, rested his fist against his chin, and simply looked at her, just as he had from across the room for so many evenings of late.

What in the world had gone on between him and his father? She didn't flinch. Instead, she lifted a fan to hide the smile playing about her mouth. Then she dared to boldly stare back at him. It was a start, but in the end, he'd have some explaining to do. She didn't care that she was leaving soon; he owed her.

He leaned over and whispered in her ear, "You are wearing my favorite dress this evening, *ma petite.*"

He could have bedded her right there if he chose to.

Mercy, but she was shameless in her thoughts! Just his breath at her ear made her go soft in the head.

Bells chimed to indicate the show was about to begin. She turned to the stage, fanning the heat from her face. "And what makes it your favorite?"

"The color reminds me of the deep turquoise shining in your eyes." He hesitated at her ear slightly longer than was proper.

Felicité nudged Celine's chair with her toe. The little scamp was privy to everything.

Celine dizzied, grew embarrassed by her quick reaction to the feathery touch of his lips at her ear. Trevor discreetly slid his free hand down the side of his leg until it came to rest beside hers. His little finger curled around hers.

Dear God! Oh, how she ached to crawl into his arms. How very much she had missed him, and how very much she yearned to tell him so. As far as she was concerned, whatever had transpired between Trevor and his father had produced no less than a miracle.

The devil take Miss Lola Montez's performance. She would gladly let him sweep her in his arms and carry her out of the theater and back to the safety of her cabin, where they could spend the rest of their lives together. Her desire for him had not diminished one bit.

Such fantasy.

Her ruminations came to an abrupt halt when the orchestra began playing exotic music such as she had never heard. Lola Montez was behind the curtain, and the excitement rippling through the theater grew thick in the air.

The curtain lifted to expose a riveting, charismatic woman dressed in a sheer red harem costume swathed with strings of gold coins that jangled when she moved. Her cloud of black hair and lithe hips swayed to the music. She was enigmatic, erotic.

And she knew it.

At first, she played purposefully and viscerally to the audience as if she performed for each person alone. But once her hypnotic gaze fell on Trevor, it moved no further. The energy in the theater shifted dramatically as Lola's performance suddenly turned as intimate as if the two were alone.

Celine bristled. Perhaps Lola picked a man from the audience at every performance in order to create such shocking intimacy. The action was certainly producing a memorable, even scandalous, evening. No wonder the woman's reputation preceded her arrival. No wonder the seats were sold out.

With her fan over her mouth, Celine leaned toward Trevor. "Have you met this woman before?"

"No," he murmured.

Sitting next to Trevor while another woman openly seduced him grew increasingly uncomfortable. Celine tried to tell herself that Lola's private performance was only Celine's imagination, but damn it, Felicité kept poking the back of Celine's chair every time Lola completed a twirl and caught Trevor's eye again.

Other patrons in the upper balconies raised their opera glasses and searched the audience for whoever it was that had captivated Lola, while those below occasionally tore their mesmerized gazes from the stage and craned their necks.

Trevor was well aware also. His elbow rested on the chair's arm between them while his chin in the palm of his hand hid the bottom half of his face. "*Mon Dieu,*" was all he said.

What was that supposed to mean? If he was uncomfortable, he didn't show it, he sat so quietly, while she fought the urge to squirm. Finally, she came to the conclusion that had she been in his place, and a male performer on stage drew that kind of attention her way, she certainly would keep her eyes focused on the stage to avoid all gawkers. And she would show no emotion in order to give the gossipmongers as little as possible to chatter about. But her musings didn't stop her from feeling like a voyeur.

Oh, wasn't the audience lapping this up? Well, this was New Orleans; what did she expect? Society here loved such scintillating entertainment. Lola's singular performance was bound to provide ripe conversation for weeks. Celine decided she didn't wish to attend the after-party in the entertainer's honor. No matter how exclusive the invitation, hers could go in the trash.

But Celine couldn't find a graceful way out. Cameron and Trevor joined her and Justin in the carriage that transported them to the Garden District home of one of New Orleans's wealthiest patrons of the arts. If she begged off now, she might destroy what Justin had worked so hard to achieve. She couldn't take such a risk—the climate in the carriage was still prickly.

They were an hour into the festivities when Lola made her grand entrance dressed in a form-fitting red silk gown that defied fashion—and gravity.

She circled the room as though she glided on air, stopping at every man, whispering something private in each ear that brought a blush to the hearer's cheek. Sliding a gloved hand up and down a sleeve, she would tilt her head in provocatively. All the while, she virtually ignored the women.

Had Lola intended saving Trevor for last? She stopped in front of him, tossed her thick black mane behind her with a lift of her chin, and, breathing in slow and deep, she ran both hands up Trevor's arms until she circled his neck. When she blatantly brought her lips to Trevor's ear and whispered something Celine could not understand, anger stung like a bee.

Damn Trevor's nonchalance. He only smiled politely, but he did not retreat. Was he being polite to avoid a scene? Or was he actually interested? Emotions Celine couldn't identify swept through her like a maelstrom. Well, she wasn't about to stand there looking the fool. Where was Cameron? Or Justin, who'd disappeared into the crowd some time ago. It didn't matter, she would find her way back to the townhouse, even if it took a feigned headache to do so.

She gathered her wits about her, turned to Trevor, and spoke politely. "If you'll excuse me, I'll be leaving now."

Trevor's brow furrowed. "Why?"

Lola carved out a cold smile for Celine and then turned back to Trevor. She touched his arm and gazed into his eyes in a provocative manner that would have put Giselle Beaudrée to shame.

"I am delighted you have come to Lola, this evening, señor. I do hope you consider the night to be young, and you will remain to greet the sunrise with me."

What kind of invitation was *that?*

Trevor's smile was slight. "We shall see."

"Your arrogance is astounding," Celine said through her teeth. A sudden weariness flooded her to the point that she felt boneless. She'd had enough of Trevor's women. There was no getting around it—he was the kind of man women flocked to. After all, even she had succumbed to his charisma.

Trevor placed a hand at the small of her back and leaned to her ear. "Don't be a child. The lady means nothing by her antics. I merely humor her."

"You call me a child, and her a lady? You call *her* a lady?"

Lola smiled and ran an insolent gaze up and down Celine that Trevor didn't catch with his head turned. The fool. Celine bit back a rude retort and stepped away.

Cameron appeared at Celine's side and took her arm, his face flushed with fury. "Would you care for a bit of fresh air?"

"Actually, I am rather tired of this . . . this meaningless evening. I . . . I need to find my wrap." She clasped her hand in the crook of Cameron's arm, and left Trevor standing alone.

Brushing Cameron's arm from her waist, she went in search of her cloak. She cursed herself, refused a servant's aid, and fumbled haphazardly through the sea of wraps in a room off the entry. *You are leaving in six days anyway, you stupid ninny. Keep your distance until then.*

Trevor's words sounded behind her. "Don't go."

"Oh, for heaven's sake, leave me alone, Trevor." Her voice rose, and a sob caught in her throat, but she turned to face him nonetheless. "Just leave me alone."

He took her arm. "Please—"

She shrugged it off. "We really shouldn't be near one another," she said, her voice now under control. "For some reason our personalities are like oil and water. The day I sail from here will be a propitious event in my eyes."

"These things take time, Celine—"

She laughed, but it came out bitter. "Time? Time? We have no time, Trevor." She made to brush past him, but he grabbed her arm again.

She struck out at him, her hurt and anger unleashed like talons. "Leave me alone!"

He pulled her to him, crushing her against his chest.

She struggled to get out of his hold.

"Stop it, Celine." He shook her. "You little fool. Can't you see it is you that I—"

Cameron appeared from nowhere. "Leave her be, you selfish bastard." He shoved Trevor against the wall and buried a fist in his midsection.

Trevor grunted, doubled over, and gripped his stomach. He dropped his hands, heaved in a breath, and straightened. His voice rasped low and dangerous as he stepped forward. "You shouldn't have done that, Cousin." Trevor pushed, and Cameron stumbled backward into a curio cabinet. It toppled under his weight, sending glass shelves and the contents shattering to the marble floor with a resounding crash.

Women shrieked.

A crowd gathered at the doorway. Several onlookers rushed to separate the men, pulled them from the room and back into the main hallway.

Justin shoved through the crowd, his face a portrait of utter despair.

Lola instructed the musicians to play. She began a seductive dance, turning heads. But not before Cameron picked up a leather glove and slapped Trevor's face with it.

A wave of exclamations washed through the crowd.

Trevor stared at his cousin for what seemed an eternity. Then a cold fire rose in his eyes. He picked up the glove and handed it back to Cameron. "In two mornings' time." He turned on his heel and walked away.

Oh, God no, not a duel!

Justin took her arm. “I’m taking you home, Celine.”

Frantic, and her mind numb, Celine couldn’t make sense of his words.

“Now,” he said. “Before things get any worse.”

“I don’t think that’s possible.” She shoved a loose curl behind her ear and froze with her hand on her right ear. “My earring. I’ve lost an earring.” She pulled away from him and raced back to where the conflict had taken place. She searched desperately, as if finding the bauble would somehow reprieve Cameron’s soul. Her instincts told her Trevor would be the better shot of the two.

Exhausted, she finally gave up, and allowed Justin to take her to the carriage. “How inane of me to be looking for an earring when a man’s life is at stake.”

Instantly, she was sorry for her remark when she saw how pale Justin had become. “Oh, Justin, you should have let me die under that wagon. Dear God, what a mess I’ve created in your life.”

He leaned over and squeezed her hand. “Don’t blame yourself. We all have free will. It seems Trevor has his way of dealing with things, but Cameron?” He shook his head and his voice trailed off. “What fool thing has he done?”

“I am so sorry.” Celine’s tears stained her cheeks and blurred the tapestry of the moon and stars above. They rode in silence, each contemplating the horrific enormity of the evening’s events.

When Justin saw her into the townhouse, he finally spoke. “It will do no good to hold anyone in contempt. They each need our prayers now more than ever.”

A carriage pulled up to the grand Garden District home where Lola Montez had held court all night. “The St. Charles,” Trevor directed the driver. The fiery entertainer beside him smoothed one eyebrow with the tips of her fingers, then trailed them slowly through the wisps of dark curls at her temple.

He helped Lola into the carriage and slid in beside her. She placed her hand on top of his thigh. The heat of it burned through the fabric of his trouser leg.

Casually, she tilted her head and regarded him through luxurious lashes. Her dusky smile came soft and easy. "I believe this will prove to be a very interesting evening." She gave a throaty laugh. "I correct myself on the word *evening* since the sun, it is about to rise, yes?"

Trevor studied her. Although he didn't consider her to be beautiful, he found her exotic. Her self-assured detachment held a certain mystery, and her uninhibited freedom offered a promise to explore whatever sensual pleasures he chose. Most of all, her nomadic lifestyle was appropriate for the direction the evening had taken.

"Your room or mine?" she asked in a husky whisper.

"I would prefer yours, madame."

A barely perceptible shift took place in her countenance. Her smile grew vague. "Of course."

She had to know what he meant by preferring her room over his. She had lived too long traveling from hotel to hotel, and from man to man, not to have learned it was the simplest way for a man to escape when they were finished with each other.

By the time they reached the hotel where both had rooms, Trevor's anger had gone through a metamorphosis. It had crawled back inside him, back into that cold cave he knew so well.

He stood at the window in Lola's hotel room, watching the first remnants of morning paint the night sky a pale pink. He could not bring himself to crawl into her bed.

"Señor Andrews. Who was the woman you intended to hold in your mind when you made love to me?" Her voice was soft, but knowing.

Trevor's cynical retort was flat, lifeless. "Make love? Is that what you'd call it?" He continued to stare out at nothing in particular.

Lola ignored the remark. "Someone will lose his life in this pitiful charade you are enacting. But you, señor, you seem already to have died."

Trevor turned around and reached for his jacket. "I have to go."

She patted the edge of the sofa. "Not yet. Sit for a moment with Lola. Please, sit." He did not move from the window.

"The woman with the green eyes, she is the one you love, no?"

Her words stung. "Love? What the hell is love, anyway?"

"I will tell you what love is," she said. "It is when a man makes love to a woman and gives her his soul. But then something happens to separate them. He tries to return to his old ways, but he cannot bear the intimate touch of another woman, so he keeps his secret by parading a different woman on his arm in public each night, while taking none to his bed."

His jaw twitched. "You're mad."

"Perhaps a little," she said, smiling. "You are in love, but that is not your problem. It could be the solution, though." Her voice grew compassionate. "She loves you as well, Señor Trevor."

"Celine? You couldn't be more wrong. She detests me."

"Aha, then there is hope!" Lola stood and helped herself to one of Trevor's cheroots from his jacket. She lit it and paced in front of him. She spoke quickly, punctuating the air with the cigarillo. "Do you know that hate is not the opposite of love?"

He needed to leave. Why the hell was he giving her another minute of his time?

"Apathy is the opposite of love. If this woman with the

green eyes were indifferent toward you, then all hope would be lost."

She inhaled the cheroot, lifted her chin, and blew a cloud of smoke in the air. "You should know something else, *mi amigo*—there are only two emotions when we care about someone—love or fear. Hatred and jealousy are merely the fearful sides of love. Your woman, she was very jealous of Lola tonight." She ceased her soliloquy and waited for Trevor's response.

Damn it, he didn't want to make sense of her words. He reached for his jacket. "You're a fine actress, Lola. But you really should save it for the stage."

She acted as though she hadn't heard him. "Someone has hurt you very deeply, yes?"

When he failed to respond, her voice grew soft. "You are much too young to have grown so bitter. If you do not heal these wounds that lie so deep in your heart, then very soon, señor, you will find yourself living a very difficult and lonely life."

She tilted her head back, as if it gave her a deeper perspective into Trevor's soul. "That is, unless you plan to step in front of your cousin's bullet."

His blood chilled. "I don't know what the hell you're talking about. I have to go." He turned to leave, but she stepped around him and stared straight into his eyes.

A strange otherworldliness shone in her expression. "Your mother, she is not among us?"

"My mother is none of your concern."

"She left you at a young age?" Her eyes narrowed. "You were a sensitive child, and her death broke your heart, yes?"

Trevor remained silent, not sure why his feet remained planted where they were. His heart pounded so loud he could hear it.

"And then there were others, were there not? Women who were like vultures, pecking away at an already dying heart."

"What are you, some kind of goddamned witch? Leave me alone." He stepped forward to make his exit, but she placed a hand against his chest.

"Will you permit me to ask you one last question before you go?"

"What?" His solitary word froze the air around them.

"When you take your last breath, whose hand will hold yours? And what will you see when you gaze into your loved one's eyes? Or will you die alone, and lonely?"

"I need to go."

"Go to her. She will forgive you. This life you are leading now, it will be a lonely one, that I know. Take her for your wife before it is too late."

With a jerk of his shoulder, he shrugged her hand off his chest, threw his jacket over his shoulder, and strode hard for the door.

"Señor."

He turned and looked at her one last time before he walked out.

"Excuse me, madame. I believe I have a certain pair of pistols to purchase."

Chapter Fifteen

The ticking of the French mantel clock grew louder by the hour, and now it seemed to be marking cadence with the beat of Celine's heart. She glanced across the room at the ornate timepiece. Only a few minutes after midnight. Barely fifteen minutes had passed since she'd last checked.

Heaven help her.

She struggled for a breath. Thank goodness she'd had the sense to remove her corset or she wouldn't have been able to breathe at all. She rose from the divan and wandered to the window, where she gazed at the yellow saucer of a moon. She would never make it through this night.

Yesterday had come and gone with no trace of Trevor or Cameron. It was as though they were making themselves scarce lest anyone keep them from their self-destruction. She and Justin had desperately searched everywhere, checked each of the men's hotel rooms throughout the day, to no avail. If only they could find one of them, perhaps they could stop the morning's carnage.

She hoped at least Cameron had come to his senses and retreated, perhaps intending to remain reclusive until their ship set sail. But her hopes were dashed when she was told that a pristine set of dueling pistols, nestled neatly in a velvet-lined mahogany box, had been delivered to a local surgeon.

Justin had offered to spend the night at the townhouse, but she'd declined. Before nightfall she had secretly left the Vieux Carré for a solitary ride to Dueling Oaks.

Dueling Oaks.

What a cruel name, and crueler purpose, for so beautiful a place in nature. How peaceful it seemed by day's ebbing light, as though nothing had ever transpired there to disrupt the serenity. Yet the very ground on which she'd stood had played host to so many fatal meetings, no count of the dead was kept.

She shuddered when she walked the grassy opening between the trees where the duel was to occur. Had the grass grown greener where it drank the blood of the fallen? Or were those the places where no grass grew at all? And the morrow would bring yet another victim who refused to see the absurdity of bloodshed, refused to peer inside himself to resolve the real quarrel.

Dueling had become so commonplace of late it seemed to be more a disease of epidemic proportions than a battle for honor. Wives, who kissed their husbands good-bye in the morning, heard from passersby that they would not make the dinner hour. Mothers, watching sons depart in the youthful promise of a new day, often saw a lone figure making his way home at dusk.

Celine had heard of duels occurring over the slightest insult, and wondered how a grown man could have so little regard for his own life or that of another. What havoc false pride created. She'd never dreamed such a scourge would touch her life.

She rubbed the gooseflesh on her arms and checked the clock. Barely twenty minutes had gone by. Oh, she could not bear another moment of this torture. Grabbing a light wool cloak, she set out on foot from the house. She had to try one more time to stop this madness.

She traveled up Royal Street and over to the St. Charles Hotel. She approached the clerk at the front desk. "Have Mr. Trevor Andrews or Mr. Cameron Andrews been to their rooms this evening?"

"*Non,* mademoiselle. I have not seen either gentleman."

The clerk turned his attention elsewhere, but kept a keen eye on Celine. With the socially prominent cousins being so close, the gossip over the duel raged through the city like a yellow fever plague. By the way the clerk regarded her, he couldn't wait to pass on another morsel of scandal.

She didn't care.

After she paced the lobby for a few moments, the clerk grew bored and returned to his duties. The moment he turned his back, she hurried down the corridor to Trevor's room. Her hollow knock echoed in the late hour. She started to knock again but hesitated and tried the knob instead. With a click, the door released.

Her heart beat wildly as she inched it open. "Trevor?" She stepped inside the darkened room, closing the door behind her, and leaned against the hard panel until her eyes adjusted to the darkness. A lone shaft of moonlight cast a shadowed path across the floor.

It was Trevor's essence she became aware of first, and then, as her eyes adjusted to the darkness, she made out a form stretched across the bed. Cautiously, she moved over to where he lay flat on his back, clad only in trousers. His crossed hands pillowed his head, and he stared up at the ceiling. His coldness registered through her flesh, as though death had already claimed his heart. The lash of a razor would not have cut her so deep.

"Trevor, I . . . I came to . . . to beg you to please call this whole thing off."

He ignored her.

"Please, Trevor, listen to me." She sat at the edge of the bed and awkwardly reached over to caress his cheek. It, too, was cold and hard. She snatched her trembling fingers away and clasped them in her lap. "Cameron loves you like a brother. You can't be a party to this . . . this debacle. Brothers support one another, work out their disagreements. They remain loyal to one another. They don't kill each other over . . . over trivial matters."

Trevor lay silent, motionless.

"Your actions may very well mean the death of your own father. I don't know how much more he can take."

Slowly, Trevor turned his head and stared at her through piercing shards of ice. "Have you made this same speech to Cameron?"

She trembled at his coldness.

He went back to staring at the ceiling. "I didn't think so. Your only interest in coming here is to save Cameron's hide."

A boulder on her chest would not have crushed her more. "That's not true. I came to you because . . . because I honestly felt you to be more mature than Cameron. I thought that you would be more willing to swallow your senseless pride."

Again, she elicited no response. She had to force her most difficult words. "I also think you may have a killer's instinct, where Cameron does not."

Trevor's bark of laughter filled the air. "You couldn't be more wrong."

He rose on one elbow, then reached over and gripped the back of her neck and pulled her toward him with a slow, steady force until she could feel his hot breath against her lips. He held her there for a long while, glaring at her, his eyes flashing. His scent captured her senses once again. A compelling urge to close her eyes and press her lips to his shot through her, startling her and bringing her thoughts back into focus.

His hard, emotionless voice cut through the air with finality. "I would take no pleasure in killing my cousin, contrary to what you have decided I am."

He released his vise-like grip on her, and shoved one arm behind his neck, laying his head back on the pillow. He resumed his sightless staring at the ceiling. "I was right—you did come here to save Cameron's hide. Now I suggest you leave."

"I don't know why I said what I did, Trevor. I am truly sorry. I . . . I'm frightened. And so very, very tired."

She took in a heavy breath and exhaled her words. "I am horrified by all of this, and I feel I am at fault. This entire mess has been caused by my having tried to become a part of your family." Tears slid down her cheeks, and a sob escaped her throat.

"Aren't you filled with a little too much self-importance, Mrs. Kirkland? You don't belong in our family. You never have, and you never will." His words, rapier sharp, cut through her midsection and left her bleeding at her core.

Stunned and utterly speechless, she was unable to move. Somehow, despite his cruel words, she thought she understood his pain and isolation.

Her tears stopped. She sniffed and wiped her cheeks and nose with a handkerchief she'd dug from her pocket. "If only I could reach you in some way. If only I knew what magic it would take to make the darkness go away. God knows how deeply I desire to do so."

She stood to leave, her words hanging in the air, tangled threads of pain, love, and fear. The misery of his silence, of her search for the right things to say, squeezed her heart until she teetered on the very brink of collapse.

She bent and kissed him on the cheek, then pressed her own against his, whispering into his ear. "Dear Trevor, I know I don't have the right to feel this, or to say this, but I love you."

Sickened when there was only silence in response, she left the hotel and wound her way slowly through the darkened streets toward the townhouse. The sorrowful click of her heels against the hard wooden boards echoed through the night.

Like a child, she peered into one shop window after another, as though the distraction would make her nightmare go away. The aching in her heart only quickened as uninvited memories of growing up parentless in the Vieux Carré haunted her. She wandered aimlessly in the general direction of the townhouse.

When she found herself climbing the stairs to her room, she was unaware of how long she had roamed the French Quarter, or when exactly it had begun to drizzle. Her clothes were wet, and her shoes, crusted with mud, felt so very heavy.

She entered her room in the darkness and locked the door, suddenly feeling stifled and claustrophobic in her clammy clothing. She tore frantically at the buttons. "I shouldn't have worn wool. It's too late in the year for wool. It's too hot for wool. Damn it. Damn it. Damn it!"

She yanked and pulled at her clothes, flung them across the room, crying and cursing the air until she stood naked in the darkness.

The pins in her hair came next. Frenetically slinging them as she pulled, she raked her fingers through her hair, tossed her tangled mane about until it hung in disarray around her shoulders. Depleted, she sniffed, and then moved to the basin near her nightstand. She cupped her hands and splashed cool water over her face, cleansed her stained cheeks.

* * *

Trevor stood in the blackness of a corner nearest the open French doors, watching her shadowed movements.

Dear Trevor, I love you.

He tasted the bittersweet words she had fed him back in the hotel. Pain, slow and deep, washed through him once more. Why had he come here, tonight of all nights? Why did he continue to torment himself? He could barely watch her from across a crowded room without wanting her, and now she stood before him, naked, primitive, alive with an angry fire he had never seen before.

Dear Trevor, I love you.

Her words had stunned him. They rang sacred—deep waters to quench his parched soul. The agony and isolation when she'd left him had driven him here. Why he came, what he was seeking, he did not know. Now he was becoming less sure of his actions, confused by the tumult in his soul.

Dear Trevor, I love you.

What effect had those devastating words had on her when she'd uttered them? Or had she used them only in the passion of death's threat, only to be forgotten when the crisis was over?

Christ, what was he doing here?

She turned from the basin and moved to the French doors. Her bare feet padded soundlessly against polished hardwood; moonlight shimmered on her satin flesh.

He drew in a staggered breath.

Celine stopped in her tracks. "Who's there?" Raw terror flashed across her features. "Show yourself this instant, or I shall scream."

He stepped from the shadows.

Her shoulders slumped, and she exhaled with a *whoosh.* "Trevor!"

Not knowing what to say, he stood in silence and stared at her. He saw her bare shoulders, her wild hair framing her like a dark halo, moonlight glancing off the rosy tips of her breasts. Slowly, he moved closer as he lost himself in her.

She didn't move.

He reached out, barely touched her, and then drew his fingertips slowly down her shoulder. She caught his hand in hers and brought it to her lips.

Dear God, he might die in the morning and never be able to touch her again.

Something in him snapped.

He grabbed her and crushed her against him. Her minted breath caught in his mouth as his lips came down on hers. She tried to slip a hand between them but he would not allow the separation. Instead, he backed her against the wall, imprisoning her. He pulled his mouth from hers and peered deep into her eyes.

A faint gasp escaped her lips. "Yes," she whispered, telling him she understood that no other words were necessary.

Raw, savage need for her spiraled through him.

He braced himself and pushed her harder into the wall, covered her with his heat. Helplessly, he found the soft sweep of her neck with his mouth, buried his face in her sweet-smelling mane, caught her familiar floral scent. He hung suspended against the provocative warmth of her body. Fire flashed over him as his hands slid down to her silken hips.

She made no sound.

There was only his ragged breathing.

He opened his mouth, breathed her deep inside of him, took in the essence of her as his tongue tasted one corner of her mouth. His lips found hers.

Madness. Sheer madness.

But he did not—could not—let her go. Jerking at the buttons on his shirt until his chest lay bare, he pressed himself tightly against her. He crushed his mouth to hers once again. With one hand, he pulled himself free from his trousers, slid his hands beneath her hips, and lifted her legs up around him.

She moaned and dug her hands into his shoulders.

He was miserably scared now. Scared she would reject him, scared she would not. And so damn afraid of backing down from what he was now doing and from what he'd committed to do on the morrow.

He began to move, as if to withdraw from her.

She clutched at him.

With a visceral groan, he plunged into her full force and took her in deep, hard thrusts.

She cried out as her body shuddered with a climax.

And then a volcano of hot pleasure rolled through him.

He squeezed his eyes closed and pressed his forehead, wet with perspiration, against the wall, frayed breathing fracturing the air around them.

Remorse washed over him like hot lava, burning away any sweet taste of sensual pleasure. His fist slammed against the wall beside her.

She flinched against his damp chest.

"Christ Almighty, what have I done?"

Her breath quivered in the strange silence.

Pushing away from her, he turned his back as he fumbled at his trousers. He swept his hands over his eyes in exasperation. "I'm sorry."

She was still breathless. "There is nothing to be sorry about. I wanted you, and you needed what just happened."

"I am so goddamn sorry about everything—including tomorrow."

He walked beyond the French doors, stepped over the low railing, and disappeared into the night.

Chapter Sixteen

In the predawn silence, Celine heard the wrought iron gate to the courtyard swing open, and the clip-clop of horses' hooves. She stood, gathered a breath into her lungs for courage, and walked stiffly toward the rear of the townhouse.

Marie met her in the dimly lit hallway. "Mister Andrews and Cameron's father are by the kitchen door with the carriage." Her strained voice scraped through the air like a taut bow drawn across a violin out of tune.

Celine's heart plunged into mourning as though death had already come calling. Both men were here, which meant the duel would still take place. Justin and Miles greeted her with somber nods.

Justin spread his hands and shook his head. "Trevor went to Cameron during the night to make amends, said he would not participate, but Cameron refused, threatened to have Trevor posted."

Celine's hands pressed into her gut to try to assuage her pain. "Dear Lord, why would Cameron say such a thing? Trevor has no choice then."

To publicly post Trevor's refusal to fight according to the code duello, would brand him a coward for the rest of his days. The news would travel to France and England like the plague, and he would be shunned.

Justin placed a hand at her elbow, assisted her out the door and down the steps. Celine squinted to see through the morning shadows. She stumbled with the shock of realizing it wasn't the family carriage she was about to climb into, but a plain wooden wagon, the bed just long enough to carry the body of a full-grown man.

She swayed on her feet.

Justin and Miles grabbed her and helped her onto the middle of the hard, wooden bench. They climbed in on either side of her.

She felt movement in the wagon's bed and glanced behind her at the silhouette of a figure readjusting his position.

The surgeon!

She shivered and pulled her shawl around her shoulders.

They rode in silence to Dueling Oaks. The dull thud of horses' hooves on the dirt road, metal rattling against leather, and the groaning of the wagon, wood to wood, were the only sounds to break the grip of utter stillness. Justin dejectedly guided the horses, as if his slow pace would buy the precious time it might take to change this terrible morning.

Celine thought her senses would have been dulled by a night's worth of spent emotions, but just the opposite was true. The creaking and popping of the wagon grated at her ears, and the pungent scent of the horses nauseated her.

She swore she could smell the awful contents of the surgeon's bag as well. The hard, unpolished bench rubbed her spine raw. Bile rose in her throat, and she swallowed hard.

Couldn't anyone stop this living nightmare? She longed to send her agonized cries echoing in the winds ahead of her, to land on the ears of the only two people who could prevent this senseless ritual of death.

Gray mists from the levees and bayous snaked along the floor of the woods and out onto the road, leaving vague patches of fog floating low to the ground. As they rode deeper into the woods, forest dwellers gave off their haunting calls, signaled the oncoming intruders, only to fall silent at their passing.

Celine pulled her shawl even tighter and rubbed at her arms. She didn't belong here.

No one did.

Justin halted the wagon a good distance from Dueling Oaks and waited in the hushed glen. The surgeon climbed down from the wagon, clutching a small black valise and the case containing the pistols.

To her left, Celine could make out Trevor standing under an ancient, gnarled oak. He was impeccably dressed in black breeches tucked into black riding boots. A white lawn shirt, open at the neck and with sleeves rolled up, covered his upper torso. His second stood a few feet away.

Cameron stepped out from where four horses were tethered and removed his coat, folded it, and handed it to his second. He was dressed in similar fashion to Trevor.

How genuinely awful. A uniform for death.

Celine could almost hear the deep, resonant ring of a bell inside her head. The death knell. She twitched and pulled her closed fist into her gut.

Without so much as a glance at those standing at the wagon, Cameron made his way somberly toward the surgeon, who opened the pistol case. Trevor, as acceptor of the duel, followed Cameron's lead. They both nodded, and the pistols were handed to the seconds for loading.

Celine closed her eyes to avoid the sight of the deadly balls being inserted into the weapons. She gritted her teeth against the urge to rush forward and stop the madness. She opened her eyes just as the seconds handed the pistols to Cameron and Trevor.

"Oh, dear God," she muttered.

Justin grabbed her hand and squeezed.

Cameron and Trevor faced each other for a long moment. Then, with a word from the surgeon, they turned and marched in opposite directions to the count of twenty paces. They paused, and at the surgeon's command, turned again, raised their weapons and aimed.

It was over so quickly, Celine's brain hadn't time to register the bark of the pistols firing. It was only when she saw a crimson stain blotching the left front of Cameron's shirt and growing in size that she realized what had happened.

Cameron staggered backward a few steps. His still-smoking pistol slipped from the hand hanging limp at his side. Slowly, his knees folded beneath him. With the grace of a fallen warrior, his body found the forest floor. His gaze, still locked with his cousin's, broke off only when he closed his eyes and sank into the dark depths of unconciousness.

Celine didn't recall how she came to cross the distance from the wagon to Cameron, but suddenly she was simply there, on her knees, cradling Cameron's head on her lap and calling his name. Miles and Justin kneeled next to the surgeon.

Trevor approached the group.

Miles rose from his knee. "Don't come any closer. You've done enough for today."

Trevor faltered, and then backed away. He stood in outcast silence, pistol in hand. Even from where he stood some ten paces away, there was the lingering acrid scent of gunpowder.

The surgeon spoke as he worked. "He should be all right if infection doesn't set in. The ball went through his shoulder. It's clean. He's passed out from the shock."

He looked up at Miles. "Someone knew exactly what he was doing to send the bullet through just so."

Miles's shoulders drooped, and he leaned into his brother, his gray face mottling with the return of color.

Justin helped Celine to her feet and into the rear of the

wagon. Then he helped Miles and the surgeon load Cameron onto the bed, his head in Celine's lap. She cradled him, murmured to him of his will to live, of his zest for life.

And she wept.

Her tumbled hair did little to hide her tears. The wool blanket covering Cameron drank thirstily of the wetness.

As the wagon pulled away from Dueling Oaks, Celine lifted her head, tossed her tangled hair from her face, and blinked away the tears.

Trevor's sorrowful gaze locked with hers.

Her spine stiffened with the shock of it. The center of her chest twisted with a pain so intense, she tried to cry out Trevor's name. But her mouth only opened and closed, moving in mute mockery.

Even as the wagon headed for the townhouse, and the lone figure standing like a statue at Dueling Oaks shrank in the distance, those eyes filled with stark pain held hers.

And even when he became little more than an indistinguishable figure, and then a mere silhouette the size of her thumb, she could feel the strength of his gaze locked with hers—holding her prisoner.

His had been a silent and solitary cry for help.

To her alone.

And because of her dazed state, it was too late when she realized she had rejected him.

Chapter Seventeen

That nagging headache was creeping up on her again. Celine rubbed her temples and descended the stairs leading to the parlor. Two more days, and she'd be gone. She couldn't set sail fast enough. These past four days with Cameron and his devil-may-care attitude had her clenching her teeth to keep from railing at him. Then there was Justin and his unannounced visits at all hours, during which he went directly to Cameron's sickroom and remained there for hours behind closed doors. Healing a family rift, once her passionate goal, no longer mattered. If there were rewards to be had for failure, she'd be in line for the grand prize.

Cameron sat in the middle of the blue velvet divan, his arm in a sling; a wicker basket in his lap contained a ball of gray and white fluff. "What are you doing out of bed?" she demanded.

He grinned. "It's teatime."

Celine sat on the divan, taking the side next to his uninjured shoulder. "And what is *that?*"

"A cat. Leave it to Felicité to give me a damnable get-well gift." The bundle of fur, belly up and legs in the air, was sound asleep.

Celine ran the back of her hand up and down its leg. "It's a kitten, not a cat."

"Well, it'll be a cat soon enough, so you may as well call the blasted thing what it is." Despite his complaining, Cameron's fingers raked gently back and forth along the kitten's middle. "It'll make a good mouser aboard ship."

"What a pretty little thing. It looks as though it's been painted with an artist's brush, the way its paws and ears are tipped white. Have you given it a name?"

"Emeraude."

"Then it is a she."

"Don't know, haven't looked."

"Why not?"

"It takes two hands—one to lift the bloody thing, one to inspect. And in case you haven't noticed, I've got a rather useless shoulder at the moment. Unless you think this sling strapped on me is meant for storage. Besides, it doesn't matter the gender, since there will be only one aboard."

Despite her gray mood, Celine had to smile. "Your mind works in odd ways at times. Does the name Emeraude have any special meaning?"

"It's my favorite brothel in Paris."

"I should've known it would be something like that." She shook her head in disgust, but a bubble of amusement tried to work its way free. "You seem to be getting along rather well today."

He grinned wickedly. "Marie takes good care of her Mischie Cameron."

Celine rolled her eyes. "Didn't the doctor order bed rest?"

"I refuse to loll about like a sickling any longer. Besides, I have business to attend to on the morrow that requires me to leave the premises."

"So soon?"

"In case you are unaware, our first clipper arrived two days ago, and I have yet to set my eyes on it. You should be surprised that I remain on this divan."

Celine could stand it no longer. "What of Trevor, have you heard anything?"

"Oh, I do believe you are about to get serious on me." He gave her a faux pout. "And just when tea is due."

Her mood sank back to sorrowful. "Unlike you, most of us have been quite sober throughout this grim debacle."

"Trevor is fine, Celine." Suddenly serious, he measured his words. "In fact, he's due here shortly. We have a business meeting."

Her heart tripped. "I . . . I have to ask you this, Cameron—why in heaven's name did you threaten to have him posted?"

He shrugged. "So he couldn't back down."

"*What?* But that's insane. You could have been killed."

"He knew full well where he was aiming."

"But he could have missed!"

"Celine." He laid his hand over hers. "Did anyone ever tell you that while Trevor might have a bit of an edge on me in business matters, when it comes to anything sporting, I excel? I'm a crack shot."

It took a moment for Cameron's words to sink in. "You mean you both knew you could have taken him, so you intentionally let him take the first shot?"

He removed his hand from hers and went back to raking his fingers ever so lightly through the kitten's fur.

The throbbing in Celine's head stepped up a beat. "Do you think so little of yourself that you would risk your life over a foolish argument?"

"Perhaps it was more than that, Celine. Perhaps the bond between Trevor and me is so strong that I was willing to risk my life if it meant Trevor would change his spots."

Celine gasped. "You forced him to take that shot."

Cameron shrugged. "Someone had to take drastic measures. We've seen him on a path of self-destruction before. But don't think the others had anything to do with it. The decision was mine alone."

A dawning light struck Celine's mind. "Then that duel was not entirely over what happened the other night."

"More of a culmination of events that has been building up over the years."

"I cannot believe I am hearing this." Celine pinched the bridge of her nose. Damnable headache. "Do you think your foolish act might have done any good?"

"One would hope so. Trevor's had a more difficult time accepting his destiny than have I."

"What do you mean?"

He shifted his weight, and with a wince and a hiss, slipped his good arm over the back of the sofa behind Celine. "Try to understand our positions. At about the same time I was deciding to settle down, suddenly I was leaving behind a decent life in a country I loved, and not knowing who or what I might run across in San Francisco. I've had ghastly dreams of seeing the only woman around for miles crawling out of some godforsaken gold mine with grit on her cheeks and half her teeth rotted out."

Celine laughed. "But what does all that have to do with—"

"A lot. I knew I had to be the one to head up operations in San Francisco. My father and uncle are too old, and Trevor is vital to running the entire company. Mine wasn't an easy decision to make. I suppose I felt lonely at the prospect of embarking for the godforsaken place."

He shrugged. "So, when I met you, and learned you were on your way to San Francisco as well, I thought it providential and got stars in my eyes. So many, in fact, that I refused to see you had them, as well. Only yours were for Trevor."

Oh, good heavens. "There's no need to go on—"

"Please, Celine, hear me out. It didn't take much to see that Trevor wanted you straight away, but knowing he had no plans to settle down or change his wandering ways, I thought if I could manage to hold him off, you'd see things differently once you and I were settled in San Francisco, and he'd sail off to China and then back to England without giving you another thought."

Celine's blood froze at the idea of never seeing Trevor again. She knew it would happen. She just wasn't ready to hear it. She joined Cameron in stroking Emeraude. "In some ways it might have been better had it worked out that way."

He shook his head. "An attraction between two people is something we have no control over. Forgive me for misinterpreting my own feelings, Celine. I have no female siblings by which to measure brotherly love. At the time, I couldn't get ahold of the idea that you might serve me much better as the sister I never had."

"But you see me as that now?"

He nodded. "Thank the saints you aren't as exasperating as Felicité."

What a relief. She could have hugged him . . . but then, his shoulder. "Being an only child, and raised by a devoted grandmother, I've had difficulty understanding how members of a close-knit family can go to war with one another one minute, and then be willing to die for each other the next."

"Perhaps it's a bit of the hot-blooded French in us?"

Celine frowned. "Justin and Trevor butt heads like a couple of goats, and Justin is not French."

"Ah, but has no one told you, Celine? My uncle was as wild in his youth as Trevor."

Now if that wasn't news. "Justin was a rakehell?"

Cameron's mouth quirked. "Enough so that my grandfather banished Uncle Justin from their English estate, which is why he came to America. My father tagged along, as younger brothers often will."

"I had no idea."

"Perhaps as his penance, my uncle sired a son who is his mirror image—not in looks, but in deeds and temperament.

They are fiercely joined as *family,* but I suspect they will always knock heads."

"My word." Celine eyed a portrait of a dark-haired beauty with a small boy nestled comfortably in her lap. "You mean Trevor could end up a wizened old man one day?"

Cameron cocked a brow. "Oh, I wouldn't go so far as to say that."

Marie wheeled in a cart laden with cups and saucers, a steaming teapot, and hot beignets. Conversation ceased. Maria stiffened. "Don't pay no attention to me. I'll be out of your way in no time."

"Don't go getting yourself in a twist. It's far more entertaining to listen in not two feet from us rather than eavesdropping from afar." Cameron grinned and reached for a pastry. "Ah, my favorite."

Marie's guilty blush flashed across her cheeks. "Seems to me everythin' is your favorite."

While the maid poured tea and Cameron continued to tease, Celine set her sights once again on the portrait. "Is that Trevor and his mother? They look rather cozy."

Cameron nodded. "Trevor is eight years Michel's senior, so he was an only child for a good while. My mother looked much like her."

Melancholy swept through Celine at the thought of never having any portrait such as that to hang on a wall.

"You would have liked our mothers, Celine. They fawned over their children, and spoiled us rotten as August fruit. Unfortunately for Trevor, his mother's attention could only be had when his father wasn't in the same room."

Celine nearly choked on a beignet. "Why?"

"My uncle did not share his wife with Trevor. And therein lies a major difference between my cousin and me. Then just when it looked as though he'd gotten over losing his mother, he affianced himself to a lovely little thing. Unfortunately, she was not quite as devoted as he was. He came home a week early from a sail and found her still abed, but not alone. That's when he moved to London."

"Good heavens. No wonder he's the way he is." Celine turned to the maid. "What are your recollections of that situation, Marie?"

Marie wheeled the cart out of the room. "I'm gone now. Disappeared. Have your intimate conversation without me, mischie."

Cameron chuckled and called out, "*Merci beaucoup.*"

With Marie out of sight, he tapped Celine's shoulder. "Since we speak of Trevor, let's discuss the two of you before he arrives?"

Celine set her cup down before it touched her lips and rubbed at the back of her neck. "Please Cameron, nothing further about Trevor. I am so completely enervated, so entirely sick of all of this."

"What happened that night in the *garçonnière?*"

Celine lurched off the sofa. "I distinctly said I will no longer discuss the matter of your cousin. You are being quite impudent."

Cameron clasped her wrist and pulled her back down beside him. "I know what happened physically, Celine. What I want to know is what transpired between the two of you in a much deeper sense." His voice grew quietly serious. "I have my reasons for asking. You must know I would not impose otherwise."

Why didn't he just twist her heart in a few more knots? "What happened in the cabin was nothing more than a tryst. And a mistake." She rubbed at her temples with her free hand. "I should go to my room. I have a terrible headache."

Cameron let go of her wrist and gave her hand a squeeze. "Let me tell you what I think happened that night, Celine. Like deer in the woods, the two of you caught one another's scent the moment you laid eyes on each other. Scared the devil right out of the both of you. That's why you've picked at each other. You were terrified of that powerful force driving you together. But nothing you did, or can do, will dissipate that energy. I think it's your destiny."

Cameron touched her chin and eased her face toward him. "Not just you, I said *both* of you."

He let go and slipped his hand back into hers. "And so came that night in the *garçonnière*. Sooner or later, a twist of fate was bound to throw the two of you together. Someplace where the barriers would come down, and you would be forced to confront one another. And that you did."

He tucked a wayward curl behind her ear. "I've never had a sister before, Celine. It's amazing how overly protective we brothers become. I am terribly sorry I stood in your way."

Oh, she wouldn't weep in front of him. She couldn't. Cameron slipped his arm around her again. She leaned into him for comfort. He was right, and it was shredding her heart.

"It's a rare thing the way you two connected. I think the great pity is that both of you are about to throw it all away. Mark my words, if you leave each other now, you're bound to suffer a deprivation that nothing or no one else will be able to fill."

Celine sat for a long moment, her fingers buried in the kitten's fur. "It seems you can speak with a good deal of wisdom when you've a mind to."

"I read Emerson," he answered with a flippant grin.

Celine chuckled and they fell silent again. Finally, she spoke from her heart, telling Cameron of her experiences in the *garçonnière,* about dropping all pretext and armor, of a lovingness so sublime as to be painful, and of its enduring memories.

"If you are so clear about how you feel, how can you possibly consider leaving here, or walking away from Trevor?"

Celine braced herself with a long breath. "You speak

of wanting a family, so I assume that includes desiring children?"

He continued rubbing the kitten's belly. "I suppose it is natural to want progeny once a reckless life is left behind."

She knew it would sting, but she had to say it. "Do you think Trevor will one day want a family?"

He shrugged. "I don't see why not."

"I am barren, Cameron."

A flicker of surprise ran through his eyes. "I see." A brief moment of silence, and then he spoke again. "Is Trevor aware of your . . . situation?"

"I am." Trevor stepped from the passageway connecting the parlor to the rear rooms.

Celine jumped and her breath froze in her lungs while the pounding in her ears sounded like cannon shots. She clasped her hands in her lap to keep them from trembling. "Where did you come from?" she managed, barely above a whisper.

He rested a shoulder against the doorjamb. "Through the porte cochere and in the side door. But does it matter? I'm here." Dark shadows blotched his handsome face and he looked tired. His gaze engulfed her for a long while. And then his dark, sober eyes shifted to Cameron.

Cameron gave a slight nod as if making silent amends. "You heard?"

"Every word," Trevor answered quietly.

"How long have you been here?" Cameron asked.

"Since before Marie served tea."

Cameron shifted around, grinned, and went back to his flippant ways. "I say, old boy, this must be the day for providential eavesdropping."

Marie's shadow along the hallway wall behind Trevor disappeared.

Celine stood and headed toward the staircase, hoping her knees wouldn't give out.

"Don't be a coward." Cameron's sharp command stopped her.

She turned, holding the stair rail, and silently pleaded with Cameron to let things be.

"Trevor heard every word, Celine. And he is still here. Think about it."

She hadn't yet breathed since she'd stopped in her tracks. She did so, hoping to relieve her dizziness.

"You can walk back in here, or you can take your leave," Cameron said. "Either way, there's no more veil. Whatever you do from here on out, you can no longer reject the truth."

"I—" A visible shudder ran through her and she paled. "I cannot think."

Cameron turned to Trevor. "She can't think."

She pinched the bridge of her nose. "I've a headache."

"She has a headache."

Celine lifted her skirts and scurried up the stairs. "Oh, for heaven's sake, Cameron, hush your mouth."

It took every ounce of Trevor's will not to take those steps two at a time after Celine. Not now. Not when there was so much he still needed to mull over. He inhaled slowly and shifted his gaze from the stairs to his cousin, who sat stroking a pile of fluff.

Christ, he could have killed Cameron.

If Trevor had thought the last three days sorting things out with his father was the most difficult thing he'd ever done, now he wasn't so sure. A fist-size lump caught in his throat and the words of his carefully planned apology grew muddled in his mind.

"You may as well take a seat," Cameron said. "That wall can hold itself up rather nicely."

Trevor walked over to the butler's tray and picked up

Celine's untouched cup of tea. He wet his parched throat with the cold contents.

"Help yourself," Cameron quipped. "She never touched it."

Relief washed through Trevor like a clean, warm rain. So everything was going to be all right. Cameron had forgiven him. He sat alongside Cameron. "Did this sofa shrink since we were lads?"

Cameron poured himself another cup. "Aren't we a couple of bloody baboons sitting here with our knees nearly at our chests and sipping tea like our mothers used to do?"

They both chuckled and stuffed beignets into their mouths.

Cameron licked a finger. "You aren't letting her go to San Francisco, are you?"

"I can't stop her from doing what she's determined to do."

Cameron grabbed another beignet. "Of course you can if you've a mind to."

A brief moment of silence, and Cameron spoke again. "What the hell am I missing here? Why wouldn't you stop her? Does it have to do with her being barren?"

Trevor set the cup back on the butler's tray and ran his hand down his leg, smoothing his trouser leg. "She's set her mind on the notion that there are certain things a man must have from a wife that she cannot provide. So where does one go from there?"

"Rubbish, Trev. Prevent her from leaving."

"I'm a sailor, Cam. I cannot stop her from leaving, and then sail off on my own journey. The idea is absurd and would make me a hypocrite."

Cameron punched the air with his teaspoon. "Aha! Take her with you."

"To China? She's made it perfectly clear she will be no man's mistress."

Cameron set his cup down and wedged himself into the corner of the sofa with a pained grunt. "Suffering God. You are so hard-headed you could etch glass. And the two of you are more alike than you care to admit—both of you are bloody stubborn. The difference, old boy, is that she'll confess to it and you will not."

Trevor gave a slight smirk. "Humph."

"She's sailing with the evening tide in two days." Cameron slapped his forehead. "Oh, *pardonne moi,* but you would know that. How careless of me to forget you are running things, Mischie Trevor."

Trevor's head spun at the very suggestion of taking Celine along. He quelled a shaft of hope that tried to cleave its way into his logic. She would never agree. He changed the subject. "Captain Thompson will take the first clipper out tomorrow in your stead."

Cameron nodded. "He's the only one besides us who'll put his heart into breaking a speed record. What about me?"

"The last of our clippers has been delayed for three weeks. You'll be well enough to take the helm by then, and I'll captain the second one."

The conversation turned to ships and cargo, routes and time frames. Trevor started to explain his five-year plan when it became obvious Cameron had stopped listening. "Have I lost you somewhere along the way?"

The frown lines on Cameron's face melted away. "I do believe I have just hatched a jolly good plan."

"Which is?"

"Give me time to think on things. I'm out of this bloody confinement tomorrow, and I have a meeting scheduled with your father. Join us at ten sharp."

Chapter Eighteen

There was little left for Celine to do. Marie had everything in order well ahead of schedule. The maid wanted to send the bulk of her luggage ahead, but Celine was adamant that it remain with her until departure. She wasn't sure if it was in case she needed to retrieve something at the last minute, or if she'd hoped for some miracle. Still, she'd resigned herself to leaving, and no longer thought of New Orleans as her home.

Her future seemed like a vague, black hole.

Although contact with Cameron had been brief, since he'd been in a rush for his first outing since the duel, she was still somewhat disillusioned when he failed to comment regarding the previous afternoon's events. The two of them were to have dinner with Justin, Elizabeth, and Miles on this, her last evening in the city. She had desperately hoped Trevor would join them, but had heard nothing.

If only she could stop thinking of him.

Lindsey and Felicité would bid their farewells at the dock. She'd not wanted it that way, afraid she'd lose control, but the least she could do was comply with Justin's wishes.

She dressed in a promenade dress and left the townhouse for a final walk in the Vieux Carré. The trip did nothing to lift her spirits. She returned to the townhouse and wandered in the rose garden. It was odd how strangely detached she felt. Perhaps it was her saving grace. She dressed for dinner as void of any emotion as the day she awoke from her accident.

Antoine's was bustling. A fricassee of terrapin, brown and aromatic, was placed in front of her by a white-gloved waiter. In the past, she would have waged an internal battle to consume in a ladylike manner her favorite meal. Tonight, she barely tasted it.

Her gown was of a deep indigo, bare at the shoulders and cut close to her body, more sophisticated than her usual style. Candlelight reflected hypnotically in luminous patterns across the moiré silk when she moved. Her hair, piled high on her head, was woven through with strands of pearls. She wore the diamond-and-pearl necklace Justin had given her, but no earrings. The lost earring had never been found. Men at nearby tables glanced discreetly her way, but she ignored them. How different she was from the girl who had grown up here and played stickball in the streets.

Justin appeared more relaxed than she'd seen him in a long while. Color claimed his cheeks once again. Cameron was especially wicked with his humor. Elizabeth and Miles appeared very much at ease as well. As the evening wore on, her spirits rose somewhat. At least she could leave with a modicum of peace now that the family had mended.

The evening passed without incident—and with no sign of Trevor. She had a feeling he wouldn't show. Far better this way. She doubted she would have been able to sit in his presence and maintain her dignity.

Justin and Cameron escorted her back to the townhouse. Cameron opted to return to his suite at the hotel and left Celine and Marie to themselves. It was well after midnight, but Marie, with the brown velvet riding hat Celine had given her still perched cockeyed on her head, was dragging the last steamer trunk into the parlor.

"I sent some of the crates on ahead, Miss Celine. I know you told me not to, but we would have been in big trouble come six o'clock tomorrow if we tried to get what all was here down to the dock in one load."

"You made the right decision, thank you."

It took them another fifteen minutes to discuss the morrow.

Celine heaved a sigh. "Go on to bed. You look as exhausted as I feel."

"What about your clothing, mam'selle? Let me get you out of your gown."

Celine sighed. "Oh, just unbutton it for me, and open my corset. I'll take care of the rest. You go on to bed before you drop."

"Are you sure?" Marie started on the buttons.

"Uh-huh," Celine yawned and bent her neck back and forth as she spoke. "If you don't mind, I'll drop everything in a heap on the floor."

Marie unwound the pearls from Celine's hair, and slipped off the jewelry. "Don' mind at all. I'll fold everything you ain't gonna wear in the last crate in the mornin'." She disappeared down the hallway to the rear of the townhouse.

Celine climbed the stairs and turned into her room. She shut the door behind her and leaned against it for a moment, her arms crossed as if to comfort herself. The whale-oil lamp cast a soft glow about the room. A pained emptiness tugged at her. Her last night in New Orleans. It wouldn't have taken much for the tears to fall, so she forced herself not to think about anything but the act of undressing. She sighed as she stripped off her clothing until all that was left was her chemise.

A sparkle atop the mantel caught her eye. The lost earring! She snatched it up, inspected its unmarred surface, and then ran out the door, down the stairs and through the hallway to Marie's room. She stopped before she reached the bedroom door and giggled. Like a grand locomotive on its way to somewhere important, Marie snored away in a loud, chugging rhythm.

Celine slapped a hand over her mouth and retreated, afraid her fatigue would lead to hysterical laughter that wouldn't quit. She made her way back to her room.

Celine stepped through the doorway and stared in shock at Trevor propped up in her bed.

"Trevor!"

Judging by the outline of his body beneath the sheet gathered around his hips, he wore nothing but a wicked grin and a ship captain's hat perched at a jaunty angle atop his head.

Her cheeks heated. "What in heaven's name are you doing in my bed?"

He laughed, deep and throaty. "*Your* bed? Are you aware you chose my bedroom again?"

She struggled to collect her thoughts.

"Come, *ma petite.*" He tapped the top of the bedside commode. "Put down the earring before you lose it again."

His devilish grin played across his relaxed features. His eyes, ablaze with raw, midnight fire, raked slowly over her, then back up to pierce her soul once again.

Exquisite heat, like a shock of black powder set alight, enveloped her.

He cocked his head. "Come closer, *ma petite.* I dare you to see how close you can come."

Why not play his game? It was her last night here. She would never see him again. Never again have the chance to be with him.

Her chin tilted upward in stubborn defiance as she inched around the bed, moving closer, her blood pounding, their eyes locked like animals in the wild. She felt his power—but she was aware of hers as well. Stealth. Cunning. Moving away from the edge of the bed, out of his reach, she stretched her arm over the tabletop, dropped the earring, and ran.

He moved like a panther.

She didn't know how he'd managed to grab her so quickly. Or how she landed on the bed with him nuzzling her neck.

She squealed.

He was teasing her again with that potently mischievous look, but there was no teasing in the powerful hold he had on her. It was firm, yet intimate, with one arm pressing her tightly against his chest, the other draped casually across her lap where he boldly caressed her hip and inner thighs as though she had no choice.

Heat spread along her nerve endings, and her arms reached up of their own accord, wrapped themselves about his broad, muscled shoulders. She craved the taste of his skin, and set her tongue to his shoulder.

He'd been able to do this to her from the first time they met—to stir her in a purely physical sense. Why him? Why him and no other?

It was too late for further consideration, for she was adrift in that special scent of his that was fatal to her senses, that caused her faculties to blur and her defenses to disintegrate.

Oh, how she had missed the way his hands set her afire, the way his eyes could penetrate her soul. And his body, his hard, electrifying body—what it did to her. There was no use denying it anymore, she loved making love with him. She loved *him.*

Celine lay on her belly across the bed, arms outstretched, and slowly came awake to the morning sun streaking through the open doors leading onto the balcony. A light breeze tugged at the curtains. She was alone. Odd, the satin case on the pillow next to her was missing. She lifted her chin and blew her hair from her face, then tossed her head, flicking the errant strands over her shoulder. She eased up until she was sitting naked in the middle of the bed.

A whimsical tune whistled up from the rose garden. She scrambled off the bed, wrapped a robe around her, and hastened to the balcony. Trevor was in the garden plucking petals off the roses and stuffing them into the pillowcase. He wore his captain's hat—and nothing else.

Her hands flew to her mouth. "Trevor, are you insane? Get up here this minute before someone sees you."

"Too late." He grinned up at her. "You caught me."

"You are utterly naked."

"As I expect you to be when I return."

She laughed. He was so unabashedly casual in his nudity. She found it wicked, but charming—and a delight to watch. A heat she thought she'd extinguished last night curled around the apex of her thighs.

He shook the petals down in the pillowcase. "There, filled. Be right up." He disappeared into the house, whistling. In moments he was back in the room. He strode purposefully over to the bed and shook the contents of the pillowcase onto the sheets. With an impish grin, he reached for Celine, stripped her of her robe, and dropped her amid the bed of rose petals.

"Roll in them."

Rose petals crushed beneath her weight. She breathed deeply, wrapped in the sweet scent as Trevor picked up handfuls of the delicate satin gems and showered them over her body.

"Delicious." She gazed up at him and stretched her arms out, beckoning.

He stood over her for a moment as if drinking her in, and then stretched out alongside her. Rolling her over him and then under him, he picked up petals and rained them on her skin, ran a petal under her nose and across her lips until she squealed in surrender. When he stopped, he held her in the warmth of his arms and planted soft kisses all over her face. Then he paused and pulled away, studying her.

She met his gaze. He seemed so utterly relaxed, so carefree, and full of joy. She savored the moment, not allowing herself to think ahead. She didn't dare, not for a second. To do so would surely fracture her heart when she left. "You're in a mood."

"That I am, *ma petite.* But I must go soon. I have a business to run, and if I remember correctly, one of my new ships is set to sail on the evening tide."

The blood drained from her heart.

He made to lift away from her.

She pulled him back, tight against her.

He kissed her forehead. "We can't stay here forever."

The onset of pain, the tears, the awful fracturing of her heart threatened her senses. She pulled his mouth down to hers and kissed him, her tongue tangled with his.

"*Non, ma petite,*" he whispered. "I must go."

She slid her hand down his belly, wrapped her fingers around his hard arousal. "I need you one last time."

The room was thick with silent emotion, her overpowering sadness counter to his exuberance as she watched him dress. He described the ship she would be sailing on, took pride in the details, as though the vessel were a living entity.

Of course he would be excited. She didn't think he noticed her quietude, most likely had no idea her heart was breaking. If the smiles she gave him had cracked and disintegrated like shattered glass, she wouldn't have been surprised. He had said he would be there when she sailed, so at least she had that much to look forward to. Perhaps the presence of the rest of the family gathered around would soften the blow.

He finished dressing, picked up his hat from the table, and gave her a hug. "Oh, yes, I forgot to tell you—since you'll be residing in the captain's quarters—there is a fireplace. You should be quite comfortable when you hit cold weather around the horn."

He tugged the hat into place and made for the door.

She was to be in the captain's quarters? "What . . . what about the captain. Where will he stay?"

"I beg your pardon?" Trevor stopped at the open door, his hand on the knob.

She could already feel his absence. She fought tears. She wanted to scream. "Well, who is the captain? If proper introductions are to be made, I should know his name. And . . . and where will he be staying if I am to take his quarters?"

She clasped her trembling hands to keep from wringing them, used every ounce of willpower to maintain an aloof and unconcerned air. She had asked for this pain. She did not have Dianah Morgan's mettle after all.

"Celine?" Her name was a whimsical question. "How can you not have guessed?" Slowly he removed his hat, bowed at the waist, and straightened, his eyes aglow. He replaced his hat and gave the brim a final tip her way.

Celine's jaw dropped. "You?"

"Whoever else would you share the captain's bed with, *ma petite?*" He blew her a kiss and headed jauntily down the stairs, calling up as he went.

The door closed behind him.

Weeks on board ship with her in his bed? Dear God, she couldn't possibly survive the pain when he deposited her in San Francisco and sailed off to China. Surely, her already fragile heart would shred.

Trevor stood on deck next to the priest and Cameron, watching the docks for Celine.

"Sir, I have no idea the strings you were able to pull to make this work," the priest said. "You know how strict the church is about marriage banns."

"Cameron did the string pulling, not I."

"If you think I wouldn't turn this world upside down to

see these two well married," Cameron replied, "then what can I say?"

The guests were on board. The food, the music, everything was in place for the sparse two hours they would have to see the couple off. Felicité was beside herself, giddy with excitement. She had already begun to bother her father about a trip to San Francisco to visit her brother and his wife before they sailed off to China. "*Quelle heure,* Trevor?"

"Five forty-five. Have patience." He patted her shoulder and did his best to appear calm, but he, too, was growing anxious.

Justin regarded Trevor. "I doubt I have ever seen you looking so content."

Trevor rocked back on his heels, his gaze still on the dock. Damn it, he wished she would hurry. "Why would I not be?"

"I hadn't expected to see you so relaxed. It's obvious you are at peace with your decision."

Trevor grinned. "That I am."

The priest looked a little confused, but said nothing.

Felicité pointed toward the dock and jumped up and down in place. "Here they come! Here they come!"

Everyone peered toward the wharf as the cumbersome dray careened dangerously around a mountain of shipping crates, righted itself, and raced full speed toward them. A grimacing Marie bounced around on the seat beside the driver, holding on to its edge for dear life with one hand while her other crushed her brown velvet hat to her head. Steamer trunks piled high teetered perilously as the cart turned at a sharp angle and stopped abruptly in front of the ship.

Trevor peered beyond the dray, searching the crowd for the carriage that carried Celine.

Marie dug into the front of her bodice and retrieved a scrap of paper. She scrambled off the seat and raced up the plank, waving the folded sheet at Trevor. He rushed down to meet her, snatching the paper from her hand.

She bent over, hands on hips, panting to catch her breath.

Trevor read the note. "Dear God!" A horse kicking him in the chest could not have done more damage. "When, where?"

"I don't know." Marie wrung her hands, the pitch of her voice winding higher. "The most I could make out is sometime around two o'clock. That's the last I saw her. She said she was going for one last walk through the city, so I thought nothing of it. Then I found this note on the table by the door. Oh, I don't know, Mischie Trevor, I don't know where she went, but she took her traveling bag with her." Marie began to wail.

Justin and Cameron rushed to Trevor's side. "What in God's name?" Justin demanded.

Trevor handed the note to his father, threw his face to the sky, and sucked in a deep breath. His hands went to his hips for balance. He fought tears.

Justin, with Cameron over his shoulder, opened the note and read aloud:

Dear Trevor,

By the time you read this, I will have gone on to San Francisco on my own.

Do you recall the morning we took breakfast together on the balcony at Carlton Oaks? I told you then I was not of the same fabric as you, could not enter easily into an affair.

What we shared last night and this morning was beautiful and perfect. It, and you, will live forever in my heart.

Being with you felt so comforting, and you were so easy to love last night and this morning. For these memories, I thank you. However, I am afraid I would have been hopelessly lost in you by ship's landing, while you, dear Trevor, would most likely have grown quite bored with the same woman for so long a time.

Would you please do me the favor of delivering my belongings to the Morgan Hotel in San Francisco, where I will be residing?

Lovingly,
Celine

Trevor continued to breathe deeply, but now his head was down, his face buried in the palm of his hand. She was lost to him.

"What the devil has happened here?" Justin demanded, the red in his face deepening with each huffed breath. "It doesn't sound as though she had a clue there was to be a wedding."

Trevor was silent.

"Answer me!" Justin roared. In his fury, he shook the letter in Trevor's face. "Had you bothered to ask this woman to wed you?"

"No." Trevor raised his hand against the letter, and stared beyond the wharf, as if she would appear and tell him this was some terrible hoax.

"Why the hell not?"

Trevor turned his eyes skyward again, closed them, and took in great gulps of the air. He breathed out his answer. "I intended to surprise her. She was aware the clipper was scheduled to sail beyond San Francisco after it made port. I didn't want her to have any inkling I was taking her to China as a wedding gift."

Struggling for words, Justin swept his hand through the air toward the guests and the tables filled with food. "What . . . the reception, the guests? All of this? Don't tell me you kept your marriage plans as a surprise as well?"

It wasn't that Trevor refused to answer—he couldn't speak.

His father stood motionless, his face distorted in furious disbelief, his hand still suspended in the air. The veins in his temples and up his neck, blue and bulging, throbbed angrily. He looked incredulously at the note in his hand, then again at Trevor.

"These are the writings of a pained woman, not one who's been told she's to be a bride. Had you even bothered to inform her that you were in love with her, you . . . you pompous ass!"

Trevor kept his eyes sightless on the sky. "I did not."

"Well, why not?"

"She knew, Father. How could she not have known? I was saving the words . . . for the ceremony." Trevor heard the absurdity of his own deeds.

"You fool. You stupid, damn fool!" Justin bellowed.

Trevor looked at his father. "I know," he said softly. "I know." His shoulders sagged.

Cameron stepped in, and touched Justin's elbow. "Uncle, this isn't going to help matters. Foolish as it was, I was part of this."

"You?" Justin blustered.

Cameron nodded. "It was my bloody idea in the first place. We were well-intentioned, we just weren't clear-headed. Let's not forget what has recently transpired in our lives."

Justin blinked as if his head was clearing from a fog. His gaze flickered from one to the other. "Why didn't any of this come out in our meeting this morning? I thought you were only keeping the reception secret. And you two run a profitable business together?"

Cameron wiped a hand across his brow. "Bloody damned stupid of us, wasn't it?"

Trevor stood, shaking his head, trying to keep from crumbling in front of the entire world. He finally spoke.

"I've been such a bastard all my life, I don't deserve her, anyway. Christ, I'm sorry. I'm sorry I disappointed her, I'm sorry I disappointed you." He swept his hand toward the clipper, indicating the people standing along the ship's railing, looking as though they'd seen a ghost. "And I am sorry I disappointed all of you."

He caught sight of Felicité's sad, wet face. And he broke. He turned his back on everyone as great tears streamed down his face.

Justin reached out to him. "Don't, son. I blame myself in part for this. And you know why."

Cameron stepped forward. "I don't see what the hell the problem is, Trev. You know she loves you. You know she's worth going after, and she can't possibly be that hard to find. *Mon Dieu!*"

He grabbed Trevor by the arm and pointed toward a shirt-sleeved man jotting figures in an open ledger. "If you'd stop and think for a minute instead of spending your time cursing one another, all we have to do is walk the few steps over there and check the bloody log to know who left port today. How long do you think it would take to catch up with her using our clipper? I can guarantee you nothing on the water can move faster than us."

Cameron shoved himself in front of his cousin, leading the way. "You can figure out how to get your sorry *derrière* back in good stead with her later. Come on, old boy, time's awasting!"

Chapter Nineteen

Celine sat on a bench in the Vieux Carré, across the street from Dianah's former home, rubbing at her arms as if the humid air contained a chill wind. She hadn't felt so alone since she was six, when her mother died of the ague, and her father drank himself into a stupor and then disappeared.

The clapboard three-story house was painted the same soft yellow, the trim the same pristine white, but that was where any resemblance to the life she'd once shared with the Morgan family ended. A stranger climbed the few stairs to the wide veranda that stretched the width of the house—a veranda where she and Dianah had spent many hours. He entered the house without knocking, and why not? The place was an inn now.

Celine chewed on her bottom lip. What a vacuous place New Orleans had become. There was nothing left here for her. Accepting Justin's invitation to remain at Carlton Oaks would be sheer folly. Would she live there and dread Trevor's visits every few years? And when he showed up with a wife at his side, and children in tow, what then? Pain shot straight through her heart at the idea. Far better to start a new life in San Francisco, surrounded by people she knew and loved.

The problem now was how to get there. With only the

Andrews Company ships sailing in that direction anytime soon, that route seemed out of the question. Perhaps she could take a train. Or a stagecoach. Oh, she didn't know what dangers might await a woman traveling alone. But she could not linger. Most of what little she'd made off the sale of the meager plantation her husband's family had owned had gone to a bank in San Francisco. The rest was sewn into her skirts, and that wouldn't last long.

Celine stood, brushed the front of her skirts, and walked the three blocks to Jackson Square. She sat down on another bench. A couple of street vendors looked familiar. Even though they weren't likely to remember her, she turned her head. That was her past, and she wanted nothing more to do with it.

Well, whatever she was going to do, she had to come up with something soon. Her stomach growled, but she was in no mood for food. Perhaps some coffee.

She made her way to the coffeehouse on the square. As she approached, a familiar face caught her attention. Now there was a man who might have advice to offer. Jacques Pierre was well known in the Vieux Carré for helping one obtain whatever was needed.

She approached him with a tentative smile.

He stood, pulled out another chair, and offered it to her with a gallant sweep of his small hand. He wasn't any taller than she, and close up, signs of aging etched the corners of his eyes and mouth. His temples had gone a bit gray since last she'd seen him. "Mademoiselle. May I offer you something? Anything?"

"A coffee, please." She slid onto the seat, and after introductions and his claiming to recall her as a young girl in the French Quarter, she got directly to the point. "I need passage to San Francisco, and I was wondering if perhaps you might offer some advice. While I understand the fastest route is by sea, I am not altogether certain I wish to take that route. Unless you are aware of a ship sailing rather soon that does not belong to the Andrews Company." Very soon. Very, very soon.

His dark eyes narrowed.

Apprehension slid under her skin. "I was hoping to take a train west, but I was told the only trains from here go east and north."

A sharp look passed over his visage and then disappeared. He lifted his cup to his mouth. "You would not want to take the ship, oh, *non,* mademoiselle. Has no one told you the trip around the Horn is like meeting up with the devil himself?"

She set her cup down with a clink. "Whatever do you mean?" None of the Andrews men had said a word about any hardship.

Jacques Pierre gave a flip of his hand. "Oh, my, oh, my. The winds howl like a pack of wolves, and the seas ramp so high they are known to wash sailors right over the sides, never to be seen again. Sailing around the Horn is no place for you, mademoiselle, no place at all."

"Then what would you suggest?"

"Why the train, of course. It may be somewhat slower than by ship, but it is not uncomfortable like a stagecoach, nor will it cause you to fall overboard in a storm. There is, however, a bit of a predicament."

She was about to unravel. Any minute now. She held herself steady and took a sip of her coffee. "Which is?"

"The train is booked for months ahead. However, I know someone who can secure you a ticket. It will cost a bit more, but well worth it, because you will be assured of a seat once you arrive in St. Joseph."

"Missouri?" Oh, dear.

"Yes, mademoiselle, all trains west leave from there."

Jacques Pierre returned some twenty minutes later and explained that he'd arranged for her to leave within the hour. She nearly collapsed when he told her the fee. There was only one thing she could do. She produced the necklace Justin had given her along with the matching earrings from Cameron. The money sewn into her skirts would hopefully last her until she reached San Francisco.

There was no mistaking the greed that passed over the man's face when he snatched up the jewelry, but Celine didn't care. She was desperate, and distressed to the point of barely being able to breathe. She could not get out of New Orleans fast enough.

The passage Jacques Pierre procured on the barge upriver was sorely inadequate. After a day's travel, no matter what the vessel's owner did to ease her discomfort, it was of no avail. The small cabin in the middle of the keelboat with its low ceiling had no door, affording Celine little privacy, and leaving her prey to mosquitoes. A quilt tossed on the hard wooden floor served as her crude bed, leaving her hips bruised and tender. Stale biscuits, dried sausages, and fruit were her only sustenance. Drinking water came from a bucket dipped in the river. After a while, she ceased her complaining, and suffered in silence, taking things one day at a time. She spent most of her hours doing nothing but staring into the dark waters of the Mississippi.

When she reached St. Joseph, she honestly wondered if the good Lord had delivered her but one small section of a brain. She'd been told, through loud guffaws, that the railroads had not yet been built past the Mississippi. In her entire life, she could not recall having had a conversation regarding the rail system or the nation's progress westward. Such worldly discussions took place in libraries, among clouds of cigar smoke and glasses of whiskey, never in withdrawing rooms filled with women who were expected to discuss the more prosaic aspects of life.

Jacques Pierre, the little rat, had tricked her out of a necklace and earrings, and left her stranded.

Three days in a small rooming house staring at the ceiling convinced her that a return to New Orleans might prove far worse than riding a stagecoach. But passage aboard the stagecoach line was booked six months in advance. Desperate, she searched for any alternative. A wagon train would depart in a week or so. She'd been told there wouldn't be another until the following spring, and that she might be able to find a family in need of funds who would allow her to join them.

Celine stood among a crowd of hopeful passengers, disheartened by their aggressive glares. She dared not skip to the front of the line for a simple inquiry, lest her actions be misinterpreted.

A foul odor crept around her. Not certain where the smell originated, she surreptitiously surveyed the area. When she turned around, she stared into the shifty eyes of an oily mop of a man and nearly gagged.

He couldn't have been more than five feet two. A baggy, homespun herringbone Sunday suit hung from his disproportionate frame. He stood with his pelvis thrust forward, the hem of his pants hanging higher in front than in back, above his scuffed boots. Dirty blond hair hung in greasy strands about a pinched face. He turned sideways at her scrutiny, hunched his shoulders, and flicked his snakelike tongue about his dry, cracked slit of a smile.

She jerked her head up to avoid staring any longer and turned toward the front of the line. But she caught the stony glare of the woman behind him before she turned—his mother?

"Where's your husband, lady?"

Celine ignored his question, and covered her mouth and nose with a handkerchief.

"Ain't got one, huh? That's what I figured." The rasp of his voice, filled with lecherous intent, slithered up her spine, and raised the hair on the back of her neck.

The silence was as disconcerting as his meddling—she knew he was not finished. "They don't let no single women on wagon trains, ain't you heard? Not less they's with family. Too much trouble." He chuckled, a low, antagonistic wheeze.

"Leave her be, Will. She don't want your advice, son."

So the woman standing behind him was his mother, after all. No single women on wagon trains? Celine's heart beat a drumroll in her throat. She stood only three people away from the front of the procession—she had to find a solution, and fast.

The wagon master appeared from nowhere, surveying the queue.

A tall, broad-shouldered, thick-waisted woman standing directly in front of Celine pinched the sleeve of her husband's jacket and turned around to give her a querulous frown. "That pus of a man is right—no single women allowed on wagon trains."

"Well, what about him?" Celine questioned faintheartedly. "He's single."

"Don't matter with men. He's got family anyway." The woman jerked her bonneted head toward the female behind Will, then put her stiffened back to Celine.

Will's whiny mockery ran the length of her spine once again. "You can be my little sister. Can't she, Momma?" His voice turned flat, serious. "It'll cost you, though. We need the money. Bad."

The wagon master walked the line. When he approached Celine, he paused. Even worn and wrinkled from the trip upriver, her stylish clothing was about to give her away. She held her breath, panic biting at her gut.

He drew an imaginary line in front of her with his hand. “We’ll cut this group off here, ma’am. Start a new party of wagons with you and yours.”

Mutely, she nodded. He’d looked as though he was going to speak again, but he only hesitated, and then moved to the rear of the line.

She turned around, avoided the grunting little man, and introduced herself to his mother, and promptly asked about terms. She figured she could find another solution later.

The woman assessed Celine and her clothing, comparing them to her own simple cotton dress. “I’m Katarina Olssen. How’re we going to pass you off as my daughter? You sure don’t resemble us.”

Will snickered and dragged his sleeve across the bottom of his nose, then sniffed. “How’s about something like, our father sent her off to some fancy finishing school down South ’cause she kept bothering after me?”

He let go a high-pitched giggle. He still stood hunched over and sideways, but he’d begun to pick dirt from beneath his fingernails with a pocketknife.

Celine stared at his hands, finally noticing what it was that made them so odd—the tip of each pinkie finger was missing.

Still holding the knife, he lifted both little fingers in the air and wiggled them. “Papa didn’t take none to nose picking.”

Celine’s riveted gaze moved up to Will’s clotted nose and rheumy eyes, and bile roiled in her stomach.

His mother gave him a nudge on his shoulder. “That’s enough, Will. He’s right about needing the money though. And we could use an extra hand with the wagon. So if you’re thinking on it, his story could hold up . . . the part about you being in finishing school, I mean. My husband’s been three years mining for gold near San Francisco. He finally sent for me and Will, our youngest. Could be you decided to give San Francisco a try now that you're done with your education. It could work."

Celine surveyed the line behind them. There had to be another family.

Katarina's brows knitted together. "How far are you headed?"

"San Francisco."

The woman waved her hand at the crowd. "The people you see lined up here are headed in all directions. Once we reach Fort Hall, how many of them are going to be willing to take you aboard the rest of the way along the California trail?"

"Next."

The outfitter's loud announcement startled Celine. She had to make a decision. Now. "All right, we'll figure something out."

After countless futile inquiries as to Celine's whereabouts, Trevor finally located Jacques Pierre. The jeweler who'd made Celine's necklace and earrings notified the family that Pierre had attempted to sell the items back. Wild and angry, Trevor strode through Madame Olympée's, Cameron by his side. Grabbing the back of Jacques Pierre's neck, Trevor lifted the squealing man from his chair.

"*Merde!* You are breaking my neck, *monsieur.* Christ!"

"I'll break more than that, you little weasel." Trevor turned to Cameron. "Escort this questionable excuse for a man to his home so he can pack. We'll be leaving immediately."

Cameron smoothed his moustache, ever so slowly. "Can I do damage along the way?"

Red blotches mottled Pierre's cheeks. He straightened the stock tie about his neck, then reached back to rub at the pained muscles. "Leaving? Where, *monsieur?* Wh . . . what for?"

It took only Trevor's fierce expression to start him talking.

"*Non, monsieur,* I . . . I cannot go with you. I have many appointments. But I will tell you all I know, and show you the man who took her upriver. She would not be harmed by him. I assure you, he is the kindest of men. I saw to that."

"Good. Then we'll be using the same transportation you afforded Mrs. Kirkland. I'm curious to know just what her conditions might have been."

Trevor regarded Pierre with pure disgust. The perspiring little man withered under the burn of Trevor's glare. He moved forward, tapped a pointed finger on the terrified man's chest. "I already know you sent her upriver and with whom. You will cooperate, or for the rest of your life, you will wish you had."

Pierre backed up, tripping and stumbling as he went, his head nodding vigorously.

Trevor's words came slowly, precisely. "You will locate the best scout there is, you sorry bastard. If you value one inch of that miserable hide of yours, you *will* cooperate every inch of the way."

He stepped back, his fists and jaw clenched. Before he turned, he issued one last warning. "If you try to slip away, I will find you, you miserable little runt. Tell your contact to get the barge readied for horses, as well."

Trevor was gripped by an emotion so overpowering, he couldn't even name it. He turned to Cameron as they left. "I'm stopping at Carlton Oaks for Panther and the bay. Deliver the weasel back to me, and then I'll see you in San Francisco."

The Overland Trail treated everyone with the same harsh indifference. Sand, heat, and a dry wind parched wagons and split the lips of young and old alike, nearly causing Celine to faint twice this particular day.

She'd been walking steadily since early morning when they'd broken camp, and still nothing seemed to have moved. All around her, the monotony of the cloudless sky meeting endless plains of grass seemed to have stopped time and motion.

The wagon train had spread out to a hundred wide and one deep to avoid eating the dust of those ahead. It did her no good—dust collected in her nose and eyes. Parts of her body, rubbed raw from pulverized grit caught between fabric and skin, stung from the thin film of sweat that covered her. The grind of dirt against teeth in her clamped jaw echoed through her skull.

She stumbled, and then collected herself.

Katarina Olssen leaned out from the front of the wagon without slowing the oxen. "You all right?"

"Yes," Celine mumbled.

"Need to rest a while?"

"No." She knew Mrs. Olssen's turn on the ground meant Celine could collapse in the cramped, smelly bed inside the wagon. But it also meant waking Will for his driving shift. With his mother on the ground, his relentless insinuations would give Celine no rest. She simply could not tolerate him anymore.

Suddenly, she grew dizzy, and her heart began to pound furiously in her chest. An odd sense of panic welled up. Oh, wonderful. She'd forgotten to drink enough water again. Too late. This time, her knees buckled and the grass, grit, and heat closed in around her.

She never lost the sound of voices in the darkness, so she could not have gone far from consciousness. Moist cloths across her forehead and at the base of her neck revived her. Part of her fought coming back to stark reality.

Her eyelids fluttered. Cool metal touched her lips, and

she parted them for the water wetting her dry tongue and sliding down her throat. She opened her eyes and looked around. How had she gotten inside the covered wagon?

Mrs. Olssen was still driving and Will was walking, while Sarah, the young bride from the adjacent wagon, had managed to squeeze into the minuscule space behind Celine's pallet. Blond, plain, and shy, Sarah worked silently, tending to Celine. The bed, nothing more than layers of quilts running the width of the wagon, lay directly behind the driver.

In the beginning, Celine had argued for the bed to be located at the rear to afford her some privacy, but Mrs. Olssen insisted it be up front in case the driver ran into trouble. The woman knew what she was doing. She didn't trust Will either.

Things were bad enough when Mrs. Olssen was taking her turn walking and her son was up front doing the driving. But how would it have been in the back, with Will on the ground, and nothing to restrict him?

While he was driving, attending to the wagon and oxen, uncertain pathways forced him to keep both hands and his concentration on the reins. Nonetheless, every now and then, he'd manage to shove a hand inside the wagon and grope. Celine had learned to fall asleep with her back to him, and whenever they came to a halt, she sat up, as far from him as possible. She shuddered at the thought of his touching her. Sarah ceased her ministrations.

"I'm fine now, Sarah, thank you," Celine lied. She still felt queasy.

The young woman nodded, crawled over Celine, and sat next to Mrs. Olssen. "Ain't it Will's turn to drive?"

"I'm taking a double shift this time around," Mrs. Olssen answered.

There was something odd in the way she spoke. Celine had a vague sense the woman had figured out why Celine chose to remain on the ground for so long. But if they switched around, that meant during her turn up front, Will would be directly behind her. She nearly groaned aloud.

Katarina Olssen resumed her flat monologue. "We'll be stopping for the night after that. I don't want Celine driving anymore."

What? For the first time in weeks, a quiver of relief washed through her. But why? Katarina must be giving Celine some extra distance from Will.

"How long?" Sarah asked.

"Let's see, this is mid-July," the older woman mused. "I figure about two or three months, at the most."

Sarah hopped off the wagon without a good-bye.

The steady rocking, and the stifling interior, nauseated Celine once again. She rose on her elbows and saw that the rear flap of canvas was down, preventing a cross breeze. The pallet was too low to catch any fresh air. She was going to be sick.

With a lurch, she was up and hanging her head off the side of the wagon, vomiting in violent spasms. Katarina managed to hold the reins in one hand long enough to grab the wet cloth and lay it over the back of Celine's neck.

"Thank you." The wave of sickness passed, and she managed to crawl up on the seat beside Katarina, who shouted at Will to roll up the back flap.

"Rinse your mouth out. You'll feel better," she said to Celine. "Then drink plenty of water. Thank the heavens, we haven't been without."

She shot a glance at Celine. "We'll rearrange the wagon tonight, wash the quilts so they're fresh. You'll have to sleep on the ground with the rest of us while they dry, but by morning they'll be ready. We can make the bed front to back so's you can stretch your legs out and catch a breeze. I'll put the foodstuffs to the rear."

She was so matter of fact and to the point, Celine was taken aback by her sudden concern. "But . . . but I always sleep on the ground. We all do." The cross breeze hit Celine, soothing her.

"Not any longer," was all Katarina said.

They rode a long while in silence. Celine was achingly tired. The fatigue never seemed to leave her anymore. Neither did the soreness. Every muscle in her body screamed for relief. The grueling sun worked on her again, and she wiped the back of her neck with the cloth.

"Keep drinking water. Tiny sips. And chew on a piece of dry bread."

Celine turned to crawl back into the wagon. "I think I'll pass on the bread just now, thank you. I need to lie down."

"Eat the bread and force yourself to sit here until the quilts get washed and the wagon is aired out." Katarina's voice was still flat, pragmatic, but it carried a quiet authority. "You'll just get sick again if you go back the way it is."

Celine took a deep breath and released it in a long, irritated sigh. "Mrs. Olssen, I—"

"I've had seven children, Celine, and three grandchildren. I can tell when a woman's with child. And I know how sensitive a woman can be in the first months. I know what those rancid smells back there would have done to me."

Celine couldn't breathe from the shock gripping her chest. "I . . . I can't be. It cannot be!" Her hand splayed across her chest, ran down her belly and back. She pressed here and there at all the sore spots on her body, wincing at her tender breasts, shaking her head from side to side.

"No, it . . . it's not possible." But she knew Katarina was right. How could she have missed the signs?

The answer came to her in a flash. She was out of touch with her own senses, and went to bed at night with every muscle in her body aching. Every ounce of energy was used for pure survival in this hostile environment, and since her accident, her courses had been erratic so she paid little attention to their onsets. Lord, did Trevor get her with child that night in the *garçonnière?* Or did it happen in New Orleans?

"It fools you the first time." Neither Katarina's lackluster monotone nor her concentration on driving the team changed. "You'll recognize it quicker with each one."

"But this is not . . . I cannot—" Her hand slid to her belly. What she'd been about to reveal to Katarina would serve no purpose. Suddenly, the full impact of her physical state hit her. *Trevor's child grows within me!*

And she was on a wagon train with no turning back. Another child. Another wagon. Oh, please don't let this one take a bad turn.

Trevor.

Oh, she wanted him—wanted desperately to share this with him. She should never have left New Orleans.

No longer was she dead inside. Every nerve in her body was alive, dancing in the realization that she carried a child—*his* child. She desperately needed to be alone now, to sort through her thoughts. She had a deep desire to bathe in the enduring memories of love, even if coming alive meant she might once again have to face passion's dark side—pain. To have felt nothing for so long had become her greatest, most excruciating pain of all. Now she held within her the seedling of a child. Trevor's child! Another thrill ran through her.

"How long have you suspected?" Celine's calm voice belied her erratic emotions.

"Hard to say. Time doesn't seem to have a marker out here. Probably a month."

"That long? What made you think so?"

"Just a feeling at first. Something didn't sit right when you told that story back in Missouri. Figured maybe you ran off from a nasty husband who beat you the way you was acting. Weren't none of my business."

Katarina shrugged her shoulders. "Then your moods started swinging back and forth, edgy one day, settled the next. And your body started changing with your moods. Started thinning out from all the walking, but your bosom kept getting fuller."

She leaned forward, steadying her arms on her legs. Her gloved hands held tight to the reins, but her gaze reached over the heads of the oxen into the horizon. It was the first time Celine had seen the woman in anything resembling a pensive moment.

Katarina bent the kinks out of her neck, shot a quick glance at Celine, and then focused back on the oxen. "Then there's a kinda way a woman changes when she's got new life in her. Something that's in most every woman. Can't be put to words."

She fought the reins as the team headed toward a shallow rift in the pathway. "Before your belly's out there big enough for everyone to see, you'd best have a story to tell that has some kinda reason to it. You're at the sick stage. That's how Sarah knew."

Celine nodded slowly. Good God, how could she have been so blind? "So that's what she meant when she asked how long, and you told her two or three months. You two were discussing how far along I was."

Celine leaned her weary head against the side of the wagon. The unforgiving edge dug into her shoulder and pushed the brim of her bonnet down over her forehead, hiding her face. She closed her eyes to the sun's glare, and left the jarring reality of the wagon behind while she turned her thoughts within.

"Whoa, whoa there." Katarina's words eased the oxen to a halt for the day and snapped Celine back to the present. Katarina clamored off the wagon, rubbed at her arched back, and then headed for the other wagons for instructions. Will came around to the front to tend the oxen.

Celine felt slow and dull-witted—and utterly depressed. She'd wanted to spend the rest of the day on the wagon thinking of Trevor, to dream sweet dreams of her future, of mother and child, not come face to face with that odious creature leering at her from between the ears of an ox.

She stood in weary preparation to remove herself from the bench. Her dress, wet from perspiration, clung to the back of her hips, buttocks, and legs. She'd long ago dispensed with petticoats. She'd taken to wearing only a chemise under her dress to wick the sweat from her body after noticing the women around her had done the same. They told her to save her precious underclothing for the cold mountain nights.

When she turned to climb down, her back was toward the oxen team. She heard Will's snigger and knew his lips had already gone wet in lascivious response. Something flared in her, caught fire, and burned.

No more!

She continued her climb down, attempting to ignore Will, but he moved quickly from the front of the oxen toward her, his breathing ragged. She let go and jumped clear of the wagon. Landing on her feet with a soft thud, she turned and faced him with her feet planted apart, her hands curled in fists, ready to pound him into the earth if necessary.

He stopped in wary surprise. Hunching over, he turned sideways at her hard and fearless stare.

Their silent war had ended.

She had become the instinctive protector, the mother bear with her cub.

Chapter Twenty

When Trevor arrived in St. Joseph, Missouri, the midnight sky held no stars or moon to light the way. Jacques Pierre was nervous, extremely nervous. He'd checked out all of his contacts, searched everywhere, with Trevor shadowing his every move. Trevor had made Jacques Pierre's life a living hell, and it showed. The weasel was pale, drawn, and he'd acquired the recent habit of jumping with a yip at every sudden move.

Trevor's final warning hadn't been necessary—Jacques Pierre made it clear he would have licked Trevor's boots all the way to Missouri and back if it meant staying alive and in one piece. At present, he was sure to be a dead man unless Celine surfaced. Trevor told him the only thing keeping him breathing was the fact that she could still be out there. His fate was simple—if Celine was all right, Jacques Pierre could go free. If she had met with disaster, he would receive the same.

Trevor figured Jacques Pierre had no idea where Celine was, but he did know who could find her, if she was to be found. Trevor only prayed that she would surface safe and unharmed, and that the man beside him could locate the one tracker who could do the job.

Jacques Pierre pointed up the street on his left, toward a saloon with a few rooms above it. "We can try that hotel over there. The ground floor is a bar." He started to walk ahead. "It's not the St. Anthony, but for St. Jo, it's not as bad as it might appear from the outside. It has a long bar."

Trevor clamped hard onto Jacques Pierre's neck. The little man hopped to a halt with a startled chirp.

"Stop making that infernal noise," Trevor growled. "I couldn't care less what the place looks like, you imbecile. Just who, or what, are you looking for in there? You have given me absolutely nothing these past three days, and I'm beginning to think this little charade is your way of buying time."

Trevor squeezed the man's neck harder and pushed him forward. Jacques Pierre winced. He rose on his toes and peered over the swinging doors. He breathed a deep sigh. "He is inside, monsieur."

Trevor peered in, sizing up the men bellied up to the bar. "*Who?*"

Jacques Pierre stood flat on his feet, the doors to the saloon reaching mid-forehead on him. "The tracker. They call him The Wolf, or just plain Wolf. He is *le meilleur,* monsieur, the very, very best in all the world. He is sure to find your lady."

"Don't stretch it," Trevor warned.

"Oh, no exaggeration, monsieur. The best, the very, very best, I promise you."

"That skinny kid in the sagging buckskins?"

Jacques Pierre rose on the balls of his feet to peer in through the smoke and dust, then gaped at Trevor. "But . . . but, how did you know, monsieur?"

Trevor opened one of the swinging doors and stepped inside. "Keep your mouth shut unless you are spoken to. I'll handle things from here." He led the way to a table near the rear, positioning himself with his back to the wall. "Get me a whiskey."

Jacques Pierre jumped and, with a small squeak, hastened to the bar.

Trevor would have liked to strangle the little weasel, but not yet—he still needed the good-for-nothing.

Wolf was older than what Trevor had surmised from the street. Probably close to Cameron's age. What he'd taken for lankiness was illusion, as well. The man's frame was all firm, lean muscle beneath those loose buckskins and fringe. The seat of his pants and elbows of his shirt, sagging and dirty, hung looser than the rest of his apparel, which had given Trevor that first impression. Brown hair, as trail-worn and dusty as his buckskins and of the same color, brushed his shoulders. His face sported an unkempt beard. A worldly hardness emanated from him.

Wolf rested one arm on the bar, and one foot on the brass rail near the floor, but Trevor was keenly aware the casual stance was deceptive. His free arm draped the shoulder of a plumed and beaded barmaid who was feeding him straight shots of whiskey. Every third shot, Wolf downed a large glass of water.

Clever.

Trevor studied them intently, fascinated by the underlying drama. Wolf let his arm slip ever so lightly from the woman's shoulder to trail slowly down her back in feathered strokes, then move gently across her hips, before picking up his glass. An almost imperceptible tremor shivered through the barmaid. Wolf held the woman's gaze over the glass, drinking her in as thirstily as he did the water.

Now wasn't that something? The man was seducing a whore as carefully as if she were a lady of breeding. Wolf, the ruthless tracker, was an interesting study, indeed.

Trevor continued his scrutiny through the mirror over the

back of the bar. He raised the glass of whiskey to his lips, and he found himself studying Wolf directly once again.

With a quick flip of his head, Wolf stared at Trevor with hard eyes as blue as the sky. Then he turned back to the woman next to him and ignored Trevor completely. The eye contact had lasted only a heartbeat, but it nearly unnerved Trevor, so intense was Wolf's gaze.

Most curious to Trevor was something he'd noticed in the quick inventory he took when their eyes locked—a small object pierced Wolf's left earlobe. It was a woman's earring, finely made and of an early design, with either a ruby or garnet encased in gold at its center.

I've got him.

Trevor stood abruptly. "Time to leave, weasel."

Jacques Pierre yipped breathlessly.

"*Mon Dieu,* would you cease that noise? If I decide to kill you, I'll tell you first." He walked past Wolf without acknowledgment.

Jacques Pierre scurried behind, bewildered. "Monsieur?" he started as soon as they passed the double doors. He scurried sideways, shifting quick looks back and forth from Trevor to the saloon, pointing backward as he went. "Why are you walking away from *le meilleur?* The very best you can find—"

Trevor grabbed his captive by the neck and forced him down a narrow side street. "*Tais-toi*. And keep it shut until I say otherwise."

They walked in silence down the dark street. Trevor held tight to Jacques Pierre's sweating neck. They walked through the town in random patterns, going nowhere in particular. They started up one street, doubled back, and crossed through alleys.

When Wolf didn't step out from the dark, Trevor headed for their hotel. They entered wordlessly, making their way up the stairs and down the hall to his room.

Trevor inserted his key into the door's lock. A knife whizzed past his right ear, so close he felt the air move. The huge hunting knife pierced the door and stuck, vibrating.

"Christ!" Jacques Pierre squealed and flung himself against the wall, trembling.

Trevor stood calm, his hand still poised at the lock. He'd figured Wolf would show.

An agile hand with long, tanned fingers reached over Trevor's shoulder and yanked the knife from its target.

Trevor calmly walked through the spacious sitting room, into the bedroom, and flopped onto the bed casually. The simpering Frenchman scooted in behind him. "My name is Trevor Andrews—"

"Doesn't mean a thing." Wolf's voice was quiet, direct, yet carried lethal warning as he strolled in. He leaned against a washstand across from the bed and settled a stony glare on Trevor. "What do you want?"

A muscle clenched along Wolf's jawline, betraying his casual stance. The bone-handled knife lay by his side, within easy reach.

"I have a proposition for you—"

Wolf picked up his knife and turned to leave. "Just got off a job, ain't interested. Damn it, now I'm going to have to go another round to warm Violet up again."

"How much would it take?"

Wolf paused. "Not interested."

Trevor's chest tightened. He desperately needed this man. "I'm willing to give you an open-ended contract for the services of a personal detective. For the rest of your life if you need it." He slowed the cadence of his voice, measured his words, his manner respectful. "And for however much money it might take to find whoever it was who murdered your mother."

Wolf froze.

And then he turned.

Time moved in slow motion as he approached Trevor. His eyes, shards of murderous fury, held fast to Trevor's while his mouth narrowed into a grim slit.

An abrupt movement of Wolf's hand brought the flat side of his knife under Trevor's chin. He gave the sharp point just enough of a push to let Trevor know he meant business.

Wolf's voice came flat and hard, but a flash of agony pierced the hardness in his eyes. "How much do you know?"

"Not much." Trevor nodded toward Wolf's left earlobe. "That woman's garnet earring you wear is of an older design. I figure there are only two reasons a man would wear something like that—either he murdered a lady for it and wears it as a trophy, or he wears it in honor of someone who was done in and he's still looking for whoever did it. Since I don't believe a man with your reputation would commit murder, I took a guess."

The two men faced one another for what seemed to be an eternal silence.

"Jesus Christ." Wolf sheathed his knife, letting his hand rest on the handle. "You may have made a hell of a good guess about me, mister. But damn, I don't have to guess about you at all."

A chill snaked down Trevor's spine. He was about to put all his trust in someone who carried as much, if not more, pain than he did. He glanced over at the Frenchman. "You're excused."

"But—"

"Now," Trevor growled.

The little weasel gave a quick nod and scurried past Wolf.

When the door closed behind Jacques Pierre, Wolf took in a deep breath, then blew a stray lock of hair from his face as he exhaled. He spoke again, this time in a fast, low monotone. "Mister, you're going to have to come up with one hell of a good reason why I should even consider turning my tired ass out of bed once it hits the mattress, let alone give the likes of you some kind of fast action, because your offer of money and some damn fool detective I can run circles around in my sleep only irritates me."

Trevor replied with simple honesty. He delivered a detailed account of how he'd managed to meet, fall in love with, and then drive away Celine. When he finished, he bent his head and studied the back of his hands.

Wolf's brows knit together. "Let me get this straight. You had a wedding arranged and you had the arrogance and audacity not to bother letting her know about it? Jesus, are all you Colonial French stupid, or is it just you? Maybe it's the heat down in N'awlins that cooks your brains."

Trevor passed a hand over his eyes and swallowed an angry retort that could well send the man walking out the door. "I assumed she would say yes when placed in the right environment. I was a fool."

Wolf sat down in a chair across from Trevor and studied him. Then he bent his head and clasped his hands in front of him. "Tell me what you want."

Trevor would have walked right past Wolf the next morning on his way to retrieve Panther if it wasn't for those piercing blue eyes that stood out like the morning sun in a clear sky.

The man busy saddling his horse looked nothing like the Wolf he'd met the night before. Gone was the scruffy beard and dirty buckskins. Clean-shaven, he was handsome by even a man's measure. And his hair—clean and clubbed at the back of his neck, was blond and sun-streaked, a far cry from the disheveled brown mess Trevor had thought was its natural color.

"I suppose you won't go near a razor again until your return?"

"Nope."

Wolf was bent over, tightening the cinch across his roan's belly, when Trevor emerged from the stable with Panther in tow. As Wolf straightened, his stunned gaze riveted on the dazzling horse dancing forward, its sleek coat shimmering blue-black in the rising sun.

Trevor wasn't surprised by Wolf's response. He got the same reaction whenever anyone on American soil caught sight of the rare and mighty warhorse of Europe, the very breed that had transported Friesian and German knights to the crusades centuries before.

Quivering, muscled flanks strained with brute strength barely held in check as the beast moved forward in the precise manner of its ancestors. A riot of knee-length curling mane tumbled about Panther's head as he pranced. With each strike of a thundering hoof, the earth rumbled.

"Easy, Panther. Easy, boy," Trevor soothed as he brought the horse to a stop in front of Wolf. The huge stallion halted abruptly, then inclined its proud head, as if in noble deference, and waited patiently for Trevor to mount him.

Wolf swung himself onto his roan. "Where the hell did you manage to find a Friesian in N'awlins?"

Trevor mounted, pulled the slack up on the reins, adjusted his seat, and smiled mischievously at Wolf as he turned the horse west. "I didn't. I purchased him in Europe. I take him with me wherever I go." He cocked a brow at Wolf. "Tell me, monsieur, how does a man such as yourself, living in the middle of nowhere, know of a horse such as this?"

Wolf's face went blank before he turned away from Trevor and urged his own horse forward.

As soon as they were out of town and on the road, Trevor said, "Monsieur, you are ignoring me. You have not answered my simple question. How do you know of my horse?"

"Damn, we aren't even out of town and you're already pestering me. I should've charged you double."

A slow grin spread over Trevor's mouth. "I think you have many secrets, monsieur."

Wolf stared straight ahead. "Why don't you cut the *monsieur* crap, *mon sewer.* And let's you and me make a little deal. I ask you questions, because that's how I know what I'm looking for, and you keep your questions about me inside your lip. You don't need to know anything about me other than that I can find your little darlin' for you. That way there won't be any additional charges. No entertainment fees."

Trevor could use a little verbal dueling to take the edge off his constant worry about Celine. She still seemed a million miles away, even though Wolf had assured him she'd been seen leaving with the wagons and he would find her. That assurance had done wonders to lighten Trevor's mood. "Do you still think she's only a week or so away?"

"Barring a freak accident," Wolf said, "we'll catch up to her before she gets all the way to San Francisco. I sure as shit don't carry any perverse longing to keep company with the likes of you for that kind of time."

Trevor liked Wolf. Although he didn't bear any physical resemblance to Cameron, he had a dry wit that matched his cousin's. And God knew, Trevor needed light banter to ease the tension that plagued him. "If you have to follow her all the way to San Francisco, then you aren't worth your pay. I could have sailed my ship around the Horn and waited at the hotel for her. *Mon Dieu.*"

Wolf shifted in his saddle and gave him a deadpan stare. "Do me a favor, *mon sewer,* and fake an American accent over these next few weeks."

"At least I speak proper English, which is more than I can say for you. You amuse me."

"How so?"

"While I have command of two languages, without your

infernal cursing, your vocabulary most likely wouldn't stretch beyond that of a child's."

"I say what needs to be said, when I've a need to say it. A sight better than someone who talks all day and says nothing." Wolf jerked his head toward the back of his horse, where the bay was tied. "Hey, how come that bay we're dragging along for your lady has a man's saddle? Doesn't your fiancée ride sidesaddle like other genteel ladies? Or is that just common practice in N'awlins?"

Trevor had a feeling he was being baited. "Celine does what she chooses."

"Good. I like that in a woman. You did all right." Wolf fell silent.

"Like what in a woman?" Trevor finally asked. "That she does as she chooses or rides astride?"

Wolf snorted and slipped into a mocking Southern drawl. "Why, Mistah Andrews, suh, that your lady rides astride, by all means. It keeps the muscles on the inside of a lady's thighs nice and even, ah do believe. Powerful strong, too."

Wolf grinned. "Leave it to you to pick a woman with a good set of tight, evenly matched leg muscles. All the better to wrap around *your* fancy butt. Was that by chance, or is it a prerequisite you crazy-ass French have down yonder."

"*Merde,* but you are a crude one," Trevor spat.

"Tch, tch, tch," Wolf bantered. "Would you look who's doing the cussin' now." His mouth curled into an easy grin. "Bet you won't be doing much swearing the day we ride up beside your little lady and tip our hats. Won't she be surprised?"

A knot formed in Trevor's gut. What if Celine refused to return with him? Despite the heat, his blood ran cold.

Chapter Twenty-One

Trevor doubted he'd sleep much tonight. According to Wolf, after nearly two weeks on the trail, they were only a day away from the wagon train. This close, he'd have ridden straight through the night if it weren't for rabbit holes that could break a horse's leg in the dark. Or the fact that the horses needed their rest. Wolf guessed that they would reach Celine around dusk the next day.

Wolf's pestering banter had begun to increase these past few days. Trevor knew it was the other man's way of easing the tension.

And it worked.

Wolf sat cross-legged, staring into the fire. "You're sure going to have your bed made come sundown tomorrow."

"Do you intend to start that again?" Trevor responded.

Wolf grunted. "I sacrificed four weeks with a very lovely woman in Missouri just so's you could chase one all over hell and back." Wolf pulled his knife from the sheath strapped to his leg and sliced at what was left of the rabbit roasting on a makeshift spit. Balancing the steaming bit of meat on the flat of the blade, he offered it to Trevor.

Trevor placed his hand over his stomach. "I couldn't eat another bite, thank you."

Wolf shrugged and flipped the morsel into his own mouth.

"Wolf." Trevor rolled the name off his tongue. "How did you come by such an unusual name, anyway?"

"Huh?" Wolf held the blade of his knife in the fire to clean it.

"I'm curious." Trevor leaned forward. "And if you think I'm being rude, sir, may I remind you of the infernal personal questions you've imposed upon me of late."

Trevor poured another cup of coffee. "More?"

"Nope."

"Such a way with words, Wolf. *Mon Dieu,* you would make an incredible politician." He watched Wolf play with the fire a little longer. In the beginning, theirs had been a business arrangement, but Wolf and Trevor had connected in ways that were similar to his relationship with Cameron. "Tell me how you came by such a nickname."

Wolf shot him a frown. "What the hell does it matter?"

Trevor suppressed a smile. Ah, something about Wolf's name bothered the tracker. "Oh, your life out here, your experiences. Your past. I should like to know who I am dealing with."

As a way to keep his mind off tomorrow, Trevor continued to needle. "It's most unusual for someone to give themselves a descriptive name. Others usually do it for them. Take *the weasel*, for instance. One can well understand why I gave Jacques Pierre that name—"

"I get your drift." Wolf continued to dig at the fire with his knife.

Trevor lay back on his blanket, cradling his head in his hands, studying the stars. He knew he could wait Wolf out on this one. The man had many secrets, one of which was a cultured background that slipped through now and then. And the man had been educated. Likely outside of America by the way he used certain words. As days stretched into weeks,

Trevor grew more and more curious about Wolf, and why he chose to live the way he did.

"There's no message in it," Wolf finally answered. "It's my name." He dug at the fire hard now, poking and grinding.

"*The* Wolf, or just plain Wolf?" Trevor leaned up on one elbow.

"What?" Wolf stopped digging and eased back. He tried not to smile but failed, chuckling sheepishly. He mumbled something unintelligible.

"I cannot hear you, sir." Trevor cocked an ear with his hand. "Do speak up."

Wolf lifted his hot knife, shaking it at Trevor. "You tell anyone, and I use this on your balls, got that?"

Trevor nodded. "Such a threat."

"Wolf is my name. Short for Wolford. Been using Wolf since I was six. Everybody thinks there's some big mystery to it, and I don't tell them any different."

"Wolfort?"

"Wolford with a *d,* as in you *damn dumb French Creole*. Don't they give you any ears down South? Wolf works just fine."

Trevor laughed. "Oh, this is rich, *c'est trop*." He kept chuckling. "Is it because you don't think anyone would hire someone in your line of work named Wolford?"

Wolf grabbed his blanket and curled up with his back to Trevor. "Kiss my ass, and get some sleep. We have a long ride in the morning if you expect to find your little darlin' by the time they break for camp."

As dusk approached, fires dotting the campsites along the halted wagon train flickered and shone brighter. Celine sat beside the campfire, staring at the orange flames licking the sky, half-listening to the daily accounts and tales from the others. She was exhausted, and looked forward to the darkness and the blanket of stars.

Evenings never failed to remind her that Trevor was out there somewhere. Perhaps at this very moment, he stood on the deck of his ship, gazing up at the same great expanse. The starry nights and the bracelet she wore connected her to him. And now, her babe, too.

Their babe.

She placed the black-and-white speckled enamel coffeepot on a hot flat rock between the fire and the circle of rocks and went back to her musings. When she got to California, she would contact Trevor through Cameron. No matter what the outcome, Trevor would be informed that he had a child.

A scout on horseback approached their campsite. The relay of scouting information up and down the endless line of wagons was a valuable source of information to the group. From ahead, one learned of high or low river crossings, stopping points, dangers, and weather conditions. From behind came news of events that had taken place along the way. Tonight was Katarina's turn to host Mr. Burns, the wagon master. This meant the group gathered around the fire would be privy to firsthand information since the lead scout reported to Mr. Burns and was expected to join in the meal. In turn, the information would be passed from campfire to campfire.

The scout dismounted from his horse. "Evening."

Katarina handed Buck a cup for his first pour of coffee. "Hope you brought an appetite. Will shot a couple of jackrabbits today, and I stewed them with some potatoes and carrots."

Buck rubbed his flat belly. "Yes, ma'am, I could eat." He sat next to the fire by Mr. Burns and stretched out, crossing his dusty boots at the ankles. "Trail ahead couldn't be better for tomorrow."

He sipped at his brew. "Today was an uncommonly good day. No accidents, nothing broke down, no one got lost. Only thing to speak of is a couple of stray riders working their way up from behind. If they don't find what they're looking for, they ought to be right at your group in about an hour, I reckon. Seem to be in a mighty big hurry."

He glanced up from the grounds he'd been inspecting in the bottom of his cup. "Two riders and three horses. I hear one rider's on a monster of a horse, the likes of which no one's ever seen before. So black it shines blue in the sun, and with a curly mane that hangs to its knees."

Celine jerked. Could that horse be Panther?

Trevor! Had he actually found her trail and followed her?

Her heart pounded. Her mouth filled with cotton. It took all her strength not to interrupt Mr. Burns and Buck.

"They're looking for a woman. Leastwise, the man on the black horse is. The other rider is Wolf, a tracker who don't hire out cheap. This feller's got to be damn serious about who he's after if he's with Wolf."

Buck glanced over at the women. "Pardon my language, ladies." Then he turned back to Mr. Burns. "Yeah, he's the best I've seen. Rides circles around me."

Katarina took her eyes off Celine and broke into the conversation. "Excuse me, gentlemen, but we women watch out for one another here. This man you speak of, what if he's up to no good? What if the woman ran away for good reason? You men going to just up and hand her over?"

"Don't work that way, ma'am," Mr. Burns said. "If a woman's made her home here for the time being, she's under our protection. If she's run off with another man, well, we still don't turn her over if she don't want it. We'll see her to the end. After that, it's none of our business."

"Well—" Katarina started, but the scout interjected.

"Don't worry none, ma'am. Wolf may be a loner, but ain't

no way he'd take on anyone out to harm a woman. He'd smell the man's intentions first. Ain't no tricking the Wolf."

"I need a bath." Celine scrambled to her feet, shook out her skirts, and marched over to the wagon. She retrieved fresh clothing and a towel and headed for the river nearby.

"Wait, ma'am."

At the sound of the wagon master's stern voice, she halted.

It was as if the corners of the sky folded in on her and stole her breath.

"You'd better take your brother along, just to be safe. And don't dawdle, it's near to dusk."

Take Will? Oh, dear God! Her eyes darted from Mr. Burns to Katarina and back. Will grabbed his rifle and moved to her side. His lips were already wet.

"May I please go along with you, Celine?" It was quiet Sarah from the next wagon. Thank heavens for Sarah. "I could sure use a bath too."

Celine scrambled to Sarah's side. "Of course. Of course. Come along, but hurry before . . . before night falls."

"If I can share your towel, I can go with you right now."

"Will," Mr. Burns called out. "There's an outcropping of boulders at the high end of the stream. Put your back to the ladies and keep a lookout for Indians. Doubt you'll see much, but can't be too careful."

"You can count on me, Mr. Burns." Will snickered under his breath and walked ahead of Sarah and Celine. Count on him for what?

Celine sternly reiterated the wagon master's orders as they reached the water, also reminding Will to keep his rifle pointed upward. She trusted him even less with the rifle than with his lecherous intentions.

She and Sarah removed their dresses and, keeping their backs to Will, waded into the water clad only in their chemises. They both sucked in breath when the cold water touched their skin.

"Icy, but refreshing after a hard, hot day of dust and wind, isn't it, Celine?"

When Celine only nodded and began her bath, Sarah moved closer and whispered, "That's your man come after you, isn't it?"

"I've got to hurry, if I'm to look anywhere near decent."

"Let me help. You're shaking like a leaf and I don't think it's from the cold." Sarah ministered to Celine quietly, helped wash her hair and scrub her body, but she smiled a lot.

"He must be a good man for you to want him coming after you," Sarah said. "You're more fortunate than a lot of women."

Something in Sarah's tone gave Celine pause. "You're recently wed. Don't you consider yourself to be among those so blessed?"

Sarah cast her gaze to the ground. "Not so much."

A chill ran through Celine. For the first time, she made sense of the bruises dotting Sarah's arms, as if someone had dug fingers deep into the girl's flesh. "Oh, Sarah, I had no idea—"

"There's men a-coming on horseback!" Will hollered.

Celine's heart jumped. "Oh, Lord, too soon!"

She shot a glance over her shoulder at Will. "Don't turn around, Sarah. That little snake is staring right at us." Celine took a breath past the knot in her chest and blew it out. "From which direction are they riding, Will?"

"From the east. I can see their dust from here. And . . . and shit if that ain't a big black horse."

"East? You're supposed to be facing west with your back to us, you little worm. Turn around." Celine heard a thud and a grunt.

And then nothing.

Agitated that Will would choose now of all times to play games, she waited a few seconds. "Will, you rat."

She turned around.

And then she screamed. "Oh my God, Will!"

Will stared at the two women through blank eyes. Slowly, he fell over at the waist, an arrow protruding from the middle of his back.

He pitched forward into the water.

Two Indians on horseback shot over the rock Will had sat on—fierce-looking men with faces, bare chests, and arms painted in bright colors. Feathers stuck up from the backs of their heads.

Sarah's screams joined Celine's.

It all happened so fast, nothing registered in Celine's stunned brain. One minute she and Sarah were in the water, the next they were being dragged, face down, over the tops of horses.

The beasts flew westward, over the rocks and away from the wagon train.

Repeating rifle shots cracked in the air. Suddenly, the thunder of horses' hooves shook the earth—more Indians, and men from the wagon train, all riding at each other in great clouds of dust.

She caught sight of Trevor.

"Trevor!" she screamed and pushed herself upward with a strength she didn't know she possessed, butting her head against her captor's chin.

He grunted. Something hard slammed into her head, knocking her back. She almost passed out, but came up fighting. He struggled to keep her on the horse, and shoved her down with terrific force. Pain shot through her neck.

She spotted Trevor again and screamed his name over and over.

Something hard crashed against her skull again. Blood spurted this time, and ran down her face, blurring the mad scene before her in a haze of red. Still, she fought.

Another crushing blow hit her head.

The last thing she saw was Trevor, pitching forward just

as Will had, an arrow protruding from the middle of his back.

Amid the clouds of dust, thundering hooves, and the smell of blood, Wolf heard the woman's screams shift into something even greater than terror. This thing, this sound, penetrated the earth, and as it came upward, transformed the chaos into a haze of slow motion. The scream became a living entity, with no beginning, no end.

He tracked the scream through the blur and confusion. He knew instinctively to whom it belonged because Trevor's name was mixed in with her cries. He was close, so close now.

In a split second, everything happened at once—all around him. No separation of events or people, no sound, only the slow moving impact of the tomahawk's blunt end against Celine's already bloodied skull, an arrow penetrating Trevor's flesh, the slackening of bodies, the limp lifelessness of both Celine and Trevor.

As fast as it came, it was gone, this surreal chasm in time. Wolf found himself back amid the deafening chaos, dragging Trevor's body off Panther and over the front of his own saddle with a strength that came from beyond him.

Panther sprinted to Wolf's right, decoying five of the braves in fierce pursuit.

So, it had been the horses they were after, and not the women. But why were there three different tribes in the mix? He'd never seen the likes of it. Wolf worked his way outside the tumult, sensing fewer of them now, but he still could not position himself to get Trevor back to the wagons. Wolf didn't even know how much was left of the train or how safe it was. Instincts sharp, he headed north, toward the cover of the hills and woods.

When he was certain no one followed, he slid from the roan and pulled an unconscious Trevor to the ground. Wolf gave a light slap to the horse's backside, giving it free rein to graze, and then dragged Trevor over to a cluster of large boulders. He eased Trevor face down into a crevice between the rocks and a rotting log, and crawled in beside him. God help them both if they'd hunkered down in a nest of rattlers.

He waited.

The long silence told Wolf one story, Trevor's shallow breathing another. They remained in one spot for hours, until he was certain they were alone. He lifted his head off the ground and listened again.

The night sounds had returned to normal. He'd bet an Indian couldn't be found for miles around now, but he waited anyway.

What the hell had they all been doing in the same place? And fighting each other? He could understand running into Snakes and Dakotas. They'd been known to tangle. But Blackfoot? Something didn't sit right, especially about the Blackfoot. And they were all three tribes fighting each other as well as the whites. Didn't make sense.

Two Blackfoot braves had taken the women. And high rankers at that, judging by the way they were dressed and painted. Why the hell would they do that? Wolf chewed on his lip. The Blackfoot people were normally shy, peaceful. They stuck to themselves, didn't attack the trains. They'd steal from the Snakes, but only after the Snakes had stolen from them first.

"Oh, Sweet Jesus." Wolf put the pieces together and spoke to Trevor as if he were conscious. "The Blackfoot took the women before the Snakes or Dakotas could get to 'em. I'd bet my life the arrow that went into the back of that kid watching over Celine belonged to a Snake."

Wolf issued a hard, long breath. "Shit. They're heading up north. I can feel it in my bones." He doubted anyone would ever see those two women again.

He moved his hand to Trevor's back, near the arrow's entry wound.

Trevor moaned.

"Trevor? Goddamn it, can you hear me?"

A weak sigh indicated he had.

"I've got to get some help. I'm going to leave for a while. I'll be back as soon as I can. Whatever the hell you do, don't move, and don't make a sound. Got that?"

"Can't."

"Can't what?" Wolf hated what he was feeling, hated the panic gnawing at him. If he let the reaction overtake him, it would interfere with his instincts.

"Move. Can't move, anyway." Trevor's cheek was still pressed to the ground. A deep gurgle mixed with his feeble words.

"You're numb from lying in one place," Wolf said. "And you're weak."

Trevor managed a whisper. "Dying."

"Jesus Christ, Trevor, you've been through tougher shit than this. You know you have to set your mind to not dying. Trevor? Trevor? Crap."

Wolf laid his ear close to Trevor's mouth. Shallow, labored breathing mixed with a wet sound. Damn it!

"I have to go right now, before dawn. It's our only—"

"Find her." Trevor's slurred words interrupted him.

"What?"

Trevor's muscles trembled as he struggled to communicate. "Get her back . . . you owe me." A loud gurgling cough shook his body. "Take her home. Tell me . . . tell me you will."

"I'll get her back," Wolf promised. "Do you hear me? If it's the last thing I do, I'll find her. I *will* find her for you." He closed his eyes, took in a deep breath, and then exhaled, slow and steady. "And when I find her, I'll take her to your father. It's a promise."

Trevor's body went limp, and a rattling breath left him. Wolf fought a rush of black emotion, a powerful surge of despair, unlike anything he'd felt in a very long time. Not since he was six years old and watched his mother die at the hands of a murderer.

He put one hand on Trevor's back, bracing the arrow, and with the other, snapped the shaft off at fist-length. He wriggled out of their tight hiding place, and found the roan about fifty yards away. He only hoped he could get back to Trevor before the wolves got to him.

Dawn was breaking by the time Wolf reached the wagon train. The wagons had suffered no damage, and supplies were intact. The only deaths or injuries had been to those who'd ridden ahead to help. He'd been right—the wagon train had simply gotten in the way of a fight between the Snakes and the Dakotas, but as long as horses were to be had, they'd helped themselves.

Wolf took ten men with him back to the woods, to the crevice between the rocks and the log.

Trevor's body was nowhere to be found.

Chapter Twenty-Two

Something cool and soothing was being applied to Celine's head in gentle strokes, lessening the tight band of pain. A strong hand supported her back, steadied her until she sat upright on her own. Sunlight filtering through her closed lids told her another night had come and gone.

She could sense a slight moving about, could see the shadow play in front of her, could feel the rhythm of warm air hitting her cheek as a hand left her back and swept past her.

They were camped by a stream—she could hear the gurgling water. She'd caught the scent of a freshly cleaned body when her captor passed by. She did not want to open her eyes, did not want to see the fierce, black eyes and garishly painted face of the man. But if she did not open them soon, he would force her.

Was Sarah going through the same treatment? Was she even alive?

Initially, there had been nine warriors, but she'd made that count only after regaining consciousness. How many there were prior, she had no inkling. By their actions and their more elaborate dress, she judged the two who'd taken them from the stream to be the leaders.

All of them wore breechcloths, leggings, and shirts of a darkly tanned color, with black markings across the shirt and leggings. The two who'd captured them had bands of quills fashioned in ornate patterns running the length of their sleeves and across the breadth of their shoulders. Each wore a single braid instead of two like the others. The single, upright feather each wore in his hair was different from the others as well—they were pure white.

Celine could not tell how long they had been traveling, but it must have been a couple of weeks. At first, her captors had bound her wrists, tied her to a horse, and led it along. But she'd kept losing consciousness, and the wound in her head continually broke open, spilling fresh blood to run over her face. Finally, after a heated exchange between the two leaders, they stopped while one of them unbound her and pulled her roughly from her mount. The vicious pain in her head had made her reel, and she'd collapsed onto the ground, vomiting.

The other leader growled something at the one who'd handled her so brutally and knelt down to her. He cleansed her face with handfuls of grass, then carried her to his horse, and mounted behind her.

She'd ridden with him ever since. Tension reigned between the two leaders after that—the other man holding Celine in obvious contempt. His black eyes, through blue and red face paint, flashed violent messages. Frightened as she was, she felt that somehow the one who now rode with her had rescued her from something far worse than what she'd already been through. After the vomiting incident, the other had not touched her.

It was shortly thereafter that the group split up, going in different directions. She prayed whoever had taken Sarah would not violate her.

Her captor, the savage, as she mentally named him, had

not hurt her. In fact, he continued tending her with the utmost care.

With just the two of them on one horse, they rode at night and slept hidden on the ground during the day. Many times, Celine fell asleep while riding, so exhausted, she wasn't even aware that she'd been removed and placed in a bed of skins on the ground until he—the savage—woke her.

She was startled out of her thoughts when a shadow flickered over her lids again, and she felt him sit down in front of her. He would be straight-backed and cross-legged, with a hand on each knee, staring at her with that garishly painted face. It was as though he could see right through her lids.

She gave up and opened her eyes.

A soft gasp of utter astonishment escaped her lips. Gone was the grotesque, painted face. He sat before her in the same proud, straight-backed manner as always, but now with a gentle demeanor.

She stared into familiar onyx eyes. They appeared softer now, somehow less remote, as though removing the paint had brought greater dimension to him. He was handsome, with smooth, sun-bronzed skin stretched firm over high cheekbones, and a square, set jaw. It startled her when his full lips parted in a dazzling display of straight, white teeth.

She burst into tears.

His smile disappeared, and he tilted his head in a questioning gesture. She wrapped her arms around her middle, and rocked back and forth, her weeping uncontrollable. "Don't you see? It was easier, so much easier, when you were not human." Her sobs came harder, her rocking faster. Misery turned into acute, physical pain. "God damn you! You've become a someone now. A . . . a person. Someone who's purposely hurt me. How could you—how could you dare to . . . to . . . become *somebody?*"

She was gripped by a feeling of wretchedness. "What

am I saying? You can't even understand me. You haven't a clue what I say—you just sit there with that stupid look on your face."

God, how had she landed in such a predicament? All because she refused to sail on the same ship with the man she loved? Oh, to be able to lie safely in Trevor's arms right now. But it was too late. He was gone. How utterly cruel life could be.

Suddenly everything shifted inside of her and the absurdity of her life struck her. She laughed.

The man regarded her with a blank expression as her hysterical weeping turned into hysterical laughter. She rolled on the ground, holding her belly and laughing. And then as quickly as it came, the laughter died, and she went back to weeping. She wept and wept until there were no more tears, until she lay exhausted on the grass.

In the end, she no longer feared him. Instead, she glared at him. "No matter what you try to do to me, you cannot hurt me. I have lost everything and everyone I ever loved. Do you understand, you . . . you savage?"

Sitting up, she wiped her nose and eyes on the sleeve of the hide shirt he'd given her. It hung loose over her ragged chemise. She scrutinized him once again. "What about you? Do you have people you love? Who love you?"

One didn't need to understand a language to know when someone was angry, and her vehemence must have spewed out of her every pore, but he did nothing.

"Well, it's not true that I have lost everyone, because by God, I have my baby. He or she survived this battle, and I am damn well going to do everything I can to see my child born unharmed—even if it means killing you. Do you see it in my eyes that I will kill you in your sleep if I get the chance, you bastard?"

When she thought there were no tears left, she wept once more.

He sat quietly, watching her with onyx eyes filled with confusion.

The vast prairie, undulating like a green ocean in the wind, lay far behind them now. Celine was physically sound enough to ride alone, and no longer was there a reason to keep her bound or tied to his horse. She had no place to go, and she could not survive in the wilderness on her own.

Little, other than their ceaseless travel north, had transpired since her captor had removed the war paint and turned his head feather down in what must have been a sign of peace. But a kind of truce had developed between them.

Eventually, he gave her a small pouch with a drawstring made of rawhide, which she carried to hold food, mostly red berries and dried meat, although a rabbit roasted over a spit served them well every now and then.

She'd learned his name—White Eagle—through clever sign language. And by withholding food whenever she resisted, he forced her to learn his spoken language.

A crude communication took shape between them. From signing and pointing here and there, White Eagle progressed to repeating words in his native tongue, testing her until Celine could find a flower or plant on her own and repeat it back to him.

He was patient, and politely ignored her when she purposely mispronounced a word, either out of fatigue or plain irritability. At times, she thought she saw humor play about his face when she grew tired of the lessons, of riding, or both, and stubbornly refused to say a word correctly. He punished her by lifting her off the horse and onto the ground. She was forced to walk alongside him until she repeated the word properly, whereby he would matter-of-factly haul her back onto the horse.

Eventually, she got tired of walking.

She amused herself by speaking to him in her own language. Oftentimes, she even cursed at him in the most crude and unladylike fashion—all with the sweetest smile on her face that she could produce. And then she would laugh or giggle at herself. Crudeness brought a certain sense of freedom. Some days cursing was all that came out of her mouth.

What his intentions were after they reached their destination, she did not know. But she did know he'd had ample time and opportunity to harm her or rape her. Yet White Eagle had treated her with only gentleness and respect. She had come to trust that he would not hurt her, and he would keep her safe.

She quit rebelling.

In her yielding, something happened. Instead of relinquishing her freedom, she was surprised to find she had gained a new kind of control. A seed, deep within her soul, sprouted in a new and different way. The surrender had not been to White Eagle and to his ways, as she'd thought at first. No, it had been the letting go of the fear that he would hurt her. When she did so, to her amazement, a new confidence in acting on her own instincts surfaced.

A fine mist dampened Celine's face this morning and clung in tiny round beads to the tips of her eyelashes, laced shut from exhaustion. As usual, they'd been riding all night.

Dawn broke as the horse stepped through a clearing into a meadow. At the opposite end of a long emerald carpet of grass stood high mountain peaks, rising before Celine in breathtaking, majestic splendor.

A wondrous, almost painful sense of awe came over her, and she knew for certain she had changed. It was as if her travels through this vast unknown had mirrored a journey within. She saw and felt things completely foreign to the responses of her old self—a new pattern had emerged from her soul.

"Oh, my!"

Queenly crowns of pristine white snow ringed by thick, ermine-like fog peaked high in the heavens. A shroud of heavy mist hugged low, around the mountains' wide expanse. It was the first time Celine had seen such natural splendor.

Sunflowers and other colorful wildflowers filled the spaces between blades of thick, succulent grass. Large, graceful ferns nested thickly among pines and spruce. Elk and deer bounded from one spot to another and dotted the distance. The lilting songs of the meadowlark echoed from tree to tree.

She described it all out loud and then looked at White Eagle and smiled. "My babe survived so much to see this wonderful new land. I have to be his or her eyes for the time being."

He studied her.

"Trevor's child lies peaceful and trusting in my womb until we can meet face to face." She turned to gaze again at the splendor before her. "I wonder, does all that I am experiencing course right through me and into my babe?"

White Eagle gazed at the mountain with a reverence such as she had not previously seen in him. Could they be close to his home? Was this place so dear to him that he'd intentionally brought her to the edge of the clearing precisely at dawn so as to capture the overwhelming magic of the instant?

He must have known she would honor the moment or he wouldn't have brought her here. Had he felt the same reverence the first time he discovered this place? This was his gift to her then, a sharing of a very precious part of himself.

She stopped thinking of him as a savage.

* * *

They rode on for two more nights. On the third morning, they crested a butte overlooking a small green valley. A village formed by two circles of teepees, one inside the other, lay near the edge of a slow-moving river.

His home!

A sudden fear snaked through Celine. As they moved down the incline, drums began to beat out a pulsing rhythm. Within minutes, horses appeared from nowhere, their riders racing forward, shouting excited greetings.

A high-pitched buzzing in Celine's ears muffled the sound of children's laughter and the yelp of a small puppy tagging along. White Eagle shifted in his seat, his proud bearing filled with joy upon returning to his people.

He brought his horse to a halt and dismounted in front of a teepee in the middle of the circle. It was so tremendous in height and dimension as to dwarf the others.

All drumming stopped.

The riders disappeared. The people staring at her stepped back.

White Eagle pulled Celine off the horse, and forced her to walk by his side as they entered the teepee.

She quickly counted the people inside. Twelve in an open-ended circle, situated around a small fire in the center. But the teepee was so large the firelight did not reach its edges. As her eyes adjusted to the light, she moved toward the middle, then stiffened and let go a gasp.

"Sarah!"

Her friend appeared to be healthy, unhurt. Silently, she signaled Celine to calm herself. Celine drew in a ragged breath and, beginning from Sarah's left, scrutinized the circle of men. She did not recognize any of them. When her survey reached midpoint, however, her gaze met eyes filled with great intensity and an air of aged wisdom.

The elderly man was clearly the chief.

His rank was obvious, not so much by his dress, and the deferential manner of the others around him, but by his essence. A fathomless, timeless knowledge emanated from his chiseled countenance. The aura of dignity surrounding him left no question as to his position. A vague familiarity she could not place tugged at her.

These were strong people, like White Eagle. This man, the chief, held her in place, his keen eyes not moving from hers. It was as though his scrutiny penetrated her soul. He did not take his eyes from hers until she looked away, but she felt it was he who released the hold, not her.

When her gaze fell on the man sitting to the left of the chieftain, her mind went into a twisted buzz.

All clarity ceased.

She grew rigid and with a taut jerk of her head swiveled toward White Eagle in bewilderment.

His face was a mask of stone.

She shuddered, and returned her attention to the man across from her. His visage was a duplicate of White Eagle's stoic mask. His features, his body, held the exact likeness of the man standing next to her.

Twins!

The man sitting in front of her was the one who had captured her, had struck her skull. This man, this duplicate, considered himself to be Celine's rightful owner.

He shouted something at her that felt wicked, and then he spat into the fire. The old man in the center silenced him with a single, firm word she did not understand, and then he spoke for a long while to those assembled.

All eyes remained on the chief until he stopped speaking. Despite her language lessons, Celine could not follow him. She caught words here and there, but couldn't string them together to make any sense. White Eagle remained by her side. He had grown strangely detached, even more aloof.

The men in the circle rose and silently made their way past Celine and White Eagle. Every man's eyes were downcast. They did not acknowledge either of them. The quickening beat of drums began.

The man to Sarah's right rose and helped her to her feet. Celine was struck by the sense of them as a couple, and when they passed by, Sarah cast her eyes downward, her cheeks flushed. Despite Sarah's reserved silence, there was a luminous quality about her.

Celine's mouth gaped when she recognized an ill-concealed blush of satisfaction. The serenity on Sarah's face reminded Celine of the expression on Dianah Morgan's face the morning after she'd bid farewell to her young officer.

Sarah was in love!

In her heart, Celine knew that Sarah-of-little-words had found her home and would never leave here, but what about Celine? What was to become of her and her child?

Chapter Twenty-Three

White Eagle turned and exited with the others, leaving Celine alone in the huge teepee with the chieftain. She regarded his stoic countenance for a moment, and then tilted her head upward. A powerful force swirled in the center of the teepee, rising up to the speck of light shining through the very top. Whether or not the fire blazing in the middle of the space had created a kind of vortex, Celine didn't know, but whatever it was, the potency made her dizzy. She took a step to balance herself.

"Sit."

Celine flinched, and snapped her head forward, not sure she'd heard him right.

"Sit," he repeated in English.

She scrambled to the fire and sat across from him in blank amazement.

He flashed a proud smile. "I know plenty words. You listen good. Use them never with my people. Only with whites." Even in his boyish pride, he maintained his dignity.

"Wh . . . what is the drumming for?" Celine felt stupid. She could get nothing else out of her mouth.

"Fight of honor. Two men, one honor."

"Between White Eagle and his brother?" she asked, but already knew the answer.

He held his head high with dignity. "Why you ask? You know."

"There was conflict between the two of them after they took Sarah and me. Now I see hatred in the eyes of the man who sat next to you. I do not know his name, but—"

He silenced her with a raised hand. "Talk slow English."

She began again slowly. "I think he was the one who took me."

Parting her hair, she showed him the scar. "He hurt me here. I think White Eagle stopped him from doing more damage. I think White Eagle took me from him. Now the man is angry with White Eagle." Celine's words flowed from her, sounding much stronger than she felt.

"Other man White Eagle too. No hate. Dishonor."

Celine frowned. "I do not understand. Are you saying both men are named White Eagle?"

The chief nodded. "Only can be one White Eagle."

She was utterly confused and exasperated, but the ominous tempo of the drums outside had increased measurably, and with each quickening of the beat, the pounding of her heart quickened as well.

Suddenly she felt there could be more than one reason the chief was detaining her. Perhaps it was for his sake as well as hers. "Please explain. I do not understand. Are you saying they are fighting to the death?"

He nodded. "No can have two chiefs, only one. Name White Eagle only belong to next chief. Come in vision to Gray Wolf, father of White Eagle. My son Gray Wolf. He dead now."

My God, she'd been captured by the grandsons of a tribal chief! Celine searched frantically for an answer, or a question—either one. "If . . . if they are twins, one had to come first. Wouldn't the one born first be the one to take your place?"

"Yes. But if he dead, other White Eagle become chief. Simple. They fight. One win."

"What are you saying?" She felt as though a part of her had separated from her body and floated above the scene. Her hand slipped protectively to her belly.

"Law of people when both want to be chief." His closed fist came to his chest.

The tempo of the drums grew to a fever pitch. It was all Celine could do to keep from running. She practically shouted at the chieftain. "The law of your people? Oh my God, brother killing brother over a title?"

The gray in the chief's eyes turned the color of dark storm clouds. Dignity, honor, majesty—they were all lined in his face. His fierce expression threw terror into Celine's heart.

"The angry man who hurt me was the second born, wasn't he?" She grew dizzy again—and too confused to think. "What made this fight come about now?"

"You."

"Me? Me?" Celine splayed her fingers across her chest, not understanding, only feeling the despair of impending disaster. The duel between Trevor and Cameron flashed through her mind. Was she destined to forever be the center of a storm?

"One man, one woman. One chief, one wife. One chief, one journey." He sounded irritated now.

"Me? Wife? Wait . . . no—" Ice clogged her veins anew.

A chief's wife, carrying a white man's child? Surely they would kill it. Her hand slipped to her belly again as she was filled with fresh terror. Then her mind flashed to Sarah and her obvious comfort with these people.

"Why fight over me? Give Sarah to the other White Eagle." Good Lord, what was she saying? She pressed her hands to her cheeks as though the action would stop their burning. The serenity she thought she'd gained on the trail had evaporated.

"Two White Eagles want same white woman."

"Well, they can't have me!" Celine shot back. "They cannot simply pick a woman out of nowhere, hit her over the head, and drag her back as a mate!"

The chief eyed her with what appeared to be almost amusement.

"Let me go," she said, her voice softening as she negotiated. "That will solve the problem. There would be no reason to fight."

"You not reason for fight. You good excuse." His eyes flashed black now. "Fight come anyway, soon. Me old man."

"Oh." Images of White Eagle blurred with those of Trevor and Cameron, and of many events of the past that she suddenly realized would have come to pass inevitably, one way or another.

She was a catalyst, not a cause.

The old man's pain was clear now. These were his people, his customs. He honored his people by honoring their ways, even if it meant agony and death. Her eyes filled with tears. "I am so sorry." She wiped the corners of her eyes and spoke with great care. "You most likely know your grandsons better than anyone. Which one is the stronger, or cleverer?"

His proud bearing returned. "Both."

"Well, what is happening? What is the measure of their strength?"

He thumped his bony finger against his chest. "I teach both sons of Gray Wolf everything to stay alive—with honor. What make victor," he said, leaning forward, his eyes luminous, glittering, "is one who want woman most."

The beat of the drums stopped.

Her heart stopped with them.

Someone was dead.

And someone was coming for her.

"One White Eagle come soon when blood of brother washed away."

"Oh, no!" Nausea rose into her throat.

The chief clapped his hands twice, and two braves stepped inside, along with three women. The party escorted her to a sheltered spot along the river. The braves turned their backs. The three women reached for her clothing.

Panic bit at her again. She backed up. "No, oh no."

The shirt White Eagle had given her was torn away with one slice of a knife up the center of her back. Her chemise, the fabric nearly rotted from constant wear, gave way with little effort. And then they dragged her into the river.

"Oh, dear God! Keep my baby safe."

When she realized they were not out to hurt her, but to bathe her, she stopped fighting. The women cleaned her hair and scrubbed her body until it glowed. A shift and leggings made of pale, butter-soft hide replaced her old garment. They appeared to be of a finer caliber than what the other women wore.

But of course, she was supposed to be a chieftain's bride.

"This is insanity," she muttered. "I must find a way out."

But there was no way out. The braves returned her to the teepee where the old man still sat, stoic and unmoving.

"What now?" Did she have to ask? His failure to respond gave the answer. She waited in silence. Everything had happened so fast, she hadn't had time to think. But now that she did, her thoughts were muddled. Underlying everything was a single primitive response—protect her unborn child.

The flap of the teepee opened, and sheer panic tilted her vision when White Eagle stepped into the teepee and closed the flap behind him. In panic, she cast her eyes to the ground. He moved past her, to the other side of the fire, and stood before her. His cream-colored leggings were fringed on the sides, and they were of the same soft hide and color as her garment. Moccasins, fashioned from a similar hide, covered his feet.

Slowly, her eyes worked their way upward, hot terror rushing through her. How would she know which one he was? When her gaze reached the top of his pants, she stared. His upper body was bare. Silver cuffs encircled each wrist above long fingers and clean, even nails.

Thick, jagged scars, one stretching horizontally on each side of his chest, were the only markings disrupting the smoothness of his powerful, well-muscled form.

Firelight danced in the blue-black sheen of his thick straight hair, hanging soft and full about his broad shoulders. It framed the square set of his jaw, full lips, and high cheekbones. His depthless black eyes shone like lit coals.

In one silent, fluid motion he sat down with a commanding air, cross-legged, ramrod straight, and motionless. The chief rose and without a word or glance their way, left the teepee.

What was she to do now? Terrified, she searched the dimly lit corners of the teepee, looking for a way out.

Currents of blood leapt from her heart, throbbed up through her neck, and pounded in her brain, sending her senses reeling. Briefly, blackly, she wished the blow that had split open her head had been fatal.

From the depths of her being, Celine gathered courage. He waited. Dark eyes drilled into her. A part of her felt this man to be the same one she'd ridden with, spent so much time with. She hoped so, if this was to be her fate. She could not detect any hatred or anger in his visage. But how was she to be sure? Lethal emotions could easily have been assuaged by the battle. And if it was the *other* White Eagle, his anger might be gone because his honor had been won. If only there was something, some sign. She bit her bottom lip, and twisted at her bracelet.

White Eagle rose, walked to the inside edge of the teepee,

and returned with a small rawhide bag. He tossed it across the fire so it landed in her lap, then sat back down again.

Her berry bag!

She was too stunned to do more than stare at the small sack. With her head protectively bowed to hide her tears, Celine spoke, a thin thread of hysteria running through her words. "You're watching every little move I make, aren't you? Every little flicker, every little nuance. Nothing escapes you, does it? No wonder you people don't have much to say. You don't need to."

With a bold tilt of her head, Celine lifted her chin and deliberately met White Eagle's piercing, powerful gaze straight on.

"I am grateful you have survived, but I cannot be your bride. I simply cannot. If you cannot read that in me, then I must find a way to show you. Sarah was taken away from a cruel man, and she has found her home with your people. I walked away from someone who desperately wanted to love me, but I did not know how to help him find his way to loving me. He may be gone, but this child of his I carry needs to be with his people."

Fresh tears cascaded down her cheeks. She dropped her gaze from his and stared at the berry bag again. She was tired, and so very sad life turned out to be so cruel.

"Other White Eagle want bride. I no want bride. I will take Celine to own people."

Oh, my God!

"Did . . . did . . . did you just speak English, or did I understand your language without realizing it?" She wiped the tears from her eyes.

He smiled at her as though she were a small child. His voice was velvet-edged and strong. "Grandfather not say he teach me all? Not say he teach me white man's tongue?"

Oh, God!

"No . . . no," she stammered and swiped her hand over her

brow, furiously rubbing her temples. "I . . . I remember the exact words. Your grandfather said he taught you everything he knew for you to stay alive, with honor. Oh, dear."

"I stay alive with honor now. You no kill me with knife like you say for many moons." He chuckled.

"Oh, my God . . . oh, my God . . . oh, my God!" Celine scrambled to her feet when the full measure of his words hit her, but he was in front of her before she had time to run.

He held her by the shoulders and gazed deep in her eyes. All those months, all those horrible things she had said to him—the baring of her soul. She froze in horror as another thought struck her. Her hand shot to her stomach as terror raged anew.

He brought his closed fist to his chest. "Children know if love in heart. Babe feel love in White Eagle's heart. In hearts of my people."

A speck of joy bubbled up. Then her child would not be harmed.

Oh, the things she had said to him. Suddenly, she broke into peals of laughter and she pressed her hands to the heat of her cheeks.

White Eagle tilted his head, indicating he did not understand.

"I am so sorry. Things keep popping into my mind, things I said, things I did. Oh, my." Her face grew hotter as she recalled all her sweet-faced cursing at him. "The things I have said to you. I am absolutely mortified."

"Speak slow English."

"Oh, good then." Celine sighed. "Perhaps you didn't understand all of it. At least I hope not. Most of all, I hope you failed to understand all those terrible words a lady should never repeat."

Her face prickled. She pressed her hands to her cheeks. "Please, tell me again my child is safe."

He nodded. "Children belong to everyone in the village.

In our ways, no child is ever without a mother or father. No child is ever harmed."

Another shock wave of surprise rippled through her. "Oh, my, but how is it your English has suddenly and dramatically improved? You now speak *fast English* as well as I do. And with a clipped accent, I might add."

He reverted to his grandfather's halting pidgin English. "Better than grandfather. White Eagle live three year with Boston man who trap beaver. He leave books with White Eagle."

"Ah, so you read as well. Please, do go back to speaking fast English."

"As you wish."

"I do not understand. Why did you keep your English from me? I was not your enemy. Not in the sense your grandfather meant."

"If you knew I spoke your language, you would have held your words in. Much wiser of me to be still and listen to the wailings of your soul, the sounds of sadness in your heart."

A stream of memories clogged Celine's mind. "Well, there certainly was plenty of that going on."

"I know the woman in you. The woman in you who is as strong as a tree—and the woman in you who needs. You have come to know me in my silence, as I have come to know you in your loud wailings. I have taught you how to listen to a man in ways other than his spoken word. You watch my eyes, and they speak to you. My body moves, and you watch for its signals. You have learned to talk without speaking. You have grown sensitive to all that I am."

His countenance grew more serious. "Now, you are ready to deepen your understanding of the ways of the earth. Soon you will learn to reach far beyond the part of me that is flesh and blood, for your journey will be different now."

White Eagle's features softened as his hand gently touched the top of her head. "You are a chosen one to have been given so much pain in life. It has been your testing ground. You are ready now to learn of Celine's *nitsokan.*"

"*Nit-so-kan,*" she whispered.

"Your purpose here. As we travel the long journey to your home, Mother Earth will whisper her secrets to you. You will become one with your true mother and father, your sisters and brothers. Your soul will grow from a speck of dust until it becomes one with the earth."

She held on to his words, amazed at the man standing before her.

"You do not know yet that through your pain you have already grown in the way you were meant to do. White Eagle sees that hatred has been cut from your heart. Fear is the next foe you must attack, or it will destroy all you have worked for. Soon, you will learn ways to overcome what you fear most. You will learn to feel as you have never felt before. You will learn to listen with other than your ears, to think with your body, to touch with your mind."

Celine looked upward, to the opening of the teepee where the swirl of smoke escaped and a shaft of sunlight found the dirt floor. How odd. She'd been taught to fear this kind of man, to view Indians as ruthless savages, yet in his silence along the trail, he'd taught her a gentleness she had never known. For a moment, she felt a peace beyond words.

"Where are your people?" he asked.

She pinched the bridge of her nose. "I . . . I . . . San Francisco, I suppose. Yes, San Francisco."

"The direction the wagon train traveled?"

"Yes, it is a city where the land meets the sea. Oh, dear. You cannot possibly mean to take me all the way there."

"I must." He paused as a deeper layer of emotion flashed through his eyes. "Tonight I grieve my brother. Tomorrow we journey west."

Loud voices interrupted them, followed by whoops and hollers, and then new drumming.

“My brother returns.”

“Do you mean blood brother, or brother of the tribe?”

“My youngest brother, Sun Dog. He and his war party arrive last. His task was to see that no one followed us to the village.”

He placed his hand on the small of Celine’s back and gestured toward the teepee’s opening. She stepped outside, and together they walked to the outer circle of teepees ringing the village. They reached their destination just as a band of warriors topped a crested butte and thundered into the village.

People streamed in from every direction. Teepees all over the village spewed forth young and old alike.

At the sight of a brave astride Trevor’s mighty Friesian stallion with bloody scalps hanging from his waist, Celine’s knees gave way. One of the scalps had black, wavy hair. “Trevor!” she screamed, and collapsed on the ground, crying his name over and over in a pitiful wail.

White Eagle grabbed her and lifted her to her feet. “You must sleep. And I must go to my grieving place. We will leave at dawn.”

He took her to a teepee in the inner circle with two young women standing at the entrance. Inside she found a glowing fire, a thick pallet and blankets—and warm food. Numb and sick at heart, she was barely aware of what she ate, or of the attention the women rained on her. When sleep evaded her, something hot and bittersweet was urged past her lips.

She awoke to the sound of birds warbling out the news that dawn had broken. She’d slept through the night as though the whole world had been cast silent for those few precious hours. At sun up, White Eagle took her from the camp. She did not know what kind of exchange he had arranged with Sun Dog, but when they rode out of the village, she was on a fresh pinto while White Eagle rode Panther.

Chapter Twenty-Four

Wolf shivered in the bitter north wind and tightened the belt on the heavy jacket he'd included in his saddle pack. He swiped at clumps of fat snowflakes clinging to his eyelashes and peered into the woods through a haze of silent falling snow.

And waited.

He'd located Celine sometime back, but when he'd realized she was with child and the snow was so deep, he'd decided it would be best to let her remain where she was until after the child was born. Especially since the Indian appeared to be taking great pains to look after her.

As winter deepened, Wolf wondered if Celine would even consider going back south and leaving the brave's child behind. There seemed to be a peaceful understanding between them, and no way in hell would an Indian freely allow his child to go off and live with the whites.

The more Wolf observed the two, the more guilt chewed at his gut. It would be one thing to snatch Celine back when the timing was right, but to bring harm to the child or to the child's father was now unthinkable. And so Wolf waited, letting time take its course, never forgetting the promise he'd made to his dying friend.

He had other concerns now. A pair of trappers trailed Celine and the Indian. Wolf knew what ugly things trappers were capable of doing to a white woman caught living with an Indian. He couldn't let that happen. In some odd way, Wolf found himself acting as protector to Celine's companion as well. Wolf had to make certain the man with Celine remained safe—ultimately to keep Wolf's promise to Trevor.

Sometimes he wanted to laugh out loud at the craziness of it all. And at the endless, slow-moving winter. On other occasions, he felt time hadn't passed at all, that he was still only six years old, watching as his mother was stalked. And he was helpless through it all.

Celine had lost track of time long ago, but by now it had to be late December. Her distended belly made moving about cumbersome, so White Eagle insisted it was time to stay put until after the baby arrived. Lately, she didn't wander far from their teepee, which stood inside a wooded area that provided shelter from the snow and winds.

She had grown concerned with his decision to remain in one place. For some time, White Eagle had thought there was someone around. Trappers, he suspected. They'd happened upon them before, but White Eagle had always picked up their trail fast enough to move on.

White Eagle and Celine stood together in a clearing about twenty-five yards from the teepee. They'd been gathering wood when Celine noticed how the fresh snowflakes flashed brilliant under the sun, like diamonds strewn about the land. Braving the deep powder, she laughed and threw her head to the sky, breathing in the crisp, fresh air.

A twinge gripped her hips, the third this morning. "I think my time may be soon," she said calmly.

"I am prepared," was all White Eagle said.

A shot rang out, followed by two more sharp cracks that echoed through the woods. White Eagle jerked and astonishment filled his eyes. Just as suddenly, he grew calm and nodded toward the teepee. "Go. Now." At his words, blood spurted from his mouth, flecking the snow crimson. A red stain spread across his chest, and a line of blood dripped from beneath his sleeve and ran off his glove. "Your *nitsokan* has come." He closed his eyes and crumpled.

"Oh, no, oh no!" Celine twisted her heavy body around in the deep snow and grabbed White Eagle by an arm. She pulled and tugged, tried to drag him through the snow and back to the teepee, but she only managed to bury him deeper as she pulled. Oh, God, she couldn't leave him here. The smell of fresh blood would bring wolves.

She looked down at his chiseled, calm face, and bit her lip to keep from crying out. She braced her legs in the snow, and pulled on his arm again. A deep, tearing pain scored her belly, and a rush of warm liquid flowed down her legs. The girdle of pain moved like a line of fire, from the small of her back around to her front. No different from the first time she gave birth.

"Oh, please, no," she whispered. "Please, not now."

The pains came fast and hard. She dropped White Eagle's limp arm and crawled through the snow toward the teepee. She made it as far as the edge of the woods, where the snow wasn't as deep as in the clearing. Another pain gripped her belly. She couldn't move and lay panting on the ground in front of a birch tree.

God help her, this couldn't be happening. Panic threatened to take her under. This was not the way things were supposed to be. The baby was coming so fast, reaching the teepee would be impossible. "Help me," she muttered, "Oh, God, help me."

When the contraction subsided enough for her to move again, she wriggled out of her leggings and hiked her shift to the tops of her thighs. She gulped in air, and sweat beaded her forehead. Another pang twisted her belly. She managed to slide her hands around the trunk of the tree and pull herself into a squatting position, as White Eagle had taught her. She locked her fingers together and leaned back, letting the tree take her weight. Blood splattered onto the ground and over the snow. The scent of birth filled her nostrils. Sweat blurred her vision. When another contraction passed, she threw her head back to gulp in air.

Then she stilled.

In between the pains, she caught movement: wolves. Wiping the sweat from her eyes with her shoulder, she glimpsed yellow, hungry eyes. The wolves were closer than she'd thought. The baby was coming fast now, and she called to the heavens for White Eagle to help her, to tell her what to do.

Was this her *nitsokan?* Was this what he'd meant by being faced with a terrible fear to overcome on her journey? The wolves circled, closing in. Hunched, hungry, and waiting, they watched her.

Help me!

A shot rang out, so close she heard something whiz past her. The wolf nearest her dropped with a grunt, the others scattered.

"Oh, God," she moaned. After all she'd been through, after all she'd done to keep her baby safe, they were both going to die at the hands of trappers.

A hand touched her back, supporting her. "Come on, Celine, just a little bit more, just one more push." A strange voice, but it called her name. And the voice was gentle. She looked down to see the blur of her child's head on the bloody, frozen ground and heard the whisper in her ear again.

"There you go, there you go now. Such a sweet boy you have there, Celine."

The baby gasped, and then a thin cry stirred the air. He sucked in his breath and wailed again. Long and hard. His cry was music from the angels, and Celine laughed through her tears.

The stranger eased her onto her back, and, placing the babe on her stomach, removed a piece of rawhide lacing from the front of his buckskin shirt. Quickly, he tied the cord and cut it with his knife, then swept both Celine and the babe in his arms and rushed them into the teepee.

Gently, he placed her on the pallet, covered her with fur robes, and then swaddled the babe with what she had at the ready. He tucked the child in beside her, and covered both of them. He leaned back on his heels.

The calm that pervaded Celine as she put her child to her breast was like nothing she'd ever experienced. "What is your name?" Despite all she had been through, her voice was hushed, filled with the miracle of her newborn son.

"Wolf."

"Wolf," she repeated softly. "Your brothers were after my son and me out there."

"I had my eye on them. You were doing pretty good on your own before I could get to you."

He cleared his throat as if he had something stuck, and continued. "Found you a couple of weeks ago. I watched the two of you, and figured your companion was doing a decent job of taking care of you, so I hung back—stayed just close enough in case you needed help."

In the silence that followed, Celine regarded Wolf's tortured expression, studied his sad blue eyes. "I know you weren't the one who shot him."

He swiped his hand over his face. "I've been sheltering in a cave back a ways. The new snow surprised me this morning. Too soft and deep to move fast."

He dropped his head. "I'm sorry I didn't get here soon enough. At least I brought down the two trappers following you before they got ahold of you." His words were little more than a rasp. "I'll go out in a bit and build a platform for him." He paused a beat. "Any place you want."

She reached out and gave his hand a squeeze. "Nothing you could have done would have prevented what happened. His name was White Eagle, and he was to become his tribe's next chief."

Wolf's soft exhale held a curse.

"He was taking me to San Francisco. Along the way he taught me many things, Wolf. He taught me that there is a circle of life, and it is never ending. He did not believe in the finality of death. I think he is still among us, just in a different way."

Allowing her eyelids to drift shut seemed to help her gather more strength. "He was a brave man who insisted that taking me on this journey was part of his destiny. There was no pain in his face after it happened, only peace. I will always be grateful for what he did for me."

Except for the baby's small squeaks and occasional suckling noises, it was quiet for a long while before Celine spoke again. She opened her eyes and studied the top of Wolf's bowed head. "Who sent you?"

Wolf shrugged, but the sudden blotches in his cheeks gave him away. "I hadn't wanted to get to that part just yet."

She returned her gaze to her babe. His precious, tiny hand clutched a single finger, and she bent her head to plant a soft kiss on his forehead. "Trevor is dead, isn't he?" She touched her lips to the baby's long black lashes, then the top of his thick, black curls.

Wolf did not answer. But when he finally raised his head, the pain in his eyes shot right through her. "Wolf," she said. "This is Trevor's son."

"What?" He lurched forward and peered at the sleeping

baby, then back at Celine. “Jesus! Of course, of course,” he mumbled. “The timing.”

She lifted the babe and offered him to Wolf. “Would you like to hold Trevor’s son? His name is Brandon. I gave him his father’s middle name. It would have made Trevor proud.”

Wolf plopped down flat. She settled Brandon into his open arms, and he held the baby at an awkward angle, as if something might break. Celine took hold of Wolf’s little finger and nudged it into the baby’s fist. Brandon’s dimpled fingers clamped down. Wolf let go a hard breath. And then he chuckled. “Damn, he’s got his father in him, and it’s not just the hair.”

A smile bloomed in Celine’s heart, but she didn’t know if she had enough strength for it to find her mouth. Her eyelids fluttered shut. “I’ll leave you two alone for a moment. I am rather fatigued.”

“Trevor loved you so much. . . .” Wolf’s words clogged in his throat.

She opened her eyes and placed a hand over his and Brandon’s. “Tell me, Wolf.”

He tossed his head up and stared at the opening at the top of the teepee. His breath left his lungs in a shudder. “I have never known a man to love a woman the way he loved you. I don’t know what it was, what you two had, but I doubt there is anyone who wouldn’t want something like that.” He fell silent.

“I will never ask you what happened back by the wagon train. If I am to find Trevor, it will not be there. Instead, I will find him in my good memories, and I will see him in the heart and eyes of his son.”

Wolf swallowed hard. “We’ll stay until you and the boy are ready to travel. Then I’ll take you to San Francisco. But there’ll come a time when I will return you to Trevor’s father. It’s what I promised Trevor.”

Chapter Twenty-Five

March 1854

Trevor paced the floor of his hotel room. "Damn!" Everyone must think him dead, and he could do nothing about it. Not stuck here in Baton Rouge, anyway.

He'd been through hell trying to get from St. Joseph to New Orleans, only to find the blasted city in quarantine because of a yellow fever plague. Nothing would be moving in or out until the sickness ran its course—no mail, no ships, no goods, no people, no animals.

When he'd first arrived in St. Joseph, he'd sent a telegraph notifying his father that he was alive. Little good that would do since his father would be isolated at Carlton Oaks for the duration. Even if a message had managed to get through, a courier would have to deliver it, and that would not happen during the quarantine. Besides, there was no telling how garbled the message would end up after passing through one inadequate telegraph company after another. Damn the government for not consolidating the communications business. Too bad there weren't any lines strung to San Francisco yet.

He rubbed at his shoulder, still stiff from the arrow that

had nearly killed him. All those months isolated from the rest of the world while he suffered. Time wasted. At least he was alive, even if his life was a holy mess. If it hadn't been for those two Dakota women who'd found him, and all that ointment that made a skunk's odor smell pleasant, he wouldn't have survived.

Who would have thought, when he started after Celine, that he'd end up like this, and unable to get word to anyone? To make matters worse, before Wolf and Trevor had gone after her, he'd left specific instructions with Mr. Cummings, a barrister in St. Jo, that if Trevor failed to return within six months, Cummings was to mail a packet to Trevor's father containing Trevor's last will and testament. His father would have sent word to Cameron. They were probably all finished grieving by now.

A dark shaft of loneliness sliced through Trevor. He'd worked his way back to St. Joseph with one thought in mind—Celine. But she wasn't there, and no one had seen Wolf since the day he'd ridden out with Trevor. If they'd returned, Wolf would have taken her through St. Jo, with Mr. Cummings acting as their point of contact.

So what had happened to Celine? That awful sensation of a fist to his gut hit him again. Either Wolf had failed to rescue her and they were both dead, or Wolf had met his demise, and she was living with the Indians. Or perhaps they'd managed to make it to San Francisco. No, St. Joseph would've been closer. Making it all the way to California was the slimmest chance of all.

Despite the odds, Trevor refused to accept the notion that he would never see her again. He chose to believe she was either with the Indians, back in New Orleans, or living in San Francisco.

He drew in a ragged breath. The previous quarantine had lasted three months. He wasn't about to sit around the hotel waiting for it to lift. Since he couldn't very well locate every

Indian village west of the Mississippi, and since he was cut off from New Orleans, he ought to consider sailing to California.

A dull ache started at the back of his head. He should probably eat something. He paced again. If only his mind would give him a moment's rest. His brain relentlessly ground out different plans of action. Had he known about the yellow fever, he would have gone straight to San Francisco instead of coming here. Too late for that kind of backward thinking; it served no purpose. Returning to St. Joseph didn't feel quite right either. If Wolf did happen to show up, Cummings would know Trevor's whereabouts and send a telegraph.

He flopped onto the bed and covered his eyes. His rampant thoughts took over again. Why not take a train to Boston and find out if Donald McKay had their next clipper ready? He sat up at a rush of emotion. It felt good. Real good. With or without McKay, surely he could manage to find *something* out of Boston headed for San Francisco. He sprang from the bed, and threw on his jacket. He would telegraph Cummings and let him know he was headed east.

St. Joseph, Missouri

"Jeeesus, what a mess." Wolf stood, knocking the chair out from under him as he did so. Trail dust sifted off his buckskins as he strode over to a small table holding a bottle of whiskey and two shot glasses. He filled them both and, raising one, glanced over at George Cummings.

The portly barrister declined with a wave of his pudgy hand. "It's ten in the morning."

Wolf downed one shot and, picking up the other, moved to the window, hitched one hip onto the deep-set sill, and stared out at nothing in particular.

Cummings chuckled. "That's what you get for involving yourself with clients."

Wolf shot a scowl over his shoulder, and then went back to sipping his whiskey. "I'm looking for solutions, not mindless babble."

"If a decision is what you're after, may I suggest you take a bath, get a shave, and haul your behind back on your horse and point its nose west. Then ride like you mean it."

Wolf strode over to the desk, leaned against it with stiff arms, and glared at Cummings. "You're serious, aren't you?"

Cummings stroked the ends of his moustache as he slowly nodded. "That I am, sir. You and Trevor barely missed one another coming and going." He tapped the telegraph cable sitting in front of him. "Says here he left yesterday out of Boston. Care to miss him again?"

"No." Wolf steamed with frustration that he'd missed Trevor by a little over a week. He shouldn't have held off so long on returning from San Francisco, damn it. But he'd needed a rest once he got Celine settled in her friend's hotel. He'd also struck up a friendship with Cameron Andrews, another reason he'd been in no hurry to return. Now Wolf was beginning to wonder what the hell he'd come back to.

He flipped through the pile of open mail on the desk. One letter was from Trevor, telling Wolf to meet him in San Francisco around the middle of June. Dread, heavy as a brick, sank in his gut every time he picked up the other missive. This one had arrived from Justin right before the quarantine shut down all communication. He wrote that he'd received a letter from Cameron stating he intended to marry Celine so they could properly raise Trevor's son.

Wolf cursed again. "Can you imagine Trevor sailing into San Francisco and announcing he's alive, only to run smack into Cameron and his new bride of say, two, maybe three days? Ain't that going to be one helluva sweet mess?"

"Not if you get there first and break the news," Cummings said.

"I can't . . ."

"Yes you can, Wolf."

"You're right, Cummings. That's what I get for making friends."

Cummings turned his chair around and opened a cabinet door, revealing a small safe. After a few spins and clicks on the lock, the door opened. He counted out a stack of bills and handed them to Wolf. "You'll need this. And ride with care. There are a few good people depending on you."

"Guess there's not much goddamn choice," Wolf muttered.

"I suppose you could ignore the entire situation and go about your life like you did before you ever met Trevor."

"I supposed I could." Wolf stuffed the money into his saddlebag, slung it over his shoulder and headed for the door. "But I won't."

July, San Francisco

Bearded and weary, Wolf strode through the door of the Andrews Shipping Company Limited.

Cameron tossed his pencil down, and stood. "Wolf!"

Wolf fell into a chair opposite Cameron, stretched his legs out in front of him, and crossed his booted feet at the ankles.

Cameron rested a hip on the corner of his desk. "By God, you made it in time for the wedding."

"Yup." Wolf leaned hard against the back of the chair, tipped its front legs off the floor, and crossed his arms over his chest.

Cameron glanced down at Wolf's muddy boots marking the good Chinese carpet.

Wolf snorted and rubbed at eyes that hurt so bad he could barely keep them open. "Got any coffee? Something to eat?"

"Mr. Abbott," Cameron boomed at his bookkeeper. "In all your days, have you ever seen a more disheveled person?"

The man winced, erased the pencil mark on the ledger his flinching had produced, and continued on without a glance upward. "No, sir."

Cameron grinned. "Well, you have now."

Abbott set his pencil down and heaved a sigh. "I most certainly have not noticed your visitor, Mr. Andrews. I am much too busy making certain the books are in order before you leave port tomorrow."

Devilish satisfaction settled into Cameron's grin. "Would you mind rousting something up for Wolf?"

Abbott sighed again, scratched hard at a muttonchop sideburn, and withdrew his watch from his vest pocket. He set his pencil down, closed the ledger in front of him, and snapped his watch shut with a loud click. He stood, rolling down his shirtsleeves. "I may as well break for lunch at the same time so you don't get charged extra for duties beyond what I was hired for."

Wolf shot Abbott a sardonic grin. "Good to see your mood stays regular as your timepiece."

The bookkeeper slipped into his jacket. "What makes me think trouble just walked in? I'll return in half an hour."

When the door closed, Cameron turned back to Wolf. "What with the quarantine in New Orleans, I didn't know if you'd received the letter I sent through my uncle. I mailed one across country as well, but it probably won't arrive in St. Jo before the next decade. We've been looking for you every day of late. I was about to give up, but you know how Celine can be."

Wolf shifted in his seat. "Didn't think I was going to make it in time." His gaze lowered along with his voice while he searched for words. "How's Brandon?"

"He's fine." A shadow slid across Cameron's countenance. He leaned back on the flat of his hands, studying Wolf. "His mother is fine, as well."

Wolf gave a slight nod. He didn't want Celine mentioned just yet. "Need to talk to you about something."

Cameron gave a shrug as if he wasn't concerned, but he folded his arms across his chest and lowered his lids. "Go on."

The silence lengthened between them.

Finally, Wolf spoke. "I just rode in. Didn't even make it to the hotel." He fell silent again.

Cameron's eyes narrowed. "What the devil is going on, Wolf?"

"I need to tell you . . ." Wolf swept the back of his hand over his mouth. "Ah, hell. Trevor's alive."

Cameron sat frozen on the edge of his desk, a blank look on his face. And then he jumped to his feet, and in long strides, moved to the window facing the bay. "My God, Trevor is alive! How?"

Wolf shifted his weight in the chair and fiddled with his thumbs. "Don't know much in the way of details. I only know what I heard from Cummings in St. Jo and a short letter from Trevor. Seems after I went to get help, a couple of young Dakota women came along—sisters. They thought I'd left Trevor for good, so they dragged him off to some little island in the middle of a lake. Turns out it was a Dakota burial ground. Their mother had just died, so they hauled him onto the funeral platform and stretched him out next to the mother."

"Mon Dieu!"

"Don't know how the hell they managed all that, since I couldn't have lifted him back on my horse once I got him lowered to the ground."

Cameron returned to his chair behind the desk. He picked up a cheroot and lit it with trembling fingers.

Wolf studied him. "Do you know what Indians do when they grieve?"

"No."

"They wail, that's what they do. Hard telling what all else, but they do get left alone. So, when Trevor was lost in a fever and moaning, the girls sat up there with him and their dead mother and howled over the top of his groans so no one else would hear him. Brought him food. Nobody paid them any mind. Thought they were taking it to their dead mother as an offering. Somehow they got the arrow out of his back and greased him up with bear fat and herbs. Jesus. Can you imagine spending weeks in a damn hellhole of a graveyard?"

Cameron stared out the bay window over Wolf's shoulder. "Go on."

"When I got to St. Jo, Cummings had a few telegraphs from Trevor sitting on his desk. Since Trevor couldn't get through to New Orleans on account of the quarantine, he caught a train to Boston to pick up a ship that was due for completion."

"The *Serenity,*" Cameron responded. "Fitting name under the circumstances." There was the faintest tremor in his otherwise calm voice.

"That's the one Trevor said he'd be taking."

Cameron nodded absently. "It would be." There was another long pause. He pressed his shaking fingers to his forehead and drew circles on his skin. "It took me months to accept that my cousin would never again walk through life with me." He pointed to the door. "For a long while, every time that door opened and closed, I looked up expecting—" He pinched the bridge of his nose. "Do you have any idea how many times a clipper sailed into the harbor and I stood at the dock, hoping Trevor would be on it? Christ."

He rested his head against the high back of the brown leather chair and lowered his lashes, looking through them at Wolf. "Celine needs to be informed right away."

"I know." Wolf went back to his silent study of Cameron. "Need to be alone?"

Cameron nodded. "Meet me here in the morning. Seven sharp."

Wolf walked in at daybreak, a hangover hammering his head.

Cameron sat at his desk. "Did you sleep in those clothes?"

Wolf sat in the chair across from Cameron. "How did Celine take the news?"

"I didn't tell her."

Wolf shot out of the chair and leaned, stiff-armed, on the desk. "Well, you have about thirty-six goddamn hours to do so before Trevor arrives, *mon sewer,* or she's going to get the surprise of her life."

"Three hours is more like it."

"Ah, Christ." Wolf rolled his bloodshot eyes. "You damn, stupid N'awlins French. Do you know where Celine probably is right now? Having breakfast with Dianah and deciding on last-minute arrangements for the wedding. For *tomorrow's* wedding in case you forgot the date."

Cameron drummed his fingers on the desk, his eyes sparkling. "I didn't manage much sleep either. But my restlessness was from excitement, not worry. It seems my dear cousin may have spent a few weeks lying beside a dead Indian, monsieur, but it has not dampened his competitive spirit in the least. One of our other ships, the *Felicité,* arrived a little bit ago. According to the captain, the *Serenity* left Boston two weeks after the *Felicité* and has been trying to catch up and pass her for the last three days."

Wolf shoved his hand through his hair and cursed under his breath. "Yet you still haven't bothered to inform Celine?"

Cameron thumped a fist on his desk, his eyes glittering with excitement. "Think on it, Wolf. Trevor managed to survive!"

"And is due here any goddamn minute." Wolf jumped to

his feet and stormed around the office. "What the hell are you thinking?"

"I do not expect you to understand this, Wolf. But Celine has already run off once. And even though she might be more mature than she was back then, I am not about to take any chances—"

Wolf paused in midstep. "Don't tell me you're about to pull the same stupid bullshit that ran her off last time?"

"Stop." Cameron raised his hand between them. "I have a plan. And you, sir, will not have the opportunity to call me an ignorant French Creole again."

"Oh, brilliant. You have a plan. Why are my toes curling in my boots?"

Cameron laughed. "This is one I am handling personally. And I guarantee results. So I suggest you find someplace to sleep off that infernal hangover. I don't want you around when Trevor walks in, not with the way your salty tongue would give him news that Celine is alive."

He leaned back in his chair and took inventory of Wolf. "I'll wager you can't last another three hours in your state. If you remain here, you'll end up curled in the corner sleeping off your stupor when the man who hired you to find Celine walks in. Wouldn't that make you a bloody impressive employee?"

A snide remark danced over Wolf's tongue.

Cameron chuckled. "Don't bother. In your condition, you don't have a chance of exchanging barbs with me. *Au revoir.*"

Wolf walked out, closed the door, then opened it again and stuck in his head. "You have no idea just how big this country is, my friend. Not until you cross it a few times in a sitting position. As for me, I'm getting pretty damn sick of it."

Chapter Twenty-Six

Trevor maneuvered the sleek and powerful *Serenity* into San Francisco Bay under full sail and blue skies. His first mate stood beside him pointing to a wharf lined with wooden buildings. "When we dock, sir, you'll find the Andrews Shipping Company offices starboard. As you said, I'll see to the clipper's moorings, and you can be on your way. Nothing to concern yourself with."

Trevor's jaw twitched, the only outward sign of his nervousness—something he couldn't keep in check. A band around his chest tightened, and he struggled to breathe. "Thank you, Grogan. Go ahead and take the wheel from here."

Stepping aside, Trevor moved to the bow. Was it too much to think someone might be on the docks waiting to greet him? Grogan barked orders as a clang of the harbormaster's bells signaled the clipper to moor. Seagulls wheeled through the air, their shrill calls piercing the sky.

"That's Telegraph Hill up ahead, Captain," Grogan called out. "The tall tower with those strange metal arms waving about are signals we're arriving and what goods we carry. An odd piece of equipment, but it works. Mail won't get sorted until tomorrow, but they'll be lining up at the postal office tonight."

Trevor, standing on the foredeck with his feet braced wide and his hands clasped behind his back, merely nodded, but someplace deep inside, his emotions ran hot and cold.

Celine.

The idea of stepping onto land only to receive bad news soured his stomach.

The clipper moved gracefully—and agonizingly slowly—to a dock rapidly filling with people. Tomorrow, after the ship was emptied and cleaned, he would allow curious onlookers a tour of the clipper's interior. The air smelled different now, a common waterfront mixture of fish and human life replacing the fresh scent of the open seas.

He spied the company sign above a large gray clapboard building and nodded to onlookers as he headed down the gangplank. No one familiar was there to greet him. What did he expect, a parade? Damn it, he wished the pounding of his heart would quiet. Cameron was most likely in his office since the *Serenity* wasn't expected for another three days, and God only knew if Wolf was alive and had received Trevor's message.

But Wolf *was* alive. He sat on the front steps of the Andrews Shipping Company Limited, looking exactly the same as when Trevor had first seen him in the St. Joseph saloon, complete with dirty buckskins, bedraggled hair and beard. As he approached, he grinned at Wolf. "*Mon Dieu,* but you never change, do you?"

Wolf stood. "About time you got here."

They regarded one another for a long moment. Trevor's heart gripped in his chest when Wolf offered nothing about Celine—which meant there wasn't anything Trevor wanted to hear. His gut clenched and then dropped to his feet. He offered Wolf a handshake. "Good to see you."

Wolf stepped forward. And in an act completely unlike

him, he shook Trevor's outstretched hand, and then pulled him in for a hard and fast hug, ending with a slap on the back. Were his eyes moist? Knowing Wolf, he'd have to find some excuse to walk away. If emotions were high, he would hide them by exiting.

"Gotta go," Wolf said.

Trevor snorted.

Wolf took a couple of steps and paused to glance over his shoulder. "Cameron's inside and expecting you, said we should meet at the Morgan Hotel for dinner around eight. Guess that's where you'll be staying as well, so see you there."

"Right, yes." Trevor took a breath past the pain in his chest and blew it out. *Go, damn it. Get out of here before I ask something I don't want to hear*. Not yet, anyway.

Cameron was at his desk when Trevor walked in. His cousin clasped his hands behind his head and leaned back in his chair. "I say, old boy, you are one hour late."

Trevor chuckled and stood before Cameron, fists on hips. And he smiled. From the very depths of his soul, he grinned. God, it felt good to see family.

With a hoot and a slap on his desk, Cameron stood and made his way over to Trevor. He, too, only shook hands at first, but then the pat on the back became another hug. "I hear you have a penchant for Indian burial grounds, old boy."

"Which I hope never to see again." No mention of Celine. Nothing. He'd expected as much after Wolf had neglected to say anything. Christ, there went that damn sledgehammer to his gut again.

"Did you run into that miserable Wolf out front? I saw him lurking about despite my orders he find a bath."

About to jump out of his skin, Trevor managed a smile. "I see you and Wolf get on well."

A corner of Cameron's lips lifted. "He'll do. He only got in yesterday after a long ride from St. Joseph. He'd just arrived there, got your telegraph from Cummings, and then turned right around and headed back here." Cameron grunted. "I have to hand it to the man, he's loyal."

"It's the money," Trevor responded, not meaning it.

"As I thought."

Abbott brought in lunch, greeted Trevor as though he'd only been on holiday, and then discreetly excused himself for the remainder of the day. Over lunch, Cameron gave Trevor a cursory company report. Afterward, he settled back to listen to Trevor's tale.

Cameron glanced over at the time. "There's a place I'd like to show you before the afternoon gets away from us."

Trevor shrugged. "I don't have anything to do until the dinner hour." As the depth of his misery took another notch downward, he felt oddly removed from the scene.

On the way out, Cameron grabbed a small spyglass from the top of the credenza. Trevor raised a quizzical eyebrow but paid no further attention. He wasn't eager to ask questions. He'd have to settle for being relieved to be in his cousin's company again.

They climbed into the open carriage, and Cameron took the reins, guiding the horses south, out beyond the city and along the cliffs overlooking the ocean.

"The view is phenomenal," Trevor said. "Do you like it here?" Damn, couldn't someone mention Celine before he had to ask? His stomach did another couple of turns.

Cameron gave the reins a shake, clicked his tongue, and the horse sped up. "I've grown comfortable enough, made a few friends. I had a trip to China planned. Been feeling an urge to sail."

"*Had* planned?"

Cameron didn't respond, but turned off the highway and traveled a narrow road that climbed higher along the cliffs overlooking the sea, where the view was even more spectacular. He pulled the carriage up behind another that had been unhitched, the horse nowhere in sight. He placed a finger to his lips and spoke in a hushed voice. "You are about to have quite a remarkable experience. Trust me when I ask you to give me your word you will not utter a sound, nor make yourself known."

Curiosity piqued, Trevor nodded.

Cameron led him up a small footpath between an outcropping of large boulders. The path opened to a rolling, grassy vale that led down to the sand and the sea. Cameron motioned for Trevor to sit next to him on a seat nature had carved in the large boulder. Then he pointed west.

A black horse grazing on the grass reminded Trevor of Panther—lost to the Indians. A small, clapboard home caught his eye. In front of it, what appeared to be an Indian was sitting on a blanket holding a babe. He looked at Cameron and shrugged. "You brought me here for this?"

Cameron handed Trevor the spyglass and pointed toward the horse. Trevor lifted the glass to his eye. What? A jolt shot through him. He looked at Cameron. "Is that—"

Cameron grinned and slowly nodded.

Trevor brought the spyglass to his eye again and went back to studying the horse. "*Mon Dieu,* Panther. I suppose Wolf expects a bonus."

Cameron chuckled. "Shh."

Trevor swallowed a lump of emotion that felt like grief releasing. "That black devil of mine, he'll survive anything." He used the spyglass and his naked eye to gain different perspectives, intently scrutinizing the horse. He studied the woman in native dress and then the small house. "Is that someone Wolf met along the way? Their house?"

Cameron waited, wordlessly.

Thought cleaved a path to understanding. Trevor's breath escaped his lungs with a loud whoosh. He snapped the spyglass from his eye just long enough to gain a full view and then brought it up again, aiming at the woman. His senses went reeling.

"Christ!"

He started to stand.

Cameron grabbed him by the arm and held him back. "Celine doesn't know about you yet, and we don't want her reacting badly. Pull yourself together, and let's do things right this time."

Trevor's head dropped to his trembling hands. Months of hell without her. He'd spent his entire trip from Boston getting used to the idea that she was likely gone. That she couldn't possibly be here. His grief had been so great, so consuming, he couldn't put it behind him instantly. A great jumble of questions filled his head, but he couldn't put any thoughts into words. Only her name.

"Celine."

He studied her, savored the sweet agony of having found her. He kept the glass to his eye for a long while, drinking her in. "What's that child doing with her?"

Cameron did not answer.

When Trevor lowered the glass and turned to Cameron, he saw glittering eyes, and a wild grin. "His name is Brandon. He was born last December, and Celine is his mother."

"But Celine cannot—" It took Trevor less than a minute to count backward. He shook visibly now, and it took all his strength not to make a mad dash toward mother and child. "My God, I have a family!"

Cameron was right. In Trevor's current state, to rush down to the beach and reveal himself could be a terrible blunder. And he wasn't about to make any more mistakes, not if he could help it. She had run off once, and knowing Celine, she would be protective of her child. "Good Lord, what a story she must have to tell!"

He rubbed a hand over his face and then left it over his eyes as he tried to control his trembling body.

Cameron placed a hand on Trevor's shoulder. "We should go. I'll tell you everything on the drive back."

* * *

A light breeze caught Celine's hair, and she tucked a loose tendril behind her ear as she stood beside Dianah on the deck of the clipper *Felicité.* The chef from the Morgan Hotel scurried about, barking orders to those festooning the long tables. Tall vases filled with flowers lined one side of the ship like colorful soldiers awaiting orders, reminding Celine of another morning of preparation—her Carlton Oaks ball. At the memory of her time with Trevor in the hayloft, her heart pinched. It wasn't right thinking of him on her wedding day. She should be ashamed.

She turned from the scene before her, only to spy an elaborate wrought iron altar at the opposite end of the ship, a red velvet prie-dieu for the bride and groom placed before it. Judge Morgan would soon stand in front of her and Cameron, and unite them in holy matrimony. Her ears filled with an odd, high buzz. What was wrong with her? Today was to become the foundation for the family she would build. Her son needed a father. And siblings. She shut her eyes, swallowing hard.

"Oh my, Celine, would you look at that?"

She turned at Dianah's breathless words. "At what?"

"I should have said at *him.*" Dianah raised a fan to her face until just her catlike eyes peered over its feathered edges. She nodded toward the gangplank.

Wolf sauntered aboard. His lean, muscled hips rolled with an easy grace beneath a pair of snug, gray flannel trousers. The span of his shoulders seemed wider beneath a finely cut black jacket. His hair, tied neatly at his nape, glistened tawny gold in the sun. His chiseled, cleanly shaven face was cast bronze by his crisp white shirt and stock tie. He headed straight for Celine and Dianah, his assessing blue eyes magnetic as he approached, the garnet earring in his left ear winking in the sunlight.

"Oh, my word," Celine gasped. "Who would've guessed there was such beauty beneath all that . . . that dishevelment?"

A throaty chuckle swept around the edges of Dianah's fan. "Could that possibly be the same dirty, dusty man who charged into my elegant dining room a few months back, carrying Brandon and dragging you along, while he announced he was hungry as a bear after hibernation?"

Tears stung the backs of Celine's eyes. He'd dressed like this for her. He'd asked if he could walk her down the aisle, and she'd assumed he would do so in a pair of buckskins. But she hadn't cared what he wore. He was stepping in for a father she did not have. "He's family now, isn't he?"

Dianah nodded. "An odd lot we are, but family he is since he has none of his own. After today, though, I might consider making him a kissing cousin."

"You have wicked thoughts, Dianah."

"And I've been known to act on a few without regret." Dianah leaned to her left and gazed beyond Wolf. "It seems we have yet another early guest."

At the sight of Cameron, Celine's heart kicked in her chest. "Guest? He's the groom, for heaven's sake. He shouldn't see me before the wedding." She hurried toward the captain's quarters. "I've had enough bad luck to last a lifetime."

She entered the captain's quarters and wandered around the elegant space, checking to see that everything had been readied. She spied a note on the bed with her name on it and picked it up. A long-stemmed red rose had been drawn around the *C* in her name. She opened the note.

"*Ma petite,*" was all it said. Tears clogged her throat. Oh, she could not bear to have Cameron use that endearment. "Trevor," she whispered. Not a day went by that she didn't cradle her son and feel his father's presence. How could she expect to marry another man when not a moment passed when she wasn't aware of a vital part of her that remained hollow?

Was she doing the right thing? Was she being fair to Cameron? To herself? She should be excited, but instead there was a nauseating knot in her stomach that had tightened to the point of pain. This was her wedding day. But oh, how her heart ached.

She held the note for several moments. Trevor. Nothing she did dismissed him from her heart. Facing the truth would be painful, but living with a lie could prove devastating down the road.

She could not go through with the wedding.

Brandon would have to settle for an uncle helping to raise him, not a stepfather. She wasn't a weakling. After all she'd been through, she'd grown into a strong and capable woman. She could raise Brandon on her own and never marry another, because her love for Trevor simply refused to die. A sense of relief washed through her, cleansing her like a light summer's rain.

The door opened, and her breath caught. Cameron. His footsteps fell across the floorboards behind her. Odd how they sounded so different aboard ship. She kept her back to him, and eased the air from her lungs. He'd been so kind, so valorous, she couldn't bear to face him just yet. The last thing she wanted to do was hurt him. Fresh tears filled her throat as she spoke. "I . . . I cannot marry you, Cameron. I cannot go through with this—with us. You are a dear friend, and I love you like a brother. But that is all we can ever be to one another."

When he said nothing, and the long silence wrenched her insides, she turned to face him.

"Oh!" Her hand came to her throat. She stared blankly, her thoughts scattering to the four corners of the earth.

Trevor stood before her, holding a handkerchief in his outstretched hand.

"I love you, Celine." His words came from deep in his chest, husky and raw.

She tried to respond, but her voice wouldn't work. Her hand flailed behind her, searching for the bed before her knees gave out. Her back went up against the wall. How did she get so turned around? She stood there, staring into those hypnotic onyx eyes as though she'd fallen into another world.

"Before anything else is said," he continued, "I wanted to be sure to say those words."

He was so handsome, so wonderfully *there.* So alive! His gaze didn't budge from hers, and for a long moment, she thought she might just float to the ceiling. Think. She couldn't think. One hand pressed against her stomach as if to help release the air from her frozen lungs.

"I failed so miserably in the past, Celine. Dear God, but I love you. In fact, I don't think I can remember when I haven't loved you. I think I fell in love with you the first time I laid eyes on you."

Oh, Lord. A kind of pain mingled with a bubble of joy, but it did nothing to help her speak.

In two steps he was in front of her, his heady masculinity engulfing her. He leaned one hand against the wall next to her ear and curled his finger under her chin, lifting it. "There you were, standing on the balcony peering down at me." His words were soft but hoarse as they floated hot across her mouth. "I couldn't get to you fast enough to find out if you were real or not." His thumb traced her ear, melting her bones.

He didn't ease closer, and the distance between them acted like a magnet. When she arched forward, her breasts touching his chest, he bent down and planted a soft kiss on her lips.

She opened to him, and accepted the sweep of his tongue

across hers with a small moan. God, but she had missed him—missed that.

He pulled back, his eyes shimmering. "And whenever I was near you, I had the deepest longing to kiss you." He pressed his lips to hers again.

He slid his arms around her and gently set her cheek to his warm chest. His heart thundered in her ear; his heat enveloped her. She had yet to speak—she could not. Was he here? Was this real? Yes, dear Lord, he was here, holding her, and she would never let him go.

She lifted her head and, gazing up at him, blinked. Tears splashed down her cheeks. He caught them with the handkerchief. "Can we pick up where we left off in New Orleans, my love? Will you marry me?"

Her trembling fingers found his cheek and she traced his jawline. "There are things you do not know. Things you *must* know. I have—"

He stopped her words with a kiss, dizzying her senses. "Cameron told me how you lived among the Indians, and that you dress as one every now and then to honor the man who saved you. I also remember that you are a widow. I imagine you will be twice widowed before your life is done, seeing as how you are younger than I, and I don't have a lick of sense when it comes to taking chances. Will you marry me anyway?"

She sucked in a breath through the tears clogging her throat. "There is one more thing. We have a—"

"And as for our son—"

"You know." A sob broke loose.

"I have the utmost confidence you have cared for him in quite a respectable manner in my absence." His lips touched her ear and she felt him grin. "Although those damnable feathers have to go when he's in public."

"Oh!" His silly, wonderful words coursed clear through her bones and swam in her veins. Her arms swept under his jacket and her fingers traced up and down his spine, across his broad, muscled back. He pulled her in tighter until she was in a world filled only with him.

Celine pulled back a bit to gaze up at him. She shook her head, a smile breaking through the tears. "I love you. And yes, Trevor Brandon Andrews, I would very much like to marry you. Today if you are willing."

His low laughter rumbled through his chest. "I do believe that's what this day is about, *ma petite.* I had no intention of letting you escape this room until you said yes." And then his mouth was on hers again, this time hungry, filled with fire and purpose. He pressed fully against her length, parted her legs with his knee, his large hand cupping her breast, tracing circles.

She moaned and her fingers clutched his shirt. "We're not going to make it out of here, are we?"

He paused, pressed his forehead to hers, and sucked in a deep breath, the exhale falling sweet and warm against her mouth. "We should wait. At least a few bloody hours. I can hear too many footfalls on deck."

Laughter, filled with more joy than she'd ever known, left her lips. "Indeed." She gave him a quick kiss. "Have you seen Wolf in all his finery? He would never forgive us if we failed to show."

"Nor would Dianah. Or rather her popinjay of a chef. He's probably cursing us now for all the food getting cold. Besides, I've one more thing that needs doing before we wed."

"Really? Then kindly remove your hand from my bosom so we can get on with things. And on your way to whatever needs doing, will you tell Dianah to send in the maid to help me change?"

He stepped away from her, glanced forlornly at the bed, and headed for the door. "Give me twenty minutes to return before you make your entrance."

The maid must have been right outside because the door had barely closed when it opened again and she slipped inside.

Celine was no help at all. Her fingers shook and she cursed at the tears that threatened to blotch her face. "Oh, do hurry. Has it been twenty minutes, do you suppose?"

At the maid's nod indicating she was finished, Celine stepped to the mirror. "Oh, dear, I hope I don't spend the day weeping." The ring of fresh flowers in her hair with a short veil attached to the back had been Dianah's idea. A good one. And the simple white lace gown, one in which she could move easily about on deck, fit every curve.

She turned and made her way down a corridor that led to the small gathering. She took in small gulps of air as she went. As she stepped through the door, her gaze flitted among the guests. No matter how much time Celine had taken, and no matter how much composure she had mustered, tears stung her eyes again at the sight of Wolf waiting for her.

Wolf, so handsome and refined looking, stepped forward and offered his arm. "May I?"

She slipped her arm through the crook of his. "Has Trevor returned? Am I too early? I was so anxious."

A grin curled one side of his mouth as he guided her between the rows of flowers that carved a path to the altar. "He's here, and he brought back what he went after. Take a look."

Trevor stood at the altar with Brandon in his arms and with Cameron standing beside them. The love blazing in Trevor's eyes spanned the distance between him and Celine, so powerful that the air crackled and overwhelmed her senses.

She found her breath again and leaned into Wolf, her knees no more solid than water. "Oh, my God, I think I'm going to faint."

Wolf gripped her tighter and led her to the altar.

Trevor, never taking his fiery gaze from Celine's, handed Brandon to Cameron, and extended a hand to her. "I decided my son ought to be present when I wed his mother. Come, my love, and marry me."

Epilogue

Thirty years later, somewhere north of San Francisco along the Russian River

"Mother?"

"Brandon, there you are. Come in." Celine set her diary and pen down and motioned for him to join her by the crackling fire. "I was thinking of tea, would you care for a cup?"

He shook his head, and rather than sitting, leaned an elbow against the corner of the French mantel and crossed his booted feet at the ankles. "I am packed and need to get going, or I won't make San Francisco before nightfall."

Celine rested her head against the back of her blue velvet chair and studied her son, who had yet to don his jacket. "You are so like your father. At times, I find the uncanny resemblance rather eerie. You even stand like him." A honeyed warmth flowed through her. "What a fine figure of a man you turned out to be."

Brandon snorted. "Speaking of Father, where is he?"

"He's not slept a wink. The mare foaled about three hours ago." She stood and brushed the wrinkles from her skirt. "Shall we go to him so you can say your good-byes?"

Brandon stepped forward. She slipped her hand through

the crook of his elbow and together they moved onto the terrace running the length of the house, and then strolled along the wooded path toward the stable. Celine lifted her chin and drew in a long breath. "You are going to miss these wonderful pines back in the city."

"I always do. But then, I never fail to return, do I?"

"Next time, I do hope it's with a wife."

Laughter rumbled deep in his chest. "A pity I haven't found one to share your pedestal."

"Oh, aren't you the clever one?" She squeezed his arm and then paused. "I need to ask you something before we reach your father."

Brandon's brows knitted together. "I don't know that I care for the look in your eye, Mother. If this is about Nathan and Ethan, you are going to have to ask them. Brothers do not rat on brothers."

Her stomach churned and she turned her gaze to the tips of her toes. "As if they are ever here to ask them anything." She rubbed at her temples. "Please, Brandon. I must know. I am their mother, and they are so wild and reckless, they worry me sleepless. Twins feed off one another, and there is no telling what they've gotten themselves into."

Brandon bent, picked up a pinecone, and sniffed at it. "They are not in any trouble if that's what you are getting at."

She stamped a foot. "Oh, you are just as evasive as your father." She fisted her hands on her hips, paced a few feet away, and then stomped back. "Are they privateers? Spies?"

Brandon leaned his back against a tree and for a long while regarded her through lazy lids. "And if I said yes to either of those, would you only worry more?"

Gazes locked, they stared at one another until laughter, a bubble of relief, slipped past her lips. She pressed her hands to her mouth. "That's what I needed to know. There's a letter on the entry table. Will you see they get it?"

He nodded, used the heel of his boot to lift himself off the tree, and escorted her to the stable.

Trevor turned from the stall holding the mare and her newborn, the shadows under his eyes diminished by his wide grin. "We've got another Panther in the making. This one's a beauty."

Celine held back while Brandon stepped forward and peered into the stall. Seeing her husband and grown son side by side never failed to fill her with a satisfaction that bordered on overwhelming. She waited as they said their good-byes, and after a hug and kiss on the cheek, watched Brandon disappear into the house.

Trevor turned to her. "We have an anniversary."

"Anniversary?"

He nodded toward the ladder leading to the loft. "Come." Climbing up first, he lifted Celine from the top rung and onto a blanket spread out on the hay. Beside the blanket sat a basket filled with cheese, grapes, and wine.

Still puzzled, she shrugged.

He placed a hand over his heart. "You wound me."

And then understanding struck her—the hayloft back at Carlton Oaks. The fancy ball in her honor. "Oh, Trevor!"

He pulled her to the blanket and lay on his stomach. "Now, if you'll give Brandon a moment, you'll see him riding off down the road."

She smiled. "And there he goes." After he disappeared from view, she extended her arm and mischievously twisted her wrist about until the sun catching the gold of her bracelet glinted in Trevor's eyes. "Have I told you lately that I love you?"

He turned on his side, and, fitting his length against hers, breathed a warm kiss across her cheek. "I would rather you show me, *ma petite.*"

ACKNOWLEDGMENTS

Celine and Trevor would not have found their place in the magical world of storytelling without the help of some wonderful people working behind the scenes. To those of you who supported and encouraged me, I am forever grateful.

To the Research and Collections department of Oak Alley Plantation in Vacherie, Louisiana: Thank you for my personal tour of a fabulous antebellum mansion that filled my imagination with a busy life at fictional Carlton Oaks. If you, dear reader, were to check out the photos on their website, you could easily envision how Celine stood on the upper-floor balcony and watched Trevor step off a majestic sternwheeler and into her life.

To the folks at the California Wolf Center, thank you for helping me understand the nature of wolves so that I could write a more realistic scene of Celine giving birth to her and Trevor's son. As a reader, you may have thought the wolves would have descended upon White Eagle's lifeless body. However, while the deep snowfall naturally masked some of his scent, Celine moved about in a wooded area sheltered from the snow. The scent of her giving birth would have been similar to that of an animal doing the same. Newborns are easy prey for predators in the wild.

To my wonderful RWA® Hearts Through History critique partners. Without your input, I doubt I would have turned out a decent story: Wendy, Anne, Tess, Averil, Renee, Barbara, Joan, and Sam, what an amazingly talented group of women you are!

To my Beta readers, Nancy Linehan and Jennifer Arp.

Your sharp eyes and excellent input helped make this a better story.

To Jill Marsal of the Marsal Lyon Literary Agency who works diligently on my behalf. I have such great respect for you.

To my very special editor Alicia Condon, and to the rest of the wonderful crew at Kensington Publishing: You are some mighty fine people who believed in this series (and in me) enough to give it your all—thanking you is not nearly enough.

Don't miss

ALANNA,

the exciting sequel to CELINE,

coming next month!

Christmas night, 1831, Boston, Massachusetts

From an upper-story window, the six-year-old boy watched a lone figure scurry from the mansion and vanish into a swirling vortex of snow. A lump caught in his throat. He swallowed hard, fighting the dread pounding through his veins.

Mrs. Guthrie was the last of the servants to leave the five-story brick manse, gone off to spend what remained of Christmas with her family. A shudder racked the boy's body at the idea of spending the night alone in his room. Dejected, he turned and made his way toward his bed, glancing none too bravely at a doorway alive with shadows.

A soft thud echoed from below.

He froze.

Thought scattered as he strained to hear past the sudden pounding in his ears.

Another thud.

Unholy fear shot him down the dark corridor and into his parents' room. His mother lay propped against a mass of soft pillows with a book in her lap, firelight casting a soft glow to her smile.

"Mummy!" He clambered onto the four-poster with breathless little grunts.

His mother slid an arm around him and pulled him into her warmth. "Is that old tree thumping against the house again, dear?"

He snuggled tight against her. "Uh-huh."

She brushed her cheek across the top of his head. "Your father will see to its removal when he returns from England, sweetheart. Would you like me to read you to sleep?"

"Uh-huh." He slid an arm around her middle and cuddled closer. The familiar, safe scent of Mum mingling with the fragrance of fresh linens soon beckoned him into the lazy space between sleep and consciousness. He lay without thought now, wrapped in warm blankets and the security of gentle arms.

A sound, like the shattering of glass, broke through the silence. His mother's stiffened body threw him wide awake.

"Mummy?"

"Shh!"

Muffled noises swept through the house. But more frightening than the sounds was the distinct shift that took place, as though the very current of air around them wailed in violation.

Hot terror gripped his heart. "Oh, Mummy, that's not the tree—"

Her fingers pressed hard against his mouth. "Not a word." Bundling a blanket around him, she snatched him off the bed and stuffed him underneath. "There you go, up against the wall." She kissed him, covered his face, and then crawled back onto the bed.

He whimpered.

"No!" she whispered. "Whatever occurs, do not move or make a sound until I tell you it is safe. No one will see you in the shadows if you lie perfectly still."

Fingers trembling, he managed a slit in the folds of the blanket. Across the room, a full-length mirror tilted at an angle cast a dim reflection of his mother through smoky glass, her eyes round and darting about the room.

When the door swung wide, she shifted on the bed, the creaking loud in the boy's ears. Polished black shoes and the lower half of a man's pant legs appeared. The boy crammed a corner of the blanket into his mouth to keep from crying out.

"You!" his mother gasped.

The door slammed and the boy gritted his teeth against a shivering that threatened to take hold of his body. A hard click of heels on the wood floor, and the back of a thick-necked man with black hair materialized in the mirror. He moved to the bed.

Mute cries exploded in the boy's head. *Mummy!*

"Well, well, well." The man stood before her, the tips of his shoes under the bed, his words a harsh rasp. "I don't have to tell you no one will come to your aid, now do I? You know what I came for."

Pressed deep against the pillows, the boy's mother held the covers tight against her chest. "You'll not find what you seek in this house."

"And where will I, madam?"

When she failed to respond, his hand cracked hard against the side of her face. "Cease your foolishness!"

The boy stuffed more of the blanket into his mouth.

The man bolted from beside the bed. Snarling and cursing, he flung open drawers and wardrobes, the contents spilling onto the floor in great heaps. He moved back to the bed and knelt. Heavy grunts—so close—shot a new wave of panic through the boy. He squeezed his eyes shut and held his breath until his lungs seared. But oh, he nearly wept as his bladder betrayed him and emptied its contents into the blanket. Would the man be able to smell the wool now dripping with hot urine?

A soft knock sounded at the door. The man rose and moved toward the noise. The boy's eyes shot open. The mirrored image evaporated, leaving only shoes and pant legs visible once again. Another set of shoes appeared at the open door. A muffled argument flared and then faded. The door slammed shut and the man returned to the bed.

"You are making me quite angry now, madam," he bellowed. "If I have to force you to talk, things will become quite unpleasant for you." The man's reflection in the mirror wavered as he leaned over the bed and dug his squat hands into her arms.

"Please," she whimpered.

A strangled sound gurgled from the man's throat. He hit her again. Blood smeared the side of her mouth.

Oh, Mummy. How could he help her? He should stop this. But cowardly fear kept the boy plastered to the wall.

The man struck her once more, then planted his knee on the bed and dug into her throat. He shook her like a rag doll, violent animal sounds whistling through his teeth. At last he released her, tossed her against the pillows, and left the room, closing the door behind him.

The terrified boy huddled beneath the bed, his gaze fixed on the reflection of his mum's unmoving figure. One of her arms dangled over the edge of the mattress. She had not told him to move yet, nor to speak, but he spied one of her earbobs lying on the floor. With a trembling hand, he snatched up the bauble and buried it in the folds of the blanket.

The door swung open again. The man's shoes and pant legs appeared and moved to the bed. He searched for something before bending to the floor again. "Damn it!" His hand brushed along the floorboards, sweeping dangerously close. The bed gave and creaked as he lifted himself upright.

He ripped the remaining earring from her ear, and then made his exit.

Afraid to call out lest the bad man return, the boy huddled beneath the bed, staring at his sleeping mother's reflection while the blazing fire dwindled to ash and the room chilled. After a while, he came to the devastating realization that calling out would do no good. Tears streaked his cheeks, but the horror of it all, and fear of the man's return, held him fast to the wall.

Two servants found the boy and his dead mother the next morning. Terrified of the murderer, they secretly transported him to the countryside to await his father's return. Lonely and grief-stricken, the boy clutched to his heart the one tangible thing he had left by which to remember his mother—the gold-encased garnet earring.

Days turned into months, and months turned into years, but his father never came.